MK

WHERE

daffodils

BLOOM

By Leya Delray

Ink River Press
Georgia, USA

Where Daffodils Bloom
Second Edition

Copyright ©2018. Leya Delray.

Published by: Ink River Press.
For more information, to order in bulk, or for permission to quote short passages, send an email message to InkRiverPress@gmail.com.

ISBN 978-1-7327587-0-4 (Hardback)
ISBN 978-1-7327587-1-1 (Paperback)

All scripture quotations taken from the KJV Bible. Used by permission.

Other works quoted are all in the public domain:

The Sandpiper — Poem by Celia Thaxter.
Round and Round the Garden — Traditional Nursery Rhyme
The Bungalow Song — Folk song

Cover Design: Damonza
Interior Design: Jerilynne Knight

Printed and published in the United States of America.

Dedication

For Sharon,

who first told me her parents' story.

And then trusted me to write it.

Acknowledgments

First off, I want to thank Sharon (Overall) Crenshaw, who told me her parents' story one hot summer day at a WW2 event, and started me on this 3-year journey. She has been both a friend and mentor to me during that time. More than once, when I was ready to give up on the project, the only thing that kept me going was reminding myself "I promised Sharon." I'm so thankful for her encouragement, enthusiasm, and help in this process.

I also gratefully thank my parents and siblings, who encouraged me through this whole long process, put up with my stressed-out-please-don't-talk-to-me-it's-crunch-time self during busy periods, and were always excited to hear a new chapter read aloud.

My husband, Ben (whom I was dating when the book went to press), is a technological genius who saved my website from vanishing into never-never land when my hosting service bailed on me, and helped me reset everything so smoothly that most people never noticed the glitch. He was generally my life-saver and back-up during the final weeks before publication, always ready to figure out how to fix something that was broken or create something out of thin air if I needed it and couldn't find it. I don't know how I would have gotten the book to print without him. (No wonder I married him after that!)

My editor, Christy Distler, was fantastic to work with. She was so professional and thorough, and yet encouraging and enthusiastic at the same time. The book is much better because of her help.

My Aunt Jerilynne did a gorgeous job with the formatting, creating a book that looks more beautiful than I ever imagined, and overcoming all sorts of unexpected obstacles along the way that I didn't even know existed.

My three proof-readers—Mikaela, Elsie, and Kristen—did a fantastic job catching the seventy-two-million typos that somehow slipped past both me and my editor. It's amazing how many times you can read over something you wrote, and still not notice you left out an entire word!

Susan (Overall) Sproles helped in so many ways, from research to family stories and details. She was a great source for comparing notes with Sharon's memories and trying to make sure everything was accurate.

Kathy Matthews (daughter of Frances) and her husband Bob are amazing hosts, who allowed me to stay in their home when I visited Lytham for research purposes, and spent days taking me everywhere I wanted to go. Kathy also proofread the manuscript for me and helped make sure my English characters truly sounded English (instead of American, like myself).

Shirley (Robinson) Smith and Wendy (Dean) Wilson, childhood friends of Lily's younger sisters, were both wonderful resources, helping me to understand what Lytham was like in the 40's, and sharing their memories of Lily and Fred.

I also want to thank the members of the Lytham's Past Facebook Group, who helped me with so many tiny historical details that I would have had no idea how to find without their help (like where the Brown family went during air-raids). Their collective memory and research added so much to this book.

This list would not be complete if I didn't mention my fabulous Launch Team, whose enthusiasm was the driving force behind making the book release a success. Thank you so much, each one of you, for caring about this story. You will never know how much it meant to see so many people excited about reading and promoting this book.

Last, and most importantly, I want to thank my loving Lord and Savior, who dropped this project in my lap just when I was wondering how to use my talents. He has orchestrated so many wonderfully perfect details along the way. Details that I never would have even thought to ask for. None of this would have happened without Him.

Solo Deo Gloria

Chapter 1

October 1, 1956

Lily jerked awake. Trembling in her bunk, she brushed away shards of shattered slumber.

The same nightmare. Just as vivid as always.

She could almost feel the frozen wind cutting through her, almost see the dark figure looming in the doorway, almost hear the child sobbing.

Would they never stop haunting her?

The black hollowness of the ship's cabin pitched without warning, and her stomach lurched with it. No wonder she'd woken. There must be a storm.

Taking a deep breath, she inhaled the musty scent of stale sea air and hoped she wouldn't get seasick again. Her fingers groped for the blanket and found it had slipped nearly off the bunk. *Oh.* The cold had been more than a dream.

Wait.

So had the sobbing.

She sat up, grabbing for the wall to steady herself as the ship rolled once more.

David. He was crying again. And here she was worrying about her own nightmares.

She stumbled out of bed, catching up the blanket to pull around her shoulders. A few steps took her to David's bunk on the other side of the cabin, and she groped in the pitch-blackness. Not even a shred of moonlight came from the porthole. There. She'd found the corner of the bunk.

She shook David's little shoulder, then brushed tangled hair back from his forehead. "David. Wake up, love. It's all right. Mum's here."

His sleepy sob broke off, and he shuddered awake beneath her hand. "Mum?"

"Shhh. I'm right here, love."

"It's dark."

"The moon is just hiding behind a cloud. It will come back soon." She cradled his damp cheek in her hand.

"I want Dad." His voice quavered.

Dad.

This time the lurch in her stomach had nothing to do with the storm.

"I want Dad," he sniffled again, as if repeating it would change reality.

"You know Dad isn't here, love. Remember? We're going to see Nana and Granddad and Auntie Alice and Auntie Ruth and—"

"I don't want them! I want Dad." His voice cracked into another sob. "Why didn't he come with us?"

The ship pitched again, and she half-fell onto the bunk as she pulled David's little body into her arms, stroking his hair. He wanted an answer, but her tongue felt as dry and useless as the last leaf of autumn, shriveled up on a bare, cold branch. How was she supposed to explain to him something she could barely explain to herself?

Because your mother is a coward, David. Because she is running away.

Little arms circled her neck, pressing against her hair. "When can we go home, Mum?" His voice was a mournful whimper.

Her chest constricted. She clutched him tighter, his baby-soft cheek nestled against hers.

And she no longer knew whether the tears moistening her face belonged to David or to herself.

But there were no words to answer him. No words to make him understand.

Chapter 2

April 1944 — Twelve Years Earlier

Why an American?

Lily Brown pursed her lips as she skirted yet another love-struck couple clogging the street and tried not to grimace.

Why? That's what she wanted to ask most of her friends lately.

Food rationing, air raids, POW camps, casualty lists, gas masks. And still people acted like the Yank soldiers had come all the way to Lytham just to hand out sweets and stockings. She could hardly blame the poor blokes for playing along either. The girls made it too easy for them. Olive drab, a few chocolate bars, and a pair of nylons. That was all love cost in England these days.

She glanced over her shoulder to see who the couple were. *Oh no. Not Clara too.*

This time she couldn't keep back the grimace. Clara Forsyth was the prettiest girl in town. Oval face, rich brown eyes, hourglass figure, and jet-black hair. She could have any boyfriend she wanted, in uniform or out of it.

So why an American, Clara? Is it really worth it?

Lily glanced at her watch. Drat! Five minutes late.

Her wooden heels clicked against the pavement as she broke into a half-run, her own shoulder-length, brown curls bumping against her collar. Already late, and the clouds looked like they would break open any moment. If it didn't hold off long enough for her to get inside the cinema, well ...

Painted-on stockings did not do well in rainstorms.

She tucked her pocketbook tighter under her arm to keep the strap from slipping off her shoulder as she hurried. It would never do to lose her weekly paycheck right after she'd gotten it. They were running low on vegetables again.

A stray curl came loose in the wind and twirled against her cheek. The breeze smelled wet and heavy, like it always did before a storm.

She glanced over her shoulder again. Clara seemed quite oblivious to the weather. Not surprising. Her soldier had probably given her nylons, so she needn't worry about rainstorms anymore.

Stockings, chocolate, and uniforms. There it was again.

Why any good English girl would want to leave everything else she knew and loved, just for that, baffled Lily.

But then, Clara didn't have a mother and sisters to worry about, either.

Drops of rain had just started to dampen the pavement when she spotted Paul outside the cinema. Long legs crossed, he stood leaning near the door in one of his perfectly-tailored grey suits. The gold cufflinks glittered even without a shred of sunshine around. Did he shine those himself?

Surely not. He had servants to do that sort of thing.

"Lily!" He met her in two quick strides, wind ruffling his blond hair. His arm slipped around her waist as he brushed that stubborn curl off her cheek with his other hand. "I was starting to worry you weren't coming."

She tilted her head back to meet his eyes as he looked down from his six-foot-four vantage point. "You know how it is at the chemist's. Just when we're about to lock the door, somebody comes in wanting a blue pill they can't remember the name of, for an illness they can't describe."

Paul's broad forehead crinkled with amusement. "Do I get a kiss today?"

Her cheeks warmed. "In the middle of the street?"

"Why not?" His fingers lingered under her chin as he held her close.

She inhaled. Cologne, spiced and woody, mingled with a cherry-tinged whiff of expensive tobacco.

"London girls kiss their boyfriends in public all the time," he said. "Especially when the chaps are in uniform at the railway station."

"That's different. People always kiss at railway stations."

He cocked his brow. "Well, I'll be going back to one soon. Will you come kiss me there?"

"Paul, stop it." She pushed away from him, but just to arm's length. The storm was picking up. A gust of wind tossed raindrops into her face, and she dashed them away with her hand.

He put up his umbrella and stepped close again, shielding them both under the black canopy. "I'm sorry. I should have put it up sooner." His pale green eyes smiled down at her. "I don't suppose hiding under an umbrella makes kissing in the middle of the street less objectionable?"

She gave him a look.

"Well,"—he shrugged—"it was worth a try. Shall we go in?"

She slipped her arm through his, and his sleeve was soft as butter against her skin.

Ah. Cashmere, of course.

A little bounce enlivened her steps as he led her inside and up the steps to the cinema café. She would have cashmere clothes too, when she was Paul's wife. And furs and silks and jewels and a motorcar and anything to eat she ever wanted. So would Mother and the girls. She would make certain of that.

Drawing a bit closer to him, she tightened her arm around his.

He looked down and smiled.

Oh yes. The rest of the girls could keep those swaggering Americans. She had Paul.

. . . .

The rain began in earnest just after they stepped inside the café. They took a booth seat, and Paul ordered them two cups of tea, then picked up his menu.

Lily watched him. He'd barely glanced at the place. Strange, being so used to lovely surroundings that you wouldn't even notice the smooth jazz playing in the background or the well-dressed waiters moving from table to table. She leaned back into the padded softness of the booth seat and closed her eyes, breathing in the mingled scents of fresh-brewed tea, crisp fried potato chips, and freshly sliced cucumbers. No wonder they called this place The Palace.

"Lily?"

Her eyes flew open to find her twelve-year-old sister standing by the table, red hair dripping with rainwater. Her face looked pinched and a little pale.

"Alice? What are you doing in here?"

"Looking for you."

"But how did you know where I was?"

"Mother said you were having tea with Paul." Alice gave him a tight little smile. "When are you coming home, Lily?"

"Later. After Paul catches his train."

The waiter brought their tea. Paul offered his to Alice, but she shook her head.

"How long will that be?" She looked at Lily.

Lily pressed her lips together and tried not to let annoyance into her voice. "Why does it matter? Mother knows where I am. Now run along home. Paul isn't here for long, and I want to drink my tea before it gets cold. Yours will be cold too, if you stay here much longer."

"I already had mine."

"Well then, for heaven's sake, what's the matter with me having mine?"

Paul was sipping his tea and trying not to intervene in the conversation, but she saw him glance at his watch. He didn't have all evening.

"I wish you'd come home, Lily. I'm worried."

That was not surprising. Alice was always worrying. She would come home from school worried about this friend or that who hadn't heard from some relation on the front. Or else she would be worried about the hungry-looking stray puppy she saw. And then of course it was Lily who would end up out searching for the puppy, because when it came to animals she never could say no.

But not *now*. Not today.

"Well, why did you have to chase me down?" She took a sip of her tea. Bother. It was getting cold already. "Go talk to Mum about it." She waved toward the door.

"Mum's the one I'm worried about."

Lily's hand froze with the teacup halfway between the table and her mouth. She took a breath, held it a moment, then pushed it slowly out between her lips as she reminded herself she was a grown-up girl of eighteen and had no business panicking like a baby. "What do you mean? What's wrong with Mum?"

Alice shook her head. "I don't know. She got a letter halfway through tea and went into her room and didn't come back out."

Paul put down his teacup.

Something cold and heavy washed over Lily like a frigid ocean wave. She lowered her own cup to the table and it rattled a bit in the saucer. "A letter? From whom?" Her toes curled tight in her shoes and her fingers hugged the edge of the bench. "Did you see where it was from?"

Alice's eyes looked back at her. Dark. Weary. Not like a twelve-year-old's eyes should look. This war grew children up too quickly. But then, what had come before the war had not been much better. Not in their house anyway.

"I didn't see it up close. But I thought"—Alice swallowed—"it might have come from ... from Germany."

Robert. Lily's nails dug into the wooden underside of the booth at the thought of their older brother. She licked her lips and looked at Paul. His broad forehead creased with worry.

"And, Lily, you know it's ... it's the fifteenth." Alice's voice had a tremulous waver in it.

Lily closed her eyes. The fifteenth. Of course it was. Of all the days for Mother to get a letter from Germany.

"What's the fifteenth?" Paul sounded puzzled but concerned.

She opened her eyes and stood. "It's the day Mother's ... brother died. In the last war." She clenched her jaw shut around the words as her pulse thumped in her ears. *Not again. Please, God. Not Robert too.* "I'm sorry, Paul. I have to go home I—"

"Of course you do." He got up. "And I would go with you, only"—he looked at his watch again—"my train. I don't know if I could make it back in time to catch it if I try to—"

"Don't bother. Really. Don't. It might not be anything after all." *Please God.* This was a different war. A different brother. Robert was Robert. Not Uncle George. But why did it have to be the *fifteenth*, of all days?

"I'm sorry about the tea." She tried to sound calm.

"Don't think of it. We'll do it again soon."

"But I'm afraid I've wasted your money. I've hardly touched—"

"Nonsense." Paul reached for his umbrella. "Do you think I've never bought a cup of tea that wasn't finished before? Here, it's raining cats and dogs out there. Take this."

Lily had no time to argue. Alice was holding her hand, drawing her toward the door.

She turned to go, then stopped short. "Oh! I meant to tell you. We're going to a dance at Lowther Gardens in two weeks. Will you come?"

Paul signaled for the waiter to bring the bill. "Possibly. I should be coming back from Scotland about then. But it depends on when I have to be home. Sometimes my father has meetings I have to attend. I'll try."

Alice was tugging harder. "Lily, come on."

She let herself be pulled to the door, still looking back at Paul.

"About the letter, I hope it's good news," he called after her. "It might be, you know."

Lily swallowed and nodded.

Yes, of course. Good news. From Germany.

Perhaps.

Chapter 3

"Look out!"

Fred shouted the warning as he yanked his bike hard to the right, wooden wheels skidding sideways on wet cobbles.

The two girls had run into the street, appearing out of nowhere. Swerving wildly, he caught a flash of red hair, dark curls, and dresses flapping in the wind. Then he was past them, missing the smaller one by inches. An umbrella had nearly clipped the side of his head. He must have been so busy thinking about the postcard in his pocket that he hadn't been watching the street.

Gripping the handlebars, he tried to make the bike quit keeling off sideways, but the front wheel hit a pothole and twisted out of his hands. Losing control, he slammed his heels onto the road, trying to stop the momentum. Too late. The bike pitched over sideways and his shoulder smashed into cobbles, palms grating against wet stone. Hooked on his leg, the bicycle skidded in an arc until the handlebar kicked him square in the forehead.

Ow.

He blinked off dizziness, squinting up the street in time to catch a fleeting glimpse of the dark-haired older girl as she disappeared into an alley. A wet blur of brown hair, dripping dress, and legs streaked white where the rain had washed channels in her painted-on stockings. Then she was gone.

Well. Somebody must have been in an awful hurry to get someplace.

He pressed his fingers against the sticky gash on his forehead, then untangled himself from the bicycle and clambered to his feet, free hand feeling in his pocket for the postcard.

There.

He dragged the bike under the protection of a roof overhang and slipped out the postcard to check for damage. The corner crinkled up like an accordion now, and the part that read *Carol still isn't eating well* looked faintly damp. Otherwise it was all right. He looked the bike over next. No visible damage. The left pedal was missing, of course, but it had been that way when he bought it. In fact, the whole thing had been so battered already, there wasn't much else that could go wrong.

After sliding the postcard back into his pocket, he climbed onto the bike and started up the street again, pushing off with one foot and pedaling with the other.

· ·

By the time he was halfway to Freckleton, the rain had soaked straight through his uniform trousers and plastered the olive-drab wool to his skin. He didn't even bother skirting puddles anymore, just splashed through the muddy water and kept going. Seemed like rain was all folks ever got around here.

Right. And you oughta be used to it by this time, Fred Overall.

Another cold slap of puddle water smacked him in the leg. He gritted his teeth. *Should be.* But he wasn't. And on days like this, seemed like all he could think about was bright, sandy beaches and Florida sunshine. Especially when he'd just had a postcard from home.

Carol still isn't eating well. He could feel the card pressing against him through the lining of his breast pocket as the words played over in his mind. *And yesterday, Dad just...*

A dog barked, ahead and to the left.

He looked up.

The road was lined on either side by hedgerows, tight-clustered branches dark and dripping with rain. In a hollow underneath one of the bushes, a black-and-white collie eyed him, ears perked. A little boy squatted under a tree a few feet away, wearing a blue corduroy cap that looked pretty damp. A bike, red with rust and definitely not the kid's size, leaned beside him.

The boy looked up just after Fred did, then jumped to his feet, freckled face brightening. "Got any gum, chum?"

Fred slowed the bicycle, groping in his pocket with a grin. Seemed like every kid in Britain used that phrase. "Sorry. I'm all out of gum. How about a Tootsie Roll?"

"Yes, please!"

Fred angled his bike to the edge of the road and handed over the candy, glancing at the rusty antique leaning against the tree and then back at the boy. "What's your name, kid?"

"Dave." The boy barely looked up. He was concentrating on untwisting the wrapper.

"On your way home from school?"

Dave shook his head. "Don't start till September."

Couldn't be over five years old, then. Big for his age. But not near big enough for that bicycle.

Fred nodded toward it. "Something wrong with that?"

Dave bobbed his chin, mouth full of candy. "The front wheel keeps wiggling around."

Fred looked toward town. If he didn't truck it for base right now, he was going to miss mess call. He was late as it was, after that accident. He sighed. Somebody was probably going to yell at him, but he couldn't very well go off and leave a five-year-old stranded in the rain.

He climbed off his own bike, leaned it against the other side of the tree, and dropped down to scan the front wheel of Dave's ride. Chilly mud squelched beneath his knees. "No wonder it's wobbling. You lost a nut here." He pointed to where the axle connected to the fork.

Dave came over to stand behind him, too busy chewing to say anything.

"You live in Freckleton?"

"Yes sir."

Fred ran his eyes over the bike again. It would take forever to get back to base if he had to tote two bicycles at once. But maybe there was another way. "You care if I take a piece of the wire from the basket? I think I can fix the wheel with it."

Dave thought about that for a few moments, then shrugged.

He dug around in his coat pocket for his pliers. "Always carry pliers with you, Dave. You never know when they'll come in handy." He clipped off a wire from the side of the basket.

"Can you really make the wheel stay on with just that?"

"Temporarily." He straightened the wire and worked it back and forth to make it more pliable. "Bikes are sort of a hobby of mine." Folding the wire in half, he settled the axle into the center of it. "I used to collect old broken ones and fix them up to sell to the other kids in the neighborhood. Or give them away sometimes." He wrapped the two loose wire ends around the fork. "Guess I just like fixing things. I'm still doing it in the Air Corps."

Dave looked up, gray-green eyes lighting with interest. "You fix planes?"

"Propellers mostly." He crimped the end of the wire tight and checked his watch. *Oh boy.*

"I want to fix planes when I grow up." Excitement animated Dave's face.

Fred stood, wiping his hands on his pant legs. "You do, huh? Well, start practicing now, fixing other things. Like bikes." He gave the boy a quick grin and started to put the pliers back in his pocket. Then he changed his mind. "Here." He held them out. "Keep these with you. Next time something breaks down, maybe you'll be the one fixing it."

Dave's grin stretched so wide it almost touched his ears. He shoved the pliers into his own pocket.

"Now get on and show me how you ride this thing. I don't see how you even reach the pedals."

Dave climbed onto the bike, straddling the middle bar with one foot on a peddle and one on the ground. "Thanks, Mister."

"Call me Fred."

"Thanks, Mr. Fred."

Fred laughed. "You're welcome. Now don't go too fast, okay? That wire should hold until you get home, but I wouldn't put too much stress on it."

With one last grin, Dave pushed off with his foot and started pedaling, standing straight up between the seat and the handlebars.

Fred watched until he rounded a corner and disappeared behind the hedgerow, the collie bounding close behind. He sighed. Fixing bikes made him think about Florida. Seemed like everything made him think about Florida today. Even mess call made him wish for some of Mom's grit cakes.

Mess call.

He checked his watch again.

Oh boy.

Chapter 4

Lily stood, knuckles frozen an inch from the wood, and stared at a dusty scratch in the yellow paint in front of her nose. Only once before had the thought of knocking on Mother's door clinched her stomach in a vice like this. And that was when she was only a little girl. Before the war. Before ...

No.

She would not think of that night today.

Shoving the memories into the darkest back corner of her mind, she tightened her fingers around the vase in her hand. The house was deathly silent. Sunlight, weak and watery from the rain, filtered in through the skylight and cast a cold grey wash over the hall. Dark shadow-stripes stretched out from the banister, reaching toward her across the worn wooden floor boards. Like prison bars.

Lily held her breath, straining for a whisper of sound on the other side of the door. Nothing. Her fingers trembled. She knew it because the daffodil inside the vase was vibrating too, shedding beads of leftover rainwater onto her skin.

A flower in a vase. What had she been thinking? Mother loved the daffodils, but they were poor comfort if something had happened. If ... if Robert was ...

She clamped her teeth over her bottom lip until it throbbed. Mother would not care about daffodils then.

Lily looked down at the bright yellow bloom, standing straight as a soldier on its long, stiff stem. They were such brave flowers, daffodils. Sending up their green spears straight through the snow sometimes. You could chop them off, right down to the ground, but wait a year and there they would be, undaunted. It was hard to kill a daffodil. They didn't know how to quit.

She raised her chin. Perhaps, after all, it was not Mother she had brought the flower for. Perhaps she had picked it because, somehow, looking at it gave her courage. She took one last long breath, pushing the air into her lungs and forcing the cold fear down. Deep down, as far as it would go. She could still feel it quivering there, somewhere in the pit of her stomach. But at least her hands had stopped trembling.

Steady now. Head up. Shoulders back. Someday, maybe, she'd be as brave as Mother. But for now she could at least pretend.

She rapped on the door, and the sound echoed in the silence. A pause. Her heart bumped against her ribs.

"Yes?" The voice was unwavering. Calm. But Mother's always was.

"May I come in?"

"Yes, love."

Steady. Steady. She turned the knob.

Mother was sitting at her writing bureau, still wearing the blue apron she always wore at teatime. An open letter lay to her left and a Bible to her right. In the middle was a sheet of paper she'd been writing on. She smiled at Lily. A gentle smile, not jolly and laughing the way she often smiled.

Lily searched her face for clues. The lines seemed no deeper than usual. Her cheeks were dry, but the eyes. There was something in them. Was it tears?

"Hello, Mother." She hesitated, standing in the doorway. Now what? How did she begin? Her toes again curled inside her shoes. "I ... I brought you a flower."

Mother's smile widened a little, and she held her hand out with a welcoming gesture. "Two flowers," she corrected. "Two of my favourites. One daffodil and one Lily."

Lily crossed the few steps to her and set the vase on the bureau. Mother's fingers closed around hers with a warm squeeze.

There was the letter. It lay folded up, a corner of the envelope peeking out underneath. With the return address right there in black and white. It was from Germany.

Her mouth went dry as chalk.

"It just came."

Lily's mind was screaming, panting, her eyes trying to tear through the folded paper. What did it say? What did it say? The quivering in her stomach was trying to spread to the rest of her body. She clenched her teeth and held it down. *Please, God, please!*

Mother squeezed her hand again. "Took a month to get here though. It's from Robert."

From Robert.

The air shot back into Lily's lungs so fast she almost choked on it. *From Robert.* Then he was still alive. *Alive.* Thank God.

"What ..." She had to take another breath before her voice would come out normal again. "What does he say?"

Mother's hands unfolded the letter, separating one page from another and holding out the top one. "This page is written to you girls. The other is to me."

Lily grasped the paper, trying not to tear it in her haste. Another surge of relief rushed over her as she set eyes on the familiar handwriting.

Dear Frances, Lily, Alice, and Ruth,

I hope this letter finds you all well.

I'm doing as well as can be expected. Of course, POW camp is no picnic, but neither was fighting a war. I guess nobody is picnicking these days, except maybe those Americans at Warton. Frances sent me a letter. She said you are having dances at Lowther Gardens. I guess if anyone in this war is having fun, it must be all those lucky Yanks going to dances with my charming sisters!

I must admit I'm jealous. When I was home, I used to wish sometimes I had a brother instead of a whole houseful of younger sisters, but now I'm pretty certain there couldn't be anything better than four sisters to fuss over you. So remember to fuss over me when I get home again. I'll put up with it much better than I used to.

And whatever you do, don't run off and marry one of those Yanks. At least not until I can get back and approve of him first. What will I do if I come home to find you all gone off to America, and me not even getting to say goodbye? If you must get married while I'm gone, make it an Englishman. This Paul Holdsworth seems nice enough, going on what Lily wrote.

Smiling a little to herself, Lily glanced up to find Mother watching her. She dropped her eyes back to the page again.

I got the care packages you sent, and the Red Cross does their best to take care of all the POWs. Don't worry about me. I'm nearly used to this life now. I guess you can get used to just about anything after more than two years of it! The few months I spent fighting sure don't seem like much in comparison though. What good is it to be a Commando if you can't be out there giving the Krauts something to hide from?

Well anyway, give my love to everyone at home. And girls, help Mother as much as you can. You're lucky to have her there with you. We don't like to admit it, but I think most of the blokes here would trade about anything for a chance to see their mothers.

Take care of her for me.

Love,
Robert

P.S. Please tell Allie I got her letter and will write to her soon.

Allie.

Lily winced.

Allie again. Why did she keep writing to Robert anyway? Lily could have strangled her. Sometimes she wondered if she ought to just write and tell Robert the truth. But how did you say something like that in a letter? And what good would it do him anyway, stuck in a POW camp?

Might as well wait until he got home.

Lily focused on rereading the rest of the letter, savoring every precious word. By the time she got to the signature again, the tight, cold ball of fear that had been stuck in her gut finally dislodged and drained out of her all at once.

She dropped to her knees, wrapped her arms around Mother's waist, and rested her head on the blue apron. The fabric was soft against her cheek, worn silky by many washings. Mother's fingers stroked through her hair, smoothing the curls that never did seem to stay nicely in place.

Lily closed her eyes and breathed in the fresh whisper of lavender and lye soap. "He's still all right, then."

"Yes. Quite all right, love."

"I suppose he's much safer in a POW camp than he would be in the trenches."

"Much." There was a low echo of sadness in Mother's voice. She was thinking of Uncle George, of course.

Lily wanted to say something. But the words were missing. Words were always hard for her to find when the things to be talked about were deep things. Hard things. She ran her finger along the seam of Mother's apron tie and was silent.

After a minute, Mother spoke. "So. You wrote to him about Paul?"

Lily did not look up. "I thought he'd like to know."

"He seems to think you might marry him. Do you?"

Now there was a question she did not quite know how to answer. "Would you be happy if I did?"

Mother's fingers tapped thoughtfully on her shoulder. "That depends. Do you love him?"

Another uncomfortable question. "He's very good to me, Mother. And just think of all the lovely things I could buy for you and the girls and Robert with so much money! Anything you wanted."

"I already have everything I need."

"*Need*, yes." Lily raised her head. "But think of all the other things that would make life more comfortable. I could send Alice and Ruth to one of those proper girls' schools, and find Robert a nice job in London, or in Scotland even, when he comes back. And Father too. I could find him a good job somewhere he wouldn't ..." She bit her lip. "Somewhere else, I mean.

And wouldn't Frances love to have more pretty clothes and shoes?"

"Not if it was charity from her rich brother-in-law."

Lily sat back in dismay. "Oh no, Mother! It wouldn't ever be like charity. I just meant Christmas and birthdays and such. And think how lovely it would be to live in London and never have to work. And go to parties and plays and have a beautiful big house and—"

"But do you *love* him?"

She chewed her lip and traced a notch in the floorboard with her finger. "I think ... I think I *could* love him."

"But you don't?"

"Not ... yet." There. She'd said it.

Mother leaned back in her chair and looked at Lily for a long moment. "Then no. I would *not* be happy if you married him. Wealth without love never made anyone happy, Lily."

Lily looked at the floor. And love without wealth? How had *that* turned out? She bit her tongue to keep from saying it and stood to walk to the window instead.

Mother's voice followed her. "Paul is a very nice young man, but neither of you would be truly happy together if you did not care for him the way he cares for you."

Lily pressed her lips together in annoyance, counting to ten while she watched a bird hop along the ridge of the baker's shop that backed up to their house. It wasn't as if she was talking about getting married next week or anything. Why did Mother have to bring this up now anyway?

"I just said I think I *could* love him, Mum. Eventually."

Mother's chair creaked, and the papers rustled as she folded them up. "Perhaps. But don't assume just because he is kind and good and wealthy that you should marry him. Or that he is God's choice for you. There are many good men in the world, Lily, but you can only marry one of them."

Lily tossed her hair and looked over her shoulder. "There may be a lot of them in the *world*, Mum. But there certainly aren't very many in England right now. Actually, most of them seem to be in the middle of a war at the moment."

Mother's face tightened.

Lily knew she should not have brought that up, but she barreled on anyway, too irritated now to check her tongue. "At least Paul won't be running off to get killed or end up a POW with the job he has. He's 'essential to the war effort,' remember? And at least he never worries about running out of money for groceries. And at least he's not ... "

She snapped off in the middle and jerked her face back to the window. Her hands tightened on the edge of the sill as she pressed her lips together again, forcing words back down her throat. There was silence for a moment.

"At least he's not ... what?" Mother's tone was flat.

Lily pressed her tongue against her teeth and kept her eyes on the clouds outside. "Nothing."

Some things did not have be said.

Chapter 5

"Where ya been, Fred? Ye're soaked."

Fred looked up from the cartoon he was sketching to see his best pal Jerry striding toward him between the rows of blanket-draped bunks, wearing his usual lopsided grin.

"Ya missed mess call."

"I was fixing a kid's bike."

"In the rain?"

"It didn't break inside a house."

Jerry's shadow fell across the paper as he leaned over, his shoulders blocking the light from the ceiling as he peered at the page. "New cartoon, huh? Gonna send that one home to your mom again?"

"She says they cheer her up."

Jerry's bunk squeaked as he dropped into it. "How's the new baby?"

Fred's pencil slowed a little. Now why did Jerry have to bring that up? He'd finally managed to put the postcard out of his mind, and now here it was, dragged back up again.

"Still not eating well?" Jerry guessed.

"No." Fred kept his eyes on the pencil lead as he tried to crush the worry in his gut. It was bad enough having a baby sister he'd never met, without worrying he wouldn't get the chance.

"What else is wrong?"

He raised his eyes, surprised.

"What?" Jerry spread his hands. "You're too easy to read, Fred."

Fred sighed and went back to drawing. "It's Dad. He lost his job again."

"Gee." Jerry whistled. "How many kids still at home?"

"Three. But Margie's working now."

"Well, if she brings home near as big a chunk as you send, they oughta be all right."

Fred's head snapped up again.

Jerry chuckled as he dug out a cloth from his foot locker and started polishing his shoes. "Quit looking so surprised. We live in the same barracks, remember? Do your parents know you just barely scrape by over here and send the rest home?"

"I keep all I need."

"Yeah, and then you give it away in shiny coins to random kids on the street."

"Come on, Jerry. You do it too."

"I'm just saying. Do your parents know?"

A new voice interrupted them. "Well, well! Another work of art, I see!"

Fred's hackles went up before he even turned around. He knew that voice. *Greg Baker again.* He tried not to mind Baker, but he couldn't help it. There was something oily about him.

"You have such talent, Fred. Those cartoons. You really ought to be famous." Baker was smiling in that eelish way he had as he leaned over to get a better look at the paper.

Fred had to fight the urge to shift away from him. "Um ... thanks." He jiggled the pencil around in his fingers.

There was an awkward pause. Fred glanced at Jerry for help, but his friend seemed suddenly preoccupied with an invisible scuff on his boot.

Baker shifted his feet and cleared his throat.

"Well ... I guess I'll check out that card game. Looks like they could use an extra player."

"Bet they could." Jerry's response was barely audible, and bland as saltless grits. He didn't look up.

Fred forced a smile, and Baker walked off to join a circle of GIs who were slapping cards down and shouting friendly insults.

Right away, Jerry gave up on the mysteriously absent scuff and looked around to see if Baker was actually gone. "That guy makes my skin crawl."

"Really? I had no idea." Fred gave him a sideways grin as he stretched out his boots until they almost bumped Jerry's. "Wanna polish mine while you're at it?"

Jerry snorted. "Try the next bunk, pal."

Fred laughed and went back to drawing.

"Hey, Fred? I've been thinking."

"What made you take that up all of the sudden?"

Jerry made a face at him but kept on. "You worked on automobiles before you joined up, didn't you?"

"Built my own once."

"Yeah, you told me. Out of an old Model-T frame you got for two bucks. Wasn't that the one all the kids used to scratch their names on?"

"Mostly just the girls." As soon as he said that, he wished he'd kept his mouth shut.

Jerry's eyes twinkled right away and he broke into a chuckle. *Oh boy.*

"Just the girls, huh?" Jerry punched him in the shoulder. "Must have been a pretty popular guy."

Fred rolled his eyes and went back to drawing. "Well, I wasn't very pretty, but they always seemed to like me. Joni and Bobbi-

Sue especially. They used to scratch lines through each other's names and write their own every time they got a chance."

Jerry laughed. "Cute. What'd they look like?"

"Joni was blonde. Bobby-Sue was a redhead."

"You sweet on either of them?"

The pencil slowed in Fred's fingers.

"I knew it!" Jerry slapped his leg, lips turning up in a smirk. "Bet it was the blonde!"

Fred kept his mouth shut, but silence was more than enough for Jerry.

"Thought so. What happened to her?"

Fred kicked him.

"Why don't you find somebody else to interrogate?"

"Aw, come on, I want to know what happened to the blonde!" Jerry thumped his mattress like an impatient kid.

When Fred still ignored him, he sat silent for a second, apparently scrutinizing Fred's face for clues. But he finally gave up. "Love's a funny thing, ain't it?" He dug the corner of the cloth in between his boot laces, rubbing it in circles. "I talked to a fella once who said he knew as soon as he set eyes on the girl. Bam! Just like that. Knew she was the one for him. You believe in stuff like that?"

Fred shrugged. "Maybe."

"I don't think I'd like it." Jerry scratched his chin with his free hand. "Takes the fun out of the game."

Fred flicked a piece of lint off the wool blanket and kept his thoughts to himself. Seemed to him there could be something pretty magical about knowing, as soon as you looked at a girl, that she was the one you'd marry. Like something out of a storybook.

"Speakin' of girls ..." Jerry stopped polishing and looked up.

"Aren't you always?"

Jerry whacked him. "You mind sharing that cute Brit of yours a little, come the next dance at Lowther? She looks like a real good dancer. Even makes you look good. And we all know that takes some talent."

Fred pursed his lips to hide a grin.

"Flattery will get you nowhere."

Jerry rolled his eyes. "Aw, come on."

"Weeellll..." Fred tapped his fingers on his knee. "I guess—I might be okay with that."

"Gee, thanks. I—"

"*If.*"

Jerry narrowed his eyes. "If what?"

"Well,"—Fred leaned back on the bunk, stretched out his legs, and plopped his muddy feet right onto his friend's knee—"I still need a shoe shine."

Jerry threw the polishing cloth at his head.

Chapter 6

"All the girls smell like tea these days." Lily sat in the bedroom with one bare leg propped in front of her and a damp paintbrush in her hand.

"Not all." Frances had already finished painting her legs, and sat at the mirror twisting her hair into rolls. "Some of them use other things too. Like gravy. Or meat drippings."

Lily grimaced at her older sister in the mirror. "I think I'd become a hermit before I'd go out in public smelling like left-over roast beef!"

Frances laughed, reaching for her lipstick. "Don't be too sure. If they cut the tea rations too small, we won't have extra for painting. We may have to settle for meat drippings too."

"Not me. I'd give up drinking tea first. How's your lipstick holding out? I've nearly used mine up."

Frances paused to check. "It'll last a while yet. If I'm careful." She reached for a tin of Vaseline and added a coat of it over the lipstick for extra shine. "Are you nearly through with painting? I still need the lines drawn on."

"Almost."

Lily had switched to her other leg by now. "When you draw mine, be sure you do a good job. There's the dance tonight, you know, and I think Paul might come this afternoon."

"No, he won't!" Ruth flung open the door and came bounding into the room.

Lily's hand paused with the paintbrush halfway to her leg.

"Now don't tease, Ruthie." Frances barely looked up. "How would you know when Lily's boyfriend is coming?"

"I just do." Ruth jumped onto the bed, sticking her nose in the air. "And he isn't coming this afternoon!"

"Who told you?" Lily's fingers still held the dripping paintbrush in midair.

"He did."

"When?"

"Just now."

"*What?*" Lily and Frances both spoke at once.

Ruth swung her legs back and forth as she perched on the edge of the mattress and grinned at them. "He's waiting in the kitchen with Mum."

"He's come early!" Lily dashed the paintbrush into the tea again, sloshing drops all over the chair.

Drat!

Why couldn't he just telegram and say when he was coming?

"Frances, run down and tell him I'll be there in a few minutes, will you?"

"I can't, remember?" Frances motioned to the back of her tea-tinted legs.

"Oh, for heaven's sake! He won't notice you don't have lines if he only looks at you from the front!"

"But I'll have to turn around in order to leave." Frances obviously had no intention of moving. "I can't very well come up the stairs backward."

Lily huffed. *For goodness' sake.* "Ruth, go down and tell Paul I can't come yet, but I'll be there as soon as I'm able. Go on!"

Ruth jumped down and skipped out of the room, leaving the door standing wide open as she clattered down the stairs. Lily leaned over to push it shut, but froze as her sister's voice came floating up from the kitchen.

"Lily can't come down yet, Mr. Holdsworth. She has to finish painting her legs."

"Ruth!" Lily sprang to her feet. She heard Paul choking with suppressed laughter and trying valiantly to turn it into a cough instead. Nearly choking on mortification herself, she slammed the door shut and slumped against it, feeling her face turning red. "Frances! Did you hear what she *said?*"

Frances's eyes met her gaze in the mirror, one corner of her mouth twitching. "Calm down, Lily. She's only nine."

A hot rush of fury shot into Lily's veins. Ruth had just gone down there and *deliberately* humiliated her. And Frances was laughing about it! "If mother doesn't spank her, I'm going to!"

"No, you aren't."

"Yes, I am!"

Frances only laughed. "By the time you could catch her, you wouldn't be angry anymore. Besides, you know you wouldn't really do it anyway."

Lily opened her mouth to reply but was interrupted by a timid knock on the door and a small voice calling, "Um...Lily?"

She gave Frances a look, then spun around and pulled open the door. Before she could say or do anything else, Ruth's arms shot out, holding a tissue-paper wrapped package. A rushed sentence came tumbling from her mouth.

"Paul says you can't do anything to me until after you open your present!"

Lily hesitated for a moment, taken off guard. Then she grabbed her sister's wrist and pulled her, package and all, into the bedroom, snapping the door shut behind them.

"Paul said—" Ruth began again, dancing about at arm's length.

"I heard you." Lily let go and took the present.

Ruth scampered over to watch from the safety of the far corner.

Curious, Lily peeled back the edge of the wrapping. "*Oh.*" Anger evaporated into a bright bubble of excitement as she dropped onto the bed and tore the paper off in ragged pieces like a child at Christmas. "Oh. Oh! Frances, *look!*"

Frances crossed the room.

"It's nylons! Twelve whole pairs of them!"

"Oh, *Lily!*"

She had the package open in a moment, spilling the stockings into her lap. Her fingers brushed up and down the silky length of them. So light and airy and beautiful!

Frances reached out to brush them. "Lily, please, may I wear a pair tonight? I have a date."

Lily sighed. "Please tell me it's not another American."

"Well, I don't see why everyone else should have all the fun!"

Ugh.

"Please, Lily?"

Lily looked at the nylons.

Then at her sister's hopeful face. Then back again. "Only if you promise to let me wear the party dress."

Frances hesitated. "But...my date."

"Wear something else. It's my turn anyway."

"Then why are you bargaining?"

Lily gave her a look. They both remembered what happened last time it was her turn. Frances had slipped the dress on in secret and run out the front door before Lily could stop her. "You have to promise I can wear it."

"Fine. You can wear it."

"Frances."

"All right. I *promise* you can wear it."

Lily held out a pair of stockings, and Frances took them. It was then Lily caught sight of Ruth standing a couple of feet away, looking on with interest. The moment their eyes met,

Ruth bolted for the door, but Lily caught her by the ties on the back of her dress and hauled her back. "Where do you think you're going, young lady? How dare you go down there and say something like that to Paul."

"He didn't mind." Ruth wriggled around. "He thought it was funny."

"I'm the one you should be concerned about, Miss Impertinent! Not Paul. You're lucky he managed to save you this time, but you'd better not try it again. It might turn out less pleasant." She tugged her sister's pigtail.

Ruth crawled up into her lap and kissed her cheek. Then gave her a mischievous grin. "No, it won't."

"Oh? Why not?"

Ruth slid to the floor and scampered off a few steps, just out of reach, before looking back. "You won't be able to catch me!"

Lily lunged after her, laughing, but her sister was out the door and scurrying down the stairs before she even got close.

. . . .

"Why don't we get lunch at the pavilion café?" Paul laced his fingers through Lily's as they strolled along the path in Lowther Gardens. Morning shadows had vanished by now, melting away into the roots of the trees.

Lily hesitated. "Mum will worry if I don't come home to eat."

"We can avert that." Paul glanced around until he spotted a small boy romping with a dog out on the grass, then waved his arm to catch the boy's attention. "Want to earn a little spending money, lad?"

The boy trotted toward them.

"I know him, Paul. That's David Wheaton." Dave came up with his blue corduroy hat all skew-whiff and his collie, Kirk, at his heels. "What are you doing in Lytham, Dave? Is Mary here?" Lily looked around for her.

"No. Mum's visiting Auntie Grace."

Paul pulled out a couple of coins. "Look here, Dave. You know where the Browns live? Could you take a message there for me?"

"Yes sir." Dave eyed the coins.

"Brilliant." Paul handed him one of the coins and started scribbling on a piece of paper. "If you take this to Mrs. Brown and come straight back with an answer, I'll give you the other coin too." He finished the note and handed it over. "If I'm not in the gardens when you get back, check the café."

"Yes sir!" Dave flashed a smile and sprinted off down the path, Kirk bounding beside him.

"Problem solved." Paul turned back to Lily. "I certainly hope they have good food at that café though."

"I wouldn't know. It's brand new."

"Are you hungry now?"

"Not yet."

"Me either." Paul stretched out on the lawn, folding his hands behind his head and smiling up at her. "You look very pretty from this angle. All that blue sky behind you. I ought to take up painting one of these days."

She laughed as she dropped down beside him. The new spring grass was baby soft and cool beneath her, and a robin trilled away in the nearest tree. She plucked a tall stem and ran it along her ankle, watching the nylon shimmer in the sunshine.

"Like them?"

Lily looked up. "The stockings? I love them." She glanced around and lowered her voice. "Did you get them off the black market?"

Propping himself up on one elbow, Paul plucked his own piece of grass and twirled it between his fingers. "I haven't the faintest idea. Dear old sis gets hers from somewhere. I just told her I wanted a dozen pairs. Oh. Speaking of buying things, I have a present for you."

"Two presents in one day?"

"The nylons don't count. I'd asked my sister for those a while ago. But this week I saw something in a shop window I thought you just had to have." He sat up and patted his pockets until he found a small, flat box and pulled it out. "Here."

The silvery wrapping paper glinted in the sunshine as she took it from him, tugged the white satin bow loose, and lifted the lid. "Oh…my." Her breath caught in her throat. Inside lay a heart-shaped pendant woven of silver filigree and set with tiny diamonds and seed pearls, hanging on a chain as fine as embroidery thread. It was the most beautiful necklace she had ever seen.

"It's a birthday present."

She dragged her gaze up to meet his. "My birthday is in December."

"But mine is today."

"It is?" She lowered the box to her lap. *Stupid.* Why had she never thought to ask his birthday before? "Then I'm supposed to give you something. Not the other way around."

He laughed. "I prefer it this way. Like I said, when I saw that in the shop window, I just knew you had to have it. May I see how it looks?" He took the necklace from its box and slipped it around her neck, fingers brushing her skin as he closed the latch. Then he sat back, smiling. "There. I knew it was meant for you."

She dropped her gaze for a moment, trying to think of something to say. She never was good at this sort of thing. Words always seemed to fail her at the wrong moments. "Thank you, Paul. It's…it's lovely."

"Not as lovely as the girl wearing it."

She felt her cheeks colouring. "Shall I wear it to the dance tonight? Are you going to come?"

Paul frowned. "Unfortunately, no. Father has about a dozen things he wants me to do. I'm supposed to be back by tonight.

But wear it to the dance anyway. I'll be thinking of you while you're dancing this evening. I'd like to picture you wearing it."

"I'll be thinking of you too, while I'm wearing it." She traced the filigree with her finger.

"Don't."

"Don't what?"

"Don't think of me while you're dancing." He rested his elbow on one knee and his chin on his fist. "I'd rather not distract you."

"What?"

He smiled as a faraway look entered his eyes. "Did you know, the first time I ever saw you, you were dancing?"

"I was?"

"That jitterbug contest you won, remember? At the pavilion. My aunt dragged me there while I was visiting, promising I'd enjoy it, but I was pretty sure nothing in a little town like this could match what I was used to watching in London. Until I saw you. And I couldn't pull my eyes away. The way you moved so perfectly with the music. As if nothing else mattered at that moment except the next twirl."

He ran the grass blade along the back of her hand and over her fingers as he smiled at her. "That's what I love about you, Lily. You're all in. Whatever you're feeling or doing, your whole heart is wrapped up in it. I'd never want to change that about you." He rested his hand on hers. "Just go on dancing, Lily Brown. Don't waste your time thinking about me."

Chapter 7

Lily's cousin, Joan, lay stretched out across the bed, looking on as Lily heated a saucer over the stub of a candle. "I can't wait for the war to be over so we can buy real makeup again." Joan rested her chin on her hand and sighed.

Lily smiled. "I can think of a few other reasons I'd like the war to be over, but makeup would be a lovely side benefit." She willed the smoke to hurry as it wafted upward, leaving a filmy grey smudge on the china. After a minute, she blew the candle out and started waving the saucer around to cool it down.

"Is it ready yet?"

Lily tested it with her finger. "Close enough. We'll be late if we don't hurry." She scraped up a dollop of petroleum jelly from a small tin and smeared it around in the saucer, mixing it with the candle soot to make a smoky grey paste.

Joan slid off the bed and joined her at the dressing table.

Setting the saucer between them, Lily leaned close to the mirror as she spread a thin layer of the grey jelly onto her eyelids, blending it in as well as she could with her fingers. Beside her, Joan did the same thing. It wasn't like real eyeshadow. But it was close.

Next came a piece of burnt cork and an old mascara brush to darken their lashes.

Then the tube of lipstick, which was getting low.

"Lucky duck." Joan shook her head. "I've been using beet juice for months now. How did you make yours last so long?"

"I bought some right before the shops ran out. But it's almost gone now."

Joan raised an eyebrow. "I bet Paul would find you some more in London if you mentioned it to him."

"Joan!" Lily was horrified. "I'm not going to start asking him for things. We aren't even engaged yet."

In the mirror, Joan shrugged. "Suit yourself." She pulled a compact from her purse and brushed a little colour onto her cheeks. "How about rouge? Still have some?"

"No. I use lipstick."

"I'll let you use some of mine if you'll let me use some of your lipstick." Joan eyed the tube with a hopeful look. "I'd rather not be wearing beet juice to the dance, if I can help it."

Might as well. It wasn't going to last much longer anyway. "Just hurry, all right?" Lily handed the tube over. "Aren't you dating an American now? I thought they had whole duffel bags full of nylons and lipstick."

Joan swiped a thin layer of red on and followed it up with Vaseline before answering. "He gave me these nylons I'm wearing, but I haven't seen any lipstick so far. Speaking of nylons, where'd you get those?"

"Paul."

"Mmm." Joan grinned. "So he does notice things like that. Wear beet juice next time you see him. I bet he'll come back with lipstick."

Lily rolled her eyes.

"Is he coming to the dance tonight?"

"No. Is your soldier?"

"Yes. I'll introduce you. You're going to love him. He's such a darling. And comical too, as soon as you get to know him a bit. When I first met him—"

"We really need to go." Lily picked up her pocketbook. Joan could talk till the cows came home. "I promised Joyce Robinson we'd stop by and pick her up on the way so we could all walk together."

"All right." Joan sighed. "I don't know why you're always so worried about being late. It's not like they're waiting for us to begin the music or something."

"Just *come on!*"

Fred threaded his way through the crowd in the brightly lit pavilion, glancing around for Joan. The place was jam-packed with people. Seemed like every flyboy and ground-pounder not on duty had trekked the three and a half miles from the airbase in Freckleton.

Funny they called this place a pavilion. It wasn't anything like the pavilions back home, which were pretty much just a roof held up by a few supports with maybe a concrete floor and some picnic tables. This now, this was a full-blown building. There was space for dancing and sitting, and even a real stage at one end for the band.

Fred stopped, his path blocked by a laughing knot of soldiers.

How was he supposed to find Joan in this mess anyway? He rotated, scanning this way and that for the familiar face. What he spotted instead was a pair of long, slender legs crossed jauntily, with one high-heeled shoe bobbing in beat to the music.

But it wasn't the shoe that was getting most of the attention.

Fred blinked. If that blonde girl was going to wear a skirt that short and that tight, she shouldn't be crossing her legs like that. He could practically see ...

Good grief! What was he doing? He jerked his eyes to the ceiling and held them there for a second. Somebody ought to tell her that every guy in the room was seeing ... well, a lot more of her than they had any business seeing. A girl that age oughta know better. Oughta know what kind of message she was sending with that bouncing little foot of hers.

He lowered his gaze just enough to catch her face, and realized she was looking right at him.

Tossing her hair over her shoulder, she arched one brow and flashed him a bold little smile.

Never mind. She knew.

And before he could drop his gaze, she'd hopped off her chair and headed his direction.

Uh-oh. He looked around for an escape.

She was halfway across the space between them when a soldier, nearly doubled over laughing at some joke, stepped backward and crashed right into her.

It was Baker.

"Excuse me, miss!" He caught her arm as she wobbled on her high heels. "Are you okay?"

She nodded and smiled, looking up at him through a veil of coal-black lashes.

"Glad to hear it. My name's Greg Baker. What's yours?"

Not waiting to hear any more, Fred navigated the room with long strides until he'd put several chattering groups between them.

Safe. *Thank the Lord.*

If he could just figure out where Joan was now. Maybe she hadn't arrived yet. He turned back the way he'd come and looked toward the door.

Warmth and light swirled around Lily as she stepped into the pavilion just behind Joan.

Joyce jostled in last of all, scanning the room for her boyfriend, Arthur. As soon as she spotted him, she broke into a smile and disappeared into the crowd.

Lily sighed. *Another American.*

She stood in the doorway with Joan for a minute, letting her eyes wander over the room.

The band was warming up, getting their instruments harmonized. Laughter and chatter floated above the crowds like champagne bubbles, merry and sparkling. The local girls were all there, dressed in their best dancing clothes.

As usual, the GIs handed out compliments and charming smiles as gaily as if the entire war had been orchestrated as a social event.

There was Clara, off to the left with that same American soldier again, laughing as he tried to teach her some new dance step. And there was Joyce, being introduced to one of Arthur's friends. If it weren't for the uniforms, you could almost forget there was a war going on.

She had just turned to ask Joan if she wanted any punch when something caught her gaze.

Caught it ... and held it.

A pair of blue eyes, looking straight at her. They belonged to a soldier standing over near the band, all alone.

He had light brown hair, curled a little, and a thin pencil of mustache along his upper lip. Something about his face reminded her of Mother. Calm, peaceful, but with a quiet twinkle there somewhere, as if he were grinning deep down inside and it just hadn't made it to his lips yet.

Until he saw Lily looking back at him. Then he did smile.

"Come on." Joan's voice broke in. "I see him now. I told you he'd be here before us."

Lily found herself being pulled by the wrist through a pressing bustle of people, losing track of the blue-eyed soldier in the crowd and only vaguely wondering what Joan's new sweetheart looked like.

They were in the thick of the party now, winding their way around uniform-clad soldiers and girls in knee-length dresses and lipstick, their hair rolled up tight and shiny. They passed Clara as her uniformed boyfriend whispered something into her ear. She giggled.

Oh, Clara. She was as hopeless as the rest of them.

"There you are!" Joan's voice jerked Lily's head around. "I'd like to introduce you to my cousin. Lily, meet Fred Overall. Freddie, this is Lily Brown."

And there he was. The blue-eyed soldier.

Lily pulled out her polite smile and let him shake her hand while her mind tried to catch up. So this was Freddie, then. But Freddie belonged to Joan, didn't he? Had he really been looking at Joan then, not at her, when they came in together? It hadn't seemed that way.

The band started the first song, and young people paired off with dance partners. Out of nowhere, another soldier stepped up to the group, joggling Freddie's elbow and grinning as he looked at Joan.

"Evening, Miss Joan!" He said *Miss* as if it were spelled with two Z's. "Name's Jerry. My pal Fred here gave me permission to dance with you tonight. Would you care to?"

"I never said you could have the first dance!" Freddie elbowed him.

"Ya didn't specify." Jerry grinned even wider, looking rather like a puppy who'd just stolen the soup bone. "Miss Joan?"

To Lily's knowledge, Joan had never turned down a dance partner in her life. She smiled and went with him to the dance floor. That left Lily alone, looking up into Freddie's blue eyes.

She searched for something to say but found nothing. So instead she smiled and shifted her feet, swaying a bit to the music as it came singing out of the nearby instruments. She never could stand still very well once the music started playing.

"That's 'Begin the Beguine' they're playing, isn't it?" Freddie motioned toward the band without taking his eyes off of her.

Ah, good. Something to talk about. "Yes. Lovely song, isn't it?"

"One of my favorites." He smiled. His accent was something like Jerry's, but much softer and more gentile.

"Mine too."

He cleared his throat as if to say something, hesitated, then seemed to make up his mind to say it after all. "I'll have to tell you up front I'm not the world's greatest dancer. But would you take a chance on me anyway?" He held out his hand.

Fred counted the steps in his head, praying he wouldn't flatten the poor girl's foot.

He had enough trouble keeping track of dance steps under ordinary circumstances. And these weren't ordinary. He twirled her under his arm, pulled her back to him, and settled his hand on her waist.

No, you idiot! The shoulder blade, remember? He shifted his hand upward, fingers brushing smooth satin.

It was doing strange things to his insides, having her up this close to him. Every time she moved, the air stirred with perfume. A faint whisper of flowers and citrus. But he was pretty sure that wasn't what was making him queasy.

And it wasn't the way the light shone, bouncing and playful in her dark curls. Or the impish little smile that pulled at her lips. Or the spark of fire that danced behind her eyes.

Nope.

None of those were the cause of that strange flutter somewhere between his heart and his stomach.

It was something else. Something that made his legs wobbly and his throat dry as the two of them drifted across the floor.

Other couples floated past, indistinct, weaving their surroundings into a swaying tapestry of motion. The musing jazz swelled and sang around them as they twirled, and she was light as a whisper in his arms, dancing as if she was born to it, while he was holding his breath for fear of missing the beat.

But he didn't care.

He would have happily stayed there stumbling to keep up with her the whole rest of the night. Because somehow, as soon as he saw her standing there in the doorway and caught those bright eyes looking back at him, suddenly he just ...

Knew.

Chapter 8

"How was the dance?"

Lily looked up as she eased the door shut, trying not to wake the younger girls. Frances sat up in bed, reading a ladies' magazine by lamplight with the blackout curtain pulled tight. "Oh ...lovely." Her voice wobbled. Hoping Frances would not notice, she sat down at the mirror and began fiddling with her hair.

But Frances did notice. Or at least she raised her head and looked at Lily in the mirror.

But Lily pretended not to see, keeping her eyes fixed on her own reflection in the wavering lamplight.

After studying her for a moment, Frances went back to the magazine. "Paul didn't turn up at the last minute, did he?"

"No." *Drat.* There went her voice again. She jerked out the last few pins and shoved her fingers into her hair, loosening the tight rolls until they fell out in ringlets around her face.

"Meet any nice young men?"

"Mmm." She shrugged as she put the hairpins away in their box.

Unfastening Paul's necklace, she went to set it on the nightstand.

Frances turned the page. "I suppose Joan had a nice time?"

"You know Joan." Lily began unbuttoning her dress.

"Yes." Frances chuckled. "Did you get to meet her new boyfriend? I can't remember his name."

"Freddie. I mean Fred." This time she managed to muffle her voice in the dress she was pulling over her head.

"Did you dance with him? Is he any good?"

"Yes. I danced with him." Goodness. What was the matter with her voice? She pulled the dress off to find her sister peeking at her over the top of the magazine.

"Well?"

"Well what?"

"I asked if he was any good at it."

Lily slipped a hanger inside the party dress and hung it in the wardrobe. "He was all right." He needed a good bit of help though. Odd how she had not minded.

From the corner of her gaze, she could see Frances staring studiously at the magazine page. But her eyes weren't moving anymore.

"How many times did you dance with him?"

"A few."

"How many is a few?"

Lily was strongly inclined to pinch her. "I didn't count them exactly." She sat down on the mattress and picked up Paul's necklace again, watching the way it glimmered in the lamp light.

"How about a rough estimate then?" Frances's voice had a lilt of amusement in it.

Lily sighed. *Fine.* "Maybe six or seven."

Her fingers traced the filigree as she kept her eyes fastened on it, but her face warmed.

After a long pause, Frances's hands lowered the magazine to the bed. "How many did he dance with Joan?"

Lily squeezed her toes against the floorboards. "You know Joan. She'll dance with everyone in the room if she can manage it."

"How many, Lil?"

Lily took a breath, chewing the inside of her lip. But there was no help for it. "Two that I saw." She peeked up at her sister.

"Two?" Frances raised her eyebrows.

Lily looked down again and gave her a tiny nod.

Another long pause.

Then the magazine rustled as Frances picked it up again and cleared her throat. "Well." Her voice was barely a mumble behind the pages. "*Two.*"

Fred lay stretched out on his bunk, arms behind his head, wondering how he'd been dumb enough not to ask for Lily's address.

Jerry's voice rippled over the surface of his thoughts like breeze over the ocean.

"I'm going to have the biggest trucking company in the South, Fred. Based in Atlanta, but we'll carry things all over the country. I can see my name on those big eighteen-wheelers right now. If you ever want a mechanic job working on trucks, you just call me up ..."

On the far side of the barrack, somebody started whistling "Begin the Beguine."

Jerry's voice faded out.

Fred was back in the pavilion again, trying to make conversation without losing count of the steps.

"*Sorry, was that your toe?*"

"*No.*"

"Good." Must have been somebody else's then. Probably the guy glaring at him off to the right. "I'm not much good at this, am I?"

She hesitated.

"Don't worry, I already know it. Sure helps to have a good partner though."

Her eyes smiled.

"That's a beautiful necklace, Miss Lily."

"You may call me Lily if you'd like."

"Thanks. You can call me anything. Except late for dinner. That's always the exception."

She laughed, her gaze twinkling up at him. *"Is Fred short for something?"*

"Frederick."

"Oh! That's my brother's middle name."

Her brother must have been a special guy to make her face light up like that when she mentioned him. *"Is he still here in England or ..."*

"He's a Commando." Her eyes shone with pride. *"But the Germans captured him two years ago."*

"I see. What about your father? I think Joan mentioned the Japs had her uncle. Is that him?"

"Yes." Her voice went flat. A shadow dropped over her eyes, blotting out the glow that had been there a moment ago.

Unsure how to interpret the change, Fred decided to change the subject. *"Is that a family heirloom?"*

"My necklace? No. It's a gift from my boyfriend."

Boyfriend. Right. Of course she'd have one.

"He here tonight?"

"He had to be in London for a business meeting."

"What sort of business is he in?"

"Well, if you count the ones he manages for his father as well as the ones he owns ..."

"Fred!" Jerry's voice snapped Fred back to the present. "You aren't listening."

Fred blinked. "Sorry. What'd you say?"

Jerry, sitting on his own bunk, studied Fred's face. "You look like somebody just socked you in the stomach. What's up?"

Fred ran his hand through his hair. "I'm just trying to figure out a problem, that's all."

Jerry cocked his brow. "Anything to do with the dance tonight?"

"Why?"

"Call me a good guesser."

Fred rolled his eyes. "Don't worry about it."

Jerry folded his arms and gave Fred a knowing look. "It's a girl, ain't it?"

"Have you ever considered minding your own business?"

"Not lately."

Fred sighed, shaking his head. "I'm just wondering what's the best way to convince an English girl to give up a rich English guy and marry a poor American soldier who wants to take her to live on the other side of the Atlantic."

Jerry's brow puckered. "Does Joan have some rich guy after her?"

"No."

"Then who—"

"Jerry, forget it, okay? Just go to sleep." He rolled over, pulling the blankets up to his chin.

After a minute or two of silence, Jerry spoke again, a teasing smirk in his voice. "Hey, Fred?"

"Hmm?"

"Not trying to pry or anything, but I'm just wondering...does this mean I can have Joan?"

Good grief.

Lily lay awake beside Frances for a long time that night, staring into the darkness, with Paul's necklace cradled in her hand.

But when at last she dropped off to sleep, it was the notes of "Begin the Beguine" that drifted softly through her dreams.

Chapter 9

"Want to come over for lunch, Lily?"

Lily stopped mid-stride on the paving bricks, craning her neck until she spotted Joyce Robinson leaning out an upstairs window.

Joyce turned her head, looking back into the room as if to catch someone's instructions, then leaned out again. "Margret and Shirley want you to bring your younger sisters too."

Lily looked at Mother, who nodded.

"All right." Lily shaded her eyes as she peered up again. "We'll be over after the girls change their church dresses."

"Good!" Joyce smiled. "Arthur's coming over too, with a friend of his. We're going to have some singing around the piano after we've eaten." She bobbed out of sight without waiting for a reply.

Drat. Lily pressed her lips together to keep from grimacing as she started walking again. *More soldiers.*

Those olive-drab uniforms seemed to be everywhere. Up until a week ago, she had not much cared one way or another. But since the dance at Lowther, well ...

She sent a stray rock skidding across the street, glad for something to kick.

Honestly. She had no business thinking of Freddie. No business at all. He was an American soldier, for goodness' sake. And a poor one at that. Exactly everything she was trying to avoid.

And yet for the past eight days, it seemed each time she spotted an American uniform, she would catch herself looking just to see if Freddie happened to be inside it.

What's the matter with you?

It was perfectly ridiculous. She was *sick* of uniforms. At the moment, she would be quite happy to never see another one as long as she lived.

And now she was going to be stuck in a house with two more of them all afternoon. *Brilliant.*

＊ ＊

Joyce met them at the door and took them upstairs to put their jackets in the bedroom.

They had hardly finished when 8-year-old Shirley came bounding into the room, smiling from ear to ear, and announced that their American guests were in the parlour. "Just wait till you see Arthur's friend!" She hopped on one foot. "He's so awfully handsome! And *tall.*"

Joyce rolled her eyes at Lily. "She thinks every man in uniform is handsome."

Shirley made a face. "That one with the funny nose and glasses wasn't handsome."

"He was fifty, at least."

"Well, he wasn't handsome! But Arthur's friend is. You wait and see!" Shirley pulled Ruth toward the door and dropped her voice, but Lily still overheard. "He smiled right at me as soon as he came in. I bet he's jolly when you get to know him. Wait till you see his blue eyes!"

Something in Lily's stomach did a backflip.

She shook herself. *Stop that.* There were ten thousand Americans at the Warton Air Base. How many thousands of them probably had blue eyes?

"Are you coming down, Lily?" Joyce paused at the door.

"Of course."

Joyce disappeared into the hall and Alice went out right after her, red ringlets bobbing.

Lily took a deep breath and followed, trying to get a grip on the wild flutter below her ribs as she started down the stairs.

Voices floated up, indistinct, from the parlour. It was not until she had nearly reached the bottom that Arthur's voice came up clearly, raised in introduction. "And this is Ruth's older sister, Alice Brown."

Alice's voice came next. "Pleased to meet you."

"Nice to meet you too, Alice."

Lily's heart hit the roof of her mouth and her foot nearly missed the last step. She caught the banister and clung to it, waiting for the world to stand still again.

That... *voice.*

Alice Brown.

Fred stood in the front room, the name ringing like an air-raid siren in his head. He'd spent a week looking for Lily. Watching for her every time he biked through the streets, scrutinizing every dark-haired girl he spotted. Once he nearly ran into a lamppost trying to get a better look at a head of brown curls inside a shop window. It had turned out to be a wig display.

But now, all of the sudden, when he was least expecting it, one little introduction had knocked the breath right out of him.

Steady. Take it easy. It wasn't as if this little redhead looked much like Lily. But still ...

He sucked in air and cleared his throat. "Alice, this'll probably sound like a funny question, but do you happen to have an older sister named ..."

He didn't need to finish. Lily stood in the doorway.

She wasn't wearing the necklace today. Her gray dress was much simpler than the one she had worn to the dance, and her brown curls, pulled back with a thin red ribbon, were flying away a bit around the edges. But he'd never seen anyone look so beautiful in his whole life.

He crossed the room. "Lily! I wasn't expecting to see you here. You must live nearby." No chance he was letting her get away this time without an address.

She held out her hand and let him shake it. "I live in number twenty-five. I wasn't expecting to see you here either." She looked like she hadn't decided how she felt about that. "I didn't realize you and Arthur were friends."

Arthur laughed. "Don't be too surprised. There's ten thousand men at BAD-2, and I think about five thousand of them are Fred's friends, more or less. Don't know what he does with them all."

He slapped Fred's shoulder, then caught Joyce's hand and pulled her away toward the piano. "How's your week been? I've had one of those dance songs stuck in my head since last Saturday. Let's see if I can play it on the piano."

They were left alone near the doorway.

Lily twiddled her finger in the folds of her skirt, only half-looking at him.

He cleared his throat. "Funny how those dance tunes stick in your head."

"They can be catchy." She leaned against the wall and looked over at Ruth and Shirley, who shared a book on the couch.

Inside his pocket, his fingers rubbed back and forth against his thumb. She looked so indifferent. Had last week been just another dance for her?

"Hard to get rid of sometimes." He tried again. "There's one of them I keep hearing in my sleep."

She glanced at him for an instant, with an expression that was hard to figure out. Then she changed the subject. "I meant to ask before. What happened to your forehead?"

He put his hand up and found the scab still left from the bike accident. "Oh, that. I swerved to miss a couple of girls crossing the street. It was raining, and I lost control of the bike. It only has one pedal. Makes it kind of unsteady so ..." He broke off when her eyes went wide.

"What day was that?"

He tried to calculate. "I guess it must have been ... Hey, wait a minute!" He stared hard at her curls for a second, trying to picture them disappearing around a corner beneath a sheet of rain. And hadn't the other girl been a redhead? "It was ... you!"

She stared at him, so surprised she was almost stuttering. "I ... I didn't know you crashed. I would have stopped."

Arthur started fiddling on the piano, and Ruth hopped off the couch, pulling Shirley with her. "Oooo! Play something we can dance to."

Arthur laughed, watching her bob up and down in excitement. "Anything in particular?"

"'Begin the Beguine'! I love that one. Lily does too."

"Oh?" Arthur glanced over his shoulder at Lily, who's lips had tightened just a hair.

Ruth nodded, looking wise. "Uh-huh. She's been humming it all week."

"Ruth!" Lily broke in. Then she checked herself. "Let Arthur pick his own songs, love. He's the one at the piano." She folded her arms and dropped back into her stance against the wall.

But Fred was grinning inside.

He'd seen the brief flash of color in her cheeks. And the hand, pushing back a wayward curl, jerk too fast. He'd caught the darting glance in his direction that she'd tried to hide beneath lowered lashes.

Oh yes. He'd seen every bit of it.

* *

"How'd the afternoon go?" Jerry was playing solitaire when they got back to the barracks.

Fred just smiled and stretched out on his own bed, folding his arms behind his head and dangling one foot off the end of the bunk.

Arthur laughed. "Just dandy, I'd say." He jogged Fred's foot with his knee. "Especially considering he spent half the afternoon talking to a friend of Joyce's with a red ribbon in her hair."

There was a mischievous glint in Jerry's eye. "Another one, huh? They're starting to pile up, Fred. What would Joni say?"

"For your information, Joni is happily engaged to someone else."

"Oh ho! I see. Broke your heart, eh?"

Not quite. But Fred let it go. "And just so we're clear, this was not 'another one.'"

"Ahhh." Jerry set his cards down and leaned his elbows on his knees. "I see. Well? Think you can change her mind?"

Arthur looked back and forth between them, eyebrows raised. "Somebody want to fill me in?"

"Fred wants to marry that red-ribbon girl, but she's already got some uptown Brit after her. They aren't engaged though, right, Fred?"

"Right." *Thank the Lord.*

Arthur was still trying to catch up. "But how long have you known—"

"A week." Jerry smirked, enjoying the effect. "You gotta hand it to the guy, he sure makes up his mind quick."

"I'd say so." Arthur raised his eyebrows at Fred. "You sure about this?"

Fred looked at them both, trying not to laugh at the consternation on Arthur's face.

Sure? He couldn't remember the last time he'd been this sure about anything. Ever. He nodded.

Jerry slapped his knees and rubbed his hands together. "That settles that, then. Can I be your best man?"

Fred rolled his eyes. If only it was that simple.

Something about that fiery little spark in Lily's eyes told him she might just give him a run for his money.

Chapter 10

"There's Paul, coming up the street." Alice stood in the parlour, watching out the window.

Lily pulled the steaming kettle off the stovetop in the kitchen and poured boiling water over the tea leaves, clapping the teapot lid shut to brew. Nearly a week had passed since the visit at the Robinsons'. All thoughts of Freddie were tucked away, deep down where she kept everything else she tried not to think about.

"He's got a whole bouquet of roses with him."

"What colour?" Lily took a bottle of milk from the stone shelf in the larder cupboard and poured some into a smaller jug.

"Red. You should wear one this evening. Red always looks so nice against your hair."

"Why, thank you." Lily grabbed the sugar bowl off of the high shelf and put it on the tea tray. "Did you remember to get cucumbers when the greengrocer came by yesterday?"

"I already sliced them for sandwiches. They're in the ..." Alice's voice trailed off.

Lily poked her head into the parlour to see Alice leaning against the sill, looking out with her brows puckered up in surprise. "What is it, Alice?"

"There's a man coming along on a bicycle, but something's wrong with it. Oh, wait. I see. It's missing a pedal!"

Lily dropped the tea towel and bolted for the window.

Fred slowed his bicycle, eyeing the empty window. He could have sworn there'd been a flutter of movement there a second ago, but whoever it was must have ducked out of sight.

He leaned against the handlebars and looked at the house for a minute. A two-story brick building, it was built all-in-a-piece with the next one, pressing right up to the edge of the street. An arched opening in the wall led into a covered alleyway, like a narrow tunnel, which penetrated straight through to the far side. Probably into the backyard. The front door was located part-way down the alley.

So. This is number twenty-five. He took a deep breath.

He'd already been to see Joan earlier in the week. There was no painless way to do that kind of thing, but at least she took it much better than Joni had.

He stepped off the bike. There weren't any sidewalks on the little back street. The houses started where the road stopped. He leaned the bike against the wall and turned to find a gentleman standing there in front of the alley, peering at him over an armful of roses. Their eyes met, and Fred nodded at him.

The man nodded back, still looking quizzical, and turned down the alley toward the Brown's front door.

Fred took in the expensive suit and polished shoes as they walked away from him. Hmm. *Was that...?*

Collecting a bouquet of fresh wildflowers from the bicycle basket, he started down the alley, reaching the Brown's front step just as a motherly-looking woman in the doorway was saying, "You're here to see Lily, of course."

Thought so. Well, might as well start off with a bang.

"No kidding? You too?" He stepped up to his rival, keeping an easy smile on his face. "Sure is shaping up to be an interesting evening. Bet you're the one who gave her the necklace, right? Nice roses, by the way. You grow them yourself?"

The man stared at him for a second. "My gardener grew them. And you are?"

"Sorry. Name's Fred." He held out his hand. "What's yours?"

"Paul Holdsworth." The handshake was polite but cool. "The seventh."

Fred whistled. "Seventh, huh? Must be low on names around here if you have to use the same one that many times in a row." He grinned.

Paul blinked, but the plump little woman in the doorway was obviously hiding a smile as she broke in, "Good evening ... Fred, you said?" Her eyes had a lovely twinkle to them. "Is Lily expecting you?"

He chuckled. "I doubt it. But if I give you one of these daisies, will you let me in anyway?"

Before she could reply, Lily appeared behind her in the doorway. She was smiling, though she looked a bit unsure how to handle the situation. "Good afternoon, Paul. Fred, I ... wasn't expecting you."

Fred grinned at Mrs. Brown and handed her a bright-faced bloom. "What'd I tell you? That's why I brought extra flowers. To bribe my way in."

"May I have one too?" Ruth had apparently forgotten to think before she spoke. Because every eye now turned toward her before she could get her guilty hand out of the sugar bowl.

"Ruth Brown!" her mother scolded. "Leave that be. And I'm sure Fred did not bring those flowers for you."

Fred put on a very sober expression. "That depends. Miss Ruth, are you going to keep me from coming in if I don't bribe you too?"

Ruth pulled her fingers out of the sugar, clasped her hands behind her, and raised her chin with a mischievous smirk.

"Yes."

"Well, we can't have that." He stepped through the doorway into the kitchen and held the bunch of flowers down where she could reach.

"Which do you like best? Daisies or primroses or violets? I'm afraid you can't have the forget-me-nots. Those are especially for Lily." From the corner of his eye, he watched the reaction to that one.

Mrs. Brown looked at Lily. Paul looked at Lily. Lily looked at the floor. And blushed.

Ruth pulled a violet out of the bunch, and Fred straightened up again and stepped inside. "I hope there aren't too many other sisters around."

"I have three altogether."

"Good grief! I should have brought more flowers."

"Speaking of flowers." Paul spoke at last, stepping in past Fred. "These are for you, Lily."

"How lovely!"

"Aren't they though?" Fred nudged Paul's arm. "That gardener of yours sure knows how to pick' em, Paul." He turned and swept Lily a dramatic bow. "Since the other sisters haven't appeared and threatened to evict me so far, the rest of these are for you."

She took the bouquet, smiling.

"I'm afraid they aren't all the same color like his are, but I picked them myself, all the way along the road from Warton. And"—he lowered his voice to a secretive whisper and looked at Ruth—"someone *very* important grew them."

"Who?" Ruth's voice was a stage whisper.

"God."

Ruth giggled. "But doesn't God grow *all* the flowers?"

Fred shrugged. "You'll have to discuss that with Paul the Seventh here. He seems to think his gardener is responsible for those."

While Paul tried to come up with a response, Mrs. Brown shooed them all through a doorway into the front room.

Fred grabbed a cup, took a chair near the brick hearth, and settled down to see how the evening played out. He was more and more convinced it was going to be great fun.

Lily emptied the last drops of tea into her cup and glanced out the window. It would be time for supper soon. The evening shadows had faded long ago. Goodness, how the time had flown.

Freddie had kept them well entertained with his stories about growing up in Florida, sketching pictures of the little house and garden, the swampy forest land around it, and the family dog, a loyal mutt named Teddy. No one could help being fascinated by his tales of growing up in a country that was still but half-tamed.

Sitting there in the cozy parlour, she tried to picture what it must have been like to be left alone for a month, at only fifteen, with nothing but a pump .22 Winchester and a dog to keep him company.

"But the neighbor came by just when I needed him," Freddie was saying now. "I was down to one lone bullet, wondering where I was gonna get my next meal. Should've known God would work it out just in time though."

The mantle clock began chiming the hour.

Freddie looked up with a start, then bounded to his feet. "Good grief! Is it that late already? I best get a move on."

"What time are you expected back?" Mother took his empty teacup.

Freddie got an odd look on his face. "Well...they don't exactly know I left. I hope." He gave them a guilty grin.

"You're AWOL?" Lily didn't know whether to laugh or be worried. "That's dangerous, isn't it?"

He laughed. "Not half as dangerous as a Florida swamp full of alligators. And I grew up there."

"But can you get back on base without them knowing?"

He cocked his brow with a mysterious smile. "I have my ways."

Paul got to his feet too and set his plate on the tea tray. "My aunt will be expecting me shortly. Thank you all for your hospitality. And Lily, as always, your smiles are the highlight of my day." He took her hand and kissed it.

Freddie whistled. "So gallant. No wonder she likes you." He turned laughing eyes upon her. "I'd do the same, but I guess I better follow my mother's advice and not try to kiss a girl on my first visit.'" He shook her hand instead.

Lily's pulse quickened, and her cheeks felt much warmer than necessary. *First visit*. That meant there might be a second.

Ruth tugged on Freddie's sleeve, motioning for him to lean down so she could say something in his ear. He obliged. She leaned close but spoke in a whisper quite loud enough for the rest of them to hear. "Um...do you ever have any sweets?"

Freddie burst out laughing. "Candy, you mean?" He put his hand in his pocket. "Do you promise to leave the sugar bowl alone, at least until next time I visit?"

She nodded, eyes hopeful.

"All right then."

He handed over a stick of Orbit chewing gum.

Ruth squealed and skipped back to her seat.

Freddie stood and nodded to Mother. "Thank you for letting me in, ma'am, even though nobody was expecting me. But, Lily,"—he turned back to her, his lips quirking up in a grin ... "from now on, expect me."

Her cheeks went hotter, and she found herself avoiding Paul's eyes. Without another word, Freddie turned and ducked through the kitchen entry, opening the front door and stepping outside with Paul right at his heels.

Mother shut the door after them. The room was quiet for a moment as she took her tea apron off and hung it in the kitchen. Then she came back into the parlour and gave Lily a look. "Well, love. You didn't tell me Paul had a new rival."

Frances burst into laughter before Lily could reply. "She didn't tell *me* either, Mum. But I figured it out!"

Fred's hand was on the bike handlebar when Paul's voice stopped him. "One minute."

He turned.

Paul stood at the entrance to the alley. The shadow of the house fell across him at an angle, and his face looked firm and still in the moonlight. "Just so we're clear, I intend to marry Lily Brown."

Fred held his gaze. "Just so we're clear, so do I."

A whisper of surprise flickered across Paul's face. "I see. Does that make us enemies then?"

"Not enemies. Just rivals."

Paul studied him for a moment. "Friendly rivals?"

Fred smiled and held out his hand. "Friendly rivals."

They shook.

Paul stepped back, looked at him another moment, then gave him a nod. "May the best man for Lily win."

Chapter 11

August 1944

Stray curls whipped Lily's cheeks, snapping and whirling in the brisk sea breeze as she stood there on the beach, watching Freddie bolt after someone's runaway ball.

It had been over three months since the dance at Lowther. And somehow or another, that perfect plan she had laid out for her life was fraying around the edges.

Ever since the visit in April, Paul seemed to be in Lytham every chance he had, bringing flowers and chocolate and a dozen other little luxuries, whisking her off to the finest restaurants, concerts, and plays. The life she dreamed of was so close she could almost taste it. A life where no one worried about whether there would be food on the table next week. Or scraped and saved just to buy a new pair of shoes. A life where the constant pressure to make ends meet didn't hang like a sack of lead on men's shoulders, driving them to ...

She sighed, running her foot back and forth over the sand as she smoothed out someone's leftover footprint. If only old memories were as easy to erase.

If she married Paul, she could solve everything. Alice and Ruth would not have to work, like she had, to help make ends meet. She could get good jobs for Robert and Father. Frances would have all the pretty dresses she ever wanted.

And Mother. Mother would never look the way she had that one awful night ...

Lily slammed her toes into the sand, watching it spray out in front of her. How could she not marry Paul, now that she had the chance?

And yet.

She raised her eyes.

Freddie had the ball now. He kicked up a silver spray of seawater as he dodged around, romping with a troop of boys at the edge of the surf.

Sighing again, Lily turned away. But she couldn't block out the sound of his voice, laughing and shouting as the boys fought to steal the ball from him. Freddie was almost impossible to ignore.

Despite working twelve-hour shifts, sometimes seven days a week, repairing planes as the Allies pushed into Europe, he somehow found the time to visit. Neither Paul's obvious monetary advantage nor his prior claims seemed to deter him in the slightest. Freddie simply would not give up.

He came jogging back just then, trouser legs wet and bare feet plastered with sand. "Look, Lily! Look at the sandpipers."

She followed his finger to the little birds scuttling along at the edge of the tide on toothpick legs, and managed to force a smile.

"I learned a poem about those birds in school once."

"How did it go?"

He smiled. "'Along the lonely beach we flit, one little sandpiper and I. And fast I gather, bit by bit, the scattered driftwood, bleached and dry.'" Fred stooped to pick up a piece of driftwood, worn smooth and soft by the sea.

"For Mother again?"

He tucked it under his arm. "You don't think I'd go beach walking and not bring her back some firewood, do you?"

Lily shook her head. It was no wonder everybody loved Freddie. He was always thinking of everyone but himself. Mother, the girls, the neighbours. Random strangers on the street. Everyone. No wonder they were all drawn to him like a magnet.

No wonder she was too.

But I have to marry Paul.

She looked down at her hands for a moment, lacing her fingers together. When she raised her head again, Freddie's eyes had shifted away, out toward the horizon where distant blue sea melted into the sky.

"What are you looking at?"

His smile came soft and gentle. "Florida's out there. On the other side of the water."

She followed his gaze, trying to visualize another country beyond the waves, but all she could see was the water rippling in the sunlight. "I can't...quite imagine that."

He chuckled. "Is it that hard to believe I actually came from somewhere out there? You think I just crawled up out of the seaweed?"

She pushed a stray curl behind her ear. "I mean it seems so far away. As if it isn't quite real. Doesn't it ever seem that way to you?"

He lowered himself to the ground and rested his hands on his knees.

She joined him, wiggling her toes into the warm sand as she waited. He'd started rubbing his thumb and fingers together again, a peculiar habit he had when he was thinking.

She prodded his arm. "Well, doesn't it?"

He looked at her with that half-smile he often wore when she was being impatient. Then he got up, took three long strides to the edge of the water, bent down, and scooped something up in his hands. She watched as he came back to her, hands dripping, too high up for her to see into them from where she sat.

He leaned over her, silhouetted against the sun, his shadow cooling her skin. "Hold out your hands."

"What is it?"

"Don't you trust me?"

She hesitated, then stretched out her hands toward his.

He bent down and opened his fingers. A gush of sun-warmed salt water emptied into her cupped palms. Squeezing her hands together to keep it from draining out, she leaned over and looked. But there was nothing there.

Fred dropped down beside her again. "What do you think of that?"

"Of what?"

"That."

Lily looked down once more, but still saw nothing but water, draining by droplets into the sand. She raised her eyes. "It's just ... water."

He smiled. "Exactly."

She stared at him.

Turning back to the ocean, he waved his arm in a wide arch, sweeping over the expanse before them. "Nothing but water, Lily. All of it. Just a bunch of handfuls of water piled up together." He closed his fingers over hers, pressing them together, letting the rest of the seawater trickle out into the sand.

"And it doesn't matter how many handfuls there are. It still doesn't go on forever. I know. I've been over it. And I'm going to go back over it, one of these days." He paused, his blue eyes holding her gaze, his hands warm and strong around her own. "Maybe, someday, you will too."

The salty air came quick and fast into her lungs, and she dropped her eyes. But he kept hold of her hands, fingers interlacing with her own. Her pulse pounded in her ears.

Stop it, Lily. Stop it now! This isn't what you wanted. This isn't in the plan. Wake up. You're dreaming. She tried to pull away, but her hands would not obey her.

And all she could see was the blue of Freddie's eyes.

Chapter 12

Lily's eyes flew open in the darkness. Her breath came in gasps around the fear lodged in her throat, as her whole body lay rigid beneath the covers.

The nightmare again.

It was getting more frequent. And more vivid every time.

Staring into the blackness, she took long, deep gulps of air. The dark was so thick it was suffocating. Blackout curtains did a good job of keeping Nazi planes from having something to aim for, but they kept the moonlight out just as thoroughly as they kept the lamplight in.

Lamplight.

Wait a moment.

Now that she was looking, she could make out a thin strip of paler darkness that could only be the crack beneath the bedroom door. Someone had a lamp lit somewhere.

Careful not to wake Frances, she slipped out of bed. It was August now, and she didn't even bother with a shawl. The door creaked a bit when she opened it, but no one stirred. The light was brighter out in the hall, filtering up from downstairs. Her bare feet made no sound on the wooden steps as she descended them and peered around the wall into the kitchen.

Mother was there at the table, with her Bible open before her. She looked up from sipping a cup of tea. "What are you doing up? You were out awfully late with Paul."

Lily didn't want to talk about the nightmare. "I saw the light under the door. Is everything all right?"

Mother set down her cup and reached for the teapot. "Come and sit, love. There's enough tea for both of us." She filled a second teacup as she spoke.

Mother had a certain tone sometimes. A tone that could make even her grown children uneasy.

Lily went and sat down on the nearest chair, taking a sip of tea to hide her sudden nervousness. For several moments there was silence. At last she cleared her throat. "What's wrong, Mum?"

Mother settled her teacup in its saucer. "Fred was here to see you yesterday, while you were off with Paul. He wanted me to tell you he'd come by Wednesday morning when he's off again."

But that wasn't what they were there to talk about. She waited.

Mother pressed her lips together, staring down at her cup. After a pause, she looked up again. "You've been at this long enough, Lily."

Lily wrinkled her brow. "At what?"

"It's not a game, playing with two men's hearts. It's high time you made up your mind which one of them you want, and let the other go."

"But—"

Mother held up her hand. "I don't believe in this new way the young people have. Playing around as long as possible before committing to anything. It's not right. I did not raise my daughters to treat men like prize fish, trying to see how many they can catch and keep for a while before throwing the smaller ones back. It's high time you made up your mind."

Lily's head spun. She had already made up her mind. It was made up long before Freddie came along, was it not? But then ... then Freddie *did* come along. And she couldn't get rid of him. Oh dear. Everything used to be simple. Now she was so confused she could barely see straight. "I can't. Not yet. I need more time."

Mother shook her head. "You've had more than enough. It isn't fair to keep on like this. You can't marry both of them."

"But I don't *know* which one I want to marry."

Mother looked at her for a long, penetrating moment. "I think you do."

"No, I don't!" Lily buried her face in her hands.

Mother's chair creaked, and her footfalls whispered on the floorboards. In a moment, the familiar arms slipped around Lily's shoulders from behind, pulling her close.

"You'd better do some serious thinking and praying then, love. Because you ought to care about both of them enough not to keep dragging this on and on." Mother's voice was soft but firm. "They have their own lives to live, Lily. You can't tie them both to yours forever."

* *

Lily stood at the top of the seawall, eyes on the water.

She had not slept a wink after her conversation with Mother. Now it was nearly dawn. At this hour, with the pale fingers of morning just beginning to stretch above the trees, she was alone with her thoughts and the soothing throb of the tide.

After slipping off her shoes and stockings, she climbed down the steps, crossed the dim ribbon of beach, and sat down with her back to the sunrise and her face to the ocean.

For a long time she sat there, her toes digging into sand not yet warmed by the sun, her mind running back and forth with the rhythm of the tide. She lost track of the difference between thoughts and prayers. They seemed to merge, tangled together like seaweed tumbling in the waves.

She had thought she was so sure what she wanted. But suddenly she wasn't certain of anything anymore. Perhaps, after all, she never had been. Perhaps she had only told herself she was. Perhaps she had been waiting. Waiting all this time for some lightning bolt of clarity.

But it had never come.

She sat there for hours, her stomach far too twisted in knots to wish for breakfast. But at last she knew by the sun's position that she had to go. Life would not stand still. She could not stay on the beach forever, waiting for a lightning bolt.

· ·

All day long she went through the motions. Dispensed pills, checked prescriptions, listened to old ladies complain about arthritis. Drank her tea without tasting it. Mended a dress without feeling the needle prick her skin. It was all at a distance, as if she were acting in a play. Not living, just pretending to live, while the questions spun round and round in circles until her brain felt too numb to think.

By the time she climbed the stairs to bed, she was so tired she thought she would collapse on the steps. And yet it took hours before she finally fell asleep.

When she did, the nightmare came again. She woke gasping, with the same icy fear wrapped around her chest. And the other thing, the darker thing, much colder and harder than fear, pressed against her heart.

She had never put a name to it. Never dared to. Yet it was always there. Ugly, suffocating, spilling out of the blackness when she least expected it. Worst when she had the dream.

Pushing her fingers into the roots of her hair, she squeezed her eyes shut, trying to block out the memories. Raised voices. Sobbing. Cold wind in the darkness. Mother's face.

The night Lily ran.

Coward! Clenching her hands in the darkness, she tossed her head back and forth on the pillow, jaw clamped tight, fighting the tears.

It was poverty that had done it to Father. It had to be. If only they'd had enough money. If he hadn't always been fighting just to make ends meet. If he had been able to give them the life he wanted to.

If, if, if. There were a thousand things that would have been different. Things she had never been able to control. But now she had a chance. A chance to make sure her children never saw their father crushed under that weight, or what that could do to a man. A chance to make it all better. For everyone.

All she had to do was marry Paul.

Chapter 13

August 23, 1944

On Wednesday morning, the sun rose shrouded in a cold mist. The air was sodden, laced with chill, and the sky, when it grew light enough to see it, was iron grey and heavy with clouds.

Lily left the house right after breakfast. She didn't work at the chemist's on Wednesdays. On a normal day she would have stayed home and helped Mother with housework.

But today was not a normal day.

Freddie was coming, but she didn't want to see him in the house with everyone around. Not today. It had to be all alone. Somewhere no one would be listening. Somewhere no one would interrupt. Somewhere she could tell him ...

Tell him ... what?

That she didn't want to see him anymore? That she had made up her mind to marry Paul? That she would never run off to America with a half-broke soldier and leave her home, her family, and Mother, just for one soldier?

Not even if it was Freddie.

She walked on, into the misty grey morning, and wondered if she was going to cry.

Fred shoved his hands deeper into his pockets and hunched his shoulders against the drizzle. It had been overcast all morning, and colder than it had any business being in August. Now the gray curtain of sky had started spitting raindrops down his neck. By now he was almost used to this kind of weather. It was England, after all. But this particular morning felt off somehow. Wrong. He couldn't explain it.

Angling around a particularly muddy piece of road, he brushed against the hedge, snagging his coat sleeve on the hawthorn spikes. *Darn.* The folks who thought hedges were picturesque must never have tried leaning on one.

When he looked up from unhooking himself, someone was trudging up the road toward him. A girl with wild brown curls and a silver necklace at her throat, head lowered against the rain.

"Lily!"

Her face snapped up like a switchblade, and she stopped in her tracks.

He quickened his steps to meet her, eyeing Paul's necklace as he got closer.

She stared at him. Her lips parted a little, and her chest rose and fell faster than usual. But she didn't say a word.

That uneasy feeling he'd had all morning got worse by the second. "I was just on my way to come see you. Didn't your mom tell you I was coming?"

She nodded. Dark circles hung under her eyes. She looked like she hadn't slept well. Maybe for more than one night. The wind picked up, kicking the raindrops right into her face. He moved closer, trying to block the gust, but she took a sharp step back, almost jerking away from him.

Something was really wrong.

"Lily, are you okay?" That necklace tied his stomach in knots. He hadn't seen her wear it in ages. He'd sort of figured she tried not to wear it when he was around.

She swallowed, and a little shiver seemed to run through her. "I ... I'm fine."

"What are you doing out in this weather without an umbrella?"

"I was ... I came to ..." She licked her lips, and her breath seemed to come faster and faster as she looked up at him. "I mean I had to ..." The silence dragged long, and her mouth worked, like the words were stuck in her throat.

He waited, digging his thumbnail into the rough wool of his trouser leg.

She blinked. Once. Twice. "I needed to ... to ..." She stopped breathing all together, frozen, her eyes wide and dark in her face.

He tensed to catch her, afraid she might faint.

But she sucked in air again with a gulp and dropped her eyes to the ground. "I'm going to see a friend. In Freckleton."

He wasn't sure what he'd been expecting. But that wasn't it. "A friend?"

"Mary." She raised her face to his again, eyes weary. "Mary Wheaton."

Wheaton. That would be Dave's older sister. He'd seen Dave a few times since the bicycle incident. Met Mrs. Wheaton too. But not the sister.

Head drooping, Lily skirted around him as if he was a fence post and started walking again.

He swiveled around and stood there in the middle of the road, trying to figure out what had just happened. "Um ... if you're going to Freckleton anyway, how about stopping by the Sad Sack?" He was at a loss for anything else to say. "They've got good tea in there. I'll buy you a cup."

"I'm going straight to Mary's." She didn't even turn her head.

Fred took a couple steps, starting to try to catch up, but stopped. She didn't want to talk to him. That much was pretty clear. But why? What had he done? And why was she wearing that blasted necklace again when she had to know she'd meet him on the road?

He felt colder by the second.

She was still walking, getting farther and farther away. Her shoulders slumped and her steps were slow. But they carried her steadily on, into the mist.

He had to say something. Anything.

He cupped his hands around his mouth. "If you want to stop and get some tea after you see Mary, I'll be there. At the café. About a quarter till eleven?"

She didn't answer.

He stood there in the chill drizzle, watching her go, with his thumb and fingers rubbing back and forth at his side. Until she was a just gray shadow, lost in the mist.

"Lily! What brings you to Freckleton?" Mary Wheaton stood in the doorway, smiling a welcome.

Lily forced out an answering smile, but it felt a bit sickly. "I had an…errand. I thought I'd come by and see you while I was here."

"Come in and have a spot of tea. Cold morning, isn't it?"

It was. Especially compared to the past few days. Lily stepped inside and let Mary show her to a chair.

"You look pale, Lily. Are you feeling all right?"

"I'm fine."

Liar. Of course she was not all right. She had just left Fred-die standing out there on Lytham Road, as forlorn and confused as a lost puppy in the rain. And she hadn't even told him what she came to say.

Mary poured the tea. "Mother took Dave to school and went to the market. She won't be back for a while."

Lily's ears were listening but her mind was not. In her lap, her hands knotted together.

Had Freddie suspected the truth? Did he know she hadn't come all the way here just to visit Mary?

Of course he knew. She had seen the look on his face. Perhaps it was better this way. To let him down slowly, instead of springing it all at once. Perhaps by the time she saw him again, she would have figured out how to tell him for real.

"Dave is so proud to be starting school. It's only his first week, you know. He's so excited."

Lily forced herself to take a sip of tea and try to look interested. "I can't believe he's already old enough."

Mary shook her head and sighed. "I can't either. And you should see Mum. After waiting so long for a second child, I think she's not quite ready for him to grow up yet. She looked positively blue that first day."

"Does he like his teacher?"

"Oh yes. You remember Jennie Hall, don't you? She just started this year. I think she'll make a splendid teacher. What about Alice and Ruth? Do they like their teachers this year?"

"Oh I suppose. They haven't said much."

"Well then they must be having better luck than you did. I remember one particular year you told me you wished your parents would move here to Freckleton so you could come to class with me. My teachers were all lovely. I'm sure Jennie Hall will be the same way..." Mary's voice went on, but Lily barely heard it.

She had made her decision. And she was certain it was the right one.

So why did she feel so sick inside?

Chapter 14

"We shoulda left earlier." Jerry pulled his collar tight as he trotted to keep up with Fred." It wasn't raining so dang hard then."

"I told Lily I'd be there at a quarter till."

"Well, we could have sat around in there awhile. Besides, didn't sound to me like she was planning to be there anyhow."

Fred pressed his lips together. It was true. But still, maybe she'd change her mind. "Quit bellyaching, Jerry. I said I'd buy the coffee and doughnuts, didn't I?"

"Sure. But only because if I don't come, you won't have anyone to talk to, and you'll just sit there staring at the door waiting for that fool girl to show up."

"Don't call her that."

"Fine. But that's why, ain't it?"

"Does it matter?"

Jerry shrugged. "Guess not. Long as I get my coffee and pep tires. But I still don't like the weather."

Fred tried changing the subject. "Did you hear Bing Crosby is going to be here the beginning of next month?"

Jerry nodded. "Kinda fun being in the military, ain't it? Get to see all sorts of shows you couldn't afford back home." He started whistling a scrap of "White Christmas" as he strode along, then looked at Fred, waiting for him to join in.

But Fred didn't. From the corner of his eye he could see Jerry watching him, brow furrowed, until the whistling petered out into silence.

Finally Jerry stopped altogether and stood still in the road, forcing Fred to stop too. "You really are dead nuts on that girl, ain't ya?"

"Jerry, if you think Bing Crosby is a girl, Georgia really is the middle of nowhere."

Jerry snorted. "Nice try, but you know what I meant. You think I can't see what's going on here? No Florida boy like you is gonna go walking through weather like this to sit at a café and just *hope* his girl shows up. Not unless he's in love and scared he's gonna lose her. The sky looks like it swallowed an inkwell, and you're out here walking through the rain without even putting on your hat!"

Fred glanced up. He hadn't been paying much attention to the weather, except to listen to Jerry complaining about it.

Until now. *Good grief.*

The sky above them was still the typical gray, but over to the southeast something else was brewing. A coal-black turmoil of clouds was tumbling toward them, fast, and he could see the distant trees keeling over to one side like they were almost ready to snap off.

"That's got to be the worst rainstorm I ever saw in my life." He watched it roll toward them, a monster ready to pounce. "If it keeps moving that fast, it may hit us before we can get to the snack bar."

"Well, what are we standing here beating our gums for?" Jerry grabbed Fred by the arm and started up the street again. "Let's get a move on! I'm wet enough already without getting caught in *that* soup."

A minute later, the first gust of heavy wind smacked into them like a wall.

Lily sat across from Mary, sipping her second cup of tea. Dave's collie, Kirk, slept at her feet, and up on the mantle the clock ticked away the minutes. It was twenty till eleven.

Fred would be at the Sad Sack anytime now, looking for a table for two. He would sit there, drinking a cup of tea and waiting for her to come ...

"I just love that necklace, Lily."

She dragged her eyes off the clock. "Thank you. It was a gift from Paul."

Mary gave her a knowing smile. "*Oh*. I've heard all about Paul. Some of the girls are saying Clara is going to be the next war bride. Are you going to run off to London and leave us too?"

Lily stirred her tea. This was not the conversation she wanted to have right now. "I wouldn't be surprised if Clara does marry that soldier of hers."

"And you?"

She was saved from answering when the door flew open. A gust of wind knocked the morning paper from the table, sending pages fluttering in all directions, and Mrs. Wheaton blew through the doorway.

Mary set her cup down in surprise. "I thought you'd be longer at the market, Mum."

"I didn't go to the market." Mrs. Wheaton slammed the door against another gust. "There's a bad storm blowing in."

"A storm?" Lily jumped to her feet. "I need to get home. Mother doesn't even know—"

Without warning, the world went black.

First came the darkness. Then the downpour.

Fred was soaked before he could even register it. Wet to the skin, he dodged over to the nearest roof overhang and pressed himself against the wall, blinking away rivulets of water as Jerry crowded in beside him.

Rain poured down around them in a roaring torrent. Lightning ripped across the sky like daggers stabbing the darkness, and thunder shook the ground he stood on.

"Look!" Jerry pointed. "You can't even see the other side of the road anymore!"

It was true. Between the rain and the darkness, houses only a few yards away were completely invisible. They'd been within sight of the café a moment ago, but it too was lost in the storm.

"I hope none of the fellas are trying to fly in this!" Fred's eyes automatically scanned the sky above, though he could see nothing but darkness.

Jerry kept his head down, hat pulled low to ward off the rain. "Bet they canceled all the flights when they saw the storm coming."

You'd sure hope so. He watched the storm another minute or two, then shook Jerry's shoulder. "Let's make a run for the snack bar! This roof isn't helping anyhow."

Jerry's voice was almost lost in the gale. "The wind'll knock you clean over!"

"Aw, come on. I don't want to keep standing out here getting soaked!" The Sad Sack was no more than twenty yards away. Maybe, just maybe, Lily was there waiting for him.

Jerry just shook his head.

Fine.

Bracing himself, Fred ducked away from the building. At first the wind smacked into him like a brick wall, nearly knocking the air out of his lungs.

But a second later it changed directions and came from behind, pushing him up the street instead. Rain pelted down almost as hard as hailstones. Lighting flashes gave him quick glimpses ahead, where he could barely make out the café. Just a few more yards.

Another clap of thunder exploded in his ears, far louder than the rest had been. The ground vibrated under his feet. Lightning lit up the town like midday, and something made him turn around.

That's when he saw it.

The flaming body of a plane, cartwheeling up the street like something out of a nightmare.

A mindless steel monster, spitting sparks and fire and crushing to pieces everything in its path.

It was headed straight for him. Straight for the café. Straight for ...

Lily!

Chapter 15

"I don't know what you two are looking at." Mrs. Wheaton's knitting needles clicked in her hands as she sat in a chair next to the kitchen table. "It's black as pitch out there."

Lily took a sip of her tea and glanced at Mary, who shrugged. But neither of them moved away from the window. With the lamp glowing in the room behind them, they could see nothing except when the lightning flashed. Yet somehow Lily could not pull herself away. Eyes on the blackness, she raised her teacup to her lips for another sip.

But she never tasted it.

As the house trembled in another thunderous crash, the whole town illuminated. Out of nowhere, a ball of flames exploded into view beyond the houses across the street, casting them into dark silhouette.

Kirk sprang to his feet as if he'd been struck by lightning. For a moment he stood transfixed, the hair along the scruff of his neck standing on end. Then he gave a terrible yowl and hurled himself at the door.

"What is it?" Mrs. Wheaton dropped her knitting.

Lily pressed against the pane, trying to see. "It's a fire! Something's on fire. Mary, isn't that...that's the school!"

Mary's teacup shattered on the floor.

Almost before she knew it, Lily was out the door. Running. Running through the rain toward the orange flames with Mary and Mrs. Wheaton, and Kirk up ahead, fast outpacing them.

Through the pounding rain and the wind that tore at her like a wild thing, she became aware of more and more people around her, shouting, running, screaming. Then there was the street, awash in flame. And the school, an entire wing of it engulfed in an inferno. Houses in shambles, splintered fragments of the plane in the midst of it all, and the Sad Sack Café...

No!

Lily tumbled over something and slammed into the paving bricks, but she didn't feel the fall. Her eyes were locked on the restaurant where Freddie had promised to be waiting for her.

Right now.

But there was no restaurant anymore. Only a pile of flaming rubble.

She choked on fumes, her dress plastered to her wet body as billows of heat seared her skin. Black smoke billowed up in all directions. Flames, feeding on airplane fuel, shot upward untouched by the rain. People flickered around the edge of her vision like shadows in the lurid orange light, but all she could see was the rubble. All she could hear were the flames hissing like demons in the downpour.

Freddie. No, no, no!

The last thing she had said to him was that she would not join him for tea. The last thing he'd seen of her was her back as she walked away and left him standing there in the cold. Like an echo she heard her own words, taunting her now, *I don't know which one I want to marry!*

Now she knew. Only now, when it was too late. It was Freddie she loved. Had loved. Would always love. Freddie whose blue eyes made her heart want to dance. *Freddie.*

Who was dead.

The chaos crashed in on her again as she ground her fists into the street, pounding it convulsively. *Why, God, why?*

There were no answers. And no tears. Only the knife-sharp pain.

Someone stepped on her hand as they ran past, and it snapped her into motion. *The children.* She dragged herself to her feet, catching a glimpse of Mary still in sight up ahead. *Some of them might still be alive.* She broke into a run again, trying to catch up as the fumes stung her eyes and her lungs burned with smoke and heat.

Out of nowhere, someone seized her arm, spinning her around and catching a firm hold of both her shoulders.

She fought for a moment, panicked, half-mad, as the storm and the roaring flames and the yells of human beings pounded in her ears.

But then someone called her name. And for a moment the whole world stood still.

That ...voice.

She raised her head and looked up into the smoke-blackened face staring down at her.

Freddie.

Chapter 16

"Lily!" He was shouting over the din, voice hoarse as his fingers dug into her shoulders.

"Don't get any closer. You hear me?" Her knees felt watery beneath her, and she swayed in his arms.

Without a word, he scooped her up and carried her to the nearest roof overhang.

Before she could find her voice again, he was gone, racing to join the others. Men were battling the flames with bare hands, fighting to reach the flaming inferno that had once been the infant wing. They needed water to fight the fire, but the wreckage blocked the main water supply. A group of GIs somehow lifted and carried a massive trailer pump over the wreckage to the mill, where they hooked it up to the water there and ran hoses back to the school.

But by then it was too late. The infant wing, where Dave would be, had already collapsed. It lay in a heap of blackened bricks and flaming beams, smoking like an ancient funeral pyre. Lily didn't want to see it, but somehow she couldn't look away. She stared, choking, while the heatwaves rippled toward the clouds, and wondered why she couldn't cry.

Mary came back, her arm around her mother. They sat down beside Lily, faces cold and still as marble. Their eyes held little hope.

After what seemed a long time, Kirk found them, his fur singed from the flames and sodden with rainwater. He limped toward them, carrying something small and dark in his mouth. When he reached Mrs. Wheaton, he whined low in his chest and dropped what he was carrying at her feet.

Dave's blue corduroy cap.

Mary's face twisted when she saw it, and Mrs. Wheaton's eyes were dark and hollow. Lily looked away. But still there were no tears. She stared dry-eyed at the destruction, as soldiers and local rescue workers searched for survivors and the rain began to die down.

Freddie was gone a long time. After a while, the Wheatons went back to their house to wait for further news, but Lily stayed, waiting for him.

⋯ ⋅ ⋅ ⋅ ∘ ∘ ⊙ ⊙ ⊙ ● ● ● ⊙ ⊙ ∘ ∘ ⋅ ⋅ ⋅ ⋯

At last he came, soaking wet and black with soot and smoke.

She got up and went to meet him. "Freddie, I thought...Weren't you in the café?"

He shook his head. "Almost. Barely had time to get out of the way. But I thought...I was afraid *you* were inside."

His blue eyes looked down at her from a face stained dark. He was filthy. And his strong shoulders sagged with fatigue and sorrow.

But he was alive. *Alive*.

The reality of it finally broke through the dull veil of shock she'd been living in for hours, and before she could even stop to think, she flung her arms around his neck and pressed her lips against his.

Right there in the middle of the street.

His arms went around her, strong, safe, and steady.

She leaned against him, closing her eyes as the waves of emotion came crashing over her.

At last, the tears came. "I heard them, Freddie." She clung to him. "I heard the children. Screaming."

His chest heaved against her cheek, and his voice came low and husky. "I know. I heard them too."

It was the first time she'd ever seen a man cry.

The funeral was three days later.

Fred watched the long procession of GIs bearing coffins to their communal grave in the churchyard. Mourners lined the way, five or six deep, almost all of them adults.

Most of the children who had lived through the disaster were kept far away.

Fred swallowed, watching the hundreds of dark, solemn eyes following the tiny coffins.

Nobody said it would be like this.

You knew some soldiers wouldn't make it. Ten airmen from BAD-2 had been killed in the crash too. Some on the plane, some in the café. Tragic, of course. But those guys knew they were taking that risk when they joined up.

Nobody told you five-year-old kids might die. He clenched his jaw as tears pricked his eyes.

There had been forty-one children in the infant class. Only seven had been pulled out alive. Of those, only four still clung to life in the base hospital.

The other three had died of their injuries. Sometimes it was hard to make sense of the world.

He was turning to leave at the end of the funeral when a hand on his arm stopped him.

Mary Wheaton. She wore dark funeral clothes, and her pale face looked up at him with the deep purple of sleepless sorrow circling her eyes. "You're Fred, aren't you?"

"Yes."

She reached into her purse and pulled out a familiar pair of pliers. "David carried these in his pocket every day." Her voice caught. "They found them in his coat. Mum thought you'd like to have them back."

He met her eyes as he took them, searching for the right words. But there weren't any.

Only poor simple ones. "I'm so sorry."

She nodded. And walked away.

Fred looked down at the pliers, wondering if Dave had ever had a chance to use them. After a minute he put them in his pocket and started walking back to Warton.

No, they never prepared you for stuff like this when you joined up. But maybe that's because there was no way to do it.

Sometimes life hit you hard and low, and there wasn't anything you could do to get ready for it. You just had to stand up, look it in the eye, and keep on going.

Chapter 17

Lily's footsteps clicked on the cobbled walk as she approached the house, trying to breathe normally. It was a towering structure of solid brick and stone. Not the sort of place that made you feel big and brave. She swallowed.

Lily, you owe him this much. That was what Mother had said. But Mother had only come as far as the London station.

A butler answered the door.

Lily forced herself to sound calm. "Is Mr. Holdsworth in?"

"I'm afraid he's in a meeting, miss."

Oh dear. "Do you know how long it might be? I have to catch a train back to Lytham before—"

"Lytham?" The butler looked at her more closely. "Why, you're Miss Lily Brown, aren't you? Please come in. I believe it's the *younger* Mr. Holdsworth you're wanting to see."

"Oh yes." Lily tried not to stare like a silly school girl as she found herself in an entrance hall bigger than her house.

"Forgive me. I should have asked. Here, the footman will take your coat. Now right this way is the parlour. Please make yourself comfortable. Your Mr. Holdsworth is in the meeting too, but I'm sure he'll come out to see you."

With these parting words, Lily found herself standing alone in the parlour, unsure whether she felt relieved or sick to her stomach. The room was spotless. Shining wood. Pristine upholstery. An enormous grandfather clock stood in the corner, and a grave Grecian statue near the window, its stone eyes gazing into space with a musing stare. Crimson drapes framed the view of the garden.

Lily clasped her hands together and breathed out a sigh. Once upon a time she had longed to visit this place. But now she was here, there was no pleasure in it. Only a faint twinge, somewhere deep down. A leftover spasm of fading dreams.

She walked to the mantelpiece and leaned her forehead against the cool marble as she replayed again the conversation that had brought her all the way to London.

"I suppose I'll have to write Paul a letter and tell him."
"You will do nothing of the sort!"
"Well, what am I supposed to do? Wait until he visits again?"
"Of course not. You'll go to London and tell him in person."
"Mother!"
"First thing Saturday morning. I've money enough saved for train tickets and a cab."
"But I've never been to London by myself. What if I get lost?"
"I'll go with you."
"But Mother—"
"Lily, you owe him this much."

"Lily?" Paul stood in the doorway.

She swallowed, her thoughts scrambling for the proper greeting. "Paul, I...didn't hear you come in."

He came across the room, looking so delighted that this time she was certain she felt sick to her stomach. "What a lovely surprise! But what are you doing in London?"

There was something in her throat. She swallowed hard, fighting it. "I came to see you."

He knit his brows. "All the way from Lytham just to see me? But I was planning to visit you next weekend. What's happened? I heard about the accident in Freckleton. None of your family was hurt, were they? Are your mother and the girls all right?"

Her lips had parted twice to answer, but nothing came.

A sudden thought flashed across Paul's face, and he covered the space between them in a stride, catching her by the shoulders. "Lily! It's not your brother, is it? Or your father? They haven't—"

"No!" Lily finally found her voice. "No. Everyone is fine. But Mother said ..." Swallowing, she searched in her mind for the speech she'd practiced, but it had fallen all to pieces.

He gazed at her, waiting on her words.

"Paul, I've realized I ..." It was no good. The practiced speech wouldn't have been right anyway, now that it came down to it. Only the straight truth would do. "I love Freddie." *There*. It was done.

Paul's face went still. His arms dropped to his sides. He stood looking at her for a long moment, silent and expressionless, and then turned and walked to the window.

The seconds ticked past on the grandfather clock in the corner, echoing far too loudly in the painful stillness.

For what seemed an endless pause, Paul stared out at the garden, stiff and motionless as the marble statue beside him. Somewhere far away, maybe on the next floor, a door opened and shut.

Lily finally broke the silence. "I'm sorry."

He shuddered, catching a sharp breath as if she had roused him from a dream.

"Don't be. I knew you'd have to choose eventually."

"But I *am* sorry. I wish I—"

"Don't, Lily." Turning from the window, he looked at her with such longing that tears pricked her eyes. "I used to dream about bringing you back here to London, imagining all the wonderful presents I'd buy you. I know how much you love beautiful things, and I'd think to myself that it didn't matter how expensive it was. I'd get you anything you wanted."

He lowered his gaze to the floor a moment and his voice went soft. "Anything. No matter what the cost." He raised his eyes to hers again. "I hope Fred will make you very happy."

Lily blinked hard and swallowed, but could not speak.

The butler came to the door. "Mr. Holdsworth, your father would like to know if you are coming back to the meeting or not."

Paul settled his shoulders. "Yes, Dawson. I'm coming. Miss Brown will be needing her coat."

Dawson disappeared, and Paul took a step toward the door.

"Paul?"

He turned.

She put her hand in her pocketbook and pulled out the necklace, still in its box. "Do you want this back?"

He glanced at it, then back at her face. "I knew it was meant for you from the moment I saw it. It would never look right on anyone else."

She swallowed. "Thank you, Paul. For everything."

He gave her a slight bow. "I'll never forget you, Lily. No sane man ever could." He walked to the door, stopped, and looked back. His voice dropped to a whisper. "Goodbye."

* *

Lily leaned her head against the seat, watching the countryside streaming past outside the window. Mother was already asleep beside her as the train sped toward home.

Her hand slipped into her bag and fingered the box with the necklace inside. Poor Paul. But at least it was over now. Most likely their paths would never cross again. She pulled out her hand and clicked her purse shut, trying to think of other things.

Like Freddie.

But even there she wasn't safe. It seemed no sooner had she made up her mind than a dozen new doubts pressed in on every side. Was she really brave enough to leave England and go to another country to live?

And what would Mother and the girls do without her? And what about money? Freddie could not support a family on the pittance he kept back when he sent home most of his salary. And after visiting Paul's house, even the whole salary was looking smaller and smaller.

Stop it!

She squeezed her eyes shut. Not now. She couldn't think any more about it now. It was too much. She pushed the questions back, pressing them deep into that dark corner she tried not to disturb.

If only they would stay there.

Chapter 18

December 1944

Biting winter wind howled through the open door. Snowflakes, wet and sleet-like, swirled onto the carpet. The tall figure lurched, closing in across the room. Frances's eyes stared at her, wide and frightened. Fear twisted like poison in her stomach. The frantic whisper hissed against her ear...

Lily bolted up in bed.

Darkness. Her mind groped for reality as her fingers fumbled in the blackness, brushing the familiar blanket.

No snow. No howling wind. No whispering voice. *Just a dream.* The old familiar nightmare. But something else was wrong. Something had wrenched her from sleep like a slap in the face. Something...

And then she heard it.

The siren.

"Jerry! Wake up!" Fred threw the blanket off.

It was December. Much too cold for air raids if those Nazis had any sense at all. But they didn't.

"I am awake." Jerry swung his legs off the bunk and reached for his boots.

"Wonder where they spotted the planes."

Fred wasn't listening. "Jerry!" He leaned closer as he jerked his laces tight. "Do you think there'll be enough confusion for me to slip out?"

"What?"

"Do you think—"

"I heard that part." Jerry's voice was too loud for comfort. "But what do you want to duck out now for? This is no time to go off on French leave!"

"Keep your voice down, would you?" Fred gripped his shoulder. "What about the Browns? What if Lytham is bombed? Lily might need my help."

Jerry shook his head. "Don't be an idiot, Fred. It's over three miles to North Clifton Street. Besides, when was the last time a bomb dropped in Lytham? We're more of a target than they are. Lily's probably hunkered down in one of those back-yard shelters anyway. Safe and sound."

"They don't *have* one of those backyard shelters! They couldn't afford it."

"Okay, okay, but there's plenty of others around. They're scattered all over the Green like molehills."

"Jerry—"

"Don't be an idiot, Fred."

Lily pulled her thickest shawl around her shoulders as she hustled a quilt-wrapped Ruth down the stairs. Frances was ahead of them, snatching family portraits off the wall and adding them to the shoe box full of snapshots she was carrying.

Her movements threw bouncing shadows in the wavering light of one small oil lamp. Mother came last, hurrying Alice in front of her. She had her Bible and a neatly folded packet of Robert's letters in one hand. The other held the old glove where she tucked away emergency money.

They all crowded into a tight knot in the kitchen as Mother gave instructions. "Ruth, hold my hand and stay right next to me. Lily, make sure Alice is with you. Alice, you'll carry the lamp. Frances, you come behind and make sure everyone is together. Keep close now!"

She handed Alice the lamp, then snuffed it out before opening the door.

A rush of winter air chilled Lily's face as they filed out of the alley and onto the street. There was no moon, only the pale grey wash of starlight. Her breath came in puffs as she hurried down the street, the rise and fall of the wailing sirens sending shivers down her spine.

She should be used to this by now. Air-raid warnings were almost a part of life. So why did they still squeeze the breath from her lungs and send her heart slamming back and forth like the tongue of an alarm bell?

Ducking through the front door of number twelve, the Porters' house, she kept a tight hold of Alice's hand as they hurried through parlour and kitchen and out again to the backyard bomb shelter. When everyone was inside, Mr. Porter pulled the heavy door shut.

Darkness dropped over them like a curtain, and the shelter fell silent. Lily squeezed her hands together, listening to the air-raid siren shrieking outside, distant and muted now, like an eerie echo.

A match flared. Mother lit the lamp, and its light illuminated a huddle of pale, blinking faces. Some sat with arms folded, tight and stiff, staring into space. Others fiddled with the corner of a shawl or the brim of a hat, lips pressed together, jaws tense. No one spoke.

Lily wondered if she looked as frightened as the others.

Is Freddie listening to the siren too somewhere?

Were all the Americans huddled in the shelters at Warton, waiting to see if the airbase was the Nazis' target?

No. They would not be huddling. Soldiers were brave. They would be swapping jokes and playing card games while they waited.

Mother thumbed through her Bible as she always did, looking for a certain well-worn page in Psalms.

When she found it, she held the Bible close to the lamp and began to read aloud. *"He that dwelleth in the secret places of the most High shall abide under the shadow of the Almighty."* Her tone was low and soothing. *"I will say of the Lord, He is my refuge and my fortress; my God, in Him will I trust ..."*

Lily watched Mother's face in the flickering lamp light. Hers was the only one that showed no sign of the fear that seemed to crouch in the darkness, just out of reach of the lamp's glow.

"Thou shalt not be afraid for the terror by night, nor for the arrow that flieth by day. Nor for the pestilence that walketh in darkness. ...A thousand shall fall at thy side, and ten thousand at thy right hand, but it shall not come nigh thee ..."

Lily pulled her shawl a little closer. Mother was a wonder. For years, Lily had watched her walk through the worst life could hurl at her, and yet seem to come through untouched. Always hopeful, always ready for a jolly laugh.

Lily had never understood it.

"*Because he hath set his love upon me, therefore will I deliver him. ...He shall call upon me, and I will answer him. I will be with him in trouble ...*"

I will be with him.

That was it. Mother really believed that. Not just with her head, but with her heart and all the rest of her too. *Trust.* That was the difference. Mother had it. Trust in the One stronger than any trouble she had to face.

Lily twisted her finger in the corner of her shawl and stared at the flickering lantern. Trust was not something she was good at.

* * *

No bombs were dropped in Lytham that night.

As Lily walked back up North Clifton Street after the siren had sounded the unwavering all-clear, she watched the drifting snowflakes fluttering down around them and wondered what it felt like to trust like that.

Freddie knew, she suspected. He had that same way about him that Mother did. A peacefulness. It was not as if he sat around and never did anything about a problem, but he never *worried*, the way she did, about things that couldn't be controlled. He just dealt with them as he came to them. Same as Mother did.

Lily wished she could be that fearless.

* * *

No one felt like going straight back to bed when they reached the house.

By the warm, drowsy light of the lantern, Mother boiled a kettle of water and set some tea to brew in the teapot while Ruth dozed beneath her quilt on the settee.

Lily was just fetching the teacups when a sharp rap on the door startled them. Before anyone could respond, Freddie burst into the room, wool cap cocked sideways, scarf eschew, and dusted from head to toe with new-fallen snow.

"What on earth?" Frances started to her feet.

Freddie looked around the room, as if counting heads. "Everybody okay?"

Lily stared at him. "You came all the way from Warton in the snow, in the middle of an air raid, just to make sure we were all right?"

He blinked at her. "I guess so."

"Are you daft? Don't you know you might have been killed?"

He looked down at himself, spreading his arms as if to check for damages. "Everything seems to be in working order."

"For heaven's sake!" Mother dropped into her chair and laughed. The good, jolly laugh that Freddie could bring on like no one else.

He glanced around at them all again, his mouth pulling up into a halfway sheepish smile. "I guess Jerry was right."

"About what?" Lily stepped behind him to shut the door, which still stood letting the cold air in.

Before he could respond, Ruth sat up and stared into the kitchen, her face wrinkled up in confusion. "Freddie? What are *you* doing here?"

He chuckled. "Being an idiot, I think. At least that's what Jerry said."

Mother shook her head, still laughing. "Jerry is a very sensible young man. But it's rarely the sensible people who make a mark on this world. Have a cup of tea, Freddie."

Chapter 19

"You blockhead. Do you *want* to get arrested?"

Fred looked up from rummaging in his footlocker. "It's Lily's birthday, Jerry."

"So? Think she wants you nabbed by the MPs just' cuz it's her birthday? Why don't you try getting a pass?"

"I tried." Fred dropped the lid on his locker and started rifling through his bedding, shaking out the blanket and peering inside the pillowcase. "No exceptions to the blackout. They said I have to wait until Christmas."

"So wait, then. It's less than a week."

"I can't." Fred dropped to his knees and peered under the bunk, dog tags jangling against the concrete.

"Why not?"

"I just told you." He looked up at Jerry. "Did you take that cartoon I was going to give Lily for her birthday?"

Jerry shook his head. "Never touched it."

Funny. He could have sworn he knew right where he'd left it.

"Maybe one of the fellas took it to show some friends. It'll probably turn up later." Jerry pulled out his latest copy of

TIME magazine and thumbed through it, looking for something to read. "Does this mean you won't try to sneak out?"

Fred gave him a look.

"Oh, brother." Jerry sighed as he dropped onto his back, burying his face behind the magazine. "Well, good luck."

Lily stood at the mirror, staring at her reflection as she straightened the final pins in her hair.

Birthdays were such a contemplative time. What would her life look like in another year? When she turned twenty? *Will the war be over by then?* The Allies were winning on every front in Europe.

She leaned against the dressing table, trying to imagine what the end of the war would be like. All the local men who had been gone for years would return to their families. Robert would come back. And Father. The town would try to go back to the way things were before.

And Freddie? She traced the wood grain with her finger, remembering his fingers pushing the pencil lead across paper, sketching pictures of the home he loved so much.

With a sigh, she opened her top drawer and reached into the back corner for the bag where she kept her special jewellery. Slipping her hand inside, she groped around for her birthday brooch. The leaf-shaped one with pink jewels Mother had given her last year. Instead, her finger brushed something smooth and square.

The necklace. She stopped, and her heart did a wavering tap dance as she ran her tongue over her lips. *Leave it there. Leave it right there and get the brooch out.*

Before she could stop herself, she had the box out and open in her hand. There lay the necklace, glittering up at her like an echo from the past. Why did she keep it still? It was beautiful, yes. But she never wore it anymore. It never felt right. Why not sell it or something?

She moved it a little, watching the diamonds catch the light and send it dancing away in starbursts.

And a tiny voice whispered inside her head, *If you were so sure of Freddie, you wouldn't keep it.*

She bit her lip.

You had everything worked out perfectly. Why did you let it slip through your fingers?

"Because I love Freddie." She stared at her reflection, daring it to argue.

That's what your mother thought when she married your father.

But that was different. "Freddie is nothing like Father."

Then why are you still afraid?

A step sounded on the stairs. Lily snapped the lid on the box and shoved it back inside the handbag just as Ruth bounded into the room and hugged her from behind.

"Happy birthday! I was going to bring you a flower, only there aren't any."

Lily forced a weak laugh as she pulled her hand from the drawer, this time holding the pink-jewelled birthday brooch.

"When will Freddie get here?"

"I don't know if he's even going to come." Lily reached to re-braid one of her sister's pigtails, which was coming undone. "Last time he was here, he said Warton was about to go on blackout. They may not let him leave."

Ruth shrugged as if that was beside the point.

"Soldiers have to do as they're told, love."

"Not Fred." Ruth tossed her freshly braided hair over her shoulder with a grin. "Not when he's coming to see *you!*"

It was five thirty by the time Fred reached the Browns'. The cold, early twilight of winter was already fading into darkness. Snow, mounded up in corners and snaking in drifts along the edge of the road, shimmered pale and bluish in the starlight.

Ruth met him at the door. "I knew it!" She bounced on her toes as she dragged him into the front room. "What'd you bring for Lily?"

He grinned. "Why should you get to see it before she does?"

Ruth ran to the bottom of the steps and hollered for Lily.

Fred put his hand in his pocket. He never had found the missing cartoon. Too bad, really. It was a nice one. An American GI spending Christmas dinner with a smiling English family. Just the sort of holiday cheer people loved this time of year. All the guys who saw it thought it was great. And, of course, Greg Baker gushed over it like a girl.

But at least he'd found something else for Lily on his way up from Warton.

"I'm coming!" Lily called down to Ruth. "One minute."

"But I want to see your present!"

"Just wait a minute. It's not *your* birthday, silly goose!"

The back door shut, and Mrs. Brown came in, unwinding a shawl. "Good evening, Freddie. Shall I hang up your overcoat?"

"No, thanks. I'm leaving it on until Lily gets down here. I've got her present in my pocket and I don't want to wake it up."

"Wake it up!" Ruth was on her feet like a jack-in-the-box, eyes alight. "Li-*LY!* Come down! Your present's *alive!*"

"What?" Lily's footsteps sounded on the upstairs landing and her voice got louder as she apparently leaned over the rail. "Alive?"

Fred gave Mrs. Brown a teasing wink. "It's a nine-foot alligator. He was on his way to the Everglades but took a wrong turn along the way. I found him sleeping under my bunk this morning. His name is Archibald. He's very well-behaved and doesn't eat much. Just one or two small children a week."

"Oh, *Freddie!*" Here she came at last. Her hair was tied back with a pink ribbon that matched the stones in her brooch, and she laughed as she entered the room. "For goodness' sake. What is it, really?"

He folded his arms and let his eyes twinkle at her. "Come see for yourself."

"Where is it?"

"My overcoat pocket."

She came over and laid her fingers on the edge of the pocket. But before she could get a good look, he snatched her off her feet and kissed her.

"Ooo! Freddie! Put me down! Your coat is freezing!"

"Sorry. Can't." He kissed her again. "I have to give you your birthday kisses first. All nineteen of them." This time he kissed her cheek, just for variety's sake. "Oh, wait. It would be twenty, wouldn't it? With one to grow on? Are you still growing?" He got her other cheek next.

"Fred-*die!*" She was laughing so hard she could barely catch a breath. "Stop that! Let me go you, you barbarian!" Fred laughed and got her lips again, this time good and long.

"Frederick Donald Overall!" A new voice interrupted.

Uh-oh.

Frances stood in the open doorway, hands on her hips. He knew at once what she was looking at. The floor. She'd told him again and again, but he kept forgetting.

Now he could see eight months' worth of patience going up in flames behind her eyes.

He gulped. "Yes ma'am?" Putting on his most innocent smile, he kept Lily suspended in midair. "You look cold. Been out shopping?"

Frances shrugged off her coat and hurled it at the rack. "How many times have I told you to wipe your shoes before you come in this house?"

Fred looked down at the trail of muddy slush he'd tracked in. The last time that happened, she'd threatened to beat him with the broom. He looked back up at her, feeling a sheepish grin curling up the sides of his mouth. "How many? Well, I haven't kept a detailed tally, but it seems to me ..."

She whirled around and disappeared into the kitchen.

Ruth looked after her, startled. "Where's she going?"

Mrs. Brown's eyes were bright with merriment. "I could be wrong, but I believe she's gone for the broom."

Sure enough, Frances reappeared with the heavy wooden broom in hand. She didn't look like she was planning to do any sweeping either.

"Now wait a minute!" Fred dropped Lily to her feet and spun to face Frances. "Violence never solved anything."

"Oh, really?" She came at him, wielding the broom like a quarterstaff. "Well, I guess there's a first time for everything!"

He jumped backward.

Whack! The broom collided with a chair.

"Whoa! Frances! Can't we talk about this?"

"If I've told you once, I've told you a dozen times!" *Smack!* This time she'd caught him on the side of his shin as he tried to dodge.

"Ow! Lily, help! Call her off!"

Both Lily and her mother stood there laughing so hard they were almost doubled over.

Whap! The broom clipped his shoulder. This time he grabbed it before she could pull back for another swing. "Now just hold on. First of all, you can't hit me with that thing when I've got a live animal in my pocket!"

"You mean my present really *is* alive?"

Lily's voice was incredulous.

"Of course! Why would I bring you a *dead* alligator for your birthday?"

"Don't be daft!" Frances wrenched at the broom.

"There's not an alligator within a hundred miles, unless it's in a zoo maybe. Let go!"

"And secondly,"—Fred kept a firm hold on the broom handle—"I'm already risking arrest just showing up today. You really think it's fair to beat me when I finally show up?"

"Freddie! AWOL *again?*" Lily clapped a hand to her forehead.

"Yes. And this time it'll be serious if they catch me. The whole base is on blackout, and they specifically warned me not to leave."

"Why did you *do* it then, for goodness' sake?" She sank down onto the couch, shaking her head.

Fred looked at her. She didn't have any idea how pretty she was, sitting there with her hair all tousled and her cheeks still flushed from laughing. How could he explain that just catching a glimpse of her could make his heart start galloping, his knees go weak, and his whole world feel warmer and brighter? Who *wouldn't* go AWOL under the circumstances?

But he only shrugged and smiled at her.

"It's your birthday."

"Oh, Freddie."

"And,"—he slipped the broom out of Frances's grasp while she was distracted—"if your sister will stop trying to bash my brains out, I'll give you your present now."

He handed the broom to Mrs. Brown for safekeeping, put his hand in his pocket, and scooped out the warm, fluffy bundle.

"It's a kitten!"

"Yep." He set it in her lap. "Or I think it is, anyhow. Mostly looks like a ball of brown fur. But I think there's a kitten under there someplace."

As if on cue, the kitten opened its big green eyes and mewed.

"*Aww.*" Lily ran her finger over the silky fur. "It's so little! Where did you find it?"

"Under a bush, in the snow."

"Poor thing! Ruth, run and get some milk for it, would you?"

Between a saucer of milk and general barrage of petting and fussing, they soon had the kitten purring like a well-greased propeller. Then Mrs. Brown and Frances went into the kitchen to get supper ready, and Ruth was sent to fetch Alice from wherever it was she'd gone.

Fred found himself alone with Lily beside him on the couch. He stretched his arm across the back, curling it around her shoulders. "Like it?"

"I love it."

"Should we name him Archibald?"

She laughed. "Are you partial to that name?"

"I guess not. It's *your* birthday." He shifted a little closer.

"Speaking of which, where was I on those birthday kisses?" She gave him a look.

"Do you remember? What number were we at?"

She rolled her eyes.

"Yeah, I don't remember either. Guess we'll just have to start back at the beginning. One ..."

Lily ducked. And poked him in the ribs.

Chapter 20

Lily tapped her fingers on her knee and tried not to look nervous.

Supper and birthday songs and presents were long since over and everything had settled down. Mother sat in her chair, ripping out the lining seams of an old coat so she could cut it up and make a new one for Alice.

Frances was in the kitchen washing dishes, and the two younger girls were upstairs, chattering about the Christmas party the American soldiers had promised to throw for the local children.

Freddie sat beside her looking sleepy, with his long legs propped on a chair. Everyone seemed perfectly relaxed.

Everyone but her.

"Freddie?"

"Hmmm?" His response was almost a yawn.

She wanted to smack him. The longer he stayed, the more likely somebody would notice he'd left. If he kept this up, he was going to end up court-martialed or something. Yet there he sat, looking like he was going to take a nap.

"What time do you need to get back?"

He gave his watch a contemplative glance. "Is it really that late already?"

"Yes."

He rubbed his knees. "Guess maybe I should start heading that direction." He stood up and went to retrieve his shoes from beside the front door.

Sometimes she could strangle him for being so calm. "How are you going to get back on base?"

He looked over his shoulder as he bent to pick up the boots. "That's easy. *On* base is where they wanted me in the first place. All I gotta do is walk up to the front entrance and introduce myself. They'll let me right in."

"Freddie."

He grinned as he came back to the settee and sat down. "You mean you want to know how I'm going to get back on base *without* getting arrested?"

"You know exactly what I mean!"

"Well." He tied his shoes with maddening calm. "I haven't figured that one out yet."

Brilliant. Just brilliant. "How did you get out in the first place? You still haven't told me how you do that so often."

He stood, glancing at Mother. She kept on snipping with her scissors, looking up at him from the corner of her eye. She was curious too.

Freddie looked back at Lily with that little smile he always wore when he'd been doing something mischievous. "I used my furlough gate."

"Your what?"

"Furlough gate. I fixed up a little hole, back behind one of the buildings. And when I want a furlough, well ..." He smiled.

Good heavens. Sometimes it seemed half the things Freddie did on any given day would be enough by themselves to get him arrested. "You made the hole yourself?"

"More or less."

"Wouldn't you get in an awful lot of trouble if they caught you at that?"

"Well,"—he shrugged—"they probably wouldn't pat me on the head and give me a lollipop."

"So why can't you go back in the same way you got out?"

"I can. But to get to the hole, I have to go right past the bus station. There'll be at least one MP hanging out there by this time of night, and no groups of random people to mingle in with. I'll have to walk straight past him. And if he catches sight of this uniform ..." He spread his hands.

Mother looked at him for a minute, then down at the faded coat in her lap, then up again. She smiled. "I believe I can help you with that one."

The sky was clear and studded with stars as Fred got close to the bus stop. He pulled the headscarf a little farther forward to shadow his face, and tried to crunch his shoulders smaller inside the coat, which just barely fit him to begin with. Most women didn't have shoulders this wide.

Good grief! Why did the headscarf have to be so slippery? If it wasn't sliding one way, it was sliding another. Off to one side, backward, straight down over his face. How did women wear these things?

He could see the MPs now, two of them, standing there talking. The butts of their cigarettes glowed like orange coals in the shadows.

This was crazy. Completely crazy.

He hadn't wanted to worry Lily by telling her, but somebody might have noticed he was missing by this time. Maybe not, of course, but there was always the chance the MPs had been warned to look for him. Especially since he'd made such a big deal about asking for an exception to the blackout.

He bent over a little to disguise his height, trying to take smaller steps. Thank goodness he'd stopped wearing a mustache lately!

The closer he got, the brighter that sliver of a moon seemed to be shining. He kept his eyes lowered.

Good grief, look at those hands!

He should have thought of that. Any woman with hands *that* big was probably in a circus sideshow. He shoved them in the coat pockets to hide them. But he couldn't do much for his feet. His legs were all right, with his trousers rolled up above the hem of the coat and the long socks covering his calves, but his shoes were man-size and military issued. All the mud he'd managed to cake them with on the way back from Lytham couldn't hide that.

One of the MPs was looking his way, watching him go by. There weren't many people out this late. Especially on such a frosty night. Fred hunched his shoulders a little more and stared straight ahead at the steamy cloud his breath made in the moonlight.

And then his trousers started to unroll.

No, no, no! Inside the pockets his fingers tried to grab hold of the trousers and pull them up. He got them up maybe an inch higher, but the bottoms had already unrolled two or three inches more. Were they showing below the coat yet? He couldn't look to find out without drawing attention to them.

The MP who'd been watching him elbowed his buddy and motioned toward Fred. The second MP turned to look.

Oh boy. He knew that MP. His name was Pete Ross. And of course, the fact that he knew Fred too made him twice as likely to recognize him under the blasted headscarf.

Keep walking, keep walking, keep walking. Up ahead was the corner. If he could just get around that ...

He couldn't see the MPs anymore. They were behind him. But he knew they could still see him well enough. His pants unrolled another inch.

"Hey!"

He didn't turn around. Two steps more, and he put the corner behind him and broke into a full-out run.

His pants were almost down to his ankles by now, but he was way past worrying about that. The scarf blew back off his head and started flopping around his neck.

He could hear a commotion behind him, but he didn't slow down long enough to look. Down the alley, around the next corner, and through somebody's backyard he pelted, sucking in the frigid air so fast it burned his throat.

He didn't slow down until he ducked through his furlough gate and was safe on base again, bent double to catch his breath.

He couldn't believe it had worked.

As fast as possible, he hid the coat and scarf behind some boxes in one of the hangars and snuck back into the barracks.

The lights were still on, and Jerry was lying there half asleep with the *TIME* dropped on his chest.

Fred sat down on his own bunk and waited for his heart to go back to its normal pace. He'd made it. *Thank the Lord.*

Jerry yawned and looked up. "Oh. There you are. They were in here asking about you earlier. I told them maybe you were in the latrine."

"Did they believe you?"

Jerry shrugged. "Who cares? They never caught you off base. Did they?"

He gave his friend a blank stare. "Off base? Who said I was off base?"

Jerry grinned. "Not me, buddy. But ... Fred?"

"What?"

"You might want to roll your trousers down."

Chapter 21

Mother's boots squeaked on the snow as they walked home from visiting an old friend on Christmas Eve. "Lovely, that ginger wine." She smiled at Lily. "Always warms the cockles of your heart, doesn't it, girls?"

Frances pulled her coat a little tighter. "I think that's about *all* that will be warm by the time we get home."

The sun had already set, and the icy wind was mixed with gusts of snow.

Lily reached down and took Ruth's hand. "What did you think of the wine, Ruthie?"

Ruth had been looking blue all afternoon. She shrugged. "I liked the mince pies better."

"Stop sulking, Ruth." Frances frowned at her.

"Just because you can't go to the Christmas party in Warton doesn't mean you have to pout all day. I do believe you hurt Miss Bonny's feelings. You hardly smiled the whole time we were there."

Ruth gave Lily a mournful look. "But I *wanted* to go to the Christmas party. Freddie specially invited Alice and me! And he said there was going to be sweets and toys and games and *everything*!"

"I know, love." Mother patted her shoulder. "But I don't want you and Alice walking all the way to Freckleton, and in this weather."

"We could have gone straight from school with the other children on the lorry."

"I'd already promised Miss Bonny we were coming over this afternoon. I'm certain Freddie will bring you some sweets when he comes tomorrow."

"That's not the same thing—"

"Now Ruth, that's enough." Mother turned down the alley toward the front door. "You should be grateful for all the nice things you do have this Christmas."

Yes. Lily blew on her cold fingers as she waited for Mother to open the door. *And those of us who remember what it was like before Father left can be especially grateful.*

They all crowded into the warm house and shut the door.

"There." Mother unwrapped her scarf. "Let's get some tea put on to warm us up and then I ..." Her voice broke off.

Lily looked up from unbuttoning and followed Mother's gaze to the piano, half hidden behind the bushy little Christmas tree they'd decorated with cotton-wool balls.

Well, it *used* to be a piano. But she hardly knew if it still qualified for the title anymore. Every single key had vanished while they were gone, leaving the poor thing gaping empty like a mouth in need of dentures.

Mother stood there blinking for a couple of seconds. Then she pursed her lips, put her hands on her hips, and looked up the stairs. "Frederick Overall! You come down here right now!"

There was a burst of laughter overhead. "Merry Christmas Eve! Where have you been all afternoon? I got bored waiting on you." Freddie came down the stairs with a grin.

"Oh?" Mother gave him her firmest frown, but her eyes were twinkling. "Do you always cope with boredom by deconstructing furniture?"

"Furniture?" Freddie returned her stare with one of wide-eyed innocence.

Mother pointed.

Freddie studied the piano for a moment. The he winked at Lily and looked back at Mother. "No ma'am. I never touch furniture. But that isn't furniture. It's an *instrument*!"

Mother shook her head at him, laughing. She was used to his practical jokes by this time.

"Where are the keys, Fred? Put them back on this minute."

Freddie looked forlorn. "Do you have any idea how long it took me to get those all off? How much work do you expect me to do on Christmas Eve?"

Frances folded her arms. "Should I go get the broom again, Mum?"

Freddie held up his hands and backed away from her. "No, wait! I'll be good. I promise." He poked his head into the stairway. "Jerry! Get those keys back down here! Frances is going for the broom again!"

Now Jerry's laughter erupted above them, and he came down the steps with a heavy sack over his shoulder.

"Hello, everybody!"

Lily finished unbuttoning her coat and hung it on the rack. "Aren't you two supposed to be at that Christmas party?"

"Yes." Freddie dumped the piano keys out on the rug. "But we came to pick up Alice and Ruth."

Ruth's face lit up.

"What are you talking about?" Mother was tying on her blue apron.

"I already told you I didn't want them out in this weather."

"No, you told me you didn't want them walking to Freckleton in this weather by themselves. Now they have escorts. We'll make sure they get there and back without turning into icicles."

Ruth, who had just taken her coat off, began putting it right back on. "Oh, Mum! Can we go, *please?* We'll be all right as long as we're with Freddie, won't we?"

"Yes, can't we?" Alice joined in.

Freddie came over between them, shuffling on his knees with his hat in his hand. "Pretty please? You can't say no to three such adorable faces, can you?"

No. Mother could not.

The hangar was blazing with light and decked out like a Christmas tornado had gone through it. Fred stood behind a table full of candy canes and chocolate, tying up little sacks for the kids while he kept one eye on Ruth. Every child had a GI assigned to them, and he'd made sure he and Jerry were responsible for the Brown girls.

A shout from behind made him spin around.

A couple of boys tousled on the floor, rolling about as they shouted something about a candy cane. Their GIs came running, but Fred got there first.

He hauled them apart and got a good grip on each one's shoulder, holding them at arm's length.

"Whoa now. What's the ruckus about?"

"He took my peppermint stick!"

"I *didn't!*"

"You did!"

Fred shook their shoulders. "Boys! Now calm down a minute. Have you forgotten who's birthday we're celebrating?"

They looked up at him, and the taller one shuffled his feet, face abashed.

"Well?"

"Jesus's."

"Right." He let go of their shoulders. "And who remembers what the angels told the shepherds?"

The boys looked at each other.

"That the baby was in swaddling clothes and lying in a manger?" Again, it was the taller one who answered.

"That was the first angel. But when the whole chorus showed up in the sky and started singing, what was it they sang?"

The boys blinked.

A small, warm hand slipped into his from behind.

It was Ruth.

"Glory to God in the highest. And peace on earth. Good will toward men."

The boys looked down, embarrassed.

He squatted down to their level. "Seems like since we're celebrating the same thing they were, we should be trying for peace on earth and goodwill toward men too, don't you think?"

"Yes sir."

He went back to the table and scooped up a bag of candy for each of them. "Good. So here's enough candy to keep you both well supplied." He held out the bags, one in each hand.

"Peace on earth?"

They looked at each other and grinned. "Yes sir!"

With that sorted out, he went back to the table to start tying up bags again. Ruth followed and leaned against him, eyes looking heavy.

"Sleepy, Ruth? About time to go home, isn't it?"

She broke off in the middle of a yawn. "I'm not sleepy."

He grinned. "Maybe not, but you sure look it. Besides, if you aren't in bed, how will Santa Claus come?" He winked.

She wrinkled her nose.

"I told you. His name is Father Christmas."

"Well then, how come he answers to Santa Claus where I come from? How do you know you English folks have it right?"

"Because." She gave him a prim little smile. "We had him first."

He pulled her pigtail.

"You pay too much attention in school."

• •

It was past the girls' bedtime by the time he got them home,
but Mrs. Brown didn't scold. She let the girls chatter about the
party while she poured tea for Fred and Jerry.

They'd only taken a couple of sips when Frances came
downstairs waving a magazine. "Lily! Did you tell them?"

"I forgot." Lily looked up from her tea. "Wait till you see it,
Freddie. It's uncanny."

Frances flipped through the pages.

"You left this by the piano. Have you looked through
it yet?"

"No, I just picked it up at the Doughnut Dugout this afternoon." It was the latest issue of *Stars and Stripes*.

"Here it is!" She slid the magazine over in front of him and
pointed to a cheerful cartoon at the bottom of the page.

"Look at that and tell me if the little girl on the left doesn't
look just like Ruth, and the older one like Lily."

Fred looked.

And almost choked on his tea.

• •

As soon as they got outside, Jerry went ballistic. "That dirty,
no-good rat! Just wait till I get my hands on Baker. He won't
be able to do more than squint and groan for a week! I don't
care if I do get arrested for assault. I'll teach that sneaking
varmint. I'll break his nose in so many places it'll look like a
staircase to his brain!"

Fred didn't say anything.

"Just wait till I tell some of the fellas. They'll all help me.
Everybody hates that lying rat anyhow."

Fred pushed his hands farther into his pockets and kept
walking, looking up at the stars and thinking about two little
boys and a candy cane.

"I'm gonna haul him right out of his bunk as soon as we get back to the barracks.

By the time I'm through with him, he'll—"

"Let him be, Jerry."

Jerry stopped in his tracks. "What? You just gonna let him take credit for your work? He probably got paid for it too, the dirty rat! You don't have to help me beat him up, if that makes you feel better. I can work him over by myself."

"I said let him be."

"You mean it doesn't *bother* you?"

"Sure, it bothers me." Fred tightened his jaw. *Felt like a jack-knife to the back.*

"Then why should you care if I bust his kidney for him?"

Fred didn't answer right away. He stood looking up at the sky for a long minute while the stars glimmered down at him. "Have you ever wondered what they looked like, Jerry?" he asked at last. "All those angels up there, filling the sky?"

"Angels?" Jerry's voice was a little concerned.

"Outside Bethlehem. Remember? The heavenly host. They were soldiers, Jerry. Dangerous soldiers. They had fiery chariots and flaming swords. But for that one night, they all got together in the sky above Bethlehem and sang."

"Um. Yeah. Reckon they did. But what—"

"Come on." Fred turned his head. "You know what I'm talking about. What was it they sang? You remember?"

Jerry looked at the ground, kicking at a pebble.

"Well?"

Jerry sighed. "Yeah. I remember."

Fred smiled and put his hand on Jerry's shoulder. "Merry Christmas, Soldier."

Jerry shook his head, a little exasperated, but he smiled back. "Merry Christmas, Fred."

Chapter 22

July 1945

Fred crunched his fist around the paper in his pocket and stared at the door. He should have seen this coming.

Winter had passed, and spring had ushered in birds and flowers and victory after victory for the Allies.

On May 8, war-weary Britain erupted into celebrations as the newspapers declared victory in Europe at last. Within the next couple of weeks, word had come that all the POWs in Germany were safely back in Allied hands, and Lily had begun to talk about her brother Robert coming home soon.

Now summer had rolled around and the work at BAD-2 was slowing down. No overhauls or major repairs anymore. Just maintenance. With all attention now focused on defeating Japan, he should have known it was only a matter of time.

But it still sent him reeling like a plane with one engine gone.

Now here he stood, swallowing a nervous lump in his throat, as he knocked on the Browns' front door.

"Come in!"

He pushed open the door.

"Freddie!" Mrs. Brown looked up from ironing with a smile. "Leave the door open, will you? The breeze is lovely. Lily won't be back from the chemist's for another hour yet, so you'll just have to put up with me for a bit, I'm afraid."

He rubbed his fingers and thumb together at his side. "Good. I...wanted to talk to you."

Mrs. Brown looked up in surprise and put the iron down. "Well, come and sit. I was just about to make some tea."

The kettle was already hot. Fred sat down at the table and stared at his hands while she poured steaming water over the tea leaves, leaving them to brew as she bustled around setting out the sugar and milk and a plate of cookies. He could feel her studying him in snatched glances the whole time.

When the tea was ready, she poured the milk into the cups first, next the sugar, and last the tea. Then she handed him a spoon. "Don't forget to stir."

He stirred. And tried to figure out how to begin this conversation.

Mrs. Brown began it for him. "Well?" She looked at him over the rim of her teacup. "What is it?"

He sighed, pulled the papers out of his pocket, and slid them across to her.

She scanned them. "You're being transferred."

He nodded. "To the Pacific."

"For how long?"

"I don't know."

"Will they send you back here afterward, or straight home to America?"

"I don't know." He put his elbows on the table and rested his chin in his hands.

"They never tell you anything in the army."

"Have you showed Lily yet?"

"I just found out this morning."

"When do you leave?"

"Next week."

Mrs. Brown set the papers on the table. "Well. They don't waste time, do they? When are you going to tell her?"

He stared into his teacup. *How* was he going to tell her? That was the real question.

And what was she going to say when he did?

Distant children's voices echoed in through the open door as the neighborhood kids played in the street. The breeze, fresh with the scents of summer, skittered the crumpled papers toward him across the table.

He took a breath. Swallowed. Then looked up. "Mrs. Brown, I want to marry your daughter."

She smiled. "I've gathered that."

"But do you know how she feels about it?"

"Don't you?"

He shoved his chair back and paced the floor. "I've been trying to find out for almost a year now. Every time I get close, she dodges. Or changes the subject, or something. What's that supposed to mean? Is she worried about leaving England? Leaving you?"

Mrs. Brown stirred her tea, the spoon never once clicking against the cup. "She does love England very much. She's as proud of being English as you are of being American. But she loves *you* too."

"Then why does she keep changing the subject? She acts almost like she's ... well, *afraid* of getting married. Why would she be afraid of me?"

A strange expression came over Mrs. Brown. She turned her face to the window and stared out of it for a long minute. When she spoke again, the words came slow. "I don't think she's afraid of *you*."

"What then? Leaving England?"

"Perhaps partly. But I don't think that's really it either."

He waited.

She still did not look at him as she kept stirring her tea, almost as if she had forgotten she was doing it. "Lily has a difficult relationship with her father. I think perhaps that is affecting her view of other men."

Her father.

He knew something wasn't right there. Dropping into his chair again, he leaned forward. "Difficult how?"

She turned her eyes to him, and for a second it was as if he was seeing into her soul. He saw pain. And sorrow. But deeper still was strength, and courage, and hope.

She folded her hands. "That is something you will have to ask her yourself."

"Mrs. Brown—"

"Call me Alice."

He swallowed, his heart beating faster and faster. "Alice, will you give me your permission...to ask Lily to marry me?"

"Of course."

His mouth was a little dry. "You know that means I'll take her away from you? Away from England?"

"I know it."

"And you'll really trust me to take care of her, so far away from all of you?"

She reached out and put her hand over his. "There is no other man in this world I would sooner trust her to."

His head whirled a little, and he had to pause to catch his breath. "I can't marry her before I leave though. There's no time to get the paperwork through. I don't know how long I'll be gone. But I will come back. I swear I will. Do you think she'll be willing to wait for me?"

"If she isn't, she doesn't deserve you." She took another sip of tea, and a little smile started to play around her mouth. "Have you got a ring yet?"

"In my pocket."

"Good." She looked at the clock. "If you leave now, you should get there just about the time she comes out of the chemist's. Better not dawdle."

His stomach turned completely over. "I'm not exactly sure where or...or how. I mean, I've never asked a girl to marry me before!"

She broke into peals of laughter. "Oh, Freddie! It's not something you're supposed to practice, for heaven's sake. Just do it!"

Chapter 23

The summer breeze was soft against Lily's cheek as she pulled the shop door shut behind her.

"Hello, Lily."

She whirled toward the voice. "Freddie!"

He stood there on the pavement, hands clasped behind his back, smiling. But there was something odd about the way he gazed at her. "How was work?"

"Quiet. People don't get sick much this time of year." She tried to read the strange expression on his face.

He glanced up at the sky.

"Makes sense. Beautiful day, isn't it?"

"Lovely."

"Would you like to go for"—he paused to clear his throat—"for a walk?"

"Well ..." She hesitated.

"Your mother knows you're with me. I was over there before I came." He rattled that off as if he had rehearsed it. Odd.

"Well, all right. Shall we go to the beach?"

"Um, no." He seemed to flounder for words a moment. "I mean, the beach is probably crowded. And we haven't walked Green Drive in a while."

Lily stared at him. Since when had Freddie been concerned about crowds?

He loved people. What had gotten into him?

As she watched the nervous shift of his eyes, the whisper of an idea slipped into her mind. Was he about to ...?

Rubbish. It was probably nothing of the sort. "Green Drive is quite nice this time of year."

He smiled and slipped his hand around hers as they started up the street.

Fred listened to the trees rustling in the wind along Green Drive as he tried to figure out how to begin. Lily's hand warmed his as she walked alongside him. Once or twice he caught her glancing at him with a curious look on her face.

The fingers and thumb of his free hand rubbed back and forth together as he turned over ideas in his head. How were you supposed to lead up to this kind of thing? You couldn't just drop it out of the air, could you?

"Nice day, isn't it?" As soon as he said it, he winced. *Idiot! You said that already.*

She nodded.

He searched for something else to start the conversation with. "It's nice having more time for stuff like this, now work has slacked off so much."

She nodded.

He puffed his breath in frustration. Usually she was the more talkative one. He tried again. "Hard to believe the war in Europe's been over almost a month already, isn't it?"

She nodded.

Good grief. This was going nowhere fast. He kicked a pebble out of his way and watched it tumble into the leaves on the side of the path.

How was he supposed to get her to say yes to a marriage proposal if he couldn't even get her say yes to a comment about the weather?

"Fred?" Her voice almost startled him.

"Yes?"

"What happened to Joni?"

He stopped.

The tree branches murmured in the silence. "Joni?"

"Jerry said something about her one time."

"But what made you bring it up just now?"

"I don't know."

He ran his hand up the back of his neck and ruffled his hair. "Jerry thinks life is a radio soap opera."

She just looked at him.

He sighed and pulled her over to sit on a fallen log just off the path. "It's really not all that dramatic. We grew up together. She was in love with me. I thought I was in love with her too. Everybody figured we'd get married, but then I joined up instead. I found her crying on the tailgate of my truck the day before I left."

"Did you promise to marry her when you got back?"

He shook his head. "Almost. But something kept me from doing it. Then after I went away, I realized I didn't really love her the way she loved me. I barely missed her."

Lily twisted the hem of her skirt around her finger, staring straight ahead.

"When I went back on leave right before they shipped me over here, I told her."

"How did she take it?" Her gaze drifted to his face.

"How did Paul take it?"

She didn't answer, turning away to stare into space again.

He swallowed, moistening his lips. "I'm glad I figured out it wasn't love I felt for her." His hand found hers, resting on the tree bark beside him. "Or I might never have had a chance to realize what—"

"We had a letter from Robert today."

He clamped his jaw shut. There she went, changing the subject again.

"He's homesick. I think it's a bit hard on him knowing how long it might still be before he can get home."

"Have you heard from your father?"

"No." As always, the shadow dropped over her eyes and her tone was hollow, as if she was talking about a stranger. "I suppose he's still in Japan somewhere."

Her face was blank. Almost cold.

He took a breath. Alice's words echoed in his mind, *That is something you will have to ask her yourself* ... "Lily?"

"Hmm?"

"What is it between you and your father? Why are you so angry with him?"

Her head snapped around. "Who said I was angry?"

He held her gaze but said nothing.

She swallowed, faltering under his stare. "I don't want to talk about it."

"I do."

She looked back at him again. He could see the anger snapping around the corners of her eyes. "Why?"

"Because your mother wouldn't tell me."

She laughed once. But it was not a happy laugh. "Of course she wouldn't."

He waited, but she stared straight ahead with her lips pressed together and said nothing else.

"Well?"

Her chest shuddered, and she swallowed again, her eyes darting around like she was trying to find a way to escape. Then she looked straight at him. Her jaw worked, and her hand shook a little in his. The anger was far stronger now, flaming behind her eyes. But there was something else in there. Harder. Blacker.

Realization hit him like an icy wind. She wasn't just angry at her father. She hated him.

Sucking in a breath between clenched teeth, she spoke, her voice low and shaking. "My father is a *drunk*."

She was breathing hard now, and he could feel the fury building up like an explosion. Her words started tumbling over each other. "A *drunk*. And nobody knows what he's really like when he's drunk except us. They don't know. They haven't seen him come home in a rage and throw the Christmas tree outside in the snow. Shouting at Mother. They haven't seen ..."

She broke off and turned her head away, hands balled into fists in her lap as her chest heaved back sobs.

She was silent until the wild breathing calmed down.

When she opened her mouth again, it was as if she'd stripped all emotion from her voice. Flat. Sanitized. "They haven't seen any of it."

He knew that wasn't all. He could feel it. "What, Lily? What haven't they seen? There's something else."

Her head turned toward him. Her face was still as a stone, but there was a wildness behind her eyes. Something caged inside, trying to beat its way out of her. Her whole body was stiff as a board. As she stared at him, her hands began to shake again and her nostrils flared faster and faster.

"Lily—"

"I ran away." The words were hardly louder than a breath. Her mouth worked, eyes still riveted on his face as if in a trance. "I didn't ... try to stop him. I—I was afraid." She gulped and it was almost a sob. "Perhaps if I'd stayed, he wouldn't have—" She broke off suddenly, and without warning she sprang to her feet and bolted down the wooded path.

"Lily!" He ran after her, his long strides fast closing the distance. Catching her wrist, he spun her around. "Lily, stop!"

"Let me go!" She struggled against him. "I told you I didn't want to talk about it! I told you! Let me go!"

"All right!" He pulled her close to him, holding her tight by the shoulders. "All right. We won't talk about it. But you can't go yet."

"Why not?" Her eyes were streaming now.

"Because." He cupped her face in his hands, brushing tears away with his thumb. "There's still something we do need to talk about. And it can't wait any longer."

She shook her head, pushing away from him, but he wouldn't let go.

"Lily—"

"You're going away!" She snapped the words out before he could say anything. "You're going home to Florida. Aren't you?"

"Not home. The Pacific."

She stared at him, gulping breath unsteadily.

He couldn't read her face. It was stained with tears and her eyes still looked desperate. But he had a strong feeling she'd known all along what he was trying to build up to.

He cleared his throat. This wasn't how he'd planned it, her standing there looking like someone had ripped her heart out with a crowbar and him afraid to let go of her in case she bolted again.

But it was now or never.

"Lily, listen to me. No, don't look away. Not this time. I'm getting on a boat in less than ten days, and I've got no idea when I'll be back. But I have to know something. I have to know if there's a reason to come back. Will you wait for me, Lily? Will you?"

She had gone very still now.

He lowered his hands from her face, clasping her fingers instead. "I know it's just me against everything else you love.

Maybe I'm crazy to be asking. I can't promise you lots of money or big houses or fancy cars, but everything I have will be yours. All my love. Forever and always. Is that enough, Lily? Promise you'll marry me someday. Promise me that, and they'll have to kill me to keep me from getting back to you."

She stood there and looked at him, tears still coursing in streams down her cheeks and her chest still jerking with sobs. But something had changed in her eyes.

He didn't know what did it, unless it was an act of God. But all at once she collapsed against him, arms slipping around his neck as she buried her face in his uniform.

Her words game out in a whisper. "I promise, Freddie. I promise."

Chapter 24

October 1945

Lily twisted her hand back and forth, watching the little diamond glisten on her finger.

The October sunshine was bright and balmy, and cotton clouds drifted by overhead, painting shadow patterns on the Green. Around her, everyone was smiling.

The war is over.

Over. They had hardly recovered from the shock of the atomic bombs when the announcement of surrender came through, and now it had already been over a month since the official papers were signed.

Almost exactly six years after the war began, it was finished at last. Weeks later, people were still almost giddy with relief.

She looked down again at the piece of paper in her lap. Freddie's latest letter. Signed at the bottom as he always did, in bold, strong letters.

With all my love, forever and ever.

Freddie

"Lily!"

She started, turning her eyes toward town.

Frances waved her arm, standing at the edge of the Green. "What are you doing? You're going to be late for tea." Without waiting for a reply, she turned and started up the street.

Frances. Lily jumped to her feet. She had been waiting for a chance to talk to her sister alone all day. Stuffing the letter in her pocket, she hurried across the grass.

Frances was walking fast, and they were almost to North Clifton Street before Lily caught up with her, panting.

"Slow down, would you?"

"I don't want to be late. What were you doing out there?"

Lily matched her steps to Frances's. "Reading Freddie's letter." She took a breath, trying to figure out how to approach the subject.

"You make me laugh."

"Why?"

"After all your protests about dating Americans, here you are engaged to one."

Frances shook her head, chuckling. "I guess you just never know how things are going to turn out. I still can't believe Clara jilted Harry."

"She didn't jilt him." Lily looked ahead. They were nearing the alley already. "She just decided she loved England more than she loved him."

Frances rolled her eyes. "Took her long enough to figure that out. We all thought they were going to get married. The poor guy must have been—"

"Frances." Lily caught her sister's arm, stopping her just as they turned into the alley. "I need to talk to you."

"Now?" Frances pulled her arm away, looking exasperated. "It's teatime. And I'm tired."

Lily narrowed her eyes. "You would be, staying up until four in the morning."

Frances's brows went up for an instant, then she smoothed the surprise off her face.

"I didn't know it was your job to stay up and watch the clock."

"You woke me." Lily folded her arms.

"You were humming."

"Was I?"

"This wasn't the first time either."

Frances gave a careless shrug. "Well, you needn't glare at me like that. You can't object to me dating Americans now you're engaged to one of them."

"Dating is not the same as staying out all night. Mum's been worried."

"Dear Mother. She is so old-fashioned about these things. All the young people stay out late these days."

Frances tried to look unconcerned, but her eyes wavered beneath Lily's gaze. "I don't see why everyone else should have all the fun, do you?"

Lily stared harder, and let the silence stretch long enough to get uncomfortable. "That depends on what kind of fun you're talking about."

Frances dropped her eyes a moment, and her face tinged pink. Then she raised her chin and laughed. "Oh, Lil." She tapped Lily's nose with her finger. "You're just like Mother." Whirling around, she took three steps to the door.

"Frances!"

The door clicked shut.

Lily stood looking after her a minute, with a cold feeling in the pit of her stomach. Then, gnawing the corner of her lip, she followed her sister inside.

In the parlour, Robert sat on the settee with Alice on one side and Ruth on the other. "Hello, Lily! What's this about another letter from Fred? Is he coming back to marry you yet?"

"No, no!" Ruth tugged on his arm. "Don't stop. Finish the story first!"

Robert had been home for six weeks now. But Ruth never tired of hearing stories about all his escape attempts in Germany. Everything from climbing out hospital windows to helping dig tunnels under the fence.

Mother poured Lily a cup of tea and handed it to her.

"All right." Robert tickled Ruth's ribs. "So the Australian and I decided not to go back into camp with the rest of the working party. Just for fun. We went down to this little local pub instead, and the Australian played the piano while I sang every good pub song I could think of. The locals loved it."

"And then?"

"After a while the German police got there and arrested us for being drunk and disorderly."

Ruth giggled.

"I don't see why you bothered escaping if you weren't actually going to try and go anywhere."

Frances sipped her tea, shaking her head at Robert.

He grinned. "We were just tired of camp, that's all. We used to slip out pretty often, especially in the springtime. We called them spring handicaps."

Ruth tugged on his arm. "Now tell the one about when you got all the way to Switzerland."

"I didn't get all the way. Just almost all the way. Nearly a thousand miles before they caught me."

"Yes!" Ruth snuggled against him. "Tell it!"

"Now hold on a minute, I want to hear about Lily's—"

"Hello."

Lily had her back to the doorway when the new voice, dry and deep, interrupted. The room went still.

She knew who it was before she turned.

The memories tumbled over her like a tidal wave.

Black. Icy. Until she was almost choking on them.

Blood-stained towels crumpled up on the floor. House eerie with silence. White face, pasted with bandages, lying still in the hospital bed ...

There he stood in the doorway. Pale. Haggard.

They had been making so much noise that they hadn't heard the alley door open.

But it stood ajar, the breeze stirring the uniform that hung limp and ill-fitting on his rail-thin form.

Father was home.

Chapter 25

January 1946 — Three Months Later

January was a nice month in Orange County, and the familiar Florida sunshine warmed Fred's skin as he walked the last stretch of road, inhaling the woody scents of pine and cypress. He rounded the last bend before the driveway and stopped.

Two children played at the edge of the hard-packed dirt.

A dark-haired little boy, knees all dusty as he squatted down, built a tower out of pebbles. *That would have to be Charles.* Fred barely recognized him, he'd grown so much.

And of course the wide-eyed toddler, sitting a couple of feet away and watching a butterfly drifting low over the palmettos, must be Carol.

Between the two children, a shaggy mutt stretched on his haunches, keeping watch.

Teddy!

Fred whistled. Teddy looked up, sniffed, and exploded into a frenzied greeting, bounding up the road as he somehow managed to wag his whole body at once.

The children raised their eyes. Charles stood and took a step closer to his sister, forehead scrunched.

When Fred reached the two, he stopped and dropped his duffel bag on the driveway. "Hi, Charles. Remember me?"

Charles looked at him for a minute, then nodded. "You're my brother. Mom said you were coming home soon."

"Well, here I am." It was nice to be remembered. Even just a little.

But it was the bright-eyed toddler who had captured Fred's attention. *Two years old already!* She held onto Charles's ankle with one dimpled hand as she gazed up at Fred.

He squatted down, and Teddy took the opportunity to lick his ear. "Hello there. You must be Carol."

She gave him a bashful little smile.

Charles patted her hand. "Mom tells her about you and Hubert and George all the time. She knows your names from the pictures."

"Does she talk much yet?"

"A'most good as I do. She's just shy. Say hello, Carol."

Carol batted her eyes and was silent.

"It's all right." Fred smiled at her. "We can talk when you get more used to me, okay? Is Mom in the house?"

She nodded.

"Want to come help me tell her I'm home?"

She considered, then stretched out her hands.

He scooped her up, marveling at how soft and tiny she felt in his arms. Charles had been about this size the last time he saw him. But there was something different about a baby girl. More delicate. She looked at him, wide-eyed and trusting, and slipped one little arm around his neck.

His heart went soft as sun-warmed butter. If this was what he felt like just holding his little sister, what would it be like when he had kids? A smile tugged at the corner of his lips. In a few years, maybe he'd have a little girl or two of his own, looking at him like that with big, beautiful eyes.

"I'll carry your bag for you!" Charles grabbed the handle, planted his heels in the hard-packed drive, and tugged for all he was worth. The bag moved about fifteen inches before he had to stop, panting.

"Thanks, Charles, but I think I can handle it all right." Fred cradled Carol in one arm while he swung the duffel over his shoulder with the other.

Charles trotted alongside him as they started for the house, his bare feet making little puffs of dust with each step. "Did you bring anything from England?"

"Not much. I had to leave the most important thing over there. But I'm going back for it."

"What is it?"

"Another sister for you. Her name is Lily."

Charles nodded, a shock of sandy hair flopping on his forehead. "I'm gonna have a lot of sisters. Hubert and George want to bring me some too." He was taking two steps for every one of Fred's.

Fred tried to slow down a little.

"Mom says it's okay for them to marry Japanese girls 'cuz God made all people in His image, not just the Allies. Do you care if they're Japanese?"

"Of course not." He could see the house now as they headed across the yard. The sloped metal roof scattered with pine needles, the faded yellow paint, and the worn porch steps looked just the same as he remembered. In the kitchen window, Mom's head was bent over the sink, her shiny brown hair now frosted with gray. A lump went to Fred's throat.

Carol wiggled and pointed. "Oooo. Butterfwy!" The monarch was swooping into Mom's flower garden.

"She loves butterflies," Charles said.

Carol looked at Fred, her baby-soft brow puckered up in thought. "How come dey call dem butterfwies? Does butter fwy?"

He couldn't help bursting into a laugh.

"Fred!"

There was Mom, standing at the open door, her old checked apron still damp and her hands covered with soap suds.

He dropped the duffel and didn't try to wait for Charles anymore. Mom came down the porch steps, arms outstretched, limping a little like she always had from the polio. He met her at the bottom and wrapped his free arm around her, suds and all, just about lifting her into the air.

She was laughing and crying all at once, and trying to dry her hands on her apron so that she could wipe her eyes. "Why didn't you tell us when you were coming? I'd have made you a nicer supper. I was just frying up the leftover grits tonight."

"Good! I haven't had your grit cakes in more than two years. Serve 'em up!"

She looked past him. "Charles! Are you crazy, child? You can't tote that!"

Charles had looped the duffel bag shoulder strap around him, harness-style, and was straining his way across the yard like a plow horse.

Fred laughed. "He tried to take it at the end of the driveway. I told him not to."

Mom rolled her eyes. "He's just bullheaded, that's what he is. Not a-one of you boys knows a brick wall when you see it."

"Oh, we know 'em, Mom." He winked at her. "It's just we kinda like climbing them."

She laughed.

Fred kept his arm around her, standing there by the porch steps as he looked out over the sun-dappled grass, the pine trees, and the blue sky dotted with clouds.

He felt warm all the way down to his toes. The breeze was blowing, the sun was shining, and Mom's smile was so big it almost swallowed her.

He was home.

Balancing a wash basket on one hip, Lily turned the door-knob and stepped into the bedroom, then stopped in surprise.

Frances lay stretched out on the bed with her face buried in a pillow.

"What's the matter with you?"

"Nothing." Frances's voice was muffled. "Go away."

Lily pushed the door shut behind her. "You're crying."

"I am not!"

"For heaven's sake, Frances, stop acting like a child. What's the matter?"

Frances raised her head. Her eyes were red-rimmed and watery. She sniffed, and her voice came out low and miserable. "They know."

Oh.

Lily set the basket on the floor and began stripping Alice and Ruth's bed, wondering why it had taken Mother this long to figure it out. She thought perhaps she ought to feel more sympathy. But she did not. "Well, it is starting to show. You should have said something before this anyway."

"Oh, shut up! What do you know?" Frances glared at her.

Lily snapped a pillowcase, plopping the pillow out onto the bed. "Enough not to end up like you. What were you thinking, anyway? You're supposed to be the older sister here. Why do I always have to be the sensible one?"

"Oh you're such a *prig*!" Frances spat the word at her. "If you and Mother were in charge, nobody on earth would have any fun at all!"

"Fun!" Lily spun around, wanting to shake her. "You call this fun? Look at you!"

Tears spilled over and coursed down Frances's cheeks. "I said shut up!"

But Lily was too angry to care. She tossed the pillowcase aside and put her hands on her hips. "What did you think was going to happen? Honestly? I can't believe you're sitting there crying like you didn't know—"

"Idiot!" Frances spoke through clenched teeth, jaw tense. "I'm not crying because I don't want the baby. I'm crying because I do!"

Lily went silent, trying to make sense of that statement.

Frances's chest shuddered, and the tears came faster and faster. She opened her mouth to speak, choked on a sob, and dropped her face into the pillow again as her voice came out in a strangled wail.

"I can't ... keep ... the baby!"

Lily's arms dropped to her sides. "What do you mean? Father won't let you?" She knew it couldn't be Mother.

"He'll let me." Frances clenched the edges of the pillow. "He'll let me. As long as ... as ... *oh!*"

She slammed her fist into the bed, jerking her head up again. "He said this is his house. And any babies born here will be under his ... *authority.*"

Her lip trembled, and she squeezed her eyes shut as she pressed her hand to her face, fingers touching the slight bump in the bridge of her nose.

A chill ran up Lily's spine, and for a split second she could see the younger Frances touching the same place in her nose and asking in a teary voice, "Will it always look like that?"

She blinked the image away in time to watch Frances's shoulders go limp as she buried her face in the pillow again.

Oh, Frances. Lily lowered herself to the edge of the bed and sat there, searching for words. But there were none.

She clenched her hands together in her lap and looked out the window.

Now she understood.

For a long time she sat there, staring at the window and listening to Frances crying into the pillow. When the sobs quieted at last, she spoke.

"Will you have the baby at the convent, then?"

Frances nodded without raising her head. "They'll find someone to take her."

"Her? How do you know it's a girl?"

Frances turned her face to look at Lily, and her eyes were hollow wells of sadness. "I just know."

She curled both arms around her middle, as if she were cradling the baby. "I just know."

Lily reached out and took her hand.

Chapter 26

September 1946 — Eight Months Later

Fred stopped just out of sight of the house and mopped his forehead with his shirtsleeve. Even in September, the humidity was like a steam bath.

Pulling some crumpled bills out of his pocket, he started counting out half of them.

He was on his way home from putting in another fence. The third one in a row now. Before that it had been painting and roofing, and before that, picking oranges.

Long hours, all of them. But at least they'd kept the money coming in. Now it seemed like he'd just about exhausted all the odd jobs in the area.

This was why he'd ended up in Texas years ago, working for his uncle in the shipyard before he joined the Air Corps. There just weren't enough good-paying jobs around Seminary Lake.

Waving away a mosquito that whined next to his ear, he slipped half the money into his pocket and kept the rest out in his hand.

Mom still didn't suspect he'd been giving her half his pay all summer, because he never let her see it all together. He'd barely been able to talk her into twenty-five percent, back at the beginning of March when he saw how tight things were. But then that weasel got into the hen-house and most of the chickens had to be replaced, and some kind of worm got the summer-squash vines. Next came Dad's broken ankle, and on top of it all, Charles and Carol got the whooping cough.

Still, his parents would never have taken more, knowing he was trying to save up. Not even if he begged them. So he just slipped it in without saying anything.

The old porch steps creaked beneath his feet as supper scents wafted out to greet him. Fried okra and ... venison roast?

His stomach growled.

What was that all about? Venison was only for special occasions. He opened the screen door and let it slap shut fast to keep out the mosquitoes.

Mom looked up from the stove. "Fred! I was worried you'd be late."

"Late for what?" He held out the money.

"You finished the fence!" She took the crumpled bills and counted with her eyes. "Goodness! Mrs. Yearwood pays well, doesn't she?"

"She's a sweet lady." He avoided the question and went over to the sink to wash his hands. "Late for what, Mom?"

Mother tucked the money away in the cracked sugar bowl she kept behind the canisters. "Hubert and George and their wives are coming for supper."

Hubert and George ...and their wives. Giving Mom the smile she would be expecting, he turned away to unlace his work boots. He was happy for his brothers, of course. Kaziko and Yuriko were very nice girls.

But when they came visiting, it was hard to forget it had been over a year since he last saw Lily.

Carol came into the kitchen, waving a newspaper. "Fred!" She beamed up at him. "Read me about da boat."

"What?"

Mom stirred the okra and tasted a piece. "There's an article about the *Queen Elizabeth*. She's been looking at the picture and chattering about it all day. I already read it twice."

"Again!" Carol looked up at him with big, hopeful eyes.

He scooped her into his arms and sat down at the table.

The article was about the ship's upcoming maiden voyage. Well, not exactly her *maiden* voyage. He'd ridden on her himself during the war. But she'd never been used as the civilian ship she was originally built to be. Until now. She was going to cross from Southampton to New York in early October.

He read the short piece over twice before Carol was satisfied, and then he went to wash up for supper.

Late that evening, he sat on the porch steps, staring up at the darkened sky. A breath of breeze cooled the air, whispering in the tops of the pines. The screen door creaked behind him, and he knew Mom's step without turning around.

She lowered herself to the stoop. "Something's bothering you, isn't it?"

He didn't look at her, but he could feel her looking at him. "I'm just watching the stars come out."

She chuckled. "The stars have been out for hours."

He rubbed his chin. There wasn't much to say to that. The cicadas and crickets filled the silence.

"It's Lily. Isn't it?"

He sighed, watching a Luna moth glide past and disappear above the porch roof. "It's hard to save up when you don't have a job."

"Something else will come along. It always has. All summer."

"Those were odd jobs, Mom. It's not the same thing."

"I'm sure you'll find a salaried position soon. Why, you can do almost anything you put your mind to."

He shook his head. "Even if I got one tomorrow, I'd still have to save for months before I could pay for a ship's passage there and back and have enough to live on afterward. I don't even have a house to put her in."

He jerked to his feet and started pacing on the hard-packed ground in front of the steps. "I've got to get back to her, Mom. All day while I'm working I'm seeing her in my head. The birds and the crickets sing about her. The wind whispers her name in my ear. Am I going crazy?"

She laughed. "Love does feel that way sometimes."

Well, at least he was normal. He dropped back down beside her again, drumming his fingers against the wood. "There's got to be another way."

"Have you prayed about it?"

"Till I'm blue in the face."

"Sometimes the answer is *wait*." She put her arm around his shoulders. "Get some sleep, Fred. Sitting here stewing won't help. Try sleeping on it. Maybe something will come to you." She kissed his cheek and got to her feet, turning toward the door.

A piece of paper fluttered to the stoop.

"You dropped something." He reached to retrieve it for her.

"Oh! Carol's newspaper. She tried to take it to bed with her." Mom shook her head, taking the page from him. "That girl. The funniest things strike her fancy."

The screen door whined and bumped shut behind her.

Fred stared up at the stars winking silently, and wondered what could come to him in one night that hadn't come to him in the past eight months.

He thought he'd have trouble falling asleep, but when he finally dropped into bed the day's hard work caught up to him.

Next thing he knew, dishes were clattering in the kitchen, and the scent of hot grits and eggs had seeped under the door.

He blinked a minute in the sunlight angling in between brown calico curtains that had once been a flour sack, and tried to remember what he'd just been dreaming about.

Then he smiled.

Chapter 27

October 1946

Fred took shallow breaths and tried not to choke on garbage fumes as he gave a couple of stumbling drunks plenty of berth.

No wonder they call this place Hell's Kitchen.

Wobbly tenement houses shouldered up beside him, blocking out all but a sliver of sky. Here and there, the dull yellow of an oil lamp glowed through threadbare curtains.

Mom would be worried to death if she knew he was wandering around this part of the city when it wasn't half daylight yet. He chuckled, remembering the surprise on her face when he'd come to breakfast with his duffel bag packed and his hat on.

"Why, Freddie! Where are you off to?"

"New York." He shoved in a mouthful of grits and watched her blink at him while he chewed.

"New York? What are you talking about?"

"Can't you guess, Mom?" He grinned. "I'm gonna climb a brick wall."

Now here he was on the filthy streets of Hell's Kitchen, trying to find ...

Aha.

Up ahead, a night laborer had just started climbing the steps to his tenement.

Wooden toolbox. Faded cap. Sturdy work clothes. Yep. This was just the chance he'd been looking for. "Hello there!" Fred made his voice as cheerful as possible.

"Eh? Do I know you?"

The man's voice had a singsong Irish lilt.

"Not yet." Fred held out his hand as he got closer. "Name's Fred Overall. A pleasure to meet you, Mr. ...."

"Gaffney." The man looked Fred over like he was trying to figure him out. "You don't sound like you're from these parts."

"Nope." Fred pointed at the man's toolbox. "Are you a mechanic, by any chance?"

"I am."

"Always glad to meet a fellow mechanic."

Fred kept on smiling. "I was wondering if you'd be interested in selling your toolbox."

Mr. Gaffney blinked. "Sure, I wouldn't! I do be needing these tools to make a living with."

"Of course." Fred nodded. "But I don't want the tools. Just the box. Oh, and also your work clothes."

"Me *clothes?* What for now?"

"Well ..." Fred wasn't about to give specifics. "I need them to, um ...to get married."

"Married?" Mr. Gaffney raised his eyebrows and looked down at his grease-stained clothing. "I do be thinking the lady might not approve of these for wedding clothes."

"I didn't say I'm going to wear them to the wedding." Fred put his hands in his pockets.

"Now will you sell them to me or not?"

Mr. Gaffney rubbed the blond stubble on his chin.

It probably wasn't everyday somebody wanted to buy his clothes off him. "Well now, for how much?"

Fred grinned. If they were talking prices, the battle was already won.

* *

Footsteps.

Fred crouched deep in the shadowed corner between two cargo crates and tried his best not to breathe.

Dressed in Mr. Gaffney's work clothes, with his belongings stuffed into the toolbox, he'd managed to board the *Queen Elizabeth* without a hitch.

It was amazing where people would let you go if you carried yourself like you were supposed to be there. Everything had gone smooth as silk. Until now.

That blasted hat!

He hadn't realized it fell off until he heard the footsteps coming and saw it lying out there in plain sight, ten feet from his hiding place. He waited, body rigid.

It was only a small cap. Easy to miss. Maybe whoever it was would just walk right on by without noticing. He only needed a few more hours, and then they would be out at sea ...

The footsteps stopped, just out of sight. There was a soundless pause. Fred held his breath.

Then a flashlight beam hit him full in the face. "All right. Come out of there!"

Blast that hat! Keeping his head down so as not to be blinded by the light, he inched his way back out of the crevice until he stood face-to-face with the security guard, who turned out to be a freckle-faced kid several years younger than himself.

The youngster looked him up and down. "What are you supposed to be?"

"I'm a mechanic."

"Uh-huh." The guard motioned toward the toolbox, his voice sharp with sarcasm. "And I suppose that box is full of tools, eh?"

Fred shrugged. "Depends on how you define the word."

"You're not fooling anybody, you know."

"Not trying to. I *am* a mechanic."

"You're a stowaway."

"That too."

The guard pointed at the cap still lying on the floor. "Get your hat and come with me."

"Where to?"

"Commodore's orders." The guard motioned for him to walk in front. "All stowaways go directly to him."

Uh oh. That didn't sound good.

* * *

"Stowaway, eh?" Commodore James Bisset stood with his arms crossed, eyeing Fred. He was of average height, with a round face and a rounder belly.

"What's your name, young man?"

"Fred Overall, sir."

"Well, Mr. Overall,"—the commodore cocked his brow—"you've just been caught stowing away on one of the finest ships in the Cunard Line. What do you have to say for yourself?"

Fred took a breath. If he was going to have a chance left of getting to England, he was going to have to make a good impression. He smiled. "I guess I have good taste in ships, sir."

The commodore blinked. "Indeed. And is that all you have to say?"

Was that a tiny glint in his eye? Fred cleared his throat. "I wasn't just stowing away, sir. I was volunteering."

"Oh? Volunteering for what?"

"Anything that would earn me a passage to England, sir."

This time he was sure he saw a twinkle as the commodore sat down and leaned back in his chair. "You're a determined one, aren't you? Why England?"

"My fiancée is there, sir."

"I suppose you were stationed over there during the war?"

"I left sixteen months ago."

The corner of the commodore's mouth twitched. "But who's counting, eh? Well, Mr. Overall, much as I commend you for your determination to find a way to get back to her, I'm afraid you will not be doing so aboard this ship."

Fred's last bubble of hope deflated. "Isn't there any way I could work for my passage?"

The commodore shook his head. "We are already fully staffed. Furthermore, we are not even at sea yet. Stowaways do not simply waltz onto ships and get jobs handed to them while they are still in port, even if they are madly in love." He stood up. "Bernard will escort you off the ship."

Bernard, the security guard, opened the door and Fred started to follow him through, shoulders sagging.

"Oh, Mr. Overall?"

He looked back.

The commodore was smiling. "I recommend you don't try anymore stowaway attempts. They almost never work. Believe me."

Bernard shut the door.

Fred shoved his hands in his pockets and started walking, kicking himself for dropping that hat. "That wasn't as bad as I was expecting."

Bernard chuckled to himself. "I'd heard rumors, but I didn't believe them until I saw it myself."

"What?"

"The commodore likes stowaways."

Fred looked up. "Come again?"

"Likes them. Actually *likes* them. Couldn't you tell?"

Fred thought back for a minute. "Well...But why would he?"

Bernard slowed. He glanced up and down the passage and lowered his voice. "Because he *was* one. They say that's how he became a sailor in the first place. He was just a kid office clerk in some shipping company, but he wanted to go to sea, so ..."

He spread his hands and raised his brow.

Fred almost laughed. Of all the ships he could have stowed away on, he managed to pick the one with a commodore who started out as a stowaway himself.

What were the chances?

His grin faded though, as they got closer and closer to the gangplank. Stowaway or no stowaway, the commodore had still just squelched his only plan for getting to England for free.

Now the question was, what next?

Chapter 28

December 1946

Married.

Lily sat in the parlour, fighting to keep a smile nailed to her face.

Married. Without a whisper of warning, without the barest shred of a chance to stop it, Robert had eloped.

With Allie Kelly.

There they sat on the settee, smiling like mischievous children. *As if eloping in Hampshire were a childhood romp!* Allie clung to Robert's arm, nuzzling her chin into his shoulder as she gazed up beneath long lashes.

He beamed down at her.

Lily ground her teeth behind the smile. Robert didn't know that Allie had looked that exact same way at a dozen other guileless young men while he was stuck behind barbed wire in Germany. She choked back a lurching sensation in her stomach, determined not to be sick right there on the floor. *Why, oh, why didn't we tell him?*

But she knew the answer. It was because they thought they had time.

With Allie gone off to live with her aunt in Hampshire before he returned from Germany, they thought they were safe for a while.

So they had put it off, waiting for the right time to discuss it. And somehow the weeks stretched into months. Then one day in early December he had come home announcing he was off to Hampshire to visit Allie.

Before they could figure out how to stop him, he was gone, promising to be home for Lily's birthday.

And here he is. Lily dug her fingernails into her palm.

Here he was with a ring on his finger and Allie Kelly...no, Allie Brown, on his arm.

And somehow I'm supposed to be happy about it.

The neighbours were filing into the room like a parade, smiling and congratulating and shaking hands. Lily took a deep breath, feeling more and more like she was on the verge of suffocating.

She scanned the room, searching for an escape, and her eyes found Mother's.

Poor dear Mother, who probably felt this worst of all. But still she had that beautiful calm about her, just as always.

Reading Lily's eyes like a book, she gave a tiny nod toward the stairs.

Yes.

Of course Lily wanted to go upstairs. To find someplace to breathe and get her head on straight again. But what would Robert think if she just up and left?

With an understanding smile, Mother seemed to catch on. "Lily, why don't you go upstairs and get my Bible so I can write the marriage date in it? You may have to look around a bit to find it."

Bless you, Mother.

Lily got to her feet and wound her way to the staircase. Up the steps she flew, straight to Mother and Father's room. With her hand on the doorknob, she heard Father's voice above the hubbub below, suggesting they should all go down to the pub and celebrate.

Brilliant. She slammed the door.

Robert was married to Allie Kelly, and Father was going off to get drunk over it. What could possibly be any better? She snapped the lock into place and threw herself onto the bed, burying her face in a pillow to muffle the frustrated scream she had been holding back for an hour.

Oh, Robert! What have you done? My sweet, wonderful, reckless brother! What have you done?

Her fists beat the pillow.

Angry, helpless tears stung her eyes and she dashed them away in fury. It was all her fault. She'd had months to tell him. Why did she wait?

Something thumped onto the bed beside her, and silky fur brushed her arm.

It was Archie, Freddie's surprise birthday gift to her two years earlier. *Two years.* In that time Archie had grown into a fat tomcat who was not supposed to be in the house but somehow got in anyway.

He purred as he rubbed against her, but she ignored him. She didn't want Archie now. She didn't want anybody. No ...*yes.* Yes, she did though. She wanted ...she wanted ...

Freddie.

The sudden, desperate longing washed over her like a raging storm. Robert was gone. He belonged to Allie now, and she could never get him back.

But she had Freddie. Freddie was hers for always. And she wanted him here. This moment. Yesterday.

He had been home in the U.S. for almost a year. What w taking him so long?

"Fred Overall!" She sobbed into the pillow, po¹ bed with her balled fist. "You come back here you. This minute. Why don't you *come?*"

It was daft, talking to someone on the other side of an ocean. If only she could—

A sudden thought flashed into her mind, and she pushed herself up on her elbows. There was Mother's bureau, and a paper and a pen, lying there waiting.

Quick as thought, she slid off the bed, dropped into the chair, and seized the pen, dashing words off as fast as her fingers could move. They were haphazard, perhaps even a little incoherent, but she was past caring. In no time she had the letter signed, sealed, and ready to post.

She slumped back in the chair, exhausted from the wild tidal waves of emotion, and clutched the letter to her chest. It would be in the post before the day was out.

"Come," she whispered. "Come *soon*." Her eyes fell on Mother's Bible, there on the bureau where she always kept it. It would have taken no time at all to find it. But they both knew she was not really up here to look for it.

"God, please." She blinked away tears. "Make a way for him to get back here somehow."

Please, God. I need him.

Chapter 29

February 1947

The recruiting sergeant blinked at Fred.

"This is highly irregular."

Tell me something I don't know. Fred leaned over the desk. "Look, if you'd gotten a letter from your fiancée like the one I got from mine, you'd understand. Now. The war is over, right?"

"Don't you read the papers?"

Fred tried hard not to roll his eyes. .

"Just listen! The war is over, and all the boys want to come home, and the draft is dropping down by the week. But you need men because there's still a lot to do over there. Right?"

"Correct. There's been serious difficulty convincing anyone to stay in the military now that—"

"Well then! I'm standing here ready to go back in the Air Corps today. You just have to fix it so the first place I end up is Lancashire, England."

The sergeant's brow furrowed. "Sorry. All I do is sign men up. I don't decide where they—"

"Fred Overall?" The voice interrupted from somewhere behind him.

He turned. Another recruiting officer was coming toward him with long strides. He blinked. "Pete Ross!" The MP uniform was gone, but otherwise Pete looked about the same as always. Tall, lanky, and dark-haired.

Pete pumped Fred's hand. "What are you doing in a recruiting office? I'd think you'd have your fill of the Air Corps by this time."

"I have. But like I was telling him,"—he jerked his head toward the sergeant behind the desk—"I'd do just about anything to get back to Lancashire right now."

"Lancashire?" Pete looked puzzled for a minute. Then he grinned. "Oh."

The recruiting officer piped in, "I've just been telling him there's no way we can control where he's—"

"Yeah, yeah, Hampton, I know."

Pete flapped his hand. "Why don't you go take a lunch break? I'll run the desk for a while."

"It's four in the afternoon."

"Then go see a movie. Or take a nap. I don't care. Just go, okay?"

Hampton stood, wrinkling his nose. "Really, Ross. This is highly irregular. I—"

"Roll up your flap, would ya? I'm finishing your shift for you. What are you complaining about?"

Hampton shook his head and left.

"What's his problem?"

"Eh." Pete shrugged. "I think he wears his tie too tight." Swinging around the edge of the desk, he landed in the chair. "Okay, let's see. Any particular reason you want to go back to Lancashire?"

Fred nodded.

"Thought so." Pete winked at him. "Blond or brunette?"

"Brunette."

"Mmm." Pete shuffled through paperwork. "Same girl you used to sneak out and visit without leave?"

"I didn't realize you—"

"*Everybody* knew about it, Fred. You can't disappear that regular without people noticing."

"You never mentioned it."

Pete shrugged. "I was an MP, remember? Anyway. It's not going to be that easy to get you sent back to Lancashire. They've already handed BAD-2 back over to the British. None of our boys are even there anymore."

He looked up at Fred from under his eyebrows. "There's not, um..." He cleared his throat. "There's not a kid, is there?"

"Of course not!"

Pete held up his hands. "No offense meant. It's just a lot easier to fix this up if there's a dependent involved. Do you know how many half-American kids there are in England right now? It's an epidemic. There's a whole detachment of bureaucrats assigned to deal with that kind of situation."

"Are you telling me there's nothing you can do, just because I didn't get her pregnant while I was over there?"

Pete tugged his lower lip. "I don't know. I've got a few strings I could pull, but I can't guarantee anything."

"You'll try though?"

"I'll try."

Fred swallowed. "Okay, then. Give me the papers."

It was incredible how little time it took to sign over three more years of his life to the U.S. Government.

Pete met him at the door after the physical. "I'll do my best, Fred. They'll probably want to send you for some more training first, but I'll see if I can get you sent to England right after, at least for a little while."

"Thanks."

"No problem." Pete slapped him on the shoulder. "Three years is a long time though. I hope she's worth the price."

"She's worth a hundred years."

Pete whistled. "No wonder you went AWOL."

Fred reached for the doorknob. "I still can't believe you knew about that all the time and never said anything."

"I told you, I was an MP. If I'd admitted I knew about it, I'd have had to arrest you."

"Not unless you caught me off base."

The corner of Pete's mouth twitched as he glanced around at the other people in the room. He nodded. "True."

Fred pulled open the door and stepped out onto the street. "Goodbye, Pete. Thanks again."

"Goodbye, Fred."

The door swung shut, but he'd only made it a few steps down the street when it creaked open again behind him.

"Oh, Fred!" Pete was leaning against the doorframe with a cockeyed grin.

"What?"

The grin widened a bit. "Nothing important. I was just wondering…" His eyes were laughing as he arched one brow. "What size ladies' coat do you wear?"

Chapter 30

July 1947—Five Months Later

"Ruthie! What are you doing with my fashion magazines?"

Ruth bolted up from the bed and gave Lily a guilty smile. "I—I was just looking a little bit."

Lily pushed the door shut and crossed the room to the bed. "Wedding dresses? Aren't you a little young to be interested in that?"

Ruth wrinkled her nose. "I'm twelve."

Lily laughed. "Oh, pardon me. I forgot you were practically an adult now."

Ruth rolled her eyes.

"But really, Ruth. You've been at those magazines ever since Frances got married last month, haven't you? I knew somebody was fiddling with them, but I thought it was Alice."

Ruth grinned and dropped onto the bed again, flipping through pages. "I hope by the time I get married, they'll stop rationing fabric. I want something that *really* twirls. Like Christian Dior's 'New Look.' Can you imagine five yards of fabric in one skirt?"

She squeezed her eyes shut and sighed, as if she could see herself wearing it now. "Wouldn't you like yards and yards of fabric in your wedding dress?"

Hmph. Lily gathered up the magazines and put them away without answering. At this point, she was beginning to wonder if she would ever have a wedding dress at all.

The barest breath of a sigh slipped between her lips. Frances had looked so happy on Doug's arm.

Even the faint whisper of loss that had haunted her eyes for a year, ever since she came home from the convent without her daughter, had all but disappeared as she beamed over her bouquet.

Lily bit her lip.

It had been months and months since Freddie rejoined the Air Corps, and still they kept him tied down at some mechanical school.

Freddie said it was in Kansas, "smack dab" in the middle of the country. That sounded awfully far from England.

Turning her head, she let her eyes linger for just a moment on the top drawer of the dressing table.

Two whole years she had been waiting for Freddie to return now. And there was no telling how much longer it would be.

Sometimes, just for a moment or two, she let herself wonder how things might have been different if she'd chosen Paul instead.

"Can I help you, sir?" The gray-haired telegraph agent looked up.

Fred's heart thumped a little faster. He unfolded the scrap of paper he'd been scribbling on for half an hour as the pulsing energy of trains and people swelled and echoed around him in the wide halls of Union Station.

"I want to send a telegram to England."

The operator nodded and reached for his pad. "Where in England?" His voice sounded as bland as two-day-old oatmeal.

"To a Miss Lily Brown. Twenty-five North Clifton Street, Lytham, Lancashire."

Fred rattle the address off by heart and watched the pen scratching down his instructions.

It was a beautiful train station. Marble floors, spacious halls, and an ornamental ceiling that was well worth craning your neck to admire, even if it was four stories up.

There was a restaurant, places to get your shoes shined or a haircut and shave, and retail shops selling everything from vegetables to shoes and cigars. No wonder it seemed like half the people in Kansas City were bustling around inside.

"And what all do you want it to say?"

Fred looked one last time at the paper in his hand. It wasn't *all* he wanted to say. Not even close. But on a telegram, you had to pay for every word.

He slid the paper across the desk and pointed to the bottom of it. "That. Where I circled."

The agent bent his head, scanning the message. Then he raised his eyes to Fred's, and for just a second, his bland, tired face broke into a smile.

"Lily!" Ruth came flying toward her as Lily turned into the alley.

It had been a long day at work, and it seemed like her stacked wood heels must weigh about ten pounds apiece. Even her pocketbook felt heavy.

Ruth hurtled straight into her, spinning the two of them in a haphazard circle with the leftover momentum. "Come on. I've been waiting for hours! Mother won't let me open it."

Lily was almost too tired to ask questions. "What are you talking about?"

"A telegram! From Fred. Come *on!* Don't you want to know what it says?"

Do I? Something lurched in Lily's stomach. Freddie always sent letters.

A telegram had to mean something important. But what? She let Ruth drag her down the alley toward the door while her mind whirled so fast she felt dizzy. What if Fred had been injured, or thrown out of the corps, or for some other reason could not leave the country for months and months? Or...

Or what if he could leave the country? What if he was about to leave it? Coming back to marry her?

She swallowed.

If they got married, that was it. Everything was final. She would have to go with him. Leave Mother, leave everything here, perhaps forever. She had managed to keep from thinking much about that up until now.

Ruth flung the door open. "Here she is, Mother!"

Mother came across the kitchen, drawing a yellow envelope out of her apron pocket. "What kept you so long, Lily? I was beginning to worry. Your father isn't home yet either."

"We were busy today. I stayed extra late." She couldn't take her eyes off the envelope. "Perhaps Father had to work late too."

"Perhaps." Mother's voice wavered slightly.

Lily looked up, but Mother avoided her gaze and held out the telegram.

Heart pounding, Lily took it.

She pressed her lips together and gulped a deep breath as she slid her finger under the flap and broke the seal.

With hands almost trembling, she held the paper up to the fading summer light.

LEAVING FOR SOUTHAMPTON AUGUST 13

STOP

MARRY ME?

Chapter 31

Alice and Ruth went wild with excitement when they found out what the telegram said.

Mother beamed and got a little teary-eyed, then started bustling about talking of wedding plans.

Caught up in everyone else's excitement, Lily managed to push all the worrying thoughts away. Within minutes, Mother was pulling out patterns and ladies' magazines and talking about the wedding outfit.

Lily drew up a stool next to her, and Alice and Ruth hung over the back of the chair while Mother flipped through pages.

"What about something like this?" She motioned to a black-and-white sketch. "Simple and elegant, but with two pieces like that you could reuse it easily."

Lily looked. It was a tailored dress with buttons up the back, a pleated peplum, and three-quarter sleeves with turned-up cuffs. "That's lovely. But what would we make it out of? Do we have enough fabric left over from Frances's dress?"

Mother raised her brow. "Leftover? Rubbish! We'd get something new for you, of course. What colour would you like? That canary yellow is very popular now. Or perhaps powder blue? Blue would look lovely with your eyes."

Powder blue. Yes, that was what she would want if they were buying. But what was Mother thinking? With all the money they had just spent on Frances's wedding?

"I don't have to have something new, Mum. There can't be much money left after—"

"You're bloody right, there isn't!"

The door to the alley slammed shut so hard that Lily jumped. One look at Father's bloodshot eyes proved it was not work that had kept him out late.

Mother stiffened beside Lily with an almost silent intake of breath. Ruth and Alice faded into the shadows behind the chair. In the back of her mind, Lily could feel the dark memories crawling out again, bringing the cold fear with them.

She hated herself for being afraid of him. She was not a little girl anymore. She was a grown woman, about to be married. He should not have this kind of power over her still.

But he did.

Is Mother afraid? Her face didn't show it. Expressionless, Mother's eyes followed Father as he maneuvered his hat onto the rack and fished in his pocket, mumbling. Whatever he was looking for, he could not seem to find it. Exasperated, he gave up and came into the parlour. "You're bloody right, there isn't!" He went on as if there had been no pause. "We must have spent every bloody red penny in the house on that blasted wedding!"

"Chris." Mother's voice was soft.

He glared at her. "What are you trying to spend more money on now?"

Lily clamped the fear down as hard as she could and tried to divert him. "Nothing, Father, I only—"

"We are looking at patterns to make Lily a wedding dress." Mother's hand pressed Lily back down as she started to stand. "We just had a telegram from Fred—"

"Fred! Fred! Fred! That's all I ever hear anymore." Father glowered at them. "What makes him think he gets to just show up and carry my daughter off with him? Nobody asked me. I've never even set eyes on the good-for-nothing Yank!"

Good for nothing? A hot pulse of anger pushed Lily's chin up. But before she could open her mouth, the warning hand tightened on her arm and Mother spoke instead.

"Fred is a very nice, God-fearing, hard-working young man. I gave him permission, remember? You weren't here to ask."

The room was darkening as storm clouds rolled in outside, blotting out the last glow of sunset.

Father's eyes narrowed, bleary with alcohol. "Fine!" He spat the words at Lily. "Run off and leave us, then! It'll be one less mouth to feed around here."

Run off and leave us ...A sickening grip squeezed Lily's insides. *Run.* She could almost hear Frances's panicked voice hissing that word into her ear.

It was the last thing she had said before—

Mother stood up, pushing herself between them. "It's time for bed, Chris. We'll talk about it in the morning." She took a step toward the stairs, nudging him in that direction.

"I'm not going to bed."

"Just come upstairs, all right? I'll brew you a cup of tea."

"I don't want tea!"

"Come on now. It'll make you feel better." Somehow Mother was still moving him toward the stairs.

"Leave me be!" His heavy voice slurred the words.

"Now, Chris—"

"I said leave me be!" They were in the stairway now. "We aren't going to talk about it in the morning either. There's nothing to talk about! We haven't got any more money for another wedding. You spent it all on the last one!"

Lily's breath quickened in her chest, the fear curling upward toward her throat as his voice rose.

"Calm down, Chris. You're drunk."

"You're bloody right, I'm drunk! And why do you think I'm drunk? Because it's the only way to keep sane, that's why!"

"Chris—"

"Take your hands off me, woman! I said I'm not going to bed!"

Thunder rumbled in the distance. The low-burning lamp left half the room in darkness.

Father was raging now. "You'd be drunk too, if you were me! I work like a dog to keep this family fed, keep the money coming day after day. And still there's never enough! What happens to it! Huh? I'll tell you what happens! You spend it! Spend it and spend it and spend it!"

Lily clenched her teeth. Anger and fear twisted themselves together inside until she could barely tell which was which.

In the shadows behind the chair, she could hear Ruth sniffling and Alice trying to calm her. Ruth was the only one too young to remember that it had always been this way, before the war.

Lily's fingernails dug into her palms as she scrunched fistfuls of skirt in her hands. Ruth should not have to live like this. None of them should have to live like this.

Least of all Mother.

Her voice was still soft on the stairs, trying to sooth Father while he ranted at her.

How dare he take it out on Mother?

Lily felt hot rage rising, fighting its way up through the familiar icy fear. Mother who stashed away every extra penny while Father spent his at the pub. Mother who never spoke a bad word of her husband. Mother who refused to let the terrible struggles, year after year, steal her joy, her love, her faith, or her wonderful merry laugh.

How dare he?

And how dare she, Lily Brown, a grown woman, sit here and let him do it?

Robert was gone.

Frances was gone. And now she was about to leave them all too.

Leave Mother and the children to face this all alone.

"Chris, please! Just go up to bed."

"Belt up! And keep your hands off me! I told you I'm not tired. This is my house, you hear? I'll go to bed when I want to! Don't you touch me!"

"Christopher Brown, you're practically falling over, you're so drunk! Now come upstairs before you pass out!"

Mother must have taken hold of his arm.

"I said don't touch me!"

All at once there was the sharp snap of a blow, and then a jumbled series of thuds as Mother tumbled down the steps into the entry.

Alice and Ruth screamed.

A bolt of lightning doused the room in piercing light for a split second, showing Mother on the floor, gasping and clutching her wrist.

In that same instant, Lily was on her feet, electrified with fury. In her mind she could see Frances, lying on the floor in the kitchen, clutching her face.

It was the last glimpse she'd had before she ran out the door.

Coward!

Another ear-splitting crash of thunder shook the floor as all other feelings evaporated, swallowed up in a white-hot, blinding flash of rage.

Not again. Not Mother.

Not this time.

This time she had had all she could take.

In two flying steps, she crossed the parlour. As her foot hit the stairs, she heard Mother's voice, as if from a long way off. "Lily, don't!"

But it was too late.

In the next instant she plowed into Father, slamming him against the wall in the stairway.

Bellowing with surprise, he swung at her and she ducked out of the way. He swayed, regaining his balance, and she hurled herself into him again, knocking him back against the wall and screeching like a banshee.

"How dare you hit Mother? How dare you?"

He swung at her with his other fist and she dodged backward, tottering for a moment on the edge of the step before she threw herself forward again, pummeling him with both fists. "She's the one who saves money while you spend yours at the pub! She's the one who works like a dog while you hide in a beer glass! If you ever touch her again, I'll...I'll...I'll kill you!"

"Lily!" Mother's gasp was horrified.

Even with fury driving her half-mad, the voice must have distracted Lily for an instant. Long enough for Father to swing again and catch her on the jaw with a backhanded slap.

She stumbled. Her heel caught, jerking the whole shoe off as she grabbed for the railing, trying to catch herself, and landed on one knee.

Father came at her, swinging again. Rage pounded in her ears. Almost without thinking, she seized the fallen shoe in one hand as she ducked the next blow.

Father pulled back to swing again, and in that breath of a second, she sprang to her feet and smacked him square in the face with the hard wooden heel.

He bellowed, reeling backward as he clutched his nose, and collapsed onto the step. She gripped the shoe and braced herself, ready for him to come at her again.

But he didn't. He sat there, rocking back and forth and moaning with both hands holding his nose.

After a moment, something dark and thick began to trickle out between his fingers.

"Oh, Lily," Alice's voice was a breathless whisper from the bottom of the stairs.

She had broken Father's nose.

The shoe dropped from her hand and clattered in the sudden quiet. Leaning against the rail, she panted for air, feeling almost dizzy with the muddled chaos of emotions.

For a long moment, no one said a word. Another flash of lightning showed Ruth in the front-room doorway, face white as a sheet, and Alice on the floor beside Mother. A gust of wind flapped the curtains in the stillness.

For the first time, Lily heard the rain blowing in through the front window.

Looking old and tired, Father pulled himself to his feet. He stared at her for a minute, and there was a strange mix of emotions in his eyes that she could not read.

Then he turned and hunched his way up the stairs with slow steps, still holding his nose.

The bedroom door clicked shut behind him.

Chapter 32

The rage drained away as Lily gripped the handrail, light-headed and weary, and limped down the stairs.

Mother sat propped up against the door, hurt wrist cradled in her lap.

Dropping to her knees, Lily reached for it. "Is it broken, Mum? Can you move it?"

Mother flexed the wrist. "It's just sprained, that's all." But her eyes were dark and watery with tears.

Lily's jaw tensed. "Don't you mind what Father said. It's a lie. You know it is."

Mother kept staring at her, and the tears began to roll down her cheeks as she shook her head.

Lily's throat felt tight and hot. How could Mother believe such a thing for a moment? "Yes, it is! If he ever touches you again, I'll—"

"Oh, Lily." Mother's hand closed around hers. "Do you really think it's your father I'm crying about?"

Lily broke off, staring at her.

"You're the one with your whole life ahead of you. You're the one it will hurt the most, if you don't let go of it."

"Let go of what?"

"Hate. It's like poison. If you keep it inside, it will only destroy you."

Lily felt the angry pulse beginning to pound in her forehead again. Mother wanted her to forgive him. Again. But what good had that ever done? He never changed. He never would. "Why do you stay with him, Mum? I'm not going to be here to stop him next time if I go away with Freddie. Why don't you leave him? *Why?*"

Tears overflowed and splashed down her face.

"Because I chose him, Lily." Mother's voice was solemn. "I made a promise before God and everyone else to be his wife until death parts us. I keep my promises."

Lily wanted to scream in frustration. "So that's what marriage means? That you promise to stay with someone forever, even if you're miserable?"

"I'm not miserable."

"I don't see why not!" The tears kept coming, and Lily wiped them away. "Was this how you planned your life? Scraping to make ends meet while your husband drinks his money away?"

Mother drew herself up straight and caught both Lily's hands in hers. "Listen to me. You've got to stop holding on so hard. You're so afraid of what might happen that you're trying to control everything yourself. But life never happens like we plan it, Lily. It just doesn't work that way."

Lily bit her lip.

"Oh, my Lily." Mother's voice was low as she drew Lily's hand to her chest. "Let go. Happiness doesn't come from being the one in control. It comes from trusting the One who is."

. . . . ● ● ● ● ● ● ● ● ● ● . . . . . .

Lily lay awake for hours that night. Staring at the darkened window, she watched the rain hurl itself against the panes with every gust of wind, pounding and pounding, never able to get past the glass.

It was no good. She could not forgive Father.

Not after tonight.

As she tossed and turned beneath the cotton sheet, scenes flashed through her mind like photographs. Mother lying on the floor, clutching her wrist. Blood trickling from Father's nose. And years ago, Frances lying on the same floor, screaming, blood seeping through her fingers.

What good does it do to forgive if nothing ever changes?

She could not let go. Not of this. Instead she pushed the hatred deep down inside, and hoped she could forget about it.

Hoped Mother was wrong.

You're the one with your whole life ahead of you ...

She squeezed her eyes shut, shaking her head against the voice inside. She could not forgive Father. Not for Mother. Not for Freddie. Not even for herself. Stop holding on, Mother said. As if it was really that simple. Perhaps it would be, if she was as brave as Mother. But she was not.

You're so afraid of what might happen that you're trying to control everything ...

Yes. She was afraid. It seemed to Lily she had been afraid for as long as she could remember. Afraid of Father. Afraid of not having enough money. Afraid of letting someone else control her life. Even if it was God. Afraid of giving up her plans. Afraid of giving up Paul ...

Paul.

Across the room, the shadowy hulk of the dressing table loomed in the corner. Something quivered in her chest, and her fingers clutched the sheet.

There it was again. The top drawer. Always there to haunt her at the worst possible moment.

She squeezed her hands into fists. Every time she thought about that necklace, a tiny voice of doubt surfaced from somewhere deep inside.

You could have chosen differently. You could have had life just as you planned it.

Enough!

She threw the blankets off, and her feet found the floor.

Perhaps she could not forgive Father. Perhaps she could never forgive him. But she did not have to keep holding on to everything. Some things she could let go of. Some things she could forget. Surely.

She looked again at the rain pounding against the window. It would be madness to go out in a storm like this.

But ...

She swallowed.

· ·

The rain was still thundering against the paving bricks when she stepped out onto North Clifton Street, cold water drumming against her skin.

A flash of lightning showed the empty street, rippling with rain. Clutching the necklace until it dug into her palm, she tucked her head against the wind and broke into a run.

The town felt deserted. Most of the windows were squares of blackness, staring after her as she passed. The wind howled in her ears and plastered her dress to her legs as she splashed, heedless, through the puddles.

By the time she reached Lowther Gardens, she was gasping for air. Pulse throbbing, lungs burning, she dragged her tired feet up the garden path.

There.

There in that very spot, Paul had given her the necklace.

She dropped down, wet grass and earth squishing beneath her knees.

With bare hands, she clawed at the saturated ground, scooping out a hole.

Then she stopped, chest still shuddering for air, and looked down one more time at the necklace. Another flash showed it lying her in her palm, dripping wet and smudged with dirt from her fingers.

Even still, the flecks of diamonds shimmered in that split second of light. For a moment she hesitated. It was such a stupid thing to do. Why not sell it and use the money toward her wedding dress? That would be the practical thing to do.

But this moment was not about being practical.

I'll think of you when I'm wearing it.

She clenched her fingers around the pendant until the diamonds dug into her skin. Crystal clear she could see Paul there, on the sun-drenched grass. What good would it do her if the dress she wore to marry Freddie still tied her, even a little bit, to someone else?

Sucking in a breath, she dropped the necklace into the hole and clawed the dirt back over it, smoothing the grass back down until the place was all but invisible.

"I'm letting go, Lord." She pressed her hands over the place and turned her face to the sky as the rain stung her cheeks. "I'm letting go."

- -

All was dark and silent when she crept up the stairs and tiptoed back into the bedroom.

The thunder subsided into a distant rumble as she hung her dripping dress in the wardrobe. After slipping back into her nightgown, she wrapped an afghan around her shoulders to keep the damp hair off her neck.

Warmth began to creep into her fingers and toes once more, and all at once she was drowsy.

But she didn't want to sleep. Instead she gathered up the neat stack of Freddie's letters, tied with a red hair ribbon, and carried them back to bed with her.

Sitting there in the dreamy hush of earliest morning, while the rest of Lytham lay silent and sleeping, she unfolded one letter after another, tracing the lines with her finger in the watery moonlight.

Though the clouds were beginning to clear off, it was still too dark to make out more than a word here and there.

Except when it came to the last line. The one that was always the same.

With all my love, forever and ever.

Happiness throbbed warm and strong in her chest. How wonderful it was to feel that at last—*at last*—she could truly promise him the same.

All her love. Not just almost all, with a tiny slice held back for the old dreams and plans. But all of it. Every breath. Every moment. Every heartbeat.

Forever and ever.

Clutching the last of the letters to her breast, she smiled into the darkness.

Chapter 33

"Look, it's not like I'm asking for the moon. I just want to take my wife home with me!" Fred leaned against the desk, watching the little sandy-haired guy on the other side scratching away with a pen.

Fred was tired. He'd just spent almost a week crossing the Atlantic in a hard military berth, and now he'd been standing here in the Liverpool consulate building for two hours trying to convince a bland-faced bureaucrat to get Lily a visa.

It shouldn't be this complicated.

The guy behind the desk looked up through his spectacles.

"For the tenth time, Mr. Overall, I can't help you. Do you realize how much paperwork and processing is required for something like this? Passports, birth certificates, marriage certificates, photographs, medical examinations. You can't expect to just walk off the ship, marry her, and take her home with you like a souvenir."

"Now look, Howard."

Fred checked the name tag to make sure he had it right. "What is this, anyway? With the hoops they made me jump through in the Air Corps just to get permission to marry her in the first place, you'd think I was trying to access the U.S. Treasury!"

"Welcome to the bureaucracy."

I'll say. "Come on. If I was an ambassador's son, couldn't you figure out how to get my wife through the system faster?"

Howard rolled his eyes to the ceiling like he was praying for patience. "I don't see how that is relevant."

Fred leaned farther across the desk and lowered his voice. "If you can do it for an ambassador's son, you can do it for me too."

Howard's chuckle was dry as a pile of dead leaves. "Do you realize what kind of chaos it would cause if I tried to grant special privileges to every lovesick soldier who wandered into my office?"

"But I'm not *every* lovesick soldier."

"Are you the ambassador's son?"

"No."

"Well then."

Fred pulled himself up straight and took a deep breath. "I'm not leaving this consulate until I get what I came here for."

"I'm afraid you'll have to, Mr. Overall. The doors will be locked in five minutes." There was a note of tired triumph in Howard's voice. "You can't spend the night here." Fred folded his arms. *Watch me.*

Lily sat by the bedroom window, watching the golden glow of sunset fade into night. Dark against the sky, rows of shop roofs jutted up like the tips of a picket fence. The close of another long summer day.

And once more, it had brought no word from Freddie.

Stop worrying. Lily reached to turn up the lamp. She was supposed to be studying, not staring out the window. Settling back into her chair, she looked down at the *Good Housekeeping* pamphlet in her lap. Tall letters on the front read: *A Bride's Guide to the U.S.A.* It seemed a small book for such a large topic.

Thumbing through the pages, she found the section on American citizenship, and read that it was not acquired through marriage. There would be a waiting period of three years before the final papers could be issued, and until that time she would remain a British subject.

Three years?

Lily chewed her lip. She had been a British subject since the day she was born. And now in a mere three years, they would expect her to give it all up and swear loyalty to another country? There was no section titled *How to Renew Your Visa*, so they must have been assuming she would feel ready to be an American by that time.

And if I don't?

Drumming her fingers on the page, she glanced out the window again, toward the street. It usually took less than a week to cross the Atlantic. Freddie should have made it to Southampton yesterday at the latest. What was taking so long?

Stop it. Concentrate.

Flipping to the end of the pamphlet, she found the glossary of American words that were different from the British ones. *Such a lot to remember.* A chest of drawers was called a bureau in America, and a bureau was called a writing desk. Ground floors were first floors, and first floors were second floors.

Then there were the clothing words. It was going to be so confusing shopping for Freddie. She would have to ask for undershirts when she wanted vests, and for vests when she wanted waistcoats, and for suspenders if she wanted braces and ...

Oh dear.

Sighing, she flipped the pamphlet shut and tossed it onto the chest of drawers, wishing it was that easy to toss aside the worry gnawing at the back of her mind. After more than two years of waiting, these last few days should have been easy. But somehow they seemed the hardest of all.

"Lily, are you afraid?"

The voice startled her. She turned from the window to find Alice sitting on the edge of the bed, crimson waves framing her face as she gazed at Lily with sober eyes.

"Alice. I didn't hear you come in."

"I know."

The silence stretched between them for a minute or two, until Alice spoke again. "Well, are you?"

"Am I what?"

"Afraid."

Lily looked down at her hands.

"I would be, if I was you."

Lily raised her eyes. "You would be afraid to marry Freddie?"

"Not Freddie." Alice pulled her knees up to her chin and wrapped her arms around them. "I meant everything else. I'd be afraid to go to Tidworth—"

"Tidworth is closed." Lily had heard more than enough horror stories about that place. War brides and babies stacked into barracks without proper cribs or hot running water. Humiliating medical exams. Food nobody could recognize. She shivered. *Thank God they closed that place and left the rest of us to make our own arrangements.* "I'll just get on a ship like everybody else."

"But what will happen when you get to America? Won't they make you go through Ellis Island or something? Is that any better than Tidworth?"

Lily didn't want to admit that she had no idea. She shrugged. "It can't be that bad."

"What if the Americans don't like foreigners?"

"It says in the pamphlet that they are very hospitable people."

"Do you think the pamphlet is always right?"

Lily didn't know that either.

"What if Freddie's parents don't like you?"

"Alice, for goodness' sake!"

"Well, they might not, you know."

"Stop it!" Lily bit her lip. She put her elbow on the window sill and dropped her forehead into her hand.

"I'm sorry. I didn't mean to snap like that. It's just...I've got enough things to worry about without you coming up with new ones for me."

The bedspread rustled, soft footsteps crossed the floor, and a hand slipped into hers.

"No, I'm sorry." Alice's voice was soft. "I guess I just worry too much. I want you to be happy, but I keep thinking of things that might go wrong."

Lily tried to smile. "America seems like an awfully long way off, doesn't it?"

Alice nodded. "Will you come back and visit? Soon?"

Lily turned her eyes back to the window, gazing out at the first stars beginning to glimmer in the velvet dome of the sky, and wished she had more answers.

Fred woke to the sound of footsteps on pavement. Shifting, he stretched a little. His whole body felt cold and stiff, and his bed was hard as a board. Brain still fuzzy with sleep, he opened his eyes and found himself staring up at the underside of a roof overhang.

Oh. Right. He'd spent the night on the consulate steps, with his jacket for a pillow.

Blinking the sleep out of his eyes, he realized the approaching footsteps had stopped. Turning his head, he looked up into a pair of watery blue eyes.

"Good morning, Howard."

He grinned. "Hope you slept well."

Howard raised his eyes to the heavens, sighed, and muttered something under his breath as he stepped over Fred's legs to get to the doorway.

"You didn't, huh? Well, I tossed and turned a bit myself. But at least it didn't rain."

Howard swung the door open and left it that way, starting toward his desk.

Getting to his feet, Fred stretched his sore muscles and stomped his feet to get some warmth back into them.

His stomach growled. "What did you have for supper last night, Howard?"

Howard didn't answer. He was still muttering, rustling through papers on his desk, and slamming drawers. At last he raised his head and looked toward the door.

"Are you going to stand out there all day, or are you coming in to fill out these papers before I change my mind?"

Fred grinned and bent down to pick up his coat.

He'd been starting to worry he might have to miss breakfast.

Chapter 34

When Lily stepped into the house after work, she found Mother stitching buttons onto the wedding dress, with Alice and Ruth hovering close.

Their heads snapped up as she came through the door, and everything went quiet. Ruth's eyes slid sideways.

She pushed the door shut. "Anything the matter?"

"No, love."

"Then why did you all stop talking as soon as I walked in the door?"

Mother's eyebrow went up a hair.

Alice glanced at her and cleared her throat. "It's nothing, Lily. Just ...Ruth doesn't like your dress much."

Ruth looked sheepish and wrinkled her nose. "It doesn't twirl enough. And it doesn't come to the floor. I'd want mine to the floor."

"Well, it's not your wedding." Mother snipped the thread between her teeth. "Just below the knee will be much more practical for reusing."

Alice was staring hard at Ruth and wiggling her eyebrows.

Ruth blinked at her a minute, then changed the subject without warning.

"I want to go to the beach. Come with me, Lily."

"What?"

"Go on." Mother reached for another button. "Stretch your legs a bit instead of moping about waiting for Freddie to pop in any minute."

"Since when have I been moping? And I haven't even mentioned Freddie popping in."

"No." Mother squinted at the needle she was rethreading. "But you look toward the door every time a board creaks. It's making me nervous. A walk would do you good."

"But it's teatime!"

Mother dropped the dress into her lap. "For heaven's sake! I haven't had any time to make tea yet. We'll have it later. Go on. All of you."

Well. Mother was certainly in an odd mood this afternoon. Lily could not remember the last time she delayed tea for no good reason.

Before she knew it, Ruth had dragged her out the door with Alice following, and they were headed off toward the Green. She glanced back once, and for a moment she thought she glimpsed Mother watching from the front window.

But perhaps it was only a trick of the light.

Eyes closed, Fred leaned against the rough plaster of the windmill. The breeze, tinged with the scent of salt water and warm grass, cooled his skin.

Above his head, the wooden sails creaked in the wind.

"Fred?"

He jerked his head up and jumped to his feet. "Alice! What took so long? Where is she?"

Alice laughed and took his arm, pulling him around the windmill a few steps. "There." She pointed. "Out on the beach with Ruth."

He blocked the sun with his hand and squinted.

Yes. *Yes!* There she was. Barefoot in the sand, laughing with Ruth and pointing at the sandpipers.

Just as he'd imagined she would look.

"Are you going?" Alice nudged him.

He ran his hand through his hair, turning toward her. "How do I look?"

"Do you really think she's going to be paying any attention to your hair?"

"Well, I haven't seen her in two years!" He turned toward the beach. "Good grief!" Jerking back, he flattened himself against the wall. "She's looking this way."

"So?"

"I don't want her to see me coming. Can you go distract her?"

She sighed, shaking her head at him. "Oh, all right. I'll try."

She crossed to the edge of the Green and disappeared down the steps over the seawall. A few seconds later he saw her trotting up to join Lily and Ruth at the edge of the water.

They exchanged a few words, and Alice pointed at a tide pool. Lily turned and they walked over to look at it. Her back was to him now.

He started walking. Out of the cloaking shadow of the windmill and onto the rippling green grass. The summer sun warmed his shoulders as he tried to walk slow and not attract attention. Ruth had already spotted him. She stepped back out of Lily's view and waved, wiggling in excitement.

He reached the seawall stairs and stepped down them, feet sinking into the sand at the bottom.

Just across the beach now...

Lily stood up from looking in the tidepool, and he froze, afraid she'd turn around. But Alice caught her arm before she could, and said something to her. Ruth joined in, pointing out toward the water.

Lily shook her head, but the girls had hold of both her arms now, and were pulling her toward the edge of the surf as they apparently tried to talk her into wading.

After a minute, she relented.

That should have been his cue to start walking again, but for a moment or two he just stood there. Watching. The shallow water shimmered like sea-glass, scattering sunbeams in ripples all around Lily.

White gulls dipped and soared up above, calling to each other, as wavelets whispered against the sand. It was such a lovely picture that he almost didn't want to disturb it.

Almost.

Walking toward the edge of the water, he wondered what he should do. Call her name? Wait for her to turn around? No. Not from here. He wanted to be close enough to touch her when she saw him.

Jerking his shoes and socks off, he waded in, not even bothering to roll up his trousers. Little waves gurgled around his ankles, swishing against the olive drab and shifting the sand grains under his feet.

Even with her back to him, she looked so beautiful that he had to keep reminding himself to breathe. The soft gray dress fluttered around her, rippling in the breeze, and her dark curls tossed and tumbled like they were dancing in the sunshine.

"Look. A ship." Ruth pointed toward the horizon, still trying to keep up the distraction. "Do you think Fred is on a ship like that?"

Lily's reply sounded distant, like she was only half-listening. "Of course not, love. That's a freighter."

As he stepped closer, Alice eased backward and let him take her place behind Lily's right shoulder.

Breathe. Remember to breathe. He'd never realized how much concentration that could take. His heartbeat kept thundering in his ears until he couldn't tell the difference between that and the rumbling surf.

Now his hands were even starting to shake. If he didn't get his arms around her in another minute, he was going to go nuts. Should he say something?

Or just scoop her up out of nowhere?

If she didn't turn around in another thirty seconds, it was going to be one or the other.

"What are you looking at, Lily?" Ruth spoke again.

He watched her take a long breath. Heard her sigh.

"The water, I suppose. There's an awful lot of it between here and Florida."

Fred caught his breath. *Of course.* Holding himself as steady as he could, though his hands went right on shaking, he spoke in a voice so low that only she would hear it.

"It's just handfuls, Lily. Just a whole bunch of handfuls."

That ...voice!

For a moment, Lily couldn't move. She stood rooted to the spot, trying to make the world stop spinning around her while a tingling flood of emotion sent her heart pounding into a frenzied gallop.

I'm imagining things. Surely it had not been his voice she heard whispering over the surf. Surely it was all in her head.

Surely ...

Pulse throbbing, she at last seized control of her limbs and spun around.

There he was.

Her blue-eyed soldier.

Chapter 35

August 30, 1947

"Ow!" Lily winced.

"Sorry, love." Mother's voice came around a mouthful of bobby pins. "One more should do it."

Lily tried not to grimace. There were so many pins poking her head already, the bridal hat should stay on in a hurricane.

She stared into the mirror, watching Mother's hands fuss over the carnations, nestling them snugly into place. The netted veil brushed against her shoulders. Voices murmured on the far side of the door as the last few guests slipped into the chapel. Deep and rich, the organ notes wooed them to their seats.

This is real. She had to keep reminding herself. Once or twice she had even pinched her arm to see if she would wake up in the familiar bedroom on North Clifton. But this was no dream. In a few moments, she would be standing at the altar before God and everyone else, pledging to share the rest of her life with one man alone.

One precious, determined American soldier.

The doorknob creaked. Ruth peeked out into the vestibule, bouncing on her toes, dark blue dress bobbing around her knees. "Isn't it nearly time? Father's out in the vestibule already, and everybody else is in the chapel. When do we go?"

Soon. Lily's hands trembled a bit inside her lace gloves. It couldn't be much longer now.

Mother checked the clock. "We have ten minutes yet, love. You may wait in the vestibule if you're ready. Just mind your bouquet and don't drop it. Alice, will you go with her, please?"

Alice collected her own flowers and followed Ruth out the door, glancing down at her new shoes once or twice as she went.

"She loves those blue shoes." Mother shook her head, smiling after the door shut. "I'm glad Tyler's had some to match the dress fabric so well."

"That particular shade looks stunning with her hair too." Frances looked into her own mirror as she adjusted the filmy collar of her own gown. "The blue and red set each other off."

"Yes." There was a catch in Mother's voice. "She looks quite the young lady today."

Lily's chest tightened a little. Poor Mother. First Robert, then Frances, and now another wedding. All in less than a year's time. "Your girls are growing up, aren't they, Mum?"

Mother managed to smile and sigh all at once. "Well, I didn't sign up to take care of five children my whole life, did I?"

Frances got to her feet. "I'd better find Doug before he ends up at the front of the church with a crooked tie. He never can get it straight unless I fix it for him."

She gathered up her bouquet and vanished out the door.

The clock hands were marching forward. In five minutes more they would be standing in the vestibule, lined up at the door. Paper rustled as Mother rummaged in her bag.

"What are you doing, Mum?"

"Looking for this." Mother held up a small brown package tied with lace and ribbon.

"Here. Open it."

Mystified, Lily took the package. It felt lumpy and hard, as if it were filled with golf balls, or perhaps small onions. Keeping one eye on the clock, she tugged the bow loose and tore open the paper. A handful of fig-shaped brown bulbs tumbled out onto the table. "Daffodils!"

"Of course." Mother's hands caressed her shoulders, and a kiss brushed her hair. "My favourite flower. Except one."

Lily blinked back a couple of unruly tears. This was no time to go smearing her mascara.

"I dug them up last winter," Mother said. "Now you'll have a bit of England with you wherever you go."

Lily gulped back a lump that felt as big as a flower bulb. "What if they won't bloom in America?"

Mother squeezed her shoulders. "Rubbish. English settlers did all right there. Why not English flowers?"

The organ's voice swelled louder as the door opened a few inches. Frances's face popped into view. "Mother! Lily! We're all ready for you."

"Coming, love." Mother picked up the bridal bouquet and held it out.

Lily's heart fluttered like an anxious butterfly as she pushed back her chair, smoothed the pleats of her peplum, and reached for the flowers.

White carnations for purity, pink ones for affection, and red ones for love. Plus a few daisies sprinkled in. Everyone who saw them said the flowers were beautiful.

Her fingers tightened, clutching the stems, and her mouth felt a little dry.

This was it. No going back after today. If she stopped now, she might still be able to pick up the fragments of her plans and patch them back together again. Live the nice, safe life she'd always wanted. Stay in control.

But after today ...

Excitement and fear were so mixed up inside her that she could hardly tell them apart.

Her lip trembled a little. "Mum, I wish—"

"Don't." Mother shook her head, eyes bright. "God made you for this man. And him for you. All your wishing could never come up with something better."

Lily blinked back another stubborn tear. If only there was some way loving Freddie didn't have to mean leaving everything else she loved.

"Keep your chin up, Lily Brown." Mother squeezed her hand. "You know who's in control of this adventure. Now trust Him. And go live it. Remember, the English don't know how to quit."

Lily swallowed and raised her chin.

· · · · ◦ ◦ • • ❋ ❋ ❋ ✿ ✿ ✿ ❋ ❋ ❋ • • ◦ ◦ · · ·

Frances, Alice, and Ruth were already lined up behind the stained-glass doors of the chapel, waiting to follow Lily into the church.

She smiled, remembering how Freddie had complained at the rehearsal that it was all backward. The bride was supposed to come in last of all, like the icing on the cake.

For a moment she was insulted, until she remembered that "the icing on the cake" meant something quite different on the other side of the Atlantic, and he was not trying to say that she was the last possible thing anybody needed.

Then she laughed, and asked what flavour icing she was. He told her he would have to kiss her and see. But somebody had interrupted before he could do it.

"Lily."

She snapped back to the present.

Father was offering his elbow.

She took a breath and slipped her arm around his.

They had hardly passed a word since the night she got Freddie's telegram. Father's nose still did not look quite right.

It had a bump that had not been there before. A bump to match Frances's.

He gazed down at her, and there was something in his expression. Something she could not quite place. But it reminded her of the way he had looked at her that night on the stairs.

Strange how none of them ever spoke of that night.

Father cleared his throat. "You look...beautiful."

She managed a smile. Robert and Mother had gone through the doors already.

"Lily, I—"

"Are you ready?" Frances's whisper interrupted, tickling Lily's ear from behind.

Ready? Ready to join her life forever with one man, for better or for worse, for richer and for poorer, in sickness and in health, until death parted them?

Could a person ever truly feel ready for that?

With a final triumphant chord from the organ, the usher opened the doors.

She looked up at Father, then turned her eyes down the long aisle to the domed recess at the front, and saw Freddie standing there in his dress uniform, waiting.

Yes. Perhaps she was ready, after all.

Fred gripped his hands together and stared hard at the stained-glass window at the front of the church while the organ drummed out the processional march.

"How do I know when I can turn around?" He whispered the question to Doug.

"I'll tell you."

Fred studied the crisscross molding on the domed ceiling and took a deep breath. "How did you stand this at your wedding? In America, the groom gets to watch the bride come up the aisle."

"Sorry, Fred. English wife, English wedding."

Not quite. Fred felt a sudden grin tug at his face, but he wrestled it back down before it gave him away. Doug didn't know about the little American tradition he'd talked the minister into adding. Not even Lily knew that was coming.

Lily. She was there. In the room. Coming up the aisle on her father's arm.

And everyone was allowed to see her except him.

In another minute, he was going to break all the rules and turn around. Scrambling through his brain for something else to concentrate on, he tried going over memory verses.

Let's see ...

Many waters cannot quench love, neither can the floods drown it ...

No, no, no. Since when had he memorized anything from Song of Solomon?

Stay me with flagons ... for I am sick with love ...

Maybe he should have picked a different book of the Bible to read this week.

I am my beloved's, and my beloved is mine ...

Oh boy. At last, Doug bumped his arm. "Now."

Trying his best not to spin around like a delirious top, Fred turned.

There she stood. Eyes shining, cheeks blushing, smile radiant. The dress was soft blue, almost the color of her eyes, and there were flowers, beautiful flowers that filled the air between them with perfume and nestled like a crown in her hair, while a wisp of creamy veil framed her face.

She looked like an angel trying to pass herself off as a mere mortal. And not doing a very good job.

He gulped. No wonder Solomon wrote a whole book about love. He could feel it like a wild thing, rushing through his veins and throbbing in his ears.

The minister was starting in with "Dearly beloved" and all the other things they always said at weddings.

Thank goodness there'd be a bit of a speech before any-body expected the groom to say anything. At the moment, if he opened his mouth, he was afraid the only thing that would come out was more Song of Solomon.

Behold, thou art fair, my love; behold, thou art fair. ...As the lily among thorns, so is my love among the daughters.

And surely there couldn't be another lily in the whole world fairer than his Lily.

His to cherish. His to love.

Forever and ever.

The ceremony was almost over.

Lily stood, feeling Freddie's hand warm and strong around hers, and the wedding band already circling her finger. Just the final prayer and blessing left to go.

But what had come over Freddie?

The closer they got to the end, the more that mischievous little glint kept sparkling in his eyes.

As she peeked at him during the prayer, even the corner of his mouth was beginning to turn up a trifle.

Like it always did when he was about to get into trouble.

For heaven's sake Freddie, do behave. Just this once!

The minister's voice went on in the familiar words.

"...that through Thy most mighty protection, both here and ever, we may be preserved in body and soul; through our Lord and savior Jesus Christ."

"Amen," she murmured along with the congregation, try-ing to ignore Freddie's irreverent expression.

Now came the closing benediction.

"The blessing of God Almighty, the Father, the Son, and the Holy Ghost, be amongst you and remain with you always."

"Amen."

A pause followed. Freddie and the minister exchanged a small look.

And then the minister cleared his throat. "Ladies and gentlemen, before we dismiss, we have one special American addition to the ceremony, added at the request of our American groom."

What on earth?

A little murmur of surprise rustled through the congregation, and the minister's lip twitched.

Lily looked at Freddie, and he looked right back at her, his face splitting open into a shameless grin.

"Frederick Overall, you may kiss the bride."

What? Before she had even had time to react, Freddie had her tight in his arms, lips against hers.

She was so startled, she hardly knew whether to laugh or blush. When he let her go, she stood there and stared at him for a moment, trying to recover.

He chuckled and leaned down until his lips almost brushed her ear. "Buttercream," he whispered.

Then she did laugh.

Chapter 36

November 20, 1950

Pain.

Lily was breathing it. Drowning in it.

She arched her back as another spasm swallowed her up in a wall of red-hot flame. For an endless minute she could hear nothing, see nothing. Only the pain.

Then the burning grip loosened. Glaring white hospital lights came back into focus, and the nurse's voice was in her ear again. "Breathe, Lily. Come on, keep breathing."

She gasped, almost choking on thin air, and dropped back against the sweat-soaked pillow. How long had it been now? Days? Weeks? It seemed like a lifetime.

No wonder women died in childbirth.

Lord, Lord! I can't do this! I can't! Dear God, how does anyone do it?

Water dripped from a tilted glass, trickling between her parched lips and moistening her tongue. She swallowed. Her mouth was desert sand, bone-dry from the endless panting, and her body felt as if it didn't even belong to her anymore.

How could she push a new baby into the world when even lifting her hand sounded impossible? She lay with her eyes closed, limp as a rag against the mattress.

Another contraction tightened like a molten iron band around her, and the nurse's voice faded again. Her fingernails dug into the sheets.

Perhaps she would die. At this moment it almost sounded appealing. The world went hazy and distant again, and her own heartbeat echoed in her ears.

She tried to focus on something else. Anything else. Her mind shuffled through memories like snapshots.

Her first glimpse of the Statue of Liberty, jutting that proud torch toward the clouds.

A dirt road in Germany, stretching ahead of the motorcycle tires.

Then back in England again, standing at the station in Blackpool. Waiting. Scanning the passenger windows for the face she hadn't seen in five months.

Not spotting him until he had her in his arms, eyes glowing. Freddie!

Three years they'd been married already, while the army shuffled them from one country to another. Three happy years with Freddie. And now, if only she could manage to live through it, she would give him a child.

From somewhere, a new burst of energy surged over her. She gritted her teeth. *The English don't know how to quit, remember?* Was she English, or wasn't she?

She clenched her fists and sucked in a breath as another contraction, stronger than any before, locked around her like a vice.

The nurse's voice came slicing through the pain. "Push, Lily! Push now!"

She closed her eyes. And pushed.

"Where do you think you're going?"

Fred froze mid-stride in the hall and turned his head. Mrs. Brown was standing at the entrance of the waiting room, raising one eyebrow at him like a plump little school teacher.

About time she came back. *Even if she did just keep me from sneaking into the delivery ward.* He went back to the doorway, gesturing toward the desk. "Will you please convince these people to let me see Lily? You talk their kind of English."

She drew him back into the waiting room. "Fathers are never allowed in the delivery ward in England. Is it different in America?"

"How the heck should I know?" He marched up and down past the row of empty chairs. "I've never had a reason to care before this!"

"Calm down. You're not going to change anything by pacing the floor up and down like that."

He collapsed into the chair next to her. "How am I supposed to act when my wife's been locked up delivering a baby for this long?"

"It might help if you'd slept a little."

Oh, sure. As if he could take a nap when Lily hadn't slept in over twenty-four hours. "Aren't you worried at all?"

Her gaze dropped to her hands for a minute. "Well. I've been praying a good bit. I worry least when I pray most."

He sighed. "Alice, how long does it usually take? Do you know anyone else who's been this long? The nurses won't tell me anything. Is it dangerous? Does it mean—"

"Mr. Overall!" The voice drew his attention to the door.

A nurse stood there, smiling at him. "Congratulations, sir. Your wife just presented you with a healthy baby boy."

Fred bolted to his feet.

And then he grabbed for the nearest chair, hoping he wasn't going to pass out on the waiting room floor.

Lily was floating in the grey twilight between sleeping and waking when a strong hand closed over hers. Her eyelids felt like lead as she pushed them open, letting in the blinding glare of fluorescent lights.

"Hello, sweetheart." Freddie's face was haggard, his hair all tousled around the edges. Tears glistened in his eyes.

"Freddie, are you all right?"

"Me? You're the one who just had a baby."

Baby David. Last she saw him, the poor child was black and blue. "Is he all right?"

Freddie nodded. "He's sleeping now. How are you?"

She tried not to moan. "It hurts."

"What does?"

"Everything." But it wasn't the pain she was worried about now. It was something else.

He leaned closer, resting one elbow on the bed and caressing her cheek with the other hand. "Does your face hurt? Am I allowed to kiss you?"

She dragged out a weary smile for him.

"My nose doesn't hurt."

He grinned as he bent and kissed the end of her nose, his fingers brushing back her hair. "Have I told you lately how beautiful you are?"

Her heart gave an unsteady lurch. There was such tenderness in his eyes, in his voice. Would he still look at her like that if he knew ...

She took a breath. "Freddie, are you disappointed about the baby? Weren't you ... weren't you hoping for a girl?"

"What gave you that idea?"

She studied his face. "You were always talking about girl names. Susan and Sharon and Sarah and—"

Freddie laughed. "I do go for the S's, when it comes to girls, don't I?"

She nodded.

"Well, don't you get any crazy ideas. I'm just as happy to have a firstborn son as any other blue-blooded American."

She exhaled, feeling some of the anxiousness ease off. Perhaps he wouldn't mind so much, then.

"Besides." He grinned. "We've got plenty of time. I'm sure there'll be a girl or two along the way somewhere."

Her heart plunged into her stomach so fast that she wanted to vomit.

He went on, oblivious. "What do you think? Two or three of each maybe? We had six in my family."

Something squeezed her chest so hard she couldn't find breath to answer him.

If he went on talking like that, she really was going to vomit. She had to tell him. She had to.

But how?

Fred broke off when Lily's hand went limp inside his.

He looked at her. All at once her face was withdrawn. Almost frightened. She wouldn't meet his eyes.

"Lily?" He squeezed her fingers and found they were cold.

She swallowed and coughed, and she still wouldn't look at him, but he could see the muscles in her jaw tightening. "Freddie will ... will you still love me if I only give you one child?"

He blinked. "What kind of question is that? I don't care if God gives us one kid or twenty."

"No. I mean..." She bit her lip as she raised her eyes to his. They were swimming in unshed tears. "What if I only give you one child...on purpose?"

He felt himself pull back without meaning to, while his brain scrambled.

He opened his mouth to answer, but the only thing that came out was an uncertain, "What?"

Her tears spilled over. "Freddie! Didn't you see that poor child? He looks like he was run over by a lorry! And I'm black and blue in places I didn't know I could get that colour."

She choked on a sob and put her hands over her face. "I can't do this again! You don't know what it was like."

"The nurses said it was just—"

"Because he was breech?" She dropped her hands and looked at him.

"Yes. He was breech. And enormous. But can you guarantee the next one won't be?"

Words couldn't get past the lump in his throat.

Lily shook her head as she gulped back another sob. "I wanted more children too, but I don't want to do this again. Not ever." She leaned back against the pillow, covering her eyes with one hand, her lips shaking.

"Please. Don't ask me to."

Fred squeezed his eyes shut for a second. In his mind he could see them.

The little girls he'd been dreaming of ever since Carol's baby arms slipped around his neck that day in Florida. *My little girls*. Looking up at him with big blue eyes...

He set his jaw and looked at Lily. The tears were still trickling out from behind her fingers.

Sighing, he reached for her hand and pulled it away from her face. "Lily, my sweetheart, I will love you every minute of every day, for as long as I live. Don't you ever, ever, for one single second, start believing you could change that."

She stared at him for a breathless minute, her face almost limp with relief. Then she threw her arms around his neck and buried her face in his shoulder.

Swallowing, he held her, pressing a kiss into her tangled curls, and whispering that everything would be all right.

But deep down, when he turned his back on those two little girls and walked away, something tore inside him.

Chapter 37

October 1953—Three Years Later

Lily stared out the cab window as the frozen Canadian countryside streamed past outside. Freddie's voice sang merrily behind her. He'd been entertaining David ever since the two-year-old woke up from his nap.

"We'll build a bungalow
Big enough for two.
Big enough for two, my honey,
Big enough for two ..."
Lily sighed.

Big enough for three, you mean. That is, if they ever got around to building something at all and didn't keep boarding with relatives the rest of their lives.

She flicked a stray piece of lint off her sleeve and frowned at herself. *That wasn't fair.* They had rented a little place while Freddie was doing photography on St. Anne's Pier. And of course there was the military housing in Germany before that.

But ...

Well, here they were, back on Freddie's side of the Atlantic, six whole years after their wedding, and still they had never had a home that was really and truly theirs.

A real home. The kind where you built fences and painted the shutters and paved the walk. And planted daffodils.

She still had Mother's daffodil bulbs.

They had come with her across the Atlantic after the wedding, but it would not have made a stitch of sense to plant them when they were living with Freddie's aunt for all of five months before being shipped off to England again, and then Germany.

Now they had crossed the ocean yet again, and still—

"Are we almost dere?" David's baby voice interrupted her thoughts.

"Almost," Freddie said. "I bet your Uncle Robert will have a nice fire crackling when we get there."

Lily turned from the window. "And maybe Auntie Allie will have some hot tea."

Freddie raised an eyebrow at her over David's head.

Lily frowned. Neither one of them was keen to move in with Allie, but that didn't mean her sister-in-law was incapable of being a good hostess.

I hope.

With the cold Canadian wind stinging his nose, Fred bustled his family up the walk in the long shadows of twilight. The outside of the house was almost painfully tidy, and in the window boxes, artificial flowers drooped under a heavy dusting of snow.

Fred tried not to wince. *Fake flowers. In the middle of a Canadian winter.* How very like Allie.

The door swung open before they could knock.

"Lily! Fred! We were beginning to worry." Robert beamed in the doorway.

"Come in. It's cold enough to freeze the tail off a brass monkey!"

He ushered them inside to a blazing fire in the front room. The polished wood floor gleamed, and the flames cast cheerful shadows on velvet furniture and leaf-printed wallpaper in sage and gold.

There was no sign of Allie.

"It was so good of you to find Freddie this job." Lily unbuttoned David's coat as she spoke.

"And to let us stay with you too."

"Rubbish." Robert waved his hand. "How was Mother when you left, Lily? And the girls? I was just—"

"Robert!" Allie stood in the hall doorway, arms crossed. "Do keep your voice down. I just got Yvonne to sleep!"

Robert's face flickered, and the genuine smile he'd been wearing froze into a plastic one. "Sorry, love. Fred and Lily have just arrived. I was about to ring the bus station and—"

"I know. I told you to stop worrying." As she looked at Fred, her lips curled up in a smile.

"I knew Freddie would manage all right."

Oh, brother. Fred's tie seemed to get tighter as she looked at him, fluttering those long lashes of hers. *Allie.* He always tried to forget, when he was around her now, that he had first spotted her that night at Lowther Pavilion.

But she wouldn't let him.

Marriage had not changed her much. Her skirt was longer, and her blonde hair twisted into a bun. But her blouse was still too tight, and the past ten years had made no noticeable change to her figure.

Or her smile.

He swallowed, turning to Robert. "I think I'll go get the bags."

Lily sat with David on her lap, watching Allie smoke a cigarette on the settee. Robert had gone out with Freddie to collect the luggage from the car boot, and since then she'd been treated to a mixture of bland conversation and silence. No sign of tea.

"David will have to sleep in the bedroom with you two." Allie inhaled, then blew smoke from her nose.

"We only have the two bedrooms. It's been such a trial for poor Robert. The position has turned out to have much lower pay than he was expecting when we came over. And the house is so dreadfully small."

Allie waved a dismissive hand at the cozy parlour decked with brocade curtains, warm rugs and brand new furniture. "We had to move Yvonne out of her bedroom so we'd have some place to put your family. Now she's got my dressing room to sleep in, and I had to move all my clothes into Robert's wardrobe."

"That must be...inconvenient." Lily bounced her knee to keep David happy, and glanced at the door. What was taking Freddie so long?

"Yes." Allie sighed as she tapped the end of her cigarette over the ashtray. "Poor Robert had to move all his things into the broom cupboard."

Lily fought to keep exasperation off her face. "I'm sorry we've rearranged everything. But Freddie has every intention of paying for rent and board—"

"Rubbish!" Robert came thudding in with a gust of cold air, loaded down with suitcases.

"We don't want your money. What's family for, anyway?"

"Now hold on." Freddie came in next, bumping the door shut. "I didn't come here to—"

"Oh, come off it." Robert grinned. "You won't talk me out of this one. I'll show you where the bags go."

The men disappeared down the hall.

Allie looked after them and sighed again, shaking her head. "Your brother would give away his own bed if somebody asked. It's a wonder we aren't living in a tent by now."

Lily forced a smile. "I'm sure he wouldn't do that to you. He makes certain to take care of family first. But he has always been generous. Generous to a fault."

"Yes." Allie crushed out her cigarette. "Exactly."

Chapter 38

They'd been in Canada about four weeks when Fred got home early one afternoon.

The house was dead quiet. He hung his hat and coat on the rack and walked over to put his wet gloves in front of the fire.

After the chilly walk outside, the room felt warm and drowsy. The curtains were drawn shut against the cold, and the one lamp cast a subdued glow through its red shade.

He flipped on the radio. Musing strains of violin and saxophone hummed out into the silence as he settled into an armchair and closed his eyes.

"Hello, Freddie."

Uh-oh. Allie.

His chest tightened, but he kept his eyes shut.

She laughed. A low, sultry laugh. "It's no good, Freddie. I just saw you sit down."

He let out the breath he'd been holding and opened his eyes.

She leaned against the wall in the hall entry. Her golden ringlets tumbled loose over her shoulders, brushing the ruffles of her black silk robe. "You're home early."

He rubbed the tapestry arms of the chair. "Where's Lily?"

"Out shopping."

"And David?"

"He's with her."

"What about Yvonne?"

Allie shrugged. "She's with Lily. I had a headache this afternoon, so I stayed in."

Strike three.

"Oh. I'm sorry." He did his best to sound sympathetic. "Are you feeling better now?"

He hoped the answer was no. Hoped she would go back to bed and stay there. Indefinitely.

She smiled. "Oh yes. I feel quite well now."

He shifted his feet against the carpet. The room felt too warm now. And that music wasn't helping much. Getting to his feet, he reached for the radio. "I'm sorry if the music disturbed you. I'll just—"

"No. Don't." She crossed the space between them in two steps, catching hold of his arm.

"I like it."

She was so close to him he could see the black lace stirring as she breathed.

Her perfume had a deep, mysterious scent to it, and the lamplight lay warm and shining in her hair.

"I guess, if it's not bothering you—"

"Thanks." She looked up at him from under long, dark lashes. "You're so thoughtful, Freddie. I've known that since the first time I saw you."

She didn't show any sign of taking her hand off his arm.

"Do you remember when we first met?"

"We didn't meet."

She laughed. "Our eyes met. And I knew at once I'd never forget you."

Her fingers tightened on his arm as she leaned closer.

Okay. Time for a little more light in here.

He pulled his arm free and headed for the window, reaching for the sage-colored brocade.

"Don't." Allie's voice stopped him. "I want them closed."

"I want them open."

"It's my house, Freddie."

He dropped his arm. How was he supposed to ignore her when she put it that way?

She glided across the room.

"You know, ever since you got here, I've been waiting for a chance to talk to you like this. Alone."

"I don't think we have anything to talk about."

She smiled.

"Oh, Freddie. Stop acting like you're afraid of me. Can't we be friends?" Her hand slipped onto his arm again. The black lace whispered against his sleeve. Rich wafts of perfume were making him dizzy. He swallowed, feeling his mouth going dry.

And then, thank God, Lily's voice interrupted from outside the window. "Almost there, Yvonne. Come on." Allie stepped back, pursing her lips in annoyance. "Well. We'll have to finish this another day. I'm sure there will be plenty of other times to talk, with you here all winter."

"We won't be here all winter." He decided it at that moment. "As soon as I can save up enough for a car, I'm taking Lily and David home to Florida."

Her eyes widened and her mouth opened a fraction. But before she could say anything, the door swung open with a gust of winter air.

Yvonne came into the room, cheeks rosy from the cold. Lily followed, carrying a wiggling David, but stopped in the doorway when she caught sight of them standing there.

Her gaze flickered between them, taking in the black silk and the warm lighting. Her brows arched into a question mark.

"Did I ... interrupt anything?"

"No." Allie met her gaze with brazen unconcern.

"Freddie and I were just talking."

"About what?"

"About..." Allie paused. She looked at Fred for a second, and her lips curled into a slow smile. "About why Robert's changed his mind about the rent."

* *

"Allie's headache was rather short-lived." Lily's tone was biting.

Fred took a deep breath as he turned from shutting the bedroom door. The house had been as tense as a foxhole all evening, and Lily had hardly spoken to him.

Robert had been the only one who seemed not to notice the tension.

Now Lily sat with her arms folded tight across her chest, raking him with her stare. "What happened this afternoon?"

He met her gaze. "Nothing."

"Nothing?"

"Nothing."

She closed her eyes, gulping in a deep breath as if she hadn't had one all day, and he watched some of the tension drain out of her shoulders.

Thank God she believes me.

She opened her eyes and gave him a pointed look. "No thanks to Allie."

Fred loosened his tie and pulled it off, holding her gaze without answering.

She banged her heel against the foot of the bed. "I don't believe her about the rent. I don't think Robert changed his mind. I bet he doesn't even know about it."

What was your first clue? Fred hung his belt and tie over the chair.

"How much of your salary does she want? Did she tell you, while I was helping Yvonne put her things away?"

Fred bit the inside of his lip, wishing there was some way he could keep from telling her that part. He stalled, sitting down next to her to untie his shoe.

"Well?"

He went on loosening the laces without raising his eyes. "Are you sure you want to know?"

"Freddie! How much?"

He met her gaze and sighed. "All of it."

She gasped like he'd hit her in the chest, and sat blinking at him for a second. Then she sprang to her feet. "I'm telling Robert. Just wait until he hears—"

"Lily, no. You can't tell Robert."

She stopped, looking back at him with her hand on the door knob. "I certainly can!"

"No. You can't." He stepped to the door and closed his hand over hers on the knob.

"Let go!"

"Lily, think what a mess it would be! Either he'd side with Allie, because she's his wife, and you'd never forgive him. Or he'd side with you, because you're his sister—"

"And Allie's a twit!"

"And ruin his marriage." He put his hands on her shoulders. "Do you want that for Robert?"

Her chest heaved up and down beneath her sweater, but she didn't answer the question. Just stared at the floor, avoiding his eyes.

He waited.

At last her shoulders went limp. She looked up, and tears shone at the corners of her eyes. "But if we can't save any money, how will we ever get our own home? Doesn't she know that if we don't have any money, we can't ever leave?"

He clenched his jaw. In his head he could see Allie's triumphant smile as she looked at him.

She knew.

Chapter 39

January 1957

Lily stared at the frost clinging to the windowpane like icy fingers.

The world outside lay white and cold as a forgotten corpse, buried in the snow. It never changed. The sky was forever grey and listless. Even inside the house, there was always a chill lingering in corners and creeping along the floorboards.

She glanced over her shoulder toward the kitchen. Allie would get shirty if she spotted the curtains open. She was always making a fuss about how it let the cold air in. *Oh well*. If the blond-headed twit was going to keep them prisoner, Lily had no reason to go on playing polite houseguest.

They had been living in this frozen wasteland for three months, and were poorer now than when they started. Freddie had insisted on using up some of the money he had saved earlier on Christmas presents. She fingered the pearl droplets in her ears and didn't know whether to smile or frown. Here they were, desperate to save enough for a car, and he went and bought her jewelry.

"Lily!" Allie stood in the kitchen doorway, arms folded. "The curtains! How many times have I told you—"

"I'm watching for Freddie."

"And freezing us all to death!"

"It doesn't make that big of a difference." Lily leaned her elbow on the window sill. "Not enough to make it worth living in a cave all winter."

"Oh, really? I suppose you have just stacks of experience with Canadian winters, eh?"

"I've got a lot more than I ever wanted to."

"Well." Allie gave her an icy smile. "Isn't that just too bad." She marched across the room and jerked the curtains shut. "Why don't you make yourself useful and entertain Yvonne? She keeps bothering me to let her help cook."

"Let her, then." Lily leaned back in her chair. "How is she supposed to learn anything if you don't let her try?"

Allie huffed. "I don't need your child-rearing advice, thank you. Robert and I can manage quite well alone."

"Robert? When was the last time you asked Robert's advice on the subject? Seems to me you are rather tired of Robert."

Allie's eyes narrowed. "Mind your own business!"

"My brother is my business."

"Why don't you worry about your own husband?"

Lily could have choked her. Freddie was all she *did* worry about these days, with Allie waiting to pounce on him like a spider. Blood pounding in her temples, she got to her feet. "Seems to me"—she made her voice low and deliberate— "that I'm not the one who has trouble remembering which husband is mine."

Allie blinked, then coloured.

Without waiting for a reply, Lily brushed past her and stalked away to the bedroom, slamming the door. She stormed to the window, snapped the curtains open as wide as they would go, and leaned her forehead against the cold glass.

"Dear Lord!" She was almost shaking with rage.

"You've got to get us out of here. Before I strangle her right in front of the children!"

Fred was whistling the bungalow song as he climbed the steps to the house. Today had been a very good day. Wait until he told Lily the news.

He kept whistling as he stepped into the entry, slapping his hands against his thighs to warm them, and hung his hat and coat on the rack.

"Welcome home, Freddie."

He turned. Allie stood in the front room. Smiling.

Pulling his gloves off with his teeth, he edged around her toward the fire. "Is Lily home?"

"I think she's napping." Allie waved a dismissive hand toward the bedroom.

"Oh." Fred hung his gloves on the drying rack and stretched his fingers toward the fire.

"Why, Freddie! Your poor hands." Allie's voice dripped sympathy. "Would you like me to rub them and get the blood pumping again? Robert always does that for me when…" She reached for his hands.

He shoved them into his pockets. "That's nice of him. I'm sure he'll be home soon and you can return the favor."

Her face twitched, but she kept smiling that sickening smile and batting those enormous eyelashes. He was starting to wonder about those.

"Can I get you a nice hot cup of tea, then? Something toasty to wrap your hands around?"

Fred cleared his throat, fishing for a polite way to refuse.

Lily's voice saved him. "I'll get his tea, Allie."

He could feel the room go stiff with tension as Allie turned toward the hall.

"Oh bosh, Lily. You've got David to mind."

"I can make tea with one hand." Lily walked across the room toward them, holding David on one hip.

"Don't be daft. It'll take you twice as long that way. I'll make the tea."

"I said I'd make it." Lily glared at Allie.

"You'll spill hot water on the baby." Allie glowered back.

"I not a baby!" Three-year-old David kicked his legs.

Something crashed in the kitchen, and Yvonne's voice rose in a wail. "I didn't do it! The teapot fell off the table by itself!"

"Yvonne! That was an antique!" Allie spun around and made a beeline for the kitchen.

Fred tried not to be happy the thing got smashed.

Chapter 40

With Allie's scolding voice trailing in from the kitchen, Lily tried her best to smile at Freddie as she lowered David to the floor.

He ran to wrap his arms around Freddie's knee. "Dor pants is told, Dad."

Freddie laughed and scooped David up, tickling his ribs. "Well, it's forty below out there, boy! Where did you think I went to work, the Sahara Desert?" He flipped David around to sit in the crook of his elbow, then looked at Lily. "Rough day?"

She let the tension in her shoulders relax as she slipped one arm around his neck and rested her face against him. "Allie and I were arguing this afternoon."

His chuckle shook the grey vest beneath her cheek. "And here I thought you two were best friends."

"She's just such a ... Ooo! Your fingers are cold."

He'd closed them around her free hand.

"Sorry, sweetheart." He pulled away.

"No, no. Let me." Dropping her arm from his neck, she cupped both her palms around his hand and pulled it to her chest. "How was your day at work?"

He broke into a grin. "Terrific."

"Really? What happened?"

"Well, let's see." He dropped into his teasing tone. "I had tuna fish for lunch. And Bert opened a can of chips and found one of those coiled-spring snake things inside it..."

"Freddie! You didn't!"

"No. Sam did. Wish I'd thought of it first though. And then we worked for a few hours, and Sam started—"

"Quit being such a wind-up merchant!" She poked him in the ribs. "You know what I meant. What happened that was terrific?"

"Oh, that?" Freddie's lip quirked up in a grin. "Nothing, really. I just got a raise is all."

Her heart almost stopped beating, then leaped back into motion at a furious pace.

A raise!

God must have heard her prayers after all.

Her mind overflowed with pictures of the cozy little cottage they would soon have for their own.

White siding and cheery blue shutters. Lace curtains in the windows, a kettle steaming on the hob, and daffodils blooming by the kitchen window.

All they had to do now was wait until they'd saved enough for a car, and then... "Oh Freddie! That's just, just—"

"A long time coming." Allie's voice sliced through the daydream like a knife blade.

Freddie's arm, around Lily's shoulders, went limp.

Allie stood in the dining room doorway, arms crossed over her newest cashmere sweater. "It's about time they upped your pay. Money's been getting tighter and tighter around here. All the extra expenses are piling up."

Lily felt the heat rising in her face. "Extra expenses? You mean all those new clothes you've been buying?"

Allie sniffed. "No. I mean the extra expenses of having twice as many people in the house. David is half Yvonne's age, but he eats more than she does."

"Allie—"

"Not to mention the cost for heating." Allie arched a brow. "Some people seem intent on letting in as much cold air as possible."

Lily boiled. "You spent more money on that sweater than we spent on heating all week, and you know it!"

Allie looked as if she was stifling a yawn. "I'm sorry. But I'm afraid Robert and I are going to have to raise your rent, now you can afford it."

"Allie Brown!" Lily started toward her, but Freddie caught her arm and pulled her back to his side.

"How much do you want, Allie?" His voice sounded tired.

"How much was the raise?"

Without a word, Freddie pulled out his wallet and handed the whole thing to her.

Lily could have slapped him. The little white house with daffodils was collapsing around her ears. Fury pounded in her temples as she watched Allie remove the few bills from the wallet and count them.

"Is that all?" She looked disappointed. "That's not much of a raise. It won't even cover all the extra expenses. But"—she sighed—"I suppose it will have to do."

Folding up the bills in her hand, she gave Freddie back the empty wallet.

Freddie took it without a word

Lily whirled on him. "What's the matter with you?" Angry tears pricked the back of her eyes. "How can you just—just *let* her take it? Do you want to stay here forever?"

"Lily." He reached for her.

"Don't touch me!" She knocked his hand away, rage constricting her throat. What had happened to that brave, strong man she married? How could he just stand there like a tongue-tied schoolboy and let Allie walk all over him?

A horrible, black fear reared itself in her head. Perhaps Freddie did want to stay there forever. Perhaps he liked it here. Perhaps he and Allie ...

No! That was madness. Freddie would never. Least of all with Allie. But then why...

Confusion and anger whirled so fast that she could no longer form a coherent sentence as she glowered at him, fighting the tears while her breath spasmed in her chest.

"Really, Lily." Allie spoke with strained patience, like an adult scolding a hysterical child. "That's no way to treat poor Freddie. I'm surprised at you."

The room went red.

It was only Freddie's intervention that kept her from flying at Allie and doing something drastic. Somehow, he got David out of the way and managed to pull Lily out of the parlour, down the hall, and into the bedroom, latching the door behind them.

She broke free of his hands and stormed around the room. "I can't believe you just...just stood there!" It was maddening, the way he calmly pulled a chair in front of the door, sat down in it, and started untying his shoes as if nothing was wrong. "You didn't even try to stop her!"

He pulled off the shoe without looking at her, set it near the base molding, and reached to untie the other one.

How can he be so unconcerned? "

If Allie has her way, we'll be here until David graduates!" She fought to gulp back the tears.

"He'll be bringing our grandchildren to visit us, and we'll still be living with Robert and Allie!"

Fred set the second shoe next to the first one and began rolling his sock down. What ever happened to that caring, wonderful person she fell in love with? He was acting as indifferent as...as...*Am I really thinking of Father and Freddie in the same sentence?* Had it come to that?

The tears broke past her defences in a hot torrent. "You don't even care! You don't even care! You...you..." Choking on sobs, she hurled herself flat on the bed and buried her face in her arms. "I'll never have my own home again! I'll never have a place to plant Mother's daffodils! Never, ever, ever! And you don't even care!"

"Lily."

"I'll be stuck here forever, babysitting Yvonne while Allie spends our money on cashmere sweaters and settee pillows!"

"Lily."

"I should have married Paul! I should have! He wouldn't have let me spend my life like this. Stuck in a house with a woman who'd be happy if I wandered off and froze to death!"

"Lily!"

She pulled her head up, mostly to glare at him.

"Hold out your hand."

"What?"

His tone was quiet but steady. "Hold out your hand. I want to show you something."

For a moment, everything went still. Like a distant whisper, she could almost feel the sun on her skin and sand beneath her toes. Almost hear the waves, a faint echo, swishing against the shore, and see the sandpipers scuttling.

* * * * * * * * * * * * * * * * * * * *

"What is it?"

"Don't you trust me?"

She stretched out her hand.

Freddie leaned forward and tipped over a mysterious envelope, emptying it into her palm. Then he sat back against the chair, a smile dancing in his eyes.

"What do you think of that?"

She blinked at the crumpled bills, lying there in her hand like a miracle.

Money? She raised her eyes. "Where did it come from?"

"My sock."

"Freddie."

"It's the other half of my raise, Lily."

She looked at him, understanding crashing over her like a wave. Here she had been ranting on like a lunatic, and all the time...

"*Oh, Freddie.*" The next moment she was in his lap, laughing and crying and kissing him and getting tears all over his jacket. "I'm sorry! I didn't know! Why didn't you tell me?"

"Allie came back too soon. I knew she'd find out about it if I tried to pretend I never got the raise, but I figured if I let her think she had all of it when I only gave her half—"

"Of course! You're brilliant!" She should have known.

How could she ever have thought otherwise? Even for a moment?

"I didn't mean it, Freddie. I didn't mean any of it. I don't wish I'd married Paul! I never meant a single word!"

He laughed, wiping tears off her cheeks. "Oh yes, you did, you firecracker you! Just for a second there you did."

"I did not!"

"You did."

"I did not!"

"Oh, Lily." He shook his head, tracing her chin with his fingers. "Did I ever tell you how pretty you are when you're angry?"

She couldn't help laughing.

"No, but I think David must agree with you. He sometimes seems intent on making me as angry as possible..."

Goodness! She started up. "Freddie, where's David?"

"Probably helping Yvonne break more dishes." Freddie sounded unconcerned. "I left him in the front room."

"I should go and find him."

"He'll be all right."

"But Allie doesn't like to be bothered with him. I should go..." She tried to get up, but Freddie's arm stayed tight around her.

"Allie can get over it."

"But Freddie—"

He put his finger over her lips. "Let her do the babysitting for a while."

Her pulse started drumming in her ears again.

But this time it was not anger making her heart beat.

"Then what...am I supposed to do?"

He smiled, his hand caressing her cheek, drawing her closer. "I'm sure you'll think of something."

His lips met hers for a long moment, and her arm slipped around his neck. Then she pulled away and nestled her head against his shoulder as his fingers twined in her hair.

"Freddie?" She whispered the words against his neck.

"Yes, sweetheart?"

"I think we should close the curtains."

Chapter 41

September 1954

Late one Saturday morning, Lily sat in the bedroom, cradling Mother's daffodil bulbs in her hand. The brief Canadian summer had come and gone already, and now the crisp golden leaves were sifting down through the branches and settling in drifts on the cooling earth.

The front door opened and banged shut.

Allie.

Coming back from another shopping trip with her arms full.

Lily tumbled the bulbs into their wrinkled paper package and tucked them away in the hat box, snapping the lid on and sliding the box under the bed. She scanned the room.

Nothing looked suspicious. Perhaps it was cleaner than usual, but that was all. She stepped out into the hall and pulled the door shut behind her.

Allie stood in the dining room, bags and boxes scattered on the table. "Oh, Lily! Wait until you see this new bedspread." She smiled as she unwrapped a bulky package. "The one in your room is getting a bit worn, isn't it?"

Lily blinked. If it had been anyone else asking the question, she would have thought she knew what the connection was. But Allie? "I suppose it is."

"Found this on sale today. Eiderdown. Just look!"

It was a gorgeous bedspread. Buttery, cream-coloured satin, embroidered in a swirling cascade of flower-covered vines. Surely Allie wasn't intending to —

"It will look stunning with the mahogany in our bedroom. And since we won't be needing our old bedspread anymore, you and Freddie can have that one."

Oh. Of course.

"Is lunch ready yet?"

Lily pressed her lips together and counted ten. Why did Allie always assume there would be food waiting when she got home? "I haven't been into the kitchen. I was busy this morning."

"Doing what?"

Allie sounded annoyed.

"Um... organizing. Cleaning up. You know." Lily was not about to spoil the chance to watch Allie's face when Freddie showed up later.

Robert walked in. "My heavens! Who robbed the department store?"

"Come look at this!" Allie motioned him over. "Won't it look lovely in our room?"

Robert smiled, but it was a tired, practiced smile.

Poor Robert. In the eleven months they had been in Canada, Lily had sensed the strain growing between him and Allie. But whether it had anything to do with Freddie and her, she was not certain.

While Allie went on exclaiming over the bedspread, Lily ducked out of the dining room, heading for the window to watch the road for Freddie.

Fred glanced behind him in the cracked rear-view mirror.

David sat on the bench seat, wearing the dusty green coat that was already getting too small for him. His little nose was pink with cold. The back window was missing entirely, and there was a bitter wind blowing this morning.

"Chilly, partner?" *Too bad I couldn't afford to get that window replaced.* "We'll be home in a minute. How do you like the new car?"

"I wike it." David grinned. "I tan pull da stuffing out of da seats!" He tugged a fistful of horse-hair from a tear in the upholstery and held it up.

Trust a three-year-old to look on the bright side.

It wasn't much of a car, but he'd managed to get it running and find new tires. Of course, he only had ten bucks left in his wallet now, but he wasn't going to stay in Canada a day longer.

He'd hardly gotten the car braked out front when Lily appeared, smiling like he'd shown up in a Mercedes.

"Hello." He climbed out and grabbed her waist, twirling her in a dizzy circle. "Here's our magic coach. Still looks a bit like a pumpkin, but it works!"

Her eyes swept the ancient automobile. "Will it make it all the way to Florida?"

"Don't you trust me? I fixed it myself."

"It looks like it went through the Blitz."

"The outside's got nothing to do with how it drives."

He patted the hood.

"The tires are good. The motor is running. Who cares if the paint's peeling off? Is everything packed?"

"Everything."

He squeezed her hand. "Then let's get this show on the road!"

Lily was certain she would never forget the look of consternation on Allie's face when she came out on the verandah and spotted that car.

"W-what..." She stammered, her voice a little weak. "What is that pile of rubbish doing in my driveway?"

Freddie put his hands on his hips. "That's not nice, Allie. You shouldn't insult people's brand-new automobiles."

Robert came out next. "Has anyone seen the—" He broke off and halted, surveying the scene.

"Where did you find that, Fred? Bottom of the lake?"

"Close. Bert's backyard."

Robert whistled. "Looks like somebody used it as a scouring pad. How much did you pay for it?"

"Not much. The tires cost more."

"Does this mean you're—"

"Leaving? Yep. Today."

Lily watched the news register on Allie's face like a shockwave. She went red, then white, then red again.

Her mouth worked, but no words came out.

"So soon?" Robert arched his brows.

"Yes," Lily said.

Robert's eyes flicked sideways to his wife, who stood there like a fish trying to breath air, then he looked back to Lily. "Packed already?"

"Yes."

"Then I'll help you load the car."

Chapter 42

Lily handed Freddie the last suitcase and watched him maneuver it into the boot.

"All right. That just fits. Want to run in and make sure we got everything?"

"Already did."

"Well then, madam,"—he swept a dramatic bow, pulling open the passenger-side door—"your coach awaits."

She let him help her into the seat.

"Watch out. I have to bang it or it falls back open." He slammed the door and grinned at her through the open window. "Please keep arms, legs, and children inside the vehicle at all times." After catching David up in his arms, he tossed him into the back seat.

David giggled and bounced, kicking his legs against the worn-out upholstery.

"Goodbye." Freddie shook hands with Robert.

"Thanks for everything."

"Any time."

Freddie crossed around in front of the car and climbed into the driver's seat. "Goodbye, Allie!"

Allie stood on the verandah, frowning at them. "You're mad, leaving in that contraption this time of year. It could snow any   minute."

"Oh!" Fred slapped his forehead. "I forgot. The left rear window is broken. Do you have any old blankets we could use for David?"

"No." Allie folded her arms. "I don't."

"Now Allie—" Robert began.

"What about the one from our bed?" Lily tried to stave off a fight. "Weren't you about to replace it?"

Allie's face was immovable. "I need it for a picnic blanket."

Lily tried to keep her voice light.

"You didn't go on a picnic all summer, Allie. Can't you get something else if you want to start now?"

"No."

"Come on."

Allie glared daggers. "I already told you no. This is my house, and if I say I—"

"Stop it."

Robert had not raised his voice, but there was flint in his tone. "Stop it, Allie. It's not your house. It's mine." He looked at Freddie. "Wait right there."

Disappearing inside for a moment or two, he came back out with the new silk eiderdown in his arms.

"Robert!" Allie's voice was a shriek. "What are you doing?"

He strode past her without a glance.

"Stop! That's brand new!" She grabbed his arm, but he plowed on as if she had not touched him, dragging her after. "Stop!" A note of desperation crept into her voice. "Not that one. They can have our old—"

"No." Robert opened the back door and spread the eiderdown over David's lap, burying him in silk and embroidery.

"Give me that. I just bought it!" Allie reached for the quilt, but Robert caught her wrist and pulled her back, shutting the door.

"Drive safe." He looked through the passenger window.

"Have you gone mad?" Allie stamped her foot in fury. "Don't you realize how much that cost?"

"Yes!" Robert turned on her, eyes narrowed, and bored holes with his gaze for a moment.

"Three whole months of Fred's wages."

Allie fell back a step, her mouth dropping open.

Lily wondered how long ago he had figured it out.

There was a moment of tense, stony silence, and then Allie turned and fled into the house, slamming the door behind her.

Robert put both hands on the window sill and looked in at them. "Goodbye, Lily. I hope everything goes well for you. Always." He reached out and shook Freddie's hand one more time. "I'd say to take good care of her, but I know you don't need to be reminded."

He paused, glancing toward the house, then looked in at them again. "Never stop loving each other the way you do now." Straightening up, he stepped back from the car. "Watch for ice."

As they pulled out of the driveway, Lily stretched her neck out of the window, waving and waving.

Robert stood alone in the bare, cold yard, hand raised in farewell, until a curve in the road hid him from sight.

Fred watched Lily brush a tear away as she closed the window.

She sighed. "It's my fault he married Allie. I knew she was a selfish flirt, and I — "

"Didn't he elope?" He looked over at her.

"Sort of."

"Without telling you?"

"Yes."

"Then it's not your fault. You can't protect everyone you love from making bad choices, sweetheart." He closed his hand over hers. "Robert has to put up with the life he picked. Just like you've got to put up with me." He winked.

She tried to laugh as she wiped away another tear.

"By the way,"—he watched the road disappearing under the tires for a second—"there's something I've been trying to figure out about Allie for the longest time, and I'm still not sure."

"What?"

"Does she wear false eyelashes?"

Lily blinked at him for a moment, and then dissolved into laughter. "Good heavens, Freddie, those things were as long as my fingers! You didn't really think any woman had eyelashes like that?"

"I don't know. She's not the first one I've noticed. Were they all wearing false ones?"

She nodded, still laughing.

David piped up from the back seat, "I'm hungry!"

"That makes two of us." Fred glanced over the seat, checking to see if the picnic basket was still sitting next to the surprise he'd bought for Lily. "Why don't you ask Mum to get those sandwiches out?"

Lily swiveled around onto her knees and leaned over the seat, rummaging for the sandwiches.

"Really, you two, we haven't been on the road for ten minutes. How can you already be..." She broke off. "Freddie? What's this?"

He grinned to himself, keeping his eyes on the road. "Can't see what you're looking at."

"It's full of dirt."

"The flowerpot?"

"Yes. What's it for?"

"Um ..." He wrinkled his brow. "Flowers?"

"Freddie!"

"Sorry, was that a trick question?" He glanced over at her.

She knelt backward, one brown pump planted against the dash as she dangled upside down over the seat. The moss-green folds of her sweater bunched around her waist and above her elbows, and her hair tossed in all directions.

Rolling her eyes at him, she blew a stray curl out of her face. "Is it an American custom to keep window boxes in the back seat of cars?"

He chuckled. "No. Just an Overall family tradition."

"Rubbish."

"It is! I just started it. I figure it may take a while before we have a house of our own. It's not like we can just buy a place as soon as we get to Florida. Not on the ten bucks I've got left in my wallet."

"So?"

"Don't you think it's about time you planted those daffodils?"

Her eyes got watery for a second.

Instead of answering, she unwrapped David's sandwich and handed it to him, then slid back down into her seat and stared out the windshield at the road.

After a minute, still without saying anything, her hand crept over to his.

He drew it to his lips.

As they pulled up to a crossroad, he paused for a moment to check the map.

As they pulled up to a crossroad, he paused for a moment to check the map. Then he smiled at Lily, popped the car into gear with a clunk, and took the road headed south.

Chapter 43

"It's one thing to drive across the entire country without a licence, Freddie. But nobody else would be daft enough to march up to a bobby and tell him about it!"

Fred kept his eyes on the road as he veered left at the fork, then turned his head so that he could see Lily glowering at him in the passenger seat.

"I'm not planning to bring up the license part."

"And if they ask?"

"I'm not going to lie."

"Brilliant." She thumped the car door with her fist.

"Mum, I'm hungry."

Lily put her hand over her eyes. "David, I told you already. We don't have anything else to eat. You had the last of the bread this morning."

The police station came into view on the right. Fred slowed to pull into the parking lot.

"Freddie, for heaven's sake! You know they're going to ask for your license. Bobbies always ask."

Must be rough on her, always worrying about the worst possible scenario.

"They're not gonna jail me, sweetheart. Maybe a fine, if anything."

"But we're out of money!"

"That's why I'm stopping."

He parked the car and stepped out, leaning down to peer back in at her.

"Calm down. People in Virginia are nice." He grinned at her. "I should know. I was born here."

She threw her hands in the air. "I'm sure they'll give you special treatment because you lived here for the first two months of your life!"

"You worry too much, Lily."

"And you're daft as a brush!"

He shook his head. "You know what your mother said to me when I looked about like you do right now? She said she worries least when she prays most." He shut the car door. "Maybe you should try it."

Lily pressed her knuckles against her teeth, watching for Freddie.

I should have known it would end up like this.

She was supposed to wait and marry him when he had saved up and was financially secure. Whatever happened to that sensible plan she had?

She looked at her watch. Freddie had been in the station for far too long to be—

"Mum, sing me the teddy bear song." David bounced on her lap and held up his open palm.

She sighed and took his hand. He was probably the only child within a hundred miles who knew that English nursery rhyme. Sometimes she wondered where all the other war brides were.

There was supposed to be thousands of them in America now, but she had never seen one.

She began tracing her finger in a circle around David's palm. "Round and round the garden like a teddy bear ... One step. Two step ..." She walked her fingers up toward his shoulder. "Tickle under there!"

Making a sudden dart under his arm, she tickled until he was limp with giggles.

"Afternoon, ma'am."

She jumped. A uniformed bobby stood outside the window, a smile on his round red face.

Good heavens. What was he doing there? Did American bobbies usually smile before they arrested people? Could you be arrested for riding in a car with—

"Lily, this is Officer Grant."

Her breath whooshed back into her lungs as she snapped her head around.

Freddie opened the driver's door. "He wanted to meet you before he showed us the way to the diner. Say hello to the officer, David."

David waved.

Officer Grant waved back. "Nice to meet ya." His accent reminded her of Jerry's, but much heavier.

"The diner's a pretty fur piece up the road, an' I don't want y'all to get lost. Jest foller me an' I'll take ya' thar." He walked to his own car.

Was that English? Lily looked at Freddie. "What did he say? After 'Nice to meet you'?"

He laughed as he coaxed the engine alive again. "We're supposed to follow him to the diner. It's down the road a bit."

"What's a diner?"

Fred backed the vehicle around and pulled out of the car park, following Officer Grant onto the winding mountain road. "Kind of like the local pub. But with less alcohol and more coffee."

Food. "But, Freddie,"—she kept her voice low, hoping David would not hear—"how are we going to—"

"Pay for it?" His eyes twinkled. "Did you try praying instead of worrying while I was in there?"

She shifted in her chair. "A little." *Not as much as Mother would have.*

He grinned. "Guess a little goes a long way."

Lily sat on the red vinyl booth seat, peeping over the menu to examine this place called a "diner."

It was not at all like a pub.

The walls and counter were covered in hospital-white enamel, and fluorescent lighting glared off more chrome than should be allowed outside a car factory.

Waitresses in bobby socks and ponytails went around handing out coffee like it was the only beverage in existence, and the whole place smelled of grilled meat and fried—she sniffed—fried everything.

"Ready to order, folks?"

The redheaded waitress stood with a pencil stub poised over her notebook.

Freddie picked up his menu. "Yes. A burger and fries for me please, and coffee. The kid's burger and a milkshake for the little guy."

"And for you, ma'am?"

Lily's eyes darted back to the menu. Fries. That was what Americans called chips, of course. She had asked for chips once and ended up with potato crisps instead. "Yes, I'd like the hamburger and fries too, please. And a cup of tea."

Fred cleared his throat and jogged her foot under the table. "Lily, we're in the South now."

Oh yes. "Hot tea, please."

The waitress smiled. "You're from England, ain't ya?"

There it was again. Someone always asked. "Yes. Lancashire."

"No kiddin'! My cousin married a girl from Lancashire while he was stationed over thar. She come over later with a bunch a' war brides on the *Queen Mary*. 'Bout '46, I guess it was."

Lily's hands tightened on the menu in excitement. *A Lancashire girl? Right here in some Virginia mountain town?* "Does she live nearby?"

"Used to." The waitress pushed the notepad and pencil into her pocket. "Got killed in a car accident a couple years ago. Too bad. She was real nice. Talked just like you do."

"Mandy! Order's up!" Someone hollered from the kitchen.

"Whoops! Sorry, folks. That's me."

The waitress turned and hurried off.

Fred watched Lily's shoulders droop as she looked after the waitress.

"You wanted to meet that girl from Lancashire, didn't you?"

She swallowed and looked at her lap.

Over her head, he saw one of the other police officers come into the diner and hand Officer Grant an envelope. They exchanged a couple of words, and Officer Grant headed their direction.

"Sweetheart." He leaned over the table. "I forgot to mention the police chief organized a collection at the station."

"A what?"

Officer Grant came up to the end of the table, red face beaming. "Here ya go, Fred. Hope it's enough to getcha home."

"Thank you so much, sir."

"Shucks, it ain't nothin'. Glad to do it. Specially you bein' a Virginia boy an' all." He winked, then turned to Lily. "Take care a' that boy a'yourn, ma'am. He's a strappin' little feller, ain't he?"

Lily looked helplessly at Fred. He gave her a tiny nod.

"Yes. He is. Isn't he?" She smiled, with no idea what she was agreeing to. "Thank you all so much for buying us dinner. It was very kind."

Officer Grant grinned. "Pleasure, ma'am. Y'all take care now." He nodded at Fred and walked away, ducking out the door.

Lily watched him through the window as he climbed into his car. "I don't think I understood half of what he said."

"It's mountain talk. Plenty of Americans would be just as confused."

Mandy brought them their food.

Lily took a sip of tea and looked at the envelope he'd swept aside to make room for his plate.

"What's this about a collection, then?"

He pushed it across the table to her. "Didn't I say Virginians were nice? When I told our story at the police station, they insisted on organizing a collection to raise money for our trip."

She flipped open the envelope and started counting the bills inside. Her eyes got wider and wider. "There's over a hundred dollars in here."

"Is there?" He dunked a french fry into a puddle of ketchup.

"Freddie! That might be enough to get us all the way to Florida. Aren't you even surprised?"

"I thought you said you were praying."

She looked flustered. "I was. But—"

"You didn't think He was listening?"

"It's just...does He always answer your prayers? Doesn't he ever say no?"

"When you tell David no, are you still answering him?"

She wrinkled her brow. "What about people who pray to Him but still suffer? What about the ones who go hungry, or die in concentration camps? What about..." Her eyes got a little teary, and she bit her lip. "What about Mother? She's been praying for Father as long as I can remember. It hasn't done a bit of good. The only thing that ever got through to him was a broken nose."

"Lily." He folded his arms on the table and leaned forward, searching for the right words. "I don't have all the answers, sweetheart. Sometimes He does things that don't make sense to me at all. But I know He's always taken care of me. Not exactly the way I expected Him to, maybe, but He always has. Why should I worry when He has a perfect track record?"

She frowned at her plate for a second.

"Are you saying we shouldn't try to save money and behave like sensible human beings? Go along expecting God to orchestrate collections and free dinners all the time?"

"No. I'm just trying to tell you to let go of things a little. You worry and plan like there's nobody at the steering wheel but you. Like you have to do everything and take care of everyone."

She stared at her lap.

"That's no way to live, sweetheart. Not everything's going to turn out the way you want it to, no matter how hard you try. Wouldn't it be better to stop acting like it's all on your shoulders? Try trusting a little. See what He does."

Lily sighed.

"Sometimes you sound so much like Mother."

Chapter 44

Fred lay awake on the front seat, knees folded up to fit. Outside the windshield, stars winked down at him from the patches of sky that showed between tree branches.

Almost to Florida.

Lily had been asleep on the back seat for an hour already, sharing the Eiderdown with David, who was curled up on the floor. For once, Fred was glad he only had one child. Where would he have put the girls, if he'd had them? The trunk?

He shifted, trying not to bump his head on the steering wheel.

They'd used up the money Officer Grant gave them faster than he'd expected. So far, Lily had refrained from pointing out that it might have lasted longer if he hadn't given ten dollars away to the first homeless tramp they came across.

She's trying. She really is.

But he wasn't so sure how calm she'd be when they scraped the bottom of the gas tank tomorrow.

He rubbed his thumb and fingers together. They'd come so far. Another day or two would get them to Orlando. Surely God wouldn't let them get stuck now. "What should I do?"

He whispered the question into the silence. "Should I start looking for a pawn shop? Or do you want us to stop in Georgia for a while? I'd rather go on home if it's all the same to you. I haven't seen Mom and Dad since before David."

The stars kept winking down at him. Outside, crickets were humming, and somewhere a frog chorus croaked away.

Fred took a deep breath. The same God who took care of the grasses of the field and the birds of the air and the crickets and frogs of the Georgia countryside was still looking out for them. Hadn't he told Lily as much?

He closed his eyes and drifted off to the sound of night creatures serenading the stars.

"Wake up, sweetheart. It's morning."

Ugh. Lily curled her knees up toward her stomach and peeked out through a slit in one eye.

The sky was dusty purple still, blushing pink toward the eastern horizon. "Go back to sleep, Freddie."

"If we leave early, we might make it to Orlando by tomorrow."

Hmph. "Not if we run out of petrol today."

He laughed. "We're not going to. God's got this one. Come on."

She clamped her eyes shut and snuggled deeper into the quilt. "Ten more minutes."

A few moments of silence followed, and she was just drifting off again when a suspicious sliding click sounded from the front seat.

"Freddie!" Her voice was swallowed up in the rasping of the old engine as it coughed itself into motion. Before she even had a chance to sit up, they were jouncing over the grass, headed back onto the road. "Freddie, for heaven's sake!" She pulled herself upright and leaned over the front seat. "I'm still in my nightgown!"

He pulled her dress from the dash and handed it to her.

She dropped back onto the eiderdown and pushed haphazard tangles back from her forehead.

He was hopeless. Absolutely hopeless.

Somehow she managed to get dressed under the eiderdown in the back seat, without waking David, but she could not figure out how to get the seams on her stockings straight up the back of her legs while lying down.

Oh well.

She would have to forgo shoes and stockings until Freddie decided to stop for something. Or they ran out of petrol.

Clambering into the front seat, she checked the gauge. *Gracious.* They were almost on empty. How far did Freddie think they were going to get?

"David still asleep?"

"Yesh." She had to talk around the bobby pins she was holding in her teeth as she tried to tame her hair. The brush was stashed in the trunk, and she doubted Freddie would be keen to pull over for it.

He shook his head, smiling. "The kid's bed takes off rumbling down the highway, and he doesn't even bother to wake up."

"He must have been tired."

"Maybe." Fred looked at her from the corner of his eye. "Or maybe he just knows he can trust the guy in the driver's seat."

That's right, Freddie. Sneak in a comment about trust right after I looked at the petrol gauge. She twirled her hair into a smooth twist up the back of her head and jabbed a pin in. "How long do you think we can actually drive on that?"

"Long enough."

Long enough for what? She pressed her lips shut and decided not to ask. *Trust God. And trust Freddie.*

That's what Mother had said.

But Mother was not sitting here watching the last of the petrol evaporate into fumes.

She peeled her eyes off the gauge and looked down at the rectangular flower box wedged between her feet.

The soil looked dried out. She had meant to find water for them this morning, before they started. But there had been no time for that.

She glanced at the thermos on the dash. *No.* She couldn't use the last of their drinking water.

There were no fresh streams to fill it from. Only sluggish, dirty creeks and stagnant swamp land. They would have to buy water.

Or beg for it, since they had no money.

She sighed. What good would it do to water the daffodils anyway? The car would never make it to Florida without petrol. And even if it did, there was nothing left to buy a house with when they got there.

Perhaps it was better if the flowers didn't grow.

They would only be trapped in a window box with no window to hang in. What good would that do? She turned the pot longways and shoved it as far under the dash as it would go.

. . . .

When the gauge had been on empty for ten minutes straight, Lily gave up being calm. "Pull over, Freddie. We need to stop."

"Not yet."

"We'll break down in the middle of the highway!"

"I know what I'm doing, Lily. There's a gas station we're supposed to stop at. I haven't seen it yet."

A petrol station? Without a dollar in Freddie's wallet? Oh, brilliant.

"Freddie, a petrol station isn't going to do us any good without money. Pull over before we end up in a car accident."

"You're not listening to me." He paused to change lanes. "I had a dream last night. I saw the gas station we're supposed to stop at for help. This car is going to get us that far, I know it."

She pressed her hand against her forehead. *Does trusting God always look like this?* Because if she didn't know any better, she would say it resembled insanity.

"Are you telling me God showed up in a dream and told you the car would keep running without petrol in it?"

He sighed. "No. I just saw the station. But don't you remember that story I told you, about when I was a little boy coming home from playing in the woods after dark?"

She twisted her hands in her lap.

"Remember, somehow I just knew that I shouldn't cross that footbridge? And I went around it instead?"

She remembered. The next the day a neighbour had told them he killed a huge water moccasin that morning.

Lying across that very footbridge.

"Sometimes I just know things, Lily. I don't know why God lets me know them, but he does. I knew I was going to marry you that first night at Lowther. I knew I shouldn't cross that footbridge in the dark, and I know this car will get us to the station." He reached over and put his hand over hers, still twisting in her lap.

"Don't you trust me?"

Her mind stumbled over the answer.

Was that not what she had been trying to do ever since she buried that necklace? Why was it still such a difficult question?

"Freddie, this isn't just a dance at the pavilion. We could get *killed* driving like this! The car could stop in the middle of the road, and then one of Jerry's giant trucks would flatten us into the asphalt!"

Freddie stared ahead at the road, eyes scanning this way and that.

"For heaven's sake. Please. Just *pull over!*"

"There it is."

Freddie's voice was as cool as a cucumber sandwich.

Chapter 45

Fred shut the car door and headed for the gas station.

It looked like it had been in business since gas was invented. The part of the sign that was supposed to glow was only half illuminated, and it was hard to tell what color the paint was meant to be.

Next door sat a tiny grocery market in about the same state. A bell rang as he opened the door, and a pair of battered boots and overall-clad legs came sliding out from underneath a jacked up '42 Chevy. The legs were followed by a round belly and a face fringed with a salt-and-pepper beard.

"Hello there. Welcome to Bill's." The man sat up and looked toward the doorway behind the counter. "Katie! Customer!"

A tiny woman wearing a dress with enormous polka dots came hurrying around the corner. Her frizzy, graying hair looped into a bun at the nape of her neck, and she peered over her glasses like a school teacher. "I told you to make that bell louder, Bill. I don't hear it when I'm doing the books."

"I can hear it fine when I'm in there."

"Yes, when you're eating lunch. But when was the last time you tried listening for it while you were doing the books?"

Bill grinned. "Guess it woulda been the last time I tried doing the books at all. 'Bout two weeks before I married you."

She wrinkled her nose at him.

"No wonder. It takes me hours just to figure out half the receipts you scribble down." She read off a crumpled piece of paper. "'Two gallons. Sam G. Dinner Tuesday.' What's that supposed to mean?"

"Exactly what it says. Sam needed two gallons of gas, and he's bringing us dinner on Tuesday."

"But there's no amount on the receipt. Did he pay you?"

"What d'ya think he's bringing dinner for?"

Katie sighed as she turned to Fred. "Can we help you?"

"Yes ma'am. My car is out of gas."

Bill rubbed his palms on his overalls. "How far'd you walk?"

"Just across the parking lot. We made it here, praise the Lord."

"We?"

"My wife and son are still in the car."

Bill stood up, stowing a wrench in his pocket.

"Well, we can push the car over to the pump no problem. Long as yer wife can steer."

"There's another problem."

"What?"

"We don't have any money."

Katie blinked.

Bill scratched the back of his head. "None at all?"

"No. We spent the last of it on supper yesterday."

"What about breakfast today?"

"Haven't eaten yet."

Bill looked over at Katie, and she pressed her lips together without speaking.

Tapping his fingers on the window of the Chevy, Bill looked down at his feet for a minute, then up again.

"Where you from?"

"Florida. At least I am. My wife is from England. We're on our way from Canada down to Orange County."

Bill eyed him.

"You stationed over in England during the war?"

"Yes."

"In the army, then?"

"Yes."

"Me too. First World War."

Bill's fingers kept tapping the mirror.

He glanced at Katie again, then back at Fred.

"I'd like to help you out, but I can't afford to hand out free gas all the time. Katie'll skin me."

An idea popped into Fred's head. "I wouldn't ask you to do that, sir. But if you'll let us have a tankful on loan, I give my word I'll send the money when I get a job."

Katie pursed her lips. "A loan requires security."

"Of course." Fred nodded and turned to Bill. "What if I give you my military papers?"

Bill tugged on his beard and looked at Katie.

"Mum, I'm hungry."

Lily peeked into the picnic basket just in case she had missed anything. "Sorry, David. We're all out."

"When can we get more?"

"Soon, love. Soon." She tried to believe it. There was a cheery-faced man named Bill out there filling up their petrol tank for free, while Freddie rummaged for papers in the trunk. If God could arrange that, surely he would not let them starve? "Want some water?"

David shook his head.

Guess I'll drink some myself then. She reached for the thermos but stopped. *That's all we have left.* Pulling her hand back, she looked out the window instead.

It was a minute or two later when Bill said, "Ah! Here comes Katie."

Lily tried in vain to peer around the petrol pump. Ever since she had seen the little woman in polka dots headed for the market, she'd had a tiny hope growing in her chest. But she was trying not to listen to it, for fear of being disappointed.

Pressing her eyes closed for a moment, she tried to tell herself not to think about it.

Trust, Lily. Trust, trust, trust —

Somebody rapped on her window.

Freddie looked in, smiling even bigger than usual. "Lily! Take these groceries, would you?"

She almost broke down in tears in front of everybody. Fingers trembling, she turned the crank on the door, winding the window down.

Katie handed in two overflowing paper sacks, brushing off thanks as if it offended her. Then she bent out of sight to retrieve something else, but Bill and Freddie both jumped to help. Freddie came up triumphant, holding two jugs that looked like they could hold a couple of gallons each.

"Used to have apple cider in 'em," Bill said. "But Katie uses 'em for water."

Freddie put one jug in the back seat and one up front, then turned and held out the papers to Katie. "Here's the military forms." "I told him to give those to you so I didn't smudge 'em." Bill screwed on the petrol cap.

"Put 'em in the lid of my lunchbox so I don't forget where they are, would you?"

Katie took the papers, shaking her head. "Your idea of organization is my idea of chaos, Bill Stanley."

Bill only laughed as he shook Freddie's hand. "You take care of that family, you hear?"

"Yes sir."

Katie folded her arms. "I hope you have someplace you're plannin' to live when you get there, and don't keep that poor girl sleeping in a car."

"We're going to stay with my aunt and uncle for a while, until I get some money saved up. Thanks again for the groceries."

"Never mind. It wasn't my idea."

"Yes, it was!" Bill shook his finger at her. "I'd never 'ave come up with it if you hadn't been waving your arms and mouthing things to me behind Fred's back."

Katie reddened.

"Well, thank you both, then," Freddie said. "You were an answer to prayer."

"Aw." Bill scratched his ear. "Go on. Get going. You got a ways to go on one tank of gas."

Fred climbed into the driver's seat and started the car. As they pulled out, Katie's voice floated after them.

"I'd like to know how we're supposed to write *that* transaction on a receipt."

"Easy." Bill laughed. "Just like it happened. 'Full tank of gas. Fred O. Papers in lunchbox.'"

"Oh, Bill."

Fred chewed the last bite of his sandwich, watching Lily out of the corner of his eye.

She sat staring out the window as the pine trees and palmettos streamed past. David had dropped off to sleep as soon as he wolfed down his lunch, and since then it had been a quiet ride. As Fred opened his mouth to break the silence, Lily did it for him.

"You were right, Freddie."

"What?"

"About trusting. Mum tried to tell me too. I don't know why it's so hard for me."

Fred swallowed the bite. He could think of a few reasons trust might not come easy to Lily, but he got the sense she wasn't asking his opinion.

"I suppose I just, well..." Her voice got husky. "I had my whole life planned out. Everything was supposed to be straightforward and simple, and it seemed like it was going along splendidly." She brushed a tear from the corner of her eye, and seemed unsure if she was laughing or crying. "Then you showed up. You barmy, wonderful lunatic. And I've been trying ever since to work you into those plans. But you don't fit."

He thought about that one for a minute. "Might have worked better if you'd told me what the plans were."

"It wouldn't have done a bit of good. You're just ...*you.* You don't worry about money. You don't mind jumping around, living in a dozen different places and boarding with relatives one after another and being married for seven years without ever having a home of your own, and—"

"Lily." He reached over with his free hand and turned her chin toward him.

"Look at me. I *do* want a home that's really ours. That's why we're going back to Florida. That's home for me. I'm going to make it home for you too, if it takes everything I've got. You're going to get that house with the daffodils. I promise."

He looked into her eyes and repeated his question from the morning.

"Do you trust me?"

She stared at the water jug sitting between them for a long moment. Then she looked at him again, took a deep breath, and squared her shoulders.

Reaching for the thermos, she unscrewed the lid and bent over to pour the water over the window box.

Her hand froze in mid-air.

"Freddie! Look."

He followed her gaze. In the middle of the pot, what had appeared to be just a dried-out clod of cracked earth had crumbled apart, moist and refreshed, to reveal a bright green spear poking up toward the light.

Lily ran her hand over the soil, brushing aside wet clumps of earth to reveal three more spears, just piercing the surface.

"The daffodils." Her voice was low and wondering. "The daffodils are coming up."

He took her hand and kissed it, dirt and all.

"Lily, you just missed the sign. We're in Florida."

"We are?"

"Yep."

She craned her neck to see the sign, then turned to looked at him, a brave smile on her face.

"Well...welcome home, Freddie."

Fred grinned.

He didn't say, "Welcome home," back to her.

Not yet.

Someday Florida really would be home for Lily. And then he would say it. When it would mean as much to her as it did to him right now. But not before.

Watching the dented car hood eat up the road, he held her hand tight and sang.

"We'll build a bungalow
Big enough for two.
Big enough for two, my honey,
Big enough for two.

And when we're ma-arr-ried
Happy we'll be,
Under the bamboo tree-ee!"

Chapter 46

August 1956

It was a bungalow all right. Or at least it was trying to be one.

Lily stood on the spindly grass at the edge of the property and took in the unpainted siding, rail-less verandah, and, most of all, the bare trestles jutting up like naked ribs against the sky.

Freddie wants to buy a house with only half a roof on it.

Why was she even surprised?

"Come on. I'll show you the inside." He caught her hand, his voice full of excitement.

She let him lead her up the steps, across the unpainted verandah, and through the front door. Her shoes slapped bare concrete.

No floor.

Of course. Who bothered with flooring before the roof was on?

"This is the front room." Freddie motioned around them at the bare space hemmed in with studs. "And over here is the kitchen." She followed him as he stepped right through what should have been a wall. "The stove will go here, the icebox will go here, and the table will go over there."

He pointed at empty spaces as if he could see it all laid out and finished. "Now over this way is the bedroom ..."

There were four rooms total, besides the bathroom. A parlour, a kitchen, a bedroom, and one more small room to the side of the kitchen.

"That can be David's," Freddie said. "Though I guess things might get a little tight if ..."

He broke off, shifting his feet. "I mean, if we're still here when he gets ... big."

Lily bit her lip. *Poor Freddie.* She knew he was still hoping, deep down, that they would have more children someday. Especially a little girl. He never said so, but she caught it in the half-finished sentences, in the beaming smile he wore while he played with his little sister, and in the hopeful look that flashed onto his face and then faded when she said one day that she had "exciting news," only to tell him about her job at the Florida Hospital and Sanitarium.

Freddie's arm came around her waist and his hand tilted her face up to his.

"Have I told you yet today how much I love you?"

"Only four or five times."

"Huh. Must be an off day for me. I'm running behind."

She laughed. "Freddie, where will the bathtub go?"

He blinked. "What?"

"The bathtub. There's no room in that water closet." The lavatory and kitchen were located in the half of the house that actually had a roof.

There was already a toilet, sink, and shower. But no bathtub.

Freddie looked over his shoulder through the unfinished walls. "Um, do we have to have a bathtub?"

Of course we do. What good would her own home be if she couldn't even take a bubble bath?

He took one look at her face and laughed. "Okay. Don't worry. I'll find you a bathtub."

She gazed up at the halo of sunshine framing his head where there should have been a ceiling. "Won't it take a while, Freddie? To have this place ready to move into?"

"I can get the kitchen finished by next week. After that, I'm ready when you are."

"But we can see the sky from the bedroom!"

He shrugged.

"Well, the other options are to keep saving until we can afford a finished house, or wait to move until this one's done. But either way we'd be living with Uncle Ellis and Aunt Lola a lot longer."

Aunt Lola. Lily's stomach heaved. It had been two years since they pulled up to Aunt Lola's house and the car died right there in the driveway.

They had been living in the spare bedroom ever since. If she had to listen to one more lecture on how to be a better wife, a better mother, a better human being in general ...

"How soon should I start packing?"

Less than two weeks later, Fred lugged the last armload into the bungalow.

He could hear Lily clanging around in the kitchen, putting away the mismatched pots and pans he'd rounded up. Sunlight streamed through the roof, lighting the bedroom where they'd put a mattress on the floor and made it up with the eiderdown.

I need to get some tarps rigged up before a rainstorm rolls in.

"Sweetheart, where do you want your hat box?"

Lily's voice came from inside a cabinet. "Bring it in here."

He stepped through the wall and put the hatbox down next to the stove, careful not to spill dirt out of the daffodil pot in his other arm.

"And this?"

She looked up. "On the table for now, I suppose."

Fred wedged the window box between a soup pot and a bag of cornmeal. "The dirt looks kind of dry in here, Lily. Want me to water them?" The flowers and leaves were all gone by this time of year, but the bulbs were still under there someplace.

"No."

"You sure? They didn't bloom too well this past spring. Maybe they need more water in between times."

She looked over the door of the cabinet at him. "I know how to grow daffodils." Irritation sharpened her tone. "Mother never watered them once they went dormant. Why don't you put them outside on the verandah instead? I'm trying to organize."

"Any way I can help?"

He poked a finger into the dirt, hoping she was right about the water.

"Yes!" She tossed her hair back. "You can take the daffodils outside like I said and then go find David something to do. He keeps dragging sticks and leaves inside. I'm having a dreadful time convincing him we aren't camping just because we're sleeping on the floor." She disappeared into the cabinet.

Fred rubbed his chin.

Sometimes when Lily got annoyed with him, he couldn't for the life of him figure out why.

Picking up the window box again, he headed for the porch.

Lily kept her head in the cupboard until she heard the front door shut. Then she sat back on her heels. *Why did he have to mention the daffodils?*

She had been worried about them for a long time. They seemed to be getting sicker and sicker. She had pampered them in every way she could think of, even dug the bulbs up in winter and put them in the ice box for a few weeks in case Florida weather was not cold enough.

Still they looked weaker every year. Perhaps they were tired of living in a window box.

Getting to her feet, she turned in a slow circle to take in her new house.

And sighed. *This is not how I pictured it.*

That cozy, spotless little cottage with lace curtains in the windows and a kettle on the hob had turned into a half-finished bungalow without a stitch of paint.

Or a floor, or a roof, or even a bathtub. Not to mention she had yet to find the kettle.

Even so. She had been determined to be happy. To keep on trusting. Freddie would finish the house someday. They would have curtains in the windows and tea water steaming and bubble baths and gardens and—

Well, that was just it. There was supposed to be a flower garden full of Mother's daffodils by the back door. But what if the daffodils wouldn't grow?

She went to the window. Outside, the pine and cypress trees stirred in the breeze, swaying against the sky. Mother always liked to say God was like the wind. You couldn't see Him, but He was always there, moving things. Weaving the good into your life. You just had to open your eyes to see it.

"It's hard to trust sometimes, Lord." Lily leaned against the window sill. "It's hard to keep letting go of my plans over and over. Does it ever stop? Can't I have even one thing the way I want it?" She sighed again.

"Mum?"

"What is it, David?" She turned her head.

He was looking in the front door, hopping up and down on one foot. *So big.* In another week he would start infant school—no, wait—they called it kindergarten here.

David grinned. "Dad has a present for you. He says can he bring it in?"

"Well, of course he can bring it in." Why on earth did he send David to ask? Couldn't he just put his head in the door and—

Oh. *That's why.*

Freddie inched sideways through the door, arms stretched wide around an oblong metal tub as big as he was. With a final squeeze, he slipped through the doorway and clanged the monster down in the middle of the parlour. "There. Told you I'd find a bathtub."

A bathtub? Lily looked at it. A galvanized tub in the middle of a concrete floor, with sunshine streaming over it through the hole in the ceiling.

One thing ... She looked at Freddie, then again at the tub. And then she dropped into a chair and laughed until the tears streamed down her face.

Freddie looked confused. "Do you ... like it?"

"Of course I like it!" She pressed her hand against her chest, trying to catch her breath. *It's just that God has the funniest way of answering prayer sometimes.*

"Want to try it out? David and I can take a walk into town and get an ice-cream soda."

She considered that. "It will take me awhile to heat all the water on the stove. And I have to figure out where I packed the bubble bath."

"Okay. Two ice-cream sodas."

She laughed again. "Oh, all right." Getting to her feet, she reached for the biggest soup pot just as she heard a car coming up the driveway.

Fred walked over and looked out the window. "Uh-oh. Sorry, sweetheart. Looks like Mom and Dad came over to visit."

Lily sighed, put down the soup pot, and started clearing off the table.

Her bubble bath would have to wait.

Chapter 47

What a day. Lily's work bag thumped against the concrete as she dropped into a chair.

She leaned her elbows on the table and pressed her forehead into her hands.

Two patients had vomited on her in the same morning, the second one while she was changing his sheets. So of course she had to change the sheets all over again, and then go and put on her third uniform for the day.

Halfway through the morning, she discovered she had left her lunch at home and would have to borrow lunch money from one of the other nurses. An elderly patient had gone into heart failure and almost died, and someone had knocked over a mug and doused an entire stack of charts in coffee.

That was all before midday.

She looked sideways at the bag.

The uniforms were crumpled up in there, soiled and sour with vomit. They would have to be washed and dried and ready to take back by tomorrow morning.

Thank goodness Fred's mother offered to keep David until after supper.

Lily shoved her chair back and dragged herself to her feet. She still ached from bending over patients all day. Picking up the bag of uniforms, she went to fetch the tub out from under the verandah.

There was no place to keep it in the house, so she had to haul it out from under the verandah, thump it up the steps, and slide it in onto the concrete whenever she wanted to wash clothes or take a bath.

A bath! She gave the tub one last shove into the parlour and straightened up, dropping the hospital bag.

What am I doing?

Here she was, with the entire house to herself for the whole afternoon. And all she could think of was laundry?

The uniforms could wait.

It took her half an hour to fill the tub, heating water on the stove and mixing it with buckets of cold.

At last though, she dribbled in the bubble-bath liquid, peeled the uniform off her tired body, and stepped into the tub, easing herself down into the steaming water.

Ah. Her tense muscles relaxed.

She leaned back against the warm metal as the foamy layer of bubbles rose up to her chin, and closed her eyes. A soft whisper of breeze from the kitchen window stirred her hair, bringing with it the scents of late summer.

Fresh-mowed grass. Cypress trees in the sunshine.

She took a slow deep breath, listening to the sounds of a lazy afternoon. Bluebirds trilled in the crape myrtle, wind stirred the pine needles, grasshoppers and katydids hummed in the grass—

And somebody's tires were crunching over the gravel.

Not again! Lily's eyes popped open. Perhaps it was only Freddie, home early from work. She leaned over the edge of the tub, dripping water onto the concrete as she stretched sideways to peek around the curtains.

No. That was not Freddie's car.

For heaven's sake! She climbed out of the tub and made a dash for the bathroom, dripping as she went. Snatching her towel from the rack, she dried off most of the water as she hurried to the built-in clothes cupboard Freddie called a 'closet.'

Outside, a car door shut.

Slip. Dress. Shoes. Belt. She grabbed them without any time to make certain she had coordinated. Dropping the dress over her head, she slid her arms through the sleeves and scrambled to button herself up.

A knock sounded on the door.

She shoved her feet into the shoes, fastened the belt on her way to the door, and hoped her hair looked dryer than it felt as she shoved a couple of hairpins in and turned the knob.

"Hello there."

Lily blinked.

It had been so long since she had heard anyone speak real, proper English, it almost sounded strange. Even David was beginning to pick up the local accent now that he was going to school. Pretty soon he'd sound just like Freddie.

She stared at the well-groomed woman on the doorstep. *Wait a minute. I know her from somewhere ...*

"Why ... Dr. Green! When did you come over from England?"

"Not long ago." Dr. Green smiled. "May I come in?"

"Of course." Lily waved her guest inside. "I'm afraid it's a bit topsy-turvy. I was ..." She bit her tongue before she could say something awkward. "I mean ... I brought some uniforms home from work to wash them. Please take a seat." She motioned toward the easy chair.

Dr. Green smiled again, though she seemed to be trying not to stare at the concrete floor, the missing walls, and the bathtub in the middle of the parlour. "Where will you sit?"

"I'll bring in another chair. Make yourself comfortable." Lily ducked into the kitchen.

Goodness. Dr. Green was the last person she had expected. A long time ago, back in England, when Lily had worked for a while at St. Anne's Hospital, they had known each other. But she had certainly never expected to meet again in America. Putting the kettle on the hob, Lily turned up the heat and scrambled through the cupboard for a box of biscuits and a plate. *Teacups, saucers, cream.* What had Freddie done with the sugar? Oh. In the cupboard with the teacups again.

Collecting the plate of biscuits and a kitchen chair, she went back to the parlour. Dr. Green was studying the hole in the bedroom roof.

No wonder.

Freddie had been working on it almost every night, and he had gotten enough filled in that from the front of the house everything looked normal. It was a bit of a surprise when you stepped inside and could still see sky over in the bedroom.

Lily set her chair down and held out the plate of biscuits. "I'm sorry you're seeing the house in such a state. We just bought it."

"But why move in when it wasn't finished yet?"

"The other option was staying with Freddie's aunt."

"Oh." Dr. Green took a biscuit. "Couldn't you have just bought a finished house then?"

Lily's cheeks warmed. "Well ... housing is so expensive now. Didn't you hear about the shortage there's been since the war ended? It's hard to find anything reasonable."

Dr. Green looked embarrassed to have asked. "Oh. Well, how are you and your husband doing?"

"Very well. Our little boy is nearly six."

"How time flies!" Dr. Green shifted in her chair. "The reason I came by today was ..." She broke off and shifted again, a strange look on her face. Reaching back to feel between the seat cushions behind her, she pulled out a jagged chunk of pine branch as long as her hand.

Lily could have died. "I'm so sorry! David is always dragging things into the house and leaving them in the most inconvenient places. Let me take that." She got up and tossed the stick outside. "You were saying?"

"Yes. The reason I—"

The tea kettle chose that particular moment to begin shrieking like a banshee from the next room.

Lily wanted to groan. First the bathtub in the middle of the floor, then the tree branch, now the teakettle. Next thing she knew, it would be the roof caving in. "I'm so sorry, Dr. Green." She hurried into the kitchen.

Pulling the teapot from the cupboard, she was in such a rush that she almost smashed it on the concrete, but caught it in time.

With the pot safely on the kitchen worktop, she grabbed the P.G. Tips box and snatched out a teabag. It caught on the corner and tore in half.

For heaven's sake. She was more careful with the next two, but there were now tea leaves scattered all over the kitchen worktop and down the front of her dress. The teakettle was still squealing. *Stupid.* She should have moved it off the heat first thing. Brushing tea-leaves off her skirt, she grabbed for the metal handle.

Her hand registered searing pain and she yelped. *Idiot!* How could she have forgotten to use a towel?

"Are you all right?"

"Yes!" Making sure she had a towel around her hand this time, Lily grabbed the kettle again, poured the water into the teapot, popped the lid on, and collected everything onto a tray. *Mother would be scandalized.* There was such an order and calmness about Mother whenever she made tea. The perfect water temperature, the perfect brewing time, the perfect tablecloth ...

"Here we are." Lily slid the tray onto the lampstand next to the easy chair. "milk and sugar?"

"Please."

"One lump or two?"

"One."

She poured the milk into the bottom of the cup, dropped the sugar in after it, and reached for the teapot. *Good gracious!* What was she thinking? Of course she could not pour the tea yet. It had hardly brewed. "Um ..." She tried to cover her confusion. "The tea should be ready in a couple of minutes."

She went ahead and put the milk and sugar in her own cup and hoped Dr. Green would assume she always did that ahead of time. "So sorry for all the interruptions. You were saying?"

"Yes." Dr. Green sounded like she was holding back a sigh. "Well, I'm starting a medical practice south of Orlando, and I thought you might like to come and work for me. It would be so lovely to have another Englishwoman on staff. I'll happily match your current salary."

Oh dear. Lily sat down in her chair. "I'd love to, but I'm afraid I can't."

"Why not?"

Lily bit the inside of her lip. She did not want to admit they could only afford one car, on top of living on a concrete floor with half the roof missing.

But there was no help for it. "Freddie needs the car to get to work. I always take the bus, and ride with David over to kindergarten before I go on to work. It would take far too long to get all the way down to your clinic by bus. I can only drop David off so early."

"I see." Dr. Green folded her hands in her lap. "What does Freddie do for employment?"

Lily reached for the teapot. Surely it had brewed long enough by now.

"At the moment he's working at a mechanic shop."

"At the moment?" Dr. Green arched her brow.

Oh dear. That made it sound like Freddie was tinkering with one job after another for no good reason. She filled the cups while she tried to explain.

"There aren't many permanent positions available. A lot of women stayed in the workplace after the men came home, and all the munitions factories are shutting down too. So all those people need work. It's hard to get a steady position. Thankfully Freddie has found several short-term jobs."

She handed Dr. Green a teacup. "He's working so hard right now, fixing cars all day and then coming home and starting on the house after supper. It's my fault we had to move. He would have happily stayed with Aunt Lola longer, but ..."

Dr. Green's nose wrinkled.

"No, no. I don't mean he wants to live off his relatives—"

"Is something burning?"

Lily sniffed. *Goodness!* Springing to her feet, she dashed into the kitchen, which was beginning to fill with smoke. Yellow flames licked the air on top of the hob.

The towel. She had forgotten to turn off the burner and then dropped the towel right on top of it. She beat at the flames, but they seemed to laugh at her efforts.

Water. That's what she needed. Flinging open a drawer, she grabbed the salad tongs, clamped them around the flaming towel, and made a mad dash for the parlour to extinguish the flames in her bubble bath.

A cloud of gagging smoke billowed up from the surface of the water and filled the parlour. Dr. Green broke into a hacking cough.

Lily pulled the charred, sopping towel back out of the tub and carried it over to the kitchen sink, dripping water across the floor. "I'm so dreadfully sorry. Are you all right?"

"I will be." Dr. Green got to her feet, still coughing. "But I think perhaps I should go. I had pneumonia recently and"— she wheezed—"my lungs aren't strong yet." She started toward the front door.

Lily clattered the towel and tongs into the sink and hurried to open the door for her guest. "Won't you stay a bit longer? It was so nice see someone from home."

Dr. Green paused on the doorstep.

"If the smoke is bothering you, we can sit on the verandah. Or if we wait a few minutes, it will clear out fine. Sometimes it can be handy to have a hole in your roof." She laughed. "It makes it easy to get fresh air."

Dr. Green did not laugh. She gazed inside at the smoky chaos for a long moment, then met Lily's eyes and shook her head. "Oh, Lily." She sighed. "What has he brought you to?"

· · · · · * * * * * * * ● ● ● * * * * · · · · ·

Lily stood in the doorway, speechless, while Dr. Green climbed into her car and drove away.

She turned. A trail of water connected the kitchen to the bathtub. The tea tray and a plate of biscuits crowded the lamp-stand, wedged between the faded recliner and the unpainted kitchen chair. She clenched a corner of her apron, watching the smoke drift between naked studs on its way to the roof hole. Sunbeams streamed down through the haze and illuminated the mattress on the floor. A breeze stirred the thread-bare sheets they had hung around the bathroom.

Crossing to the tub, she put her finger in the water.

Lukewarm. Of course. The bubbles were all gone now, and bits of charred towel floated on the surface. She would have to empty it out and refill it to wash the uniforms.

And then something would have to be made for supper, after she mopped up the concrete and aired out the smoke.

Oh, Lily. What has he brought you to?

Squeezing her eyes shut, she shook her head, trying to chase away the echo. She had thought she was winning this battle. Learning to let go of all those perfect plans of hers. Maybe she had not gotten as far as she thought.

She had not heard a proper English accent in two years, and suddenly thoughts of home flooded back. Memories of Mother and the girls, sunny days by the seaside with the white windmill stretching its sails against the clouds. Green Drive. North Clifton Street. The Palace ... Paul.

Stop it! She wanted to slap herself.

Of course the house needed work, but it would get there. Freddie could build a bedstead, and they would find more furniture somewhere.

They would paint the siding white, put a railing around the verandah, plant flowers ...

Flowers!

She dropped the bag of uniforms she had just picked up, and spun around. *Of course.* She was going to plant those today.

Everything would look better when Mother's flowers were growing by the back door.

She half-ran to the verandah, hurrying around the corner where it wrapped to the side of the house. The window box sat at the very back edge. Plunging her fingers into the crumbling dry earth, she felt for a bulb.

Aha! She closed her hand around one.

It squished, cold and slimy, between her fingers.

What? She pulled her hand out. There lay what was left of the daffodil bulb, black and rotting.

No, no, no. With something squeezing her chest like a vice, she scrambled through the earth for the next bulb. Her fingers hit mush. *Please, no!*

When the third bulb dissolved in her hand, she stopped digging and just knelt there, staring at the black slime on her fingers.

Dead.

So Mother was wrong.

English daffodils could not be happy in America, after all. Anger and tears rose together, choking her throat.

Two years of nursing them along in a pot so she could plant them at her own home someday, and now ...

Dead, dead, dead!

With a savage kick, she sent the window box tumbling over the edge. It smashed into pieces on the ground.

Shaking, she slumped to the floor, buried her face in her arms, and cried.

Chapter 48

Steve, the hardware store manager, waved at Fred from behind the dusty counter when he came in. "Hullo, Fred. How's it going?"

Fred let the door thump shut behind him as he stepped into the store, inhaling the thick scents of metal, wood, and rubber. "Fine. I'm on my way home, but I stopped by for—"

"You been to the post office today?" Steve shoved up a sleeve that had slipped down his hairy forearm.

Fred held in a grin. *Here we go again.* It was hard to get a word in edgewise with Steve. Listening was not the man's strong point. "No, I haven't been lately. Why?"

Steve leaned his elbow on the counter. "Well, you know my brother-in-law Kevin is the postmaster. I told you that, didn't I?"

"I think you—"

"Yeah. Sure I did." Steve flapped his hand. "Well, anyhow. I was talking to him this morning when he came in to buy another one of them new disposals for his kitchen sink. You got one of them?"

"No. But speaking of buying things—"

"Great little gadgets. Bet your wife would love it. But they do have limitations. You just ain't goin' to believe why Kevin was buying a new one. You haven't heard the story already, have you?"

Fred sighed. Sometimes lying was very tempting to a person. "No, but I—"

"Didn't think so. You see his wife—my sister—was just in here buying a new one a couple weeks ago. And I asked her why, and she said the old one had broken. So I didn't think much about it until I saw *him* in here this morning, and then I had to ask why the heck they needed two new kitchen disposals in one month. Why do you think?"

Fred shrugged and didn't even try to speak this time.

"Well, turns out it's my nephew, Jim. Same age as your boy, about. He keeps using it to grind up corn cobs and sticks and what-have-you every time they turn their backs. Can you believe that kid?"

Fred ran his fingers through his hair and looked toward the big window.

Outside, the sun was sinking toward the horizon in a blaze of orange. It was never a quick stop at the hardware store, no matter how hard he tried. "Sounds like a handful, Steve. Now if I could just get some—"

"Oh!" Steve slapped himself in the forehead. "I forgot. I was going to tell you about the letter."

Fred swallowed a sigh. "What letter?"

"The one from England."

"Is it for Lily?"

"Yeah. When you gonna get a mailbox up at that new house? Kevin said it's been a few days since you or your wife came in and got the mail. There's been a letter sittin' there from England since yesterday morning. Your wife's from England, ain't she?"

"Steve! Roofing nails. I'm already late for supper. Are they in yet?"

"Oh yeah. Sure thing." Steve ducked under the counter, voice rattling on from below. "Shipment just came in yesterday. I got a package all ready for you." He reappeared and slid a box across the counter. "How's the roofing coming?"

"It's coming." Fred counted out the price of the nails. "Thanks, Steve."

"Sure thing."

Fred headed for the door, hoping to get out before Steve started in on another subject.

"Hey, Fred?"

Nope. Not fast enough. He turned his head but kept walking toward the door. Lily hated it when he was late for supper.

"Has your wife got her U.S. citizenship yet?"

"Not yet." She hadn't reached the three-year residency requirement so far. And somehow, he got the feeling she might not be getting it, even if she had. She avoided the subject like the plague. He reached for the door handle.

"Well, just so you know, if she wants some help getting registered for classes, Kevin was telling me just this morning that he knows a guy—"

"Thanks, Steve. I'll let her know." Fred got the door open and ducked outside, pulling it shut without waiting for a reply.

On the sidewalk still radiating heat from the afternoon, he checked his watch. Should he make a quick trip to the post office before he went home? He was already going to be a couple of minutes late as it was.

They hadn't had a telephone put in yet, so he couldn't call Lily and let her know. But on the other hand, she was always so excited to get letters from England. If he went home and told her there was one there but he hadn't picked it up, she'd definitely be disappointed.

Tucking the roofing nails under his arm, he started down the sidewalk toward the post office in the warm evening light.

It took him longer than he was expecting. The line at the post office was a mile long, and on the way home he hit road work and had to take a winding detour instead.

As he turned into the driveway in the dusky twilight, a pair of headlights nearly blinded him. He edged over to the side of the drive, and the other car eased up beside him. It was Dad and Mom.

Uh-oh. David wasn't supposed to be home until well after supper. He was even later than he'd thought.

"Well, hello there." Mom leaned around Dad to smile at him. "Long day at work?"

"Yes, and then errands afterward. Took forever. You here dropping off David?"

"Yep. He's plumb worn out from chasing that new puppy around all day." Mom looked back toward the house. "Fred, is Lily feeling all right?"

Far as I know. "Why?"

"She just seemed out of sorts, I guess. You probably ought to ask her how she's feeling. Women like to be asked."

She winked.

"Thanks, Mom."

His parents pulled out, and he crunched on over the gravel to the house, guessing Lily was just upset about him keeping supper waiting so late.

The crickets and cicadas chirped like crazy as he stepped out of the car into the humid evening air.

On the clothesline, three pale, fluttering ghosts told him it must have been a messy day at the hospital.

No wonder Lily's not happy.

When he got inside, she was helping David brush his teeth in the bathroom.

"Hello, sweetheart. Sorry I'm late for supper."

"It's on the table." Lily's voice sounded flat, coming from behind the curtain walls.

He headed for the kitchen. "There's three uniforms on the clothesline. Lots of sick patients today?"

"Yes." Again the reply was emotionless.

He spotted one lone plate sitting there on the table. It was topped with large servings of beans, okra, and sliced ham, but the rest of the table was bare as an empty airstrip. The kitchen was spotless.

"Took me longer than I was expecting, coming come. Did you know they're working on that bridge by the lake?"

"Yes."

He prodded the ham with his finger. *Stone cold.* "You already eat, Lily?"

"Yes."

"And cleaned up all by yourself?"

"Yes."

"You should have left the dishes. I don't mind helping."

Silence.

Fred puffed a breath through his nose, looking toward the bathroom through the studs. This was worse than he'd thought. Maybe Mom had a good suggestion. "You feeling all right, sweetheart?"

"Why?" Lily's voice was chilly with sarcasm. "Does eating at the usual hour instead of waiting until almost bedtime imply a person is sick?"

Sighing, Fred sat down at the table and reached for his fork. It was shaping up to be a long night.

Lily lay awake on the mattress, staring at the stars through the gap in the roof.

Pound, pound, pound.

Dash it all. It had to be close to midnight, but Freddie was still up there on the roof, pounding away in the dark. *Lunatic.* It wasn't like him to work this late. He might wake David.

She rolled over, pulling a pillow over her head, and tried to block out the noise.

Pound, pound, pound.

The pillow didn't make much difference. What had come over Freddie, anyway?

A tiny voice in the back her head suggested he might find a hammer more congenial company than his wife this evening.

Oh, shut up. She kicked the covers off. It was much too hot for a blanket.

Hot, stagnant, and muggy, as if they had slipped backward into August again. *That's Florida for you.*

She had spent two summers here already, but it still felt like a sauna to her. What on earth made people settle in such a place back when they all wore clothing from their necks to their ankles?

It was a wonder those Spanish settlers didn't all die of heat stroke.

Lily tossed and turned. Her face was sweating under the pillow. Everything felt hot.

The sheets, the air, everything. She closed her eyes and tried to remember how cool and refreshing her bed used to feel back home in Lytham when autumn came. And how the trees would turn into bright splashes of gold and orange and crimson.

They had no autumn in Florida. Or not a proper one, at least. They had summertime and not-summertime. No changing leaves. No crisp, cool sheets.

Pound. Pound. Pound

"Freddie!" She sat up, jerking the pillow off. "Will you stop that? It's almost midnight! How am I supposed to go to sleep with you up there hammering?"

Pound. Pound. Pound.

"Freddie!" She shouted this time.

The pounding broke off. "Did you call me, Lily?"

"Yes! I can't sleep with you pounding like that. Don't you know it's almost midnight?"

"Is it that late?" Fred sounded surprised. "The moon is so bright tonight I didn't even notice."

"Well, I did."

"Sorry, sweetheart. I'll stop. But do you mind if I finish this one nail?"

Lily groaned and pulled the pillow back over her head.

Chapter 49

Lily woke to the sunshine glaring in her eyes.

Goodness! She jerked upright. Usually she awoke when the sky was just tinged pink above the pines. If it was already up far enough to be shining in her eyes—

She had overslept. A lot.

No wonder, with Freddie up hammering until all hours of the night. She glanced at the other side of the bed. He was still over there, sound asleep with his arm thrown over his eyes as if he knew the light was coming and decided to be prepared.

She wanted to elbow him. He had no business snoring away when she had to be up cooking breakfast for everyone and trying to get David to school before she went to work. After all, he was the one who had kept her up so late.

Still, elbowing seemed a bit rough, considering she wanted the hole in the roof gone as much as he did. Probably more than he did.

She left him lying there, but made no attempt at being quiet as she clambered out of bed, threw open the bureau drawer to retrieve her dressing gown, pulled it on over her pajamas, and headed for the front door.

Freddie never twitched.

Letting the door bang shut as hard as it wanted to, she thumped down the verandah steps and hurried across the dew-soaked grass on the shady side of the house to see if the uniforms had dried on the wash line.

They were still wet. Of course.

She left them hanging there and ran back inside to make breakfast. The clock informed her she would be late for work if she tried to fry eggs and heat beans to go over the toast.

Cold breakfast then. Lovely.

She put the kettle on the hob, found the bowl of hard-boiled eggs in the icebox, and put salt, pepper, and bread and jam on the table, then went to wake David.

Fred peeled a hard-boiled egg and sprinkled salt over it.

Across the table, David scowled. "I don't want eggs!" He kicked the chair leg with his heel. "I want beans and toast."

Lily slammed a drawer in the bedroom. "Eat what's served, David. When I was a little girl, they started rationing sugar. How would you like that?" Her words were garbled. She'd taken a piece of buttered bread with her when she left the kitchen, and it sounded like she was trying to chew the whole thing at once.

David looked unimpressed about the rationing. "Is there sugar in beans, Dad?"

"Depends how you cook them." Fred smoothed a knife-full of jam over a slice of bread. "There's plenty in jam though. Here, eat this."

David, who usually loved jam, was too grumpy to be pacified. "I don't want jam on bread. I want beans on toast!"

Fred reached over and put the bread on David's plate.

"Eat it."

David pushed the plate away, porcelain grating on the rough table-top.

"Now look. I didn't even know you could put beans on toast until I went to England and married your mother. I did just fine without them when I was a kid. Eat your breakfast."

Pouting, David took a bite, but he didn't look too thrilled about it.

Fred held in a sigh. Nobody was happy this morning. Lily had hardly spoken to him.

He couldn't tell if she was still mad about him coming home late, or about him working late on the roof, or sleeping in, or what.

And she didn't seem interested in filling him in.

He'd forgotten to tell her about the letter last night. She'd been in such a mood that he had spent most of his time trying to stay out of her way and not cause trouble.

Now didn't seem like a good time to mention it either, since she wasn't going to have time to read it anyway. Judging by the way the drawer slammed, she'd probably be mad about that too.

He glanced over at the stack of mail sitting on the extra chair and wondered what to do about it.

Lily wasn't usually upset for such a long stretch at a time. Generally she just exploded and went marching out of the house in huff and came back when she'd gotten over it.

He didn't have a clue what do with this new development. Especially when he wasn't real clear on what had made her mad in the first place.

Swallowing the last piece of egg, he carried his plate over to the sink, washed it, dried it, and put it in the cabinet. At least she wouldn't have to clean up after him. "Lily?"

"Hmm?"

"Can I help you with anything?"

"No."

He was pretty sure that particular no meant something more like, "Well, yes, of course you could, if you could read my mind, but since I'm not going to sit here and try to figure out what you should do and give you instructions, no, you can't."

He scratched his chin. "You sure?"

"Yes."

He stood in the kitchen for a second, trying to think of something helpful to do. But ever since he got home last night, he seemed to be in the way more than anything.

She'd made some vague complaint, after she got David into bed, about how long it was taking to get the roof fixed. And then she had asked how long they were going to have guests walking around on concrete.

He took that as a hint to go up to work on the roof, even though it was late enough he wanted to tumble into bed instead. But that hadn't made her happy either. Sometimes he just couldn't figure her out.

"Well, I guess I'm going to head to work then, sweetheart, if you don't need me for anything."

He got a monosyllable reply, followed by the sound of water splashing in the bathroom sink.

Reaching for his hat, he ruffled David's hair and left for work.

Chapter 50

Lily dashed up to the hospital, ten minutes late for work.

"Where have you been?" Jillian, a fellow nurse, met her at the door. "We've got five new cases of flu and one of measles, and three more children came in throwing up every hour." She pushed a stray piece of hair back from her forehead and fanned her face with her hand.

"Can you believe how sweltering it is? Honestly. You'd think we lived in a rainforest."

Lily tightened her nurse's headpiece, which was much too warm for comfort. "I heard a rumour they're planning to bring in air conditioning."

"Can't be too soon for me!" Jillian kept fanning. "Where are the uniforms you took home with you?"

No! Lily could have kicked herself. "I forgot. They're still hanging on the wash line!"

Jillian dropped back against the wall and moaned. "We've hardly got any spares left with all the changes we needed yesterday. Everyone was supposed to bring back the ones they washed, and you're the second person who forgot. We're going to have to start borrowing from another department!"

Oh dear.

Lily hurried up the hall, furious at herself for forgetting, and turned the corner to head for the water closet. *Wham!* She smacked right into Silvia, another of the nurses, coming the other way.

"Did you bring the uniforms back?"

Uh-oh. Silvia was always a bit of a sour-puss, but today she looked like she was on the verge of hissing and scratching.

Lily hedged. "You wouldn't believe what a morning I've had! I slept late because Freddie was hammering until all hours of the night, and then the uniforms weren't dry when I went out to get them first thing, and David kept dragging his feet and didn't want to eat his breakfast and we almost missed the bus, and then when we got to—"

Silvia scowled. "You forgot them."

Lily bit her lip.

"Honestly! You'd think I was the only person working here who had a functioning long-term memory!" Silvia threw her hands into the air. "I had mine pressed and hanging at the door before I went to bed last night."

"Your memory, or the uniforms?" Lily stepped around Silvia and ducked into the lavatory without leaving time for a reply.

Honestly. Silvia had no business talking.

She had a washing machine and an electric clothes dryer. No husband or son to worry about either. *Of course she had the uniforms ready.* But how would she like to be boiling water on the stove and chipping her perfect nails on a washboard? *Ha!* She'd probably faint in exhaustion just thinking about it.

But of course, Silvia had plenty of money and would never dream of living in a house with a concrete floor and a hole in the roof.

Come to think of it, I didn't sign up for that myself.

Lily banged the stall door open. America was supposed to be a lovely, glowing frontier of opportunity. What was that silly phrase floating around in England? "Nab a Yank and go to America free."

Brilliant. As if going to America was supposed to solve all your problems.

Lily flipped on the tap and glanced in the mirror. Goodness! The skirt of her uniform was caught up into her nylons in the back. Thank heavens she noticed *that* before going back out into the hall. Shaking it loose, she made certain the skirt was lying smooth all the way around and then stuck her hands under the water in the sink.

Gracious! She nearly screamed as she jolted backward. *Idiot.* She had turned on the hot water instead of the cold, and the hand she had burned yesterday now felt like it was on fire. She switched on the cold and stuck her burning hand under it, but it didn't help much.

She had a feeling this was going to be another terrible day.

Fred had his head inside the engine of a broken-down farm truck when he heard Steve coming into the garage.

"... and then Kevin told me my nephew's been using it to grind up corn cobs and sticks when his back is turned. Can you believe that boy?"

You could always hear Steve coming.

"Sounds like somebody oughta take a stick to the kid's backside," a second voice chimed in as the door opened. Randy. He owned the garage and didn't take nonsense from anybody. "Hey, Fred! Steve's here to see you."

Fred pulled his head out from under the hood and wiped his hands on his overalls, checking his watch while he was at it. *Almost lunchtime.*

But if he didn't get this truck running by one o'clock, they were going to have an angry farmer on their hands this afternoon. Not to mention he was trying to finish up early so he could get home on time this evening. Maybe that would smooth things over with Lily.

"Morning, Steve. Who's running the hardware store?"

"Ben is. His school doesn't open until next week. Don't know what I'm gonna do once it does though. When it's your own kid, you know, can pay 'em half-salary and chalk it up for good training experience. But we can't afford another full-pay employee. You know minimum wage went up a whole twenty-five cents this year? Over thirty percent. Now we gotta pay everybody a dollar an hour. We can't hire somebody else full-time at that rate. It's robbery. But I need another worker."

Steve stopped for a breath, and Fred tried to head him off. "Well, what brings you—"

"Especially in the evening to restock the shelves and all," Steve went on, oblivious. "But anyway, I wanted to tell you we got in more shingles and plywood. And weren't you asking about flooring too?"

Fred had never been able to figure out if Steve was part deaf or just liked to tune out everyone else when he was busy listening to himself.

"Yeah. Flooring and sheetrock." He'd been saving up to buy a bunch at one time as soon as the roof was finished. "Soon as I get the roof done, I'm going to start—"

"Yeah. That's what I figured. So I thought I oughta tell you about the new linoleum patterns we just got in from Armstrong. Linoleum's real popular for kitchens and bathrooms these day. Cheaper than tile and comes in a lot of different looks. Bright colors, muted stuff, fancy patterns. Armstrong's got everything. The geometric patterns are my favorite, but if your wife likes—"

"You came all the way over here just to tell me about linoleum?" Fred figured it was okay to interrupt if that was the only way you could get more than half a sentence in at one time.

"Of course not. I ..." Steve stopped and blinked for a minute, apparently trying to remember why he had come by. "I, um ... Oh yeah, I remember. While I was driving by on my way to lunch, I noticed my gear shift was sorta sticking a little, and since I was coming right past here anyhow, I thought I'd stop in and ask you. Do you think I oughta let somebody take a look at it, or is it just getting a little worn down like the rest of us?"

Fred had to work hard not to roll his eyes. All that jabber, just so Steve could get around to asking for free mechanical advice.

I hope Lily's having a better day than I am.

Chapter 51

Lily was late leaving work.

She had to change into clean clothes at the last minute, after another child hurled on her half a minute before her shift was supposed to be up. That made three times today.

Ducking out the door, she dashed to the bus stop in the steamy afternoon air and got there in time to watch her bus turning the corner without her. *For heaven's sake.*

She caught the next one but was still quite late picking up David from kindergarten. He was the only child who hadn't been picked up yet when she reached the school. The teacher looked exasperated and quite done in.

That made two of them.

David had a glum face as he came to meet her, dragging his feet.

"Were you good today?"

"I'm afraid not, Mrs. Overall." The teacher rested her elbow on the desk. "He got into a fight with another little boy and then refused to eat his lunch or speak to anyone the rest of the afternoon."

Oh, lovely. Sounded as if David's day was about as pleasant as hers. She was so tired she didn't even try to ask any further questions, just apologized and went back to the bus station.

The air was thick and steamy. Sweat trickled town her collar as David leaned against her like a little hot-water bottle.

She would have loved to sit down on the bench, but it was taken. A man in a faded tartan shirt and braces, face shadowed by a straw hat, sprawled over most of it.

She cleared her throat, but he did not even look up. *Lazy sod.*

Too exhausted say anything, she stood there waving away a horsefly with David drooping against her side until the bus came.

A few passengers got out, and then she took David's hand and shooed him up the steps in front of her. From the corner of her eye, she saw the straw-hat man get off the bench at last and head toward the bus.

Nose in the air, she went in well ahead of him and looked for a seat. Not many were open.

She had to go more than halfway down the bus aisle before she found one and hustled David in toward the window.

She was just about to sit down herself when someone tried to squeeze behind her and nearly tripped over her leg.

It was the man from the bench. Stumbling, he cursed aloud.

Of all the ill-bred ... And right in front of David too. She spun around. "Watch your tongue, you clot. Can't you see there's children in this bus?"

He turned on her, shoving the hat brim back to meet her gaze with narrowed, bloodshot eyes.

Then she smelled it. *alcohol.*

Fear shot through her like a bullet, spewing cold memories in its wake. Her throat tightened and her whole body went rigid.

The man glared, lip turned up in a snarl as he leaned over, his sour breath almost gagging her. "If you don't like how we talk here, why don't you go back where you came from?"

Heat rose in her cheeks. *How dare he?* She pressed back the icy fear, shoving the memories back into the dark where they belonged. "You should be ashamed of yourself, wandering about drunk in the middle of the afternoon when decent men are hard at work."

He laughed. A harsh, despairing laugh that hissed through his teeth. "Decent men, eh? What do think I was before they fired me? A man's only decent so long's he can make ends meet and keep a roof over his head. Take that away from any man and see how long it takes 'im to quit bein' decent!"

She choked.

A stranger shoved between them. "Knock it off, Pete. Leave the lady alone."

"Outta my way, you—"

"Shut up! I said knock it off." The stranger, who wore a factory uniform and smelled of honest sweat, shoved the drunken Pete toward the back of the bus. "Get out of here."

Pete glowered but stumbled away toward an empty seat.

The stranger tipped his hat to Lily with an apologetic smile. "Sorry about that, ma'am. Pete used to be a good guy. Never touched a drop of liquor in his life. But he kept getting laid off. Couldn't keep up with the bills. It got to him. You know how that can go."

She knew.

He stepped away with a nod, and Lily dropped into her seat, taking her first real breath since she had smelled the alcohol. *Thank God there wasn't a fight.*

David, who seemed unconcerned with the whole exchange, leaned over and put his head in her lap.

"I'm tired, Mum."

She rubbed his shoulder. Were her hands actually shaking? She clenched her fingers in a fist, trying to stop the trembling. "Why didn't you eat your lunch today?"

"'Cause I didn't want it."

"Rubbish. You always want your lunch."

David started kicking the back of the seat in front of him, and a tired-looking woman in a blue hat glanced back, annoyed. Lily put her hand on David's leg to make him stop.

"Sammy was mean to me today."

"Is that who you were fighting with?"

"He laughed at me when I called the french fries chips. He said chips are different. And I said some chips are french fries. And he said no they aren't, and I said they are too. And he said nobody calls them that but me. And I told him you did. And he laughed at me some more and stole one of my chips and said you talked funny. So I punched him."

Oh dear. "David, you don't have to punch people just because they say I talk funny."

"But he took my chip."

"French fry."

He sat up and looked at her in alarm. "Mum, *aren't* french fries chips?"

"Yes. No! I mean ..." Good gracious, she could barely think straight she was so tired and on edge now. "They are chips back home, but not here in Florida."

He wrinkled his forehead, confused.

"Isn't Florida home? Teacher says we live in Florida."

She put her head back against the seat and tried not to moan.

"I meant *my* home, David, where I lived when I was a little girl. Chips are what we called french fries there. But in Florida they call them french fries, and this is *your* home, so that's what you should call them."

David thought about that for a minute.

She stroked the coarse curls back from his forehead. *Goodness.* He felt much too warm. "Are you feeling all right, David?"

He did not answer her, but sat with his little face puckered up in thought. At last he raised his eyes.

"Where's your home, Mum?"

A lump constricted her throat. She swallowed it back and took a deep breath. "David, how about I sing you the teddy bear song?"

He looked at her for a second, and suddenly an almost panicked expression came over his face.

Oh no. She knew that look. "David!"

Too late. He bent double and vomited in her lap.

Chapter 52

Lily sat with her head resting in her arms on the kitchen table and wished she could catch just a few minutes of sleep.

Her shoulders and feet ached, and her eyelids felt hung with weights. But she must not go to sleep. David had thrown up twice on the bus and twice more in the house before he dropped off into a feverish sleep on his little cot behind the curtain walls.

Now she sat listening for him to stir, so tired she had not even touched the cup of tea beside her. If she kept her head down much longer, she was going to drift off whether she meant to or not. Dragging it up, she propped her chin on her hand and stared with weary eyes at the stack of papers lying on the kitchen worktop.

Papers? She blinked. Where had that come from? It looked like envelopes and magazines. Freddie must have stopped for the post yesterday and forgotten to tell her.

Her chair grated across the concrete as she stood to fetch the stack. It would be easier to stay awake if she had something to think about other than sleep.

Plopping back down, she sorted through the post. Bills. Advertisements. A postcard from Fred's uncle in Texas. A notifi-

cation about local elections coming up in November. More
advertisements. More bills. A letter from England ...

England!

She dropped the rest of the envelopes and held up the blue
one. The familiar Lancashire postage mark was pressed over a
stamp with Queen Elizabeth's face on it. Her gaze flew to the
return address. *Joyce.* A letter from Joyce Robinson.

Weariness draining away, Lily slit the envelope with her
thumbnail and unfolded the lined pages.

Dear Lily,

*How are you? I hope you and Fred and your dear little
David are all healthy.*

Lily sighed. It was a nice thought.

*Are you still living with Fred's aunt and uncle? I was
visiting with Ruth the other day, and she said last time
you wrote home, you were talking of a house Fred wanted
to buy. A "bungalow," she called it. Did you buy it? I hope
so. It makes me happy to imagine you in a cozy little place
of your own, with all the comforts of home.*

Lily looked over the top of the paper. Steamy Florida sunshine was pouring in through the roof, painting light beams
through the floating cement dust. No matter how often she
swept, she could never seem to get rid of it. *Cozy?* She dropped
her eyes back to the letter.

*Do you have a garden, I wonder? What sorts of things
grow in Florida? Do they have roses and daffodils? What
about cabbages?*

Do you remember when we were little, we used to follow along behind the greengrocer's wagon when he came along North Clifton, and sometimes he'd give us some bruised apples, or carrots or lettuce maybe? I used to love that.

It's strange to think how close we all used to be then, and how we're scattered all around the world now. Joan in Australia. You over in America.

(Do you know some of the older folks here still call it "the colonies"? I suppose you don't hear that over there.)

Oh! Speaking of old times, can you guess what I saw in the London paper the other day? Paul Holdsworth just got married!

Paul.

Lily's stomach lurched. She lowered the letter to the table and stared out the window for a moment, trying to make sense of her emotions.

Paul was married. How was she supposed to feel about that? *Indifferent, of course.* Why should it make any difference what Paul Holdsworth did? Why should she be surprised if he had found a wife? Why should it matter? *It doesn't.*

She shifted in her chair. Her fingers toyed with the edge of the paper, folding the corner back and forth.

Perhaps she should not read any further right now. Perhaps it would be better to come back later. When David was well, and the roof was fixed, and there were walls instead of sheets, and floors instead of a concrete slab, and curtains hanging in the windows ...

Oh rubbish. She shoved the warning feeling aside and found her place in the paragraph again.

It took him a dreadful long time to find somebody else, didn't it? He married some heiress I never heard of. The wedding was all over the society column. So many flowers it took a whole lorry to carry them, and there were almost as many guests as there are people in Lytham! I believe she spent as much on her dress as I did on my whole wedding.

What a dress that must have been. *And no fabric rationing to work around either.*

Lily curled her foot around the chair leg, toes tightening in her shoes. Everyone had said the flowers at her wedding were beautiful, but they would have looked pitiful next to a whole lorry full of them.

She pursed her lips and kept reading.

They're to honeymoon in Italy and then come back to the new house he just bought. Some monstrous place with five floors and its own indoor swimming pool, as I recall. I can't imagine what they need five floors for when there's only two of them.

And really, why did he have to marry an heiress when he had so much money already? I suppose that's the way of things though. Rich people marry rich people and live in mansions with private swimming pools, and the rest of us get along as well as we can with a two-story flat and a porcelain bathtub.

Or with a metal washtub and a concrete floor.

Lily bit her lip and scuffed the sole of her shoe back and forth against the concrete.

Well anyway, we're all quite well here in Lytham, though I heard your father has been ailing. The water's turned cold and the children are back in school again. Yesterday I went down to Lowther Gardens for a ladies' meeting...

The letter went on, filled with all the old familiar names and places.

It seemed just about everyone Lily had ever known in Lytham was doing splendidly. They all had new jobs, or houses, or husbands, or babies, or had painted their parlour, or bought new curtains, or been awarded a scholarship, or had some distant relative leave them thousands of dollars.

It's a wonder nobody's won the lottery! Lily dug her nail into the edge of the paper and hated herself. She should have been happy for every one of them, but instead she just kept scuffing her shoe harder and harder on the cold cement, while the tense feeling that had started in her stomach when she read Paul's name kept twisting tighter, like a winding spring.

When she reached the end of the letter, she slapped it down on the table and pressed her fist to her mouth.

I should answer it now. While David was sleeping. Otherwise she would have to make time for it another day. She didn't feel like writing, but she had better go on and get it over with. Retrieving paper and a pencil from the cupboard, she marked the date in the top right corner and began.

Dear Joyce,

Yes, we bought the bungalow. But I don't think you'd call it cozy. The roof is not finished so we have to keep the rain out with old army tarps.

She stopped and stared at the sentence. That was not a very happy way to begin a letter. She would have to do better than that. Hmm ...

No, I don't have a garden yet. And I don't think cabbages grow here. Too hot. Mainly people grow oranges. There is also a vegetable called okra. It has a tall woody stem and looks a bit like a hollyhock when it blooms. The part you eat is a green pod, furry on the outside like a peach and full of slimy white seeds. When you slice it, the slime comes out like saliva and gets all over your hands and your knife. I can't understand why Freddie likes it ...

That was not happy either. But her pen scratched on, faster and faster.

I think it is too hot for roses also. Other than the blossoms on all the orange trees, which are everywhere, there are not very many flowers. I don't think Americans like them the way we do. You can't find a flower-seller anywhere. There are florists for weddings and parties, but no lovely carts full of fresh bouquets to take home on your way from the market.

Sometimes I get so hungry for flowers, I go and spend hours at Eola Park, where they have a whole wall covered in sweat peas. One day a man took my picture there, and now they've put the picture on a postcard. Freddie bought me one.

It was becoming harder and harder to breathe past the lump in her throat. She tried to swallow it.

But the sweet peas are not always blooming. And the summers are so hot that almost nothing blooms then. There is almost no place to get cool. No one has cellars here because they would fill up with water. But at least it would be cool water! I don't know what they did about air-raid shelters. I should ask Freddie if they filled with water too.

As for daffodils...

Her pencil stopped dead on the page. She sat there, staring at the scribbles sprawling across the paper in one line after another, and trying again to swallow the lump in her throat.

As for daffodils...

Her breath caught, and the words blurred before her eyes. She blinked, trying to clear her vision, but the tears spilled over and ran, hot and wet, down her cheeks. The pencil slipped from her fingers.

"Mum!" David's voice. "I'm thirsty!"

Wiping her face with the back of her hand, she sucked in a shaking breath.

"Yes, love. I'm...coming."

As she shoved her chair back from the table, the half-finished letter fluttered to the floor. She picked it up, holding it to the light streaming in through the open kitchen window, and it quivered in her fingers.

As for daffodils...

Choking, she crumpled the page in her fist and hurled it against the wall.

Ow!

Fred dropped the hammer and grabbed his thumb. Under the nail, skin throbbed like somebody was still pounding on it.

He squeezed with his other hand, waiting for the sharp edge of pain to dull down into an ache.

His fingers were slimy with sweat. The air hung hot and heavy, like a steamy wet blanket over his shoulders.

Shouldn't be this hot in September. Not even in Florida. He wiped his forehead on his sleeve and reached for the hammer again.

"Freddie!" Lily's voice echoed up from somewhere below.

He stopped mid-swing, heart jumping.

"Yes, sweetheart?"

He'd hardly gotten a word out of her all evening. Maybe she was ready to talk—

"Don't forget to put the tarps down when you come to bed. It smells like rain."

Oh. He tried to keep the disappointment out of his voice. "Are you going to bed now? Want me to stop hammering?"

"No."

"Am I keeping David up?"

"No."

"Do you need anything?"

"No." Her footsteps retreated into the living room.

Good grief. He smacked the nail so hard, it drove the head straight to the wood with one stroke. Getting home early from work hadn't done a lick of good, far as he could tell. Lily was still barricaded behind an icy wall. The longest sentence she had spoken all evening was when he walked in the door and found her drooped like a dishrag in the easy chair, eyes half-shut.

"David threw up five times today."

That was all she had said.

He had tried to start conversations several times. When he'd begun to tell her about the letter from England, she'd cut him off with a bland, "I know."

Then he asked what Joyce had said in the letter, but she barely replied. They ate warmed-up leftovers like a couple of strangers, staring at their plates. *How am I supposed to know what's the matter if she won't speak to me?*

Reaching for another nail, he pounded it into place, thumping blows echoing up as the sunset glimmered through the pines, peeping around the trunks and branches in golden starbursts. But he didn't have much energy to enjoy it.

Why do women have to be so complicated? The best he could figure, she must be frustrated about the state the house was in. So he'd done the only thing he could think of—grabbed his tools and gone up to the roof, same as last night.

He was almost out of plywood though. He'd have to take some money out of the savings box and buy more tomorrow.

At least the roof was something he actually knew how to fix, unlike the gaping chasm that had opened up between him and his wife.

Wham! This time it was his finger.

He dropped the hammer again, and it must have hit a slick spot. Before he could grab it, it skidded out of reach, slid down the roof, and disappeared over the edge, hitting the ground with a dull thud.

Good grief.

Turning his back to the roof, he leaned against it and looked up at the sky. In the dusky gray patch on the eastern horizon, the first faint stars were beginning to glow, but most everything else was hidden behind fast-gathering clouds.

He rested his arm on his knee, finger and thumb rubbing back and forth.

What do I do, Lord? I just want her to be happy. But how can I fix it if she won't tell me what's wrong?

A whip-poor-will called and called in the stillness, searching for his mate. Fred leaned his head against his arm and sat there, listening for another bird to call back.

But only the frogs and the crickets answered.

Chapter 53

It was cold. Bitterly cold.

The wind rasped like a demon in the silence, whipping Lily's dress against her legs as she stood, frozen, watching the doorway.

He came in out of the darkness. A shadowy figure with hunched shoulders and an unsteady walk. Stumbling, he lurched toward her, hat pulled low against the storm.

Lily's hands shook, clenched inside the folds of her skirt. Her heart pounded against her ribcage as if it was trying to escape. The snow came whistling in through the open door, splattering cold and wet against her face, and the darkness seemed to be seeping out of the corners, swallowing everything around her

"Run!" The voice hissed in her ear.

Like a coward, she bolted, ducking under the man's arm and racing for the door. Someone cried out, and she turned on the doorstep. A child lay sobbing on the floor, hands over its face. But this time it was not Frances.

It was David.

The hair stood up on the back of her neck, and a terror fiercer than any before rose up inside her, freezing the blood in her veins.

The panicked shriek brought Fred bolt upright in bed.

She raised her eyes. The shadowy figure had lurched around and came looming toward her, pushing back his hat so that she looked straight into his bloodshot eyes. It was not Father this time.

Her heart stopped beating, and the shadows closed in around her. It was ...it was ...

"Freddie!"

The panicked shriek brought Fred bolt upright in bed. "Lily?"

A flash of lightning showed her lying rigid beside him, eyes wide open, fixed on empty space.

What on earth? The room plunged into darkness again, and he groped for the flashlight he kept under the edge of the mattress, fingers tangling in the sheets.

What the heck was going on? What time was it? And why did he feel so wet?

Good grief.

It was raining. And he'd forgotten to put the tarps down. Raindrops splatted against his hair and seeped through his nightshirt in the blackness.

His fingers gripped the smooth flashlight handle and he yanked it out, fumbling for the switch.

"Lily! Wake up."

The light snapped on.

Rain. Thunder. A torch beam stabbing the darkness.

Lily stumbled into consciousness, stomach still convulsing with fear. Raindrops splashed, cold and wet, against her face. Someone was calling her name.

"Wake up, Lily!" A hand shook her shoulder.

Freddie.

She snapped upright. Rain poured down through the open roof, soaking her nightgown, pattering against her pillow. The light from the torch bounced about as Freddie clambered out of bed.

"Come on! We've got to move the mattress before it's soaked!" He dragged the blanket off after him.

Her breath still came in frightened gasps as she scrambled up, grabbing both pillows and tripping over her own feet as she ran for the parlour, almost colliding with a stud on the way, and tossed them into the easy chair. Back in the bedroom, she gripped one side of the mattress while Freddie got the other. Her fingers felt slow and clumsy and her body still half asleep as she tugged the unwieldy thing up on edge and dragged while Freddie pushed, hauling it across the cement.

"Mum! Mum!" David's voice was panicked.

"Just a minute, love! Just a minute!"

They didn't even bother with the doorway, just bumped the mattress over a two-by-four and between two studs into the parlour. It fell flat on the cement again with a breathy thump, safely out of the rain. Without a word, Freddie turned and ran for the ladder, the torch beam tossing like a mad thing.

Lily groped her way through the darkness to David's bedside. He was only half-awake, safe and dry in his half of the house. She smoothed the hair back from his feverish forehead and murmured soothing words, stroking his head and holding his hand until he dropped back to sleep. By the time she pushed through the curtains and stumbled back to the parlour, Freddie was coming in from strapping down the tarps.

She dropped onto the damp mattress and locked her arms around her knees, shivering from head to foot. Her wet nightgown was plastered to her chest, and water trickled down her neck, dripping out of her hair.

But it was not the cold that made her tremble.

"I t-told you to put the tarps down!" Her voice chattered between her teeth.

He went to the linen chest and pulled out the eiderdown, which they'd packed away as soon as they got something lighter. "Here, sweetheart. You're shivering."

She almost shied away from his hands as he wrapped it around her, but in the dark he didn't notice. Her fingers clutched the soft edge of the comforter, squeezing so hard her knuckles hurt. "How could you forget, after I reminded you?"

"I'm sorry."

"When are you going to finish that roof?" Her voice came out sharp.

He laid the flashlight on the mattress and began unbuttoning his pajama shirt. "Soon." His tone was steady and calm. "It's been heavy work at the garage lately. Randy's laid off a couple of guys this summer. There wasn't enough work for them. But now there's too much for the rest of us."

Laid off. Her tongue felt dry in her mouth. "Is he going to lay anyone else off?"

He peeled off his wet shirt. "I doubt it. Unless the work slacks off over the winter maybe."

Her heartbeat was still unsteady. "Freddie." She pressed her chin into the eiderdown.

"When was the last time you drank?"

He stopped, his shirt dripping in his hand as he turned toward her. "What?"

"Alcohol." Her breath shivered in her lungs. "When was ... when was the last time you had some?"

He stood there staring at her, bare chest glistening wet in the dull glow of the torch. "Lily, you know I don't drink."

"But haven't you ever tasted it?"

"No."

"Not even when you were younger?"

"Not once."

Never touched a drop of liquor in his life ... The words of the stranger on the bus echoed in her mind.

She turned her head away, pulling the eiderdown tighter around her shoulders and staring into the darkness. With the rain still pelting the roof, she couldn't hear Freddie's movements, but when the mattresses shifted, she glanced out of the corner of her eye and saw him lower himself onto the bed, still wearing his wet pajama trousers.

"What's wrong, Lily?"

Ha. There was a question. Everything was so muddled up inside that she hardly knew anymore. "I ... I had a nightmare."

"The one about your father?"

Her chin snapped up and she blinked at him. *How did he know about* ...

"Sometimes you talk in your sleep." He leaned his elbows on his knees. "Was it that one?"

"No. Yes. I mean ..." A shiver ran through her beneath the eiderdown. "It was different."

"He did something to Frances when you were children, didn't he?"

How much do I say in my sleep? She squeezed her eyes shut, biting her lip. "He came home drunk when Mum was out. Frances told me to run and I ..." *Was a coward.*

"You were younger than she was, Lily. Of course you ran."

"I shouldn't have left her! He ..." The words broke off on her tongue. Her fingers clenched the eiderdown, and her voice almost failed her. She forced it out, but it was a trembling whisper. "Mum had to take her to the hospital."

Freddie put his hands on her shoulders. "Listen to me. None of that was your fault. There was nothing you could have done to stop it. Nothing."

She turned her face away.

"Lily." His fingers tightened. "You've got to quit thinking you're responsible to protect everybody from everything. It's too big for you. Not everyone's like your father. I'm not. Robert's not. There are millions of good, kind people in the world."

Pete on the bus rose up in her mind. Bloodshot eyes. Snarling lips. *He used to be a good guy*, the stranger had said. *It got to him.*

She pulled away, shoving her fingers into her hair as she pressed her forehead against her palm, everything crashing in on her at once.

Her voice came out in a helpless gasp. "Paul got married."

Freddie broke off into startled silence. In a lull between gusts of rain, the clock ticked loud. "Paul?" He spoke again, voice confused as he seemed to be groping for the connection. "Was...he in the dream too?"

"No. Joyce wrote me. They went to Italy for their honeymoon."

"He married Joyce?"

"No!" The spring was winding tighter and tighter inside her. "He married an heiress."

Freddie stared at her, obviously floundering. "An heiress?"

"They have an indoor swimming pool!"

"They do?"

"Yes!" Her voice was rising and stretching tight, holding back the half-hysterical tears. "And marble floors and silver plates and...and...and probably a whole yard full of daffodils!"

"Daffodils." Freddie snatched at the word, as if he had at last grasped some idea what she was talking about. "Is that what's got you so upset the past couple days? I'm sorry. I've been so busy with work and the house, I didn't think. You want me to build you a flowerbed tomorrow?"

"*No!*" The spring snapped. Tears burst through, tumbling down her cheeks, and a chest-wrenching sob nearly choked her. "I don't want a flowerbed! I don't want anything here in Florida! I want...I want to go *home!*"

In the dim torchlight, Freddie exhaled, sharp and loud, as if a board had struck him in the chest.

She buried her face in her arms.

For several moments, the room fell silent.

She was afraid to look up. The tears kept coming, dampening the eiderdown against her cheeks, and her breath came in shuddering gasps.

"Home." Freddie spoke at last. His voice was heavy, as if a great weight had settled onto his shoulders. "You mean ... England."

Of course I mean England. She kept sobbing. *But what does it matter?*

It was not as if they kept enough money for a ship's passage stashed away for a rainy day. Here she sat, making a fool of herself, blubbering like a baby because she could not run home to Mother when the roof leaked. And what difference did it make?

None.

None except to prove she did not deserve to call England home anyway.

The English didn't know how to quit. But she knew how. She wanted to. She just had too little money to do it!

Freddie still hadn't spoken. She turned her face toward him, but he wasn't looking at her. He was staring down at his hands, shoulders limp.

"Freddie, I—"

"All right, Lily." He raised his head, and even in the half-light she could see the shadow in his eyes. "If that's what will make you happy."

Chapter 54

Fred stood in the white-arched entrance to the platform, Lily's travel case in his hand.

The trunks were long since loaded on the baggage car, and the last of the passengers were mounting the steps onto the train. A puff of steam hissed behind Lily as she stood looking up at him. Her blue plaid travel dress fluttered around her legs in the breeze, and a few wayward tendrils of hair had come loose from their pins, whipping against her cheeks.

"Well,"—she looked over her shoulder at the train—"I'd better board, before they leave without me."

If only they would. He took a deep breath. "Are you sure you'll be all right getting on the ship in New York by yourself?"

She nodded. "David will help me, won't you love?" She looked down and patted David's shoulder. "Say goodbye to Dad."

David's lip trembled. "I don't wanna. Why can't he come?"

"I told you already. Now say goodbye."

David sniffled. "Bye, Dad."

"Goodbye." Fred grabbed David up in a bear hug, memorizing the feel of the little arms around his neck, the coarse hair against his cheek.

How long until I hold him again?

Lily said she was going for six months, but there was something frightening about the way she said it. It sounded pat and rehearsed, like she was reading a script. And there was a darkness behind her eyes that scared him. It was like she had shut a door and he couldn't see inside anymore.

He lowered David back to the ground beside her.

"Goodbye, Freddie." Her voice was emotionless. She held out her hand for her bag.

He let her take it, but before she could step back again he slipped his arm around her waist and drew her toward him.

She went stiff. "I should go. The conductor's coming."

He clenched his jaw. It felt like a weight was crushing his chest. "Can't I kiss you goodbye?" It wasn't as if anyone would be scandalized. "People always kiss at railway stations."

She stared at him, and something flashed across her face. Her back gave a faint shudder against his hand.

"Lily, I—"

She pulled free, brushing his arm off, and turned away from him.

"All abo-OOOARD!" The conductor called out his singsong warning.

Shoulders rigid, Lily took David's hand and hurried toward the train without looking back.

They were starting up the steps to the car when David dug his heels in, broke free, and came running back, hurling himself against Fred and clinging like a bur.

"I don't wanna go to England! I don't wanna go to England!" He buried his face in the bottom of Fred's jacket. "I wanna stay here with you!"

The conductor was coming along the train, making sure everyone had boarded.

Heart strangling inside him, Fred pried the little arms loose and dropped down on one knee, holding David by the shoulders.

"You can't stay here, David. You know that. Dad has to stay and keep working so you'll have a house to come back too. And you have to go to England and take care of Mum."

"I don't wanna!"

Fred clenched his jaw. "Sometimes we both have to do things we don't want to."

A tear spilled over and trickled down David's cheek. "Why?"

Fred felt his own eyes going moist. He took a deep breath and fought to keep his voice from cracking.

"It's part of being a man, son."

And part of loving a woman.

He picked David up and carried him to the train.

Lily waited on the step, lips pressed together so hard they were only a pale line above her chin. Without saying a word, she took David's hand and disappeared into the railway car.

Fred stepped back far enough to see the row of windows and started scanning them. Strangers looked out at him or bent their heads over newspapers and books. He kept scanning, up and down, up and down. Surely Lily would choose a seat on this side of the train, if only for David's sake.

The conductor had disappeared, and the wheels were beginning to role when he spotted the hands waving from a window several cars away.

He ran up the track until he reached them. The two familiar faces peered out as the train started chugging. David was crying. Lily was pale and still as a marble statue.

Fred bit his lip and choked down the lump in his throat, raising his hand to wave back. The train began to pick up speed. He followed the car, first walking, then breaking into a run to keep up, until he reached the edge of the platform. Coming to a standstill, he watched the cars chugging away down the track, waving and waving until he could no longer make out the window.

Then he stood there on the edge of the platform, with the breeze flapping the corners of his jacket, and gave up fighting the tears.

Lily sat on the train's bench seat with David nestled up against her, and watched the countryside flash by outside. The car was filled with people going back to New York, or some other Northern city, after a Florida vacation. There would be many more come wintertime. This was only the beginning of the season.

The sunshine glowed through the window, warming her lap and washing the world outside in brightness. A green sea of orange trees stretched out in all directions, leaves shimmering in the sunshine.

Oranges. She would not be here to see the flower buds forming this year. Or to sniff the breeze when the trees burst into white canopies of blossoms and filled the air with perfume. They had a magical scent, orange blossoms.

Something that hinted of roses and honeysuckles, and yet was altogether its own.

There were no orange groves in England.

David shifted, still sniffling into her sleeve. "Mum?"

"Yes, love?"

"How long till we come back home?"

Home.

She leaned her forehead against the window and closed her eyes. In her mind's eye she could see the white windmill standing on the Green, keeping watch over the sea. The church steeples poking up at the sky above the roofs. The brick streets sandwiched between shops and rows of houses. The familiar alleyways. The tree-lined wanderings of Green Drive. Lowther

Pavilion lit up in the evening. Faces looking out windows as she came down North Clifton. Neighbour's faces, smiling and welcoming her back.

But all the pictures were hazy.

No matter how hard she tried to hold onto them, they kept slipping from view. Blurring like stained glass and fading into the background.

While clear and plain, rising before them all, was the picture of a solitary man on the edge of a railway platform, arm raised in silhouette against the white arches of the station...

Watching them out of sight.

Chapter 55

The house was dead quiet when Fred came home. Even the mild thump of the car door shutting sounded like a gunshot in the silence. Every footstep crunched loud on the gravel as he walked up to the porch.

The yard looked lonely. No dark-haired little boy came running around the corner of the house, trailing sticks and moss. No white uniforms hung bleaching on the line. No tempting scent of supper came wafting from the kitchen window.

He wiped his feet on the doormat. *Why?* It didn't matter anymore, now that Lily wasn't here to worry about the floor. He could track dirt all over the house if he wanted, and nobody would care.

But he wiped his feet anyway.

Leaving the door ajar for the evening breeze, he stepped inside. The concrete floor was cold and barren, with no quick feminine steps coming to meet him. His own footfalls echoed in the silence. He stood there a while in the front room, looking around at the emptiness. Stud walls drew shadowy stripes across the floor. The sun was dropping in the west, and through the hole in the roof he could see the sky stained orange and gold.

He stared at it for a minute, and then he went into the kitchen and pulled down the cracked teapot from the top shelf, dumping the contents onto the table. A few crumpled bills and some loose change spilled out into a pile.

One, two, three, four. Four-fifty, four-sixty, four-seventy, four-seventy-five ...

Four dollars and seventy-seven cents. All that was left of his construction fund. He'd been saving up to surprise Lily next time he went for roofing supplies, looking forward to the excitement on her face when he came home with the linoleum and sheetrock too. But then there had been tickets, and ship's passages, and enough cash sent along to get them both back home to Florida at some point.

If they ever do come home.

Sighing, he swept the money back into the teapot and put it away. Even his breathing sounded loud in the still house.

He knew he should be starting something for supper about now, but somehow he wasn't hungry.

He left the kitchen and went out to the porch instead.

The sun was brushing the tops of the pine trees. He sat on the porch steps and watched it inch its way lower, sinking into a golden puddle of sunset and sending crimson rays glimmering through the trees. And then he sat some more while the sky turned from lavender to dusky blue, and then the stars began to poke glimmering holes in the black canopy.

At last he went in, to the bedroom, and stood looking down at the lonely mattress lying there on the floor.

"Dear God." He whispered the words, alone in darkness. "When I told you I'd do anything to make her happy, I never thought it would be this."

He had been alone almost a week when the telegram came.

It was past suppertime, but he was just getting home. He'd been staying at work late a lot, since Lily and David left.

What was the point of coming home to an empty house and sitting around staring at all the things he didn't have any money to fix? Might as well be at the shop, doing something.

He was climbing the porch steps when he heard a bicycle grating on the gravel and turned around. The boy riding it was redheaded and splattered with freckles.

He had a bag over his shoulder, and he came pumping the pedals and splaying loose gravel in all directions like the world depended on him delivering telegrams.

Fred watched him. A nervous feeling twisted in his gut. Nobody he knew sent telegrams when a letter would do just as well. They were too expensive. Unless ...

What's the matter with you, Fred? Do you have to start worrying just because Lily isn't here to do it?

The kid probably just wanted directions.

Reaching the porch steps, the boy slammed his bike to a stop so hard that Fred expected him to go pitching right over the handlebars. But he didn't. Instead he jumped off and looked up at Fred with a confident grin. He was missing a front tooth. "Evenin', sir. You Fred Overall?"

"Yes."

"Telegram for you."

The nervous feeling rose again. "Where's it from?"

"England."

His heart started to pound. It was too soon for Lily to be in England. What reason would her family have to send a telegram to him? *Unless something is wrong.* His tongue went dry as leather in his mouth.

The ship. Lily and David. They were somewhere in the Atlantic between New York and Southampton. There were storms in the Atlantic this time of year.

He took the telegram and stood there on the porch, staring at it, while the boy got back on his bicycle and peddled away down the driveway. He heard the wheels turn onto the road, and then the whizz of the chain grew faint in the distance.

Still he stood there, staring at the Western Union envelope.

Dear God, please. Hands shaking, he slit the paper with his thumbnail and pulled out the telegram. It lay in his palm upside down. The message was written on the other side. *Please, please, please.* Taking a deep breath, he flipped over the paper.

His eyes absorbed the words in less than a second, and his breath came out in a rush as he lowered himself to the porch step, knees wobbly with relief. It was not about Lily. Or David. *Thank you, Lord!*

But it was not happy news either.

The evening shadows crept across the yard as he sat there, looking down at the sharp black letters. "Oh, my Lily."

He breathed her name into the stillness. "I wish somebody could have warned you."

Chapter 56

The world was shrouded in grey when Lily arrived in Southampton. Iron-coloured clouds rolled slow and heavy above them. Like a defeated army trudging across the sky.

Dark buildings loomed behind shifting curtains of fog, and a cold drizzle spit raindrops in her face as she stood at the ship's railing with David, watching the sailors lower the gangplank. She had forgotten how dreary England could look in October.

It seemed to take ages before the luggage was unloaded and ready for a cab. The cold sea breeze stung her cheeks and slapped raindrops down her collar. David huddled against her, trying to hide from the wind as he whimpered about how cold it was. By the time she had him bundled into the cab, he was almost in tears. It seemed as if he had done nothing but cry since they left Florida.

While their luggage was loaded into the boot, she tried to distract him by pointing out the window and helping him sound out the name of their ship, painted in bold black letters on the bow. The *U.S.S. United States*.

It rode at anchor, smoke stacks jutting up against the fog. Faintly they could see the sailors moving about on deck, tiny specks in the mist.

"How long till we go home, Mum?"

There he went again. He had asked the same question every night since they got on the train in Orlando. And still she had never really answered him.

"Aren't you excited to see your Nana, David?"

He puckered his forehead. "Is she nice?"

"Well, of course she is! Don't you remember? She's perfectly jolly. Like...well, like a female Father Christmas. And she loves to make biscuits...I mean cookies. And she's wiser than anybody I ever knew."

"Except Dad." It was not a question.

David was certain Freddie knew everything there was to know in the world. He wiggled over to the window and peered out a moment, then dropped back and looked at her again. "Is my grandfather jolly too?"

Her smile froze on her lips. *Father.* She stared at her hands in her lap as a coldness settled over her. Her toes curled inside her shoes.

David thumped his feet against the footboard, impatient. "Is he like Father Christmas, Mum?"

Her lips tightened.

She shut her eyes, and was back in the parlour.

Cold wind whistling through the open doorway. Snowflakes blowing onto the rug.

Father lurched unsteadily as he stumbled across the room, dragging the freshly decorated tree behind him. Cotton-wool balls tumbled off onto the floor as he hurled the tree out into the darkness and then slammed the door before they could even see it crash into the snowbank —

"Mum!"

Her eyes snapped open.

David looked at her, exasperated. "Is he like Father Christmas, Mum?"

She turned her face to the window and sighed. "No, David. Not quite."

The driver climbed into the front seat and started the engine. Lily stared out the back window as they sped off toward the train station, watching the *U.S.S. United States* fade away into the mist.

. . . .

It was grey and dreary all the way up from Southampton. The train sliced through fog like a knife through pudding, carrying them past countryside that was all but invisible.

Nothing but a bleary shadow marked the buildings as they passed.

Suppertime had long passed when the train reached Lytham station, wheels squealing in the quiet night air as they ground to a halt. Lily stood up, collecting her travel bag and catching a firm hold of David's hand. With one good deep breath, she stepped over the gap onto the platform.

The engine hissed, and a cloud of steam melted into the fog that still draped everything in sight. A few people stood on the platform, boarding the train or coming to meet the passengers. But though she looked up and down in both directions, there was no sign of Mother.

For a few moments she was too distracted to worry about it, as she was busy making certain all their luggage was unloaded and placed together in a pile. When that was finished though, and the train was preparing to churn away into the darkness, she stood beside the luggage feeling somehow lost in the one place in the world she ought to be most at home.

What could have happened to delay them? She had sent a telegram before she boarded the ship, announcing her scheduled arrival and which train she planned to take. Why on earth would Mother not come to meet her? And if no one came, what was she to do about the luggage?

A few raindrops pattered down from a sky that was nothing but darkness. Grabbing one bag after another, she dragged them under the overhang and looked around, trying to think what to do. David dropped onto one of the suitcases and curled up, looking as if he would soon be asleep right there on the platform. It was then she realized how bone-tired she was. So tired that she was almost tempted to join him and worry about everything else after they'd had a nice kip. But proper ladies did not takes naps on top of suitcases on empty railway platforms.

She cast one more glance up and down, searching for Mother's familiar round figure, but didn't see it. She was on the verge of going into the station and asking to use the telephone so she could ring a cab, when footsteps echoed on the platform and a willowy, dark-haired young woman came hurrying toward her out of the fog.

Lily blinked at her a moment. *Could that possibly be ...*

"Welcome home, Lily!"

"Ruthie! You're all grown up."

Lily remembered a baby-faced eighteen-year-old, still a little plump, who had not quite grown out of bringing home flowers and puppies and swiping sugar cubes on occasion. Now here came this lovely young woman with high cheekbones and wide dark eyes, hair swept back into a sophisticated twist, and a belt nipping her coat in to a waist that had to be the envy of half her friends.

No wonder it took a moment to recognize her own sister.

"I'm sorry I'm so late." Ruth hugged her. "There was a mix-up about who was supposed to come and get you, and then the hos ..." She broke off, looking flustered, and glanced down at David. "Goodness! Look at this boy. And you think *I've* grown?"

Lily wondered what Ruth had been about to say, but she was too sleepy to pry at the moment. "David, say hello to your Auntie Ruth."

David didn't stir. He was fast asleep, curled up on the suitcase.

"Poor little dear. He must be done in." Ruth bent over and stroked David's cheek. "Doug should be here any minute. And then as soon as we can, we'll get you both home where you can rest. I'm sure you must be tired too, coming all the way from Southampton right after stepping off the ship. Alice promised to have some hot tea waiting when we got there."

Even in Lily's tired brain, something about that sounded wrong. If Mother had not come to meet her at the station, then surely she ought to be the one home making tea? Not Alice.

"Ruth." She waited for Ruth to straighten up and meet her gaze. "Where's Mother?"

Something flickered in Ruth's face. "Mother? Oh. Well, she wanted to come meet you at the station, but she couldn't get away."

"Away from what?"

Ruth's eyes searched about as if looking for the answer on the platform somewhere. "She had a...an appointment. She couldn't break it."

An uncomfortable feeling rose in Lily's stomach. Ruth's face was blank. Much too blank for comfort.

"Ruth." She looked her sister in the eye. "You're a terrible liar. Where is Mother?"

Ruth squirmed under her stare. "I'm not lying. Mother *did* have an appointment."

"What was it?"

Ruth avoided her gaze and looked toward the road. "I can't imagine what's taking Doug so long."

"*Ruth!*" Now Lily had panic rising in her chest. "What's going on? Is something the matter with Mother? Tell me!"

Staring at her shoes, Ruth shifted and bit her lip. "You weren't supposed to know yet. They wanted you to get settled first before someone broke the news."

News? Lily's heart thundered against her ribs and her knees felt wobbly. "What news?" She had a feeling she needed something to hold onto. "Ruth, answer me! Where is *Mother?*"

Ruth's shoulders slumped. "I knew they should have sent somebody else. I'm no good at keeping secrets. She's at the hospital."

"The hospital!" Lily's heart stopped beating all together. "What's the matter with her?"

Ruth sat down on a suitcase. "Nothing. But she won't leave Father."

"Father?"

"Yes." Ruth stared at her hands for a moment, twisting her fingers together. Then she raised her head. "That's what I wasn't supposed to tell. We didn't want to shock you on your first day here. Lily,"—she bit her lip—"we think Father is dying."

Chapter 57

The wall clock punctured the silence, ticking away the minutes.

Lily sat still on one of the waiting-room chairs and stared at her hands while she listened to the hushed rustlings of the hospital.

How many years ago was it that she had sat here waiting to go in to see Frances?

She had been a little girl then, perched on the edge of the seat, her feet not even reaching the floor. The room had seemed bigger. Colder. And the nurses were like strange white ghosts, whispering up and down the halls.

But that was a long time ago. *Why am I more frightened now than I even was then?*

She shifted in her seat and looked toward the doorway. Any minute a nurse would come and tell her she could go in. She squeezed her hands together and stared at the clock. It wasn't as if she had never seen someone dying before. She was a nurse. She saw it all the time.

But before it had always been a stranger. Someone she cared about only as a patient. Someone she had never...

Loved? The word hung in her mind. An unanswered question, fluttering in the darkness.

Did she love Father?

That was what she had been asking herself, ever since that moment when she stood on the station platform playing Ruth's words over and over in her mind like a broken record. Trying to make sense of them. Trying to understand the cold stillness that was all she seemed to feel. *Father is dying.*

Across the room, a woman's knitting needles clicked in the stillness. Lily's eyes followed the yarn unwinding from the ball. But she was not really seeing it.

What's the matter with you, Lily? Haven't you got any heart at all? Her father was lying on his deathbed.

Should she not feel something sharper? Something deeper? She closed her eyes, searching for something.

A memory. Something happy, long ago, that she had tucked away even deeper than the dark memories. But it would not come.

"Lily?"

Her eyes snapped open, breath exhaling in a rush.

A nurse stood in the doorway. "Your mother says you may come in now."

Lily rose to her feet, heart beating a slow rhythm within her chest, and followed the nurse into the hall. The memories were coming now, but not the one she wanted. It was as the others. The cold, shadowy ones that had been rolling around inside her head for two days now.

And the icy black thing she had shoved down so deep all those years ago had come out with them.

She bit her lip as she turned a corner and spotted the room number up ahead. It made her sick, the way the blackness welled up inside her at the thought of seeing him.

How could she hate a man who was lying in a hospital bed, dying? Yet she hated. And the closer she got to the room, the more she could feel it, spilling over, seeping everywhere, until she could almost taste it, bitter as poison, on her tongue.

Was there any love left? Anywhere? Could you love someone and hate them both at once? Could you?

The nurse opened the door.

Fred woke in the drowsy darkness, long before dawn, and reached across the bed for Lily.

His hand found empty mattress.

He stretched further, feeling nothing but the cool autumn air, until his fingers brushed the far edge of the blanket.

And then he remembered.

Dropping back onto his pillow, he rubbed a palm over his face, shoving his fingers into his hair to smooth it back from his forehead. *What time is it?* He groped for his flashlight, switched it on, and checked his watch.

Four-thirty in the morning.

That would mean—he counted five hours—it was already nine thirty in England. Lily was probably drinking a cup of tea in the little kitchen on Clifton Street.

Or maybe she was visiting Christopher in the hospital. Either way, her day had long since started.

He stretched one hand back across the mattress and let it lie there, trying to imagine the warm softness of her skin beneath his fingers, the gentle motion as she breathed. But there was only the mattress, cold and lifeless.

Flipping over onto his back, he shone the flashlight up at the roof. He hadn't touched the hole since Lily left. There was still some tar-paper and nails left over, but he hadn't used them. What was the point anymore?

He turned his head. In the dim glow from the flashlight, he could see the empty place on the mattress.

Rubbing his hand over his face again, he sighed.

Then again, what was the point of lying in bed alone, wishing for morning?

He kicked back the covers and reached for his toolbelt.

"Lily."

Father's voice was so weak that Lily almost didn't recognize it. His face was pale, even against the hospital sheets. *Like Frances's was.* The grey frost at his temples had spread to the rest of his hair since she saw him last, and his left hand, lying on the blanket, was thin and limp.

She pushed the door shut behind her and stood there, lacing her fingers together. Words were hard to get hold of. She had to concentrate, stumbling over the memories, pushing past the blackness, in order to force a greeting to her lips.

"Hello, Father." Her own voice felt stale and hollow in her mouth. She hoped nobody could hear the bitterness she was trying to muffle behind it.

Mother sat in a chair on the far side of the bed, holding Father's right hand.

She smiled at Lily. Not the quiet smile you expected to see at a deathbed, but a bright smile, reaching all the way to her eyes and crinkling up the corners of her face. Lily could return only a thin shadow of it.

Father spoke again. "I'm glad you're here. Your mother says you were already on your way before they even had a chance to tell you."

Mother nodded. "Perfect timing. The Lord works in mysterious ways."

"Yes," Lily said.

"Yes," Father repeated.

How strange to hear him agree to that. Usually when Mother mentioned God, he went silent. Or changed the subject.

His eyes were fixed on Lily. It made her nervous, having him stare at her like that. What if he could see the cold blackness she was trying to hide inside? What if it was written in her eyes? She looked at the floor.

"You're very angry with me, aren't you?" His voice was barely above a whisper.

Her head snapped up. *So he can see it.* But was that truly a surprise? If she could taste the bitterness on her tongue, was it any wonder it showed on her face? What did surprise her was that he would say anything about it.

She pressed her palms together and swallowed, at a loss for how to answer. There was something in his eyes that confused her. She could not quite put her finger on what it was, yet she felt that she ought to recognize it somehow.

"You don't have to pretend, Lily."

His gaze remained fixed on her face. "I'd be surprised if you weren't angry."

She stared at him.

"I have not been...the kind of father I should have." His eyes began to look damp.

Lily wished she could grab hold of something. The world felt shaky. What was that Frances had said before Lily came? *Father has changed a bit, Lily.* She had seen the grey hair and the pale, sickly face and thought she knew what her sister was talking about.

But now she wasn't so sure. Her tongue moved in her mouth, but her jaw stayed shut. A simple greeting had been hard enough to dredge up at the beginning.

Now the blackness was whirling like a storm inside her, tying her stomach in knots and twisting her thoughts until she hardly knew which way was up.

Her hand groped for the wall behind her.

"I told your mother and the girls already. And I'll tell Robert when he gets here." Father's voice seemed to be catching in his throat. "I am *so sorry*." He dropped his eyes for a moment, and the muscles in his jaw worked as he continued.

"You were right to hit me with a shoe that night. It was the only thing that would have stopped me. I wish you had done it earlier. Maybe it would have changed a lot of things."

Lily's world was tilting. Her heart seemed to be running up and down her ribs like a staircase, and her pulse throbbed in her ears.

No one had prepared her for anything like this. The blackness swelled and throbbed, and the memories whirled. Chaotic. Blinding. She felt for the wall again, and her hand brushed the doorknob.

Father raised his head and looked at her. The faintly familiar something in his eyes grew stronger. "I don't have any right to ask this, Lily. But"—he took a breath, and a tear trembled in the corner of his eye—"could you possibly...forgive me?"

Forgive him? Something shattered insider her. Lily felt the impact run through her body like a shockwave. Her knees went weak. She was lost in a whirling storm of emotion.

Forgive him?

She fell back a step. Dizzy, choking. Her hand groped and found the doorknob.

Forgive ...Father?

Gasping for air, she wrenched the door open and fled.

Chapter 58

Fred's hand froze mid-swing.

He stood there, one foot on the ladder, one knee on the roof, his fingers still on the nail, and tried to make sense of the feeling that had just slammed into his gut.

Something is wrong.

But what? The feeling was hard to pinpoint. It was as if a cold shadow had dropped over him out of nowhere.

He lowered his arm. *Lily.*

He knew it, somehow. Just as he had that morning before he met her on the cold, foggy road, and saw Paul's necklace glittering at her throat.

Something was wrong with Lily.

What is it, Lord? What is it? He stood still, there in the darkness, with his headlamp glaring at a patch of shingles, wondering. And then his hand slid away from the nail.

Did he really have to know? After all, there was only one thing he could do about it, no matter what it was.

Crouching there on the roof, he dropped his head into his arms and prayed.

Lily was in the lavatory when Mother found her.

She knew it was Mother, without looking around from where she leaned against the wall, pressing her forehead onto the cool tiles. They were probably covered in bacteria, but right now she didn't care.

"Lily?" The familiar hand touched her shoulder.

She gulped for air, her whole body shaking. "What's wrong with me? I feel like I'm going to be sick."

Mother sighed and rubbed her arm. "You didn't let go of it. Did you?"

She pressed her fist against her mouth, willing back a sob, and shook her head. *Nine years.* That's how long ago Mum had sat there crying at the foot of the stairs. It had haunted her ever since. "I couldn't. I just couldn't. Not when he never even said he was sorry."

"And now?"

She squeezed her eyes shut, hot tears escaping down her cheeks. "I don't know."

The memories flashed through her mind like phantoms. *Bloodshot eyes. Cold wind. Christmas tree in the snow. Yelling on the stairs. Mother clutching her wrist. Frances screaming ...*

"Mmm." Mother's voice was soft. "It does get harder the longer you wait."

Lily covered her face with her hands.

"I can't believe he's even asking. Frances said he was different, but I didn't think—"

"Different?" Mother almost sounded as if she was going to laugh. "That's all she said?"

Lily looked over the top of her hands.

Mother *was* about to laugh. "Well. I suppose that's one way of putting it. Saul was *different* after the road to Damascus too."

Lily dropped her hands. "What?"

"And the Philippian jailer was different after the earthquake at midnight."

"Are you saying—"

"Everyone's different after they meet Jesus."

Lily leaned harder against the wall and stared. For once in her life, she found herself doubting Mother's word. Not that she would lie, of course, but perhaps the stress of Father being on his deathbed ...

"I don't ... I mean, I ..." She floundered for words. "That doesn't happen, Mum. Not in real life."

Mother just kept smiling. "Doesn't it?"

Lily groped for something that made sense. Deathbed conversions were the stuff of fairy tales, not reality. Not with her own father. "Mum,"—she shook her head—"that's impossible. It's just something out of ... of a bedtime story."

Mum put her hand on Lily's cheek. "Oh, my Lily. Jesus loves stories."

Fred raised his head.

Far away on the eastern horizon, the dark sky was beginning to fade to gray.

He took a long breath as the first breeze of morning stirred his hair.

Everything was going to be okay. Somewhere, somewhere beyond that horizon, the crisis had passed. Lily was all right.

Thank you, Lord.

He straightened up and checked his watch with the head-lamp. Still only a quarter till. He had an hour yet before he'd need to think about breakfast.

Rolling his shoulders back, he shoved his sleeves up to his elbows and reached for the hammer.

Father looked as if he were sleeping when Lily came back into the room.

Mum shut the door behind them, and the latch clicked in the silence.

Father's eyes opened. She had the feeling then that he had not been sleeping at all. Perhaps...perhaps he was praying. Someone must have been.

She stood by the door, awkward, hugging her elbows. What should she say first? Apologize for running out like that?

Try to explain it? Just say, "Yes, I forgive you"?

She bit her lip. It was all so surreal. She still felt unsure it was really happening.

Father looked at her, straight into her eyes again. And he must have read them just as easily now as he had a few minutes ago when there was something quite different behind them. His pale lips turned up into a smile.

All at once, she knew what it was she had been seeing before.

The strange something in his gaze that she hadn't known how to interpret. Her heart skipped a beat.

One last memory flashed into her mind. *There it is.*

The one she had been looking for. It was the oldest memory she had. From long before she saw Frances in the hospital bed. Years before Father lost himself in a beer glass. The one memory left of a father she had loved.

It was a tiny memory, it's surroundings hazy and fading. But she could still see the face, looking up at her and laughing as he tossed her in the air, pigtails flying.

Do it again, Dad! Do it again!

And there, looking at her from the hospital bed, was the same face. The same smile. The same look in his eyes.

Love.

That's what was in Father's eyes. That's what had been there when they stood in the vestibule. That's what had been there, faint and tangled with other things, when he sat looking at her on the stairs.

From the hospital bed he raised his hand and stretched it toward her, and she realized she didn't have to say anything after all.

Reaching out, she slipped her hand into his.

Chapter 59

"Mr. Overall?"

Fred heard the voice, like a distant echo somewhere underwater. He tried to open his eyes, but they didn't seem to be obeying him at the moment.

Why am I so cold? And why was the bed so hard? And wet? He rolled his head back and forth, trying to shake off the slumber. His whole body felt sore, and he'd lost his pillow someplace. Had it fallen off the bed? He groped, feeling for it, and his hand hit a bush.

"Mr. Overall?"

This time he did manage to get his eyes open. Red hair came into focus first.

Then a freckled face, leaning over him, silhouetted against blue sky. And a missing front tooth. "Mr. Overall?"

On the third try, he got his mouth working. "Hello there."

The freckled kid looked relieved. "You okay, sir?"

Fred took inventory, trying to remember what he was doing lying on the ground. Other than feeling sore and stiff all over, there didn't seem to be anything wrong with him. "Yeah. I think so." He pulled himself to a sitting position, still trying to clear the cobwebs out of his brain. "What day is it?"

"Wednesday." The boy stepped back and gave him a quizzical stare. "You always sleep outside like that?"

Fred looked around. He was sitting next to the ladder, which he'd moved outside the house when he started roofing last night. He'd been working on the roof each night for a week now, living off Spam and cheap coffee so he could put every dollar possible toward buying supplies. His toolbelt was still cinched around his waist as he sat there in the grass.

He didn't remember going to sleep. Just remembered staying up later and later, with the headlamp glaring into the night. Pounding and pounding and pounding, trying to—

"The roof!" He sprang to his feet as it came back to him in a rush. "I finished it! Right down to the last shingle!" He did a little jig on the wet grass and grinned at the freckled kid, who was looking concerned again.

Then he stopped mid-kick.

"Hey, wait a minute. What time is it?"

"Seven thirty."

"Good grief." What time had he fallen asleep?

Must have been the wee hours of the morning. He'd been so tired after staying up late night after night to work... "Good thing you came along." He smiled at the boy. "Or I might have slept my way right out of a job. What are you doing here anyhow? Aren't you the telegram delivery boy?"

"Yeah." The freckled kid put his hand in his satchel. "I'm delivering."

"All the way out here at this time of the morning?"

"Gotta do it before school." He held out an envelope.

This time Fred didn't wait long enough for more than a quick tightening of his stomach. He took the telegram and tore it open.

It was from Mrs. Brown.

CHRIS DIED EIGHT THIRTY THIS MORNING

STOP

HOME WITH GOD

Fred stared at it. *Home with God?*

Did that mean ...? He read the message over again, but of course there were no extra words tucked between the lines someplace. He'd have to wait for a letter to find out the rest. Slipping the telegram back into the envelope, he wondered how Lily was taking it.

The telegraph boy still stood there, like he was worried Fred might pass out on the grass again.

"It's my father-in-law. He died this morning."

"Oh. I'm sorry. Were you ... close?"

Fred looked down at the envelope for a second. "Not really."

The boy shifted his feet for a second. "Well, I gotta get to school. You sure you're all right?" His eyes took in the flecks of damp grass clinging to Fred's clothes.

"Yes."

"Okay." The boy turned around and walked away.

Fred went into the house and stood looking up at the bedroom ceiling, shifting the telegram back and forth between his fingers.

Christopher was dead. But now what? Would Lily come home? He didn't see any reason to think so. It wasn't like she'd gone to England because of her father in the first place. She hadn't even known he was sick until she got there.

Why did she go?

Fred had never been real clear on that one. He wasn't even sure if Lily was clear on it. It seemed like something had just snapped all of the sudden. But he didn't know what.

She wouldn't be the first war bride to give up and go home ...and never come back.

In the kitchen, he opened another can of Spam and poured a cup of cold coffee, setting out a plate and a napkin and fork. But he wasn't hungry. He sat there, staring at his plate, and tried to think.

Maybe he should go after her. Maybe she needed him. But how could he go? A ship's passage cost more money than he would have for months. And stowing away hadn't worked too well the first time.

He shoved in a bite of Spam and chewed and swallowed without tasting it.

If only he could figure out what it was that had made Lily want to leave in the first place, he might be able to fix it.

There had to be something he could do. She hadn't left just because she was homesick. He was sure of it. There was something else. Something that came over her all of the sudden. What was it?

He gulped a mouthful of cold coffee and checked his watch. It wasn't quite time to leave for work yet. If he hurried, he could write Lily a letter before he went.

Just sitting here thinking about her wasn't helping much.

He found a pencil and some paper and started.

Dearest Sweetheart,

I got the telegram this morning about your father. I'm so very sorry I could not be there with you when it happened. But I'm glad at least that you made it in time to say goodbye to him.

I miss you and David very much, but I understand your family needs you now more than I do.

Stay as long as ...

He stopped, pencil poised over the paper, and fought himself. The better part of him knew he ought to tell her to stay as long as her family needed. As long as she needed. And that he would be waiting patiently for her when she was ready to come back.

Patiently?

He clenched his jaw. *No.* Desperately. That was more like it. Sometimes he slept in the arm chair because he couldn't stand to wake up on his side of the bed in the night and find her side still empty.

He slapped the pencil down and shoved his chair back. As he turned to go back to the bedroom, the pencil rolled off the table and plunked onto the concrete. He left it there.

Walking through the studs to the foot of the mattress, he looked up at the finished roof and wished patching up the chasm between him and Lily was as simple as fixing that hole.

Used to be, he could fix just about anything he needed to. But this time he was stumped. What had started out with her just seeming annoyed about supper had stretched out into a gulf so big it seemed like you could put an ocean in it.

Come to think of it, there *was* an ocean in it.

He chewed his lip. Was he really going to write Lily and tell her to stay as long as she wanted?

Yes. He clenched his hands into fists. He had to.

If he couldn't fix it, he'd just have to deal with it as best he could. Returning to the kitchen, he looked around for the pencil. It had rolled underneath the foot of the counter. Dropping to his knees, he peered underneath.

The pencil lay resting against a crumpled ball of paper.

What's that? He retrieved them both and went back to the table, uncurling the paper and smoothing the wrinkles until he could read the scribbled words.

They were in Lily's hand writing.

Dear Joyce,

Yes, we bought the bungalow. But I don't think you'd call it cozy. The roof is not finished so we have to keep the rain out with old army tarps ...

He stopped.

Joyce? *Wait a minute.* His gaze flicked up to the date in the top right corner.

It was written the same day the thunderstorm woke them in the middle of night, raindrops pounding through the open roof and turning their bedroom into a puddle. *The same night Lily snapped.*

An alarm went off in his head.

He dropped into the chair and started reading the letter like it was a treasure map, searching for clues.

...I don't have a garden yet ...too hot for roses ...you can't find a flower-seller anywhere ...Sometimes I get so hungry for flowers ...

In the back of Fred's brain, a memory flickered.

...Eola Park ...the sweet peas ...summers are so hot ...nothing blooms ...

What was it Lily had said that night, in the dark?

The one thing she said that he thought he understood? What was it?

...I should ask Freddie if they filled with water too. As for daffodils ...

"Daffodils!" He shot to his feet.

There it was. What about the daffodils? Lily's letter stopped there, the ink fading off in a wobbly line as if the pen had started shaking in her fingers. Farther down the page there were tiny stains, as if someone had dripped water on the paper.

Or tears.

He dropped the letter on the table and ran out onto the porch.

The daffodils. The daffodils. Where had he seen them last? He dashed around the corner to the back edge where he had left the window box sitting. But it was gone.

He stopped, turning this way and that, looking for it. Then he went to the edge of the porch and checked the ground down below.

There. There was the window box, lying shattered on its side, the jagged pieces mixed up in crumbling dirt that spilled in all directions.

He jumped off the porch and dropped onto the ground beside the wreckage. Up close he could see the soggy black remains of what must have been a bulb, lying half buried in the dirt. And there was another one. And another. *Oh, Lily.*

He stared at the pile for a moment.

Were they all dead, then? Every one of them? He had to check. Brushing aside the shattered pieces of the pot, he ran his fingers through the dirt, probing.

He found another bulb, rotten and black like the other three, and kept going, fingernails digging through the soil until—

His knuckle bumped something solid. *There!*

He pulled it out. A daffodil bulb. Firm and perfect. He pushed more dirt aside and found the last two, healthy as could be.

You stopped too soon, Lily.

Gathering up the three good bulbs in his hand, he sprang to his feet and ran into the house. *The icebox.* Lily always put them in the icebox over the winter. Grabbing a bowl from the cabinet, he dropped the bulbs into it and slid them onto the bottom shelf in the icebox. Then he stood up and looked around again, new energy pulsing in his veins.

Lily would come home. She would. Maybe not right away, but someday. He was sure of it. And when she did ...

He looked out the window toward the garden shed. Come January, he would need a flowerbed by the back door to plant the daffodils in, but before that, there were other things to do. He spun in a circle, taking in the concrete floors, the stud walls, and the curtainless windows. He had promised her a cozy house of her own. Well, it was about time he got it for her.

Pulling the cracked teapot down, he counted the money again. *Not even close.* It would never work. Not even if he lived off Spam and coffee for a month. There still wouldn't be enough for all the supplies he needed.

There's got to be a way.

He rubbed his thumb and fingers together, thinking. Somehow he had to get those supplies. And if he didn't have the money for them...

Then it came to him.

Chapter 60

The bell rang as Fred pulled open the door of the hardware store that evening and stepped inside.

Steve was rummaging behind a new display of garden tools, his curly black hair bobbing up and down as he mumbled to himself.

"No, no. Not there. Too crowded. It's gonna fall over as soon as somebody tries to pick one up ..."

Good grief. The guy didn't even stop talking when there was nobody but himself to listen. "Good afternoon, Steve."

Steve looked up.

"Hullo, Fred! Picking up more roofing supplies?"

Fred took a breath as he started toward the counter. "Not exactly. I actually wanted—"

"Linoleum?" Steve rubbed his hands on his blue jeans. "Seems like half the city wants those new patterns. But I might have enough left for your place if you want it. Honestly though, I'd recommend you finish the roof before you start putting flooring in. Might get ruined otherwise."

"Yes, I know. But I—"

"'Course you know what you're doing, I reckon. And didn't you say the bathroom and kitchen are covered anyhow? Guess that flooring would be safe then. It's the bedroom you'd need to worry about. You planning to put linoleum in there too?"

Fred gritted his teeth. Was he sure he wanted to do this? It meant listening to Steve jabber every single day...

"Plenty of folks are doing that, you know. Especially since they started advertising that *I Love Lucy* home decor awhile back. Seems like everybody and their cousin wants new linoleum. You got a television at that house of yours?"

"No."

"Well, you probably haven't seen the advertisements then. Now if you ask me—"

"Steve!"

Steve broke off and looked at him, brows arched in surprise. "What?"

Fred swallowed. *For Lily. For Lily.*

"Remember what you said about not being able to afford full-salary help, even though you need it?"

"Sure." Steve's hair flopped around like a mop as he nodded. "I been slammed ever since Ben went back to school. Stayin' late to restock the shelves. My wife's mad 'cause I keep makin' supper get cold. It's about to drive her crazy—"

"Could you pay me in materials?"

Steve blinked. "What?"

"If I took the job, could you pay me in materials for the house? I could come in evenings and Saturdays."

There. He'd said it.

Steve scratched his head. "Well now...I ain't sure that's legal. You know we gotta worry about minimum wage and all."

"But if I'm not even working for money in the first place, how does minimum wage apply?"

"There's the cost of the materials. I'd have to calculate for that. If I pay you in materials at the same rate I'd pay somebody else in cash, how does that help me? I still can't afford it. Not at this year's minimum wage."

Fred grinned. "Okay. So mark the materials up before you give them to me."

Steve wrinkled his brow at that one. "You mean like I mark seventy-five cents' worth of linoleum up to a dollar, and give you that for an hour of work?"

"Right. Then I'm working for last year's rate. You're allowed to mark things up whenever you want to, right?"

"Well ...." Steve hesitated. "I still ain't sure that's legal. You know how regulations are."

"But will it look legal? On paper?"

"Ye-es." Steve twisted his cuff button. "I reckon so."

"Then who cares? We both get what we want and the bureaucrats will never know the difference."

Silence. Steve's fingers tapped a rhythm on the counter for minute as he stared down at his shoes. Then he looked up. "When could you start?"

"How about now?"

Steve grinned. "All right. You've got yourself a deal. Want to start on that new garden tool display?"

"Sure." Fred walked over to it.

"Just arrange things by size and color, but make sure it's easy to grab stuff without knocking everything over. Say, if you're working here on evenings and weekends, and at the garage during the day, when are you goin' to work on the house?"

"I'll figure it out."

"Yeah. Guess there's always nighttime. But hey, you know, I'm glad this worked out. It'll be nice to have somebody around when I'm working in the evenings. It gets kinda lonely sometimes with nobody to talk to, and I—"

The bell rang.

Steve turned toward the door.

"Oh, hello, Mr. Groover. What can I do for you today? No wait, I bet I know. New shovel? Yeah, thought so. I just got in some nice big ones too. You want a long shaft or the kind with a hand-hold on the end? Well, never mind, they're right next to each other anyway. Just come right over this way and I'll show you. How's that grandson doing these days? Good? Glad to hear it. Did I tell you what my nephew's been doing to Pat's disposal lately? No? Oh glory, wait till you hear this ..."

Fred sighed as he started rearranging garden trowels. At least there'd be customers to break things up sometimes. What was he going to do once they locked the door on weeknights and started restocking shelves, with Steve talking non-stop?

"Yes, corncobs! Can you believe that?" Steve's voice ran on unbroken on the other side of the shelf.

"I don't even know where he got them from. And Tod's bought three disposals in the past month and a half. Three disposals! He must be keeping the plumber busy too. He says he doesn't know what he's going to do with that kid. If you ask me ..."

Fred sighed. Maybe he could wear earplugs.

Chapter 61

February 1957

The rain fell in cold, heavy drops, running in rivulets down the grass-covered mound that was already beginning to blend into the rest of the churchyard. Lily stood, holding her umbrella, while Mum placed the knot of flowers near the headstone and stood there for a minute, looking down at it.

February was always cold like this. Slushy flecks of snow mingled with the raindrops, melting into the grass as they fell. Lily pulled her umbrella a bit lower, thinking about how nice the weather must feel in Florida right now. Her face was cold. Her fingers were cold. Her toes were cold. The wind snapped at the edges of her coat, trying to get inside.

Every Sunday, Mother came to the graveyard, rain or shine, and brought new flowers. Every Sunday, Lily came with her and stood waiting while Mother looked at the grave in silence. They never said anything, just stood there together until Mother was ready to go back to the house.

Lily shifted her feet, wiggling her toes to try to get some warmth into them. To the west, the sun was beginning to sink toward the sea. It was getting colder by the minute.

"It's strange." Mother's voice broke the silence. Her gaze was still fixed on the grave, and a single tear glistened in the corner of her eye. "It's strange. When I promised to love until death divided us, I never thought about what would happen after that. How the loving goes on, lingering afterward. And it hurts."

Lily looked at her. Mother had always been a wonder to her. But in this moment, she felt it even more than usual. "You really did love him, all the time, didn't you? Even through everything."

Mum blinked, and a tear fell, trickling down her cheek. "So did you."

Maybe. But I buried it so deep I forgot it was there. You never did. "I don't see how you kept on being in love with someone like that. Even when nothing turned out the way you expected it to."

Mum sighed. "Being in love isn't the same as loving, Lily. Loving is a commitment. It doesn't wear off. That's what it means when the Scriptures talk about leaving and cleaving."

Lily pressed the toe of her shoe into a hole in the grass.

"Even if what you committed to turns out to be different than you planned?"

Mum patted her arm. "Love is like a daffodil bloom. Commitment is like the bulb. Sometimes the blooms are so beautiful, nobody thinks about the bulb. Until the weather changes, and the flowers die back, and the bulb is the only thing left, buried under the dirt."

Lily pressed her lips together, but Mum didn't seem to notice.

"But that doesn't mean the daffodil is dead. It's a perennial. When the springtime comes, it bursts open again, more beautiful than before."

"Unless you kill it."

Mum looked up, cocking a brow. "What?"

Lily blinked back a stubborn tear that wanted to fall. "What if you can't keep the bulb alive? What if it's rotten? What happens to the bloom then?"

"It's awfully hard to kill a daffodil bulb."

Lily turned her head away. "Not in Florida, it isn't."

Mum caught her arm and spun Lily around to face her. "Rubbish. No flower of mine gives up just because it's been transplanted."

"Oh, Mum, they *did* though! I killed them! I don't know what I did wrong. They just...rotted. They barely bloomed at all last spring, and when I dug them up this autumn..." She bit her lip.

"Did you dig all of them?"

"I...no. But all the ones I dug were—"

"Then you don't know about the rest of them, do you?"

"Oh, Mum! Why does it matter? Even if they weren't all rotten yet, they will be. I don't see why you're so determined some of them survived!"

"Are they English flowers?"

Lily rolled her eyes. She knew where this was going. "You keep saying that. But sometimes even Englishmen quit. Don't you remember the American Revolution? We put a bunch of Englishmen on American soil and you know what? They quit! Because they didn't belong there. They weren't Americans. They were Englishmen!"

"Americans *are* Englishmen!"

"Oh, Mum!"

"Don't roll your eyes at me. I bet you can take two thirds of those people you call Americans and track their heritage back to England. Or Scotland. Or Ireland. None of them started there in the beginning. They were all transplants. And they figured out how to bloom just as well in their new home as they did in the old."

Lily shook her head. "Don't you think, just once in a while, some transplants can't do that? Don't you think, every now and then, one of them doesn't come back in the spring?"

Mum held her gaze for a moment, and then she reached up and cradled Lily's cheek with her hand. "Do you know what lilies and daffodils have in common, love?"

"What?"

Mum smiled, and squeezed her hand.

"They're both perennials."

Chapter 62

Lily didn't know how long she had been standing on the beach, watching the sunset, when she heard footsteps in the sand.

Alice. She came across the beach from the seawall, arms folded tight against the cold.

The rain had stopped now, but the wind still whipped in from the sea, frothing the water into whitecaps.

Footfalls muted in the sand, Alice came and stood beside Lily, looking out over the sea as a few red curls, come loose from their pins, tossed against her cheek.

For a while they stood, side by side, staring at the horizon while the waves crashed against the shore.

Then Alice took a breath. "Lily, are you afraid?"

Lily looked at her from the corner of her eye. "Didn't we have this conversation before?"

"You never answered me."

Lily kicked at the sand. "Did Mum send you?"

"She told me where to look."

They had parted ways as they came out of the churchyard, Mother heading for home and Lily crossing the road to the

Green instead. She had forgotten about being cold as thoughts turned over and over in her mind.

"Well?" Alice stood with brows arched, waiting.

Lily sighed and stared down at the ripples gurgling against the beach. She wouldn't get away without answering this time. "I've always been afraid, Alice." She pushed back a wayward tendril that was slipping down over her ear.

Alice looked at her, eyes dark and sober, and said nothing.

"Always." She repeated the word in a whisper. *Afraid of being poor. Afraid of what that turned Father into. Afraid it might do the same thing to Freddie. Afraid of leaving Mother. Afraid of having another child. Afraid of becoming an American.* "I'm a coward. There's so many things I'm afraid of, I can't even keep track anymore."

"And that's why you came back?"

Lily nodded. "Mother told me I needed to stop trying to control everything. To trust God instead. I tried."

She took a breath and it quivered in her throat. "I thought I'd finally learned to trust, and then ..."

She broke off, pressing her lips together, trying to hold back the tears.

"And then?"

Lily laughed, because it was the only way to keep from crying. "And then a couple of rotten flower bulbs, a drunk man on a bus ... and it all came back. Worse than before."

She looked at Alice. "So I ran away. I'm just ... not brave enough to trust."

Alice studied her for a minute, then looked at the water again with a thoughtful expression on her face. She pulled her collar tighter against the wind as the sun melted into the horizon, painting golden ripples on the sea. "Lily, do you remember when I used to be afraid of the water?"

Lily nodded. "Terrified, you mean. Even if it only came up to your toes. I never saw a child react like that." She folded her arms to keep the wind from slipping inside her coat sleeves.

"I'm surprised you remember it though. You were swimming like a fish by the time you went to infant school."

"Remember how I learned?"

Lily had to think about that for a moment. She had not been very old herself at the time. "Didn't Mother teach you?"

"Yes." Alice smiled. "I'll never forget it. She walked out into the water and stood there looking back at me, holding her hand out, and called my name."

Lily watched the last rays of sunlight shining golden on her sister's face. "And you went?"

"I trusted her." Alice stood with her eyes fixed on the water, as if she could still see Mother standing there.

Then she took a breath as if coming back to the present, and turned her eyes straight at Lily. "But I was still afraid."

Lily swallowed and hesitated a moment, trying to think of something to say.

Finally she forced out a half-hearted laugh. "Did you come all the way out here to give me swimming lessons?"

"No." Alice reached into her pocket and pulled out a folded letter. "This just came. It's from Freddie. Mother said she thought you ought to see it." She held out the paper.

Lily took it, and Alice turned and walked away toward the seawall.

Staring at the letter, Lily was just about to unfold it when Alice's voice broke the silence again.

"But about those swimming lessons, Lily."

She looked up.

Alice held her gaze, dark eyes solemn, with one foot on the bottom step. "I guess what I was trying to say is, I always sort of thought trusting someone just meant you'd go when they called you. Wherever they called you." She paused, and smiled. "Whether or not you're afraid."

Lily had to turn away quick, before the tears spilled over and betrayed her. When she looked back again, Alice was already walking away across the Green.

Lily stared after her for a few moments, while the words played over and over in her mind. *Whether or not you're afraid.*

For so long she had been fighting the fear, trying to be brave enough to trust.

Had she been going at it backward all along?

She looked around her at the beautiful, familiar landscape. Church spires and rooftops rising across the skyline. Lights glistening in windows as the evening shadows deepened. And the windmill standing like a sentry, facing the sea. Then she turned and looked out at the water. Toward the western horizon.

Florida's out there. On the other side of the water.

Oh Freddie.

She looked down at the letter in her hand and unfolded it. It was addressed to all of them.

Freddie wrote about how he had spent Christmas and New Year's at his parents' house, and how tall Carol was getting, and how he had laid the new linoleum in the kitchen last week and was looking for curtains to match it, and how he was going to paint the siding white tomorrow.

Dear Freddie. Over there working and waiting, and never once demanding to know when she was coming back. *Just trusting. Always trusting.*

As she folded the letter up, still mulling over Alice's words, a sudden gust snatched it from her fingers and hurled it away, toward the Green.

She chased it, dashing through the sand, but only caught up when it hit the seawall, flattened against the cement.

Peeling it off, she spotted the extra sentence, scribbled in with a rushed hand on the back of the page.

Almost missed the postscript.

Holding the paper up to catch the last rays of sunset, she read the note once. And then read it over again. But it took reading it the third time for the message to really sink in.

And then she knew.

With a lump in her throat and the wind pushing salty air into her lungs as her chest heaved, she knew.

She had to go where God was calling her.

Even if she was afraid.

P.S. Dearest sweetheart, the daffodils are blooming.

Chapter 63

April 1959

The sun shone warm on the grass and the wind rustled in the tops of the pine trees as Lily pulled the car into the driveway.

It was strange. Somewhere along the way in the past two years, she must have at last become familiar with the steering wheel being on the wrong side of the car. It had not bothered her at all today, even though she was driving by herself.

After parking the car around the backside of the white bungalow, she turned off the engine and sat there by the open window for a moment or two, resting her head against the seat and breathing in the honeyed scent of orange blossoms.

It's done. The paperwork was in. Her name was on the list. In a couple of weeks she would begin taking the classes.

Drawing in a deep breath, she pushed open the car door and stepped out onto the gravel. *Where is Freddie?* She had expected to see him out working in the yard, or perhaps playing ball with David. He was generally doing one or the other on a warm Saturday afternoon.

But there was no sign of him anywhere.

Strange. She had thought he might at least come out to meet her when she arrived. After all, he wanted to come along, but she'd told him she had to do this by herself.

And she had done it.

But now she wanted him to come running out and sweep her up in his arms and tell her how proud he was.

Had he gone off on an errand? Surely not.

He would be expecting her home about this time.

She walked around the car toward the back steps. Inside the shell-lined flower bed beside the kitchen door, a few bright yellow blossoms still nodded in the breeze.

Mother's late-bloomers were still holding on for another week or two.

The rest of the new ones Mother had sent were just green spears right now, planted in a circle around the three proud bulbs Freddie had coaxed alive all by himself.

Lily stopped on the step and was stooping down to pick a bloom for the table when a sound stopped her.

Music.

Soft strains of big band swing came drifting out through the kitchen window.

Did Freddie leave the radio on again? She opened the door.

The room seemed dark for a moment, compared to the bright sunshine outside. She stopped on the threshold, waiting for her eyes to adjust.

Then they did. But she kept right on standing there.

Oh, Freddie. Of course he hadn't gone out on an errand. She was daft as a brush for thinking it.

Standing there with her hand still on the doorknob, she let her gaze take in the whole picture.

A lace tablecloth draped the dented old round table, hiding all but its legs. On top, tea cakes, cucumber sandwiches, and even a couple of chip butties were arranged on mismatched china—which was of course the only china they owned.

A teapot was enthroned in the middle, steam still curling from its spout, and two teacups sat waiting to be filled. The music came from the phonograph, which had been brought in from the parlour and deposited on the kitchen worktop.

Standing in the midst of it all, wearing his mischievous half-smile and resting his hand on the back of her chair, was Freddie.

She took a step into the room and pushed the door shut behind her, trying to come up with something to say. What came out was not exactly romantic. "Where's David?"

Freddie laughed. "Visiting Mom and Dad."

As she crossed the linoleum, he slid her chair out in readiness. She sat down and he took his seat beside her. Lily felt strangely tongue-tied, as if they were still newlyweds getting accustomed to each other instead of the parents of an eight-year-old. Everything seemed different now.

Everything *was* different now. Ever since she had signed her name on that page.

Freddie reached for the sugar. "How did it go? Everything work out okay?"

"Yes." She watched him put the sugar cubes in the cups and pick up the teapot. "They put my application in. I begin classes in two weeks."

He filled the teacups.

"How long will it take to process everything?"

"Months. The lady there said I shouldn't expect to be sworn in until autumn." She stirred the hot tea to melt the sugar evenly.

Freddie reached for the milk. He didn't have to ask how much she wanted anymore. He'd been making her tea far too long for that. Just a quick white stream into the teacup, and then he tipped the jug up again and set it aside.

She stirred again and took a small sip.

He followed suit. "Are you glad you went by yourself?"

Yes. She needed to know she was sure enough of her decision not to back out at the last minute. Even if she was there alone. She nodded but didn't try to explain it to him.

"Are you nervous?"

She stared down at her tea, watching the spoon move in circles and trying not to clink against the china. *Nervous?* Her emotions were far too complex for one word.

There was too much to name. Happiness, sadness, excitement, hesitation...and a feeling of letting go. Letting go of something she had been holding onto so tightly that her fingers felt stiff and empty without it.

No. Not quite empty though. Just because she reached out for something new didn't mean she had to let go of the old altogether. She had two hands, did she not?

She stopped stirring but kept her eyes on the teacup. "I'm glad I can keep my British citizenship too."

His hand slipped into her lap and closed around her fingers. "So am I."

She looked up at him.

He was smiling. Not his mischievous smile now, but the gentle one. The one that made her wonder how he could fit so much love in a single look.

"You don't mind if part of me will always be English?" She had to ask. Not because she really wondered, but because she somehow needed to hear the answer again.

He pulled her hand to his lips. "Far as I can remember, it was an English girl I fell in love with in the first place. Wasn't it?"

She said nothing. Just sat there looking into his eyes.

The phonograph went still for a moment between songs, and she could hear the needle sliding over vinyl. Then the speaker came to life again, and familiar notes sang out on the breath of a clarinet player.

It was Artie Shaw. Playing "Begin the Beguine."

Fred looked over toward the music and pushed his chair back, then stood up, smiling down at her. "I believe this is our song, sweetheart."

Her heart thumped warm and happy in her chest. She got to her feet.

And they danced. There on the linoleum, between the open window and the lace-covered table, they danced in circles, with his arm tight around her waist and her cheek resting against his shoulder.

While the tea got cold, forgotten in the cups, and the music kept singing from the phonograph, and the breeze whispered in through the window, carrying the scent of orange trees in bloom.

"I'm still not very good at this, am I?" Freddie's breath stirred her hair.

She raised her head. *Not good at it?*

He was talking about the dancing. But as she stared up into his blue eyes, a lump rose in her throat.

This moment was not about dancing, it was about love. The kind of love that could make her give up everything, make her let go of her fears, make her choose a life far different from anything she had ever planned for herself.

The kind of love that made her want to become a citizen of a strange new country, just so the place he called home could be her home too.

"Yes, you are, Freddie." Her voice was husky as her hand tightened on his. "Yes, you are."

He looked surprised for a moment and then seemed to catch her meaning.

"Well." He brushed his cheek against hers. "It sure helps to have a good partner."

Her breath caught in her throat and her feet stopped moving without her telling them to. He stood there, smiling down into her eyes as if *she* was the one who had signed three years of her life away just to get back across the ocean so they could be together. As if *she* was the one who had worked and slaved to save up money for the house repairs, only to hand it over and stand alone on a platform, watching a train out of sight. As if *she* was the one who'd made the daffodils bloom.

She wanted to cry.

She wanted to kiss him.

She wanted to tell him it was all his doing. And Mother's, and God's.

That she had not done half her share. But that she was going to from now on. That she was glad she would soon be able to call herself an American. That she never would have made it this far without him.

There were so many things she wanted to say.

So many things she ought to be thanking him for.

But as usual, the right words would not come when her heart was full.

She took a deep breath. There was one way she could show him though. One gift she could give him. A piece of news so special, she'd been waiting for just the perfect moment.

This moment.

Taking both his hands in hers, she guided them down until they rested against the waist of her dress. His forehead wrinkled as he followed their hands with his gaze, and something, the tiniest hint of hope, flickered into his eyes. He looked up at her, brows drawn together in a question mark.

"I've been waiting to tell you. To ask you..." She paused, tightening her fingers over his and taking another breath. "I mean...if it's a girl, should we call her Susan?"

Freddie's face lit up like fireworks on the Fourth of July. His eyes shone, and his smile stretched wider than she had seen it in a long time. Then something seemed to have lodged in his throat. He swallowed to clear it, and the sparkle in his eyes grew brighter with unshed tears. They pushed their way to the corners, and trickled down his cheeks. Freddie always did cry easier than she did. But these were happy tears.

She reached up and brushed them away, her heart singing in her breast. "Should we close the curtains, Freddie?"

He took her face in his hands and pulled her close to him, gazing into her eyes. "I love you, sweetheart." He leaned closer, and his breath whispered against her lips. "Welcome home."

the end

Afterword

Fred and Lily Overall had three children. David, Susan, and Sharon. The family lived in Florida for several decades, but eventually moved north to the red hills of Toccoa, GA, where Fred and Lily were loved by everyone who knew them.

Their daughter Sharon still lives in the area and was highly instrumental in making this book a reality.

Susan lives in southern GA and was also very involved in the writing of this book. Both Sharon and Susan married and have families of their own.

David served in the U.S. Navy, and was adored by his younger sisters. He never married. On August 5th, 2018, a few months before this book went to print, he passed away in Texas and was buried with full military honors.

Frances and Doug had two daughters, Patricia and Kathleen, both of whom live near Lytham. Kathleen (Kathy) helped tremendously in proofreading this book to make sure the English characters actually sounded English, not American. (Something I could not have accomplished without her.)

Frances's first daughter, Ann, was adopted by a family in Blackpool (very close to Lytham). When she grew up, she researched her heritage and was able to reconnect with her mother and half-sisters. She currently lives in London and remains in contact with Kathleen and Patricia to this day.

Robert and his wife Alice (called Allie in this book, for clarity) eventually divorced. Throughout this story I have worked very hard to portray the characters as true to life as possible, and Allie is no exception.

She really did flirt with Fred, charge exorbitant rent, and refuse to give David a blanket when the car window was missing. (And Robert really did ignore her and get one anyway.) Later in life, Robert became a caretaker for Newhaven Fort in East Sussex, England.

He was known to tell wonderful stories about his many escape attempts in Germany. (His POW pals nicknamed him "Nosher" because he was so good at stealing food for his fellow prisoners.) It is unknown what became of Robert's daughter, Yvonne. Her cousins have not been in touch with her for many years.

Lily's sister Alice was always a favorite with Fred and Lily's children. She married, but her only child died as an infant.

She and her husband Ken came over from England every few years to visit, and she often sent packages, especially at Christmas. Her nieces still remember the Toblerone chocolate bars she sent in every box.

Ruth married and had one son and three daughters.

All of Fred's siblings (Hubert, George, Margie, Charles, and Carol) had families. Hubert and George really did bring home Japanese war brides, and both women are alive at the time of this writing.

Carol (who did indeed ask, "Does butter fly?") is also still living. The rest of the siblings on both sides have passed away.

Sadly, Fred never reconnected with his pal Jerry after the war. But Susan remembers that sometimes when they were driving near Atlanta they would see privately owned semi-trucks marked as "Jerry's Trucking." And Fred was always certain they belonged to his friend.

Lily's friend and neighbor, Joyce Robinson, passed away during the writing of this book. She was still living in the Lytham area at the time. Her American boyfriend Arthur was a real person, but they broke up before the war ended and went on to live separate lives.

Joyce's little sister Shirley helped me a good deal with descriptions of what it was like growing up on North Clifton street during the 40's.

Shirley remembers Lily and Fred very well, and how Fred would give out candy and coins to the local children. Her line in the book: "He's so awfully handsome. And *tall*" is almost a direct quote from my first conversation with her. She laughingly admits that she probably had "a bit of a thing for Freddie" as a child. But then—she says—everybody else did too.

The minor character Clara, and her American boyfriend Harry, are based on an actual couple (though names were changed to protect their privacy).

After Clara broke off the relationship and Harry went back to the States, they both found spouses, married, and had families of their own. They never spoke to each other again...until three years ago.

During the time that I was doing research for this book, some determined history-lovers harnessed the power of Facebook to reconnect them, and they were able to see each other again (at least through a computer screen). Their story deserves a book all its own. But short of that, I at least wanted to include a small piece of it in this one.

Though most of the people in the story are based on real individuals, a few are purely fictional, including Greg Baker, Pete Ross, and the Wheaton family. However, they were each created to help me tell important, true pieces of the story.

Another G.I. did steal one of Fred's cartoons and pass it off as his own in the military magazine *Stars and Stripes*. We don't know his name, so I made up Greg Baker.

Fred did, in fact, dress up like a woman to sneak past MPs at the bus stop and get back to his "furlough gate" after visiting Lily.

And he somehow managed to get sent back to the Lytham area after rejoining the Air Corps, despite the fact that Warton Air Base had already closed down. I created Pete Ross to fill in those gaps. The plane crash and school fire in Freckleton were real, but I chose to create a fictional family to experience it through, instead of using the names of actual people involved. (There were multiple Davids in the infant classroom though.)

Fred and Lily never spoke of this devastating event, so we don't have any way of knowing if they were actually nearby when it occurred.

As with characters, I have done my best to be completely accurate with other facts and events that we know of, using fiction only to fill in the gaps. Even in tiny details, I tried to include as many accurate bits as possible.

For instance, Fred did steal all the keys out of Mrs. Brown's piano once as a practical joke, and collected driftwood for her to burn (she loved the colored flames it produced).

Lily's pink-jeweled birthday brooch is quite real, and her daughter Sharon still has it.

Fred's stories about growing up in Florida are all ones he used to tell regularly. He built his own car before he was old enough to have a license, and the girls scratched their names in the paint.

His relationship with Joni is factual. Teddy really was the family dog.

Although the necklace Paul gave Lily is fiction, Paul was a real person. And there is a mysterious patch of grass in Lowther Gardens which had some special meaning to Lily.

She once stood looking at it for a long time when she visited, later in life, but would never tell her daughter what happened there.

The letters contained in the story are fictional. But some of the details included in the story do come from actual letters exchanged between Lily and her family in England, especially Alice.

The section about Miss Bonny's ginger wine and mince pies, and Mrs. Brown's quote about warming "the cockles of your heart" came straight out of a reminiscing letter Alice wrote. She also wrote about loving the blue shoes she got from Tyler's for Lily's wedding (which is how we figured out the wedding colors) and remembered that the flowers were particularly beautiful.

Speaking of flowers, Lily really did have her picture taken next to the sweet pea wall at Eola park, and the photo did indeed end up on a postcard. I have one myself.

When it comes to the more major events in the story, most of them are at least loosely based on actual family stories.

Fred and Lily did meet at a dance at Lowther Pavilion (the bicycle accident was fiction).

Fred always said he knew at once that she was the girl he would marry, but it took Lily a long time to make up her mind between him and Paul.

Fred did travel all the way to New York to stow away on a ship back to England, only to be caught and put ashore. It was purely my imagination that made the ship the famous Queen Elizabeth. However, Commodore James Bisset was a historical person, and really in command of that ship at the time. According to his memoirs, he began his seafaring career as a stoway.

Mr. Brown did have a drinking problem, though he apparently hid the violent side of it from everyone but his family.

The part of the story about him breaking Frances's nose as a child and putting her in the hospital with other injuries is factual. And Lily really did break his nose with her shoe many years later, when she decided she had had enough (though the exact date of that fight is unknown). However, Lily's recurring nightmares were my own invention.

Fred actually spent a night outside the consulate in order to convince the man working there to let him take Lily back to America with him. (Though they ended up having to ride in separate ships, with Lily arriving a few weeks after Fred.) David was a breech birth, and Lily was indeed afraid to have more children for a long time afterward.

The trip down to Florida in the old car is very closely based on true stories, including the free meal and collection taken up by the policemen in Virginia, and Fred's dream about the gas station. Lily did want him to pull over, and he wouldn't, until he found the station he was looking for. The owner loaned him a tank of gas in exchange for his military papers, and then gave the family groceries for their trip.

The house with the missing roof and concrete flooring was real, as was the bathtub Fred got for Lily. She said later that every time she had it all filled and ready to go and was just getting in, somebody was bound to drive up the driveway.

A doctor friend of Lily's, from England, did show up and offer her a job around this time. She was shocked at the living conditions and actually asked, "Oh Lily, what has he brought you to?"

Lily got fed up and went back to England with David in October of 1956. It is unclear exactly how long she stayed there, but her Mother did give her a bit of a push and tell her she needed to "leave and cleave."

The only major divergence from the factual storyline is the death of Christopher Brown. His real death was not until the early 1960's. But the circumstances of his death are accurate. Lily was really there to say goodbye, and Christopher did profess faith in Christ and ask forgiveness from his family on his deathbed. Lily forgave him. (She said later that she had to. She could not have lived with the hate she felt for him.)

Lily became a United States Citizen on September 29th, 1959, a little over a month before the birth of her first daughter. Her second daughter was born three years later.

Fred and Lily were married for over 62 years, until Lily died of liver cancer on April 25, 2010. Fred missed her terribly, but it was not long before they were reunited.

Almost exactly fourteen months later, after a long battle with dementia and kidney disease, he followed her to heaven on June 22, 2011.

According to their children, in all those 62 years of marriage Fred never stopped looking at Lily like she took his breath away. Every single day.

And he signed almost every card he gave her with the same words:

"All My Love, Forever and Ever."

They were lifelong sweethearts.

Lily Brown

Fred Overall

Fred, Lily, and (probably) Paul
About 1944

Fred, April 1944
(About the time he met Lily)

Lily and Mrs. Brown, 1945
Photo probably taken on
North Clifton

Photo taken in the Doughnut Dugout, Lytham
Fred at far right

Robert Brown, Commando

Wedding, August 30, 1947
Left to Right: Alice, Fred, Lily, Frances

Family Portrait, (England) 1950
Fred, Lily, David

Lily and David (age 4 months) 1950
Photo taken by Fred, in England

Lily and David, Orlando (abt 1954)

Lily and David, Florida
(This is probably the house with a missing roof)

Lily (middle) with other nurses
Orlando FL

Lily, 1956
Photo taken right before
she returned to England

Left to Right: Lily, Alice, Frances, Ruth
England, 1956

David, Charles, Fred

David, Fred, Susan (1962)

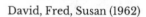

Left to Right: Lily, Susan, Mrs. Brown, Sharon, Fred, David
About 1963

Back row, left to right: Frances, Pat (*Frances's daughter*), Lily, Mrs. Brown
Front row, left to right: Susan, Kathleen (*Frances's daughter*), Sharon
England, 1966

Lily and Fred (1970's)

Fred and Lily, 1990's
(By this time they had moved to Toccoa, in NE Georgia)

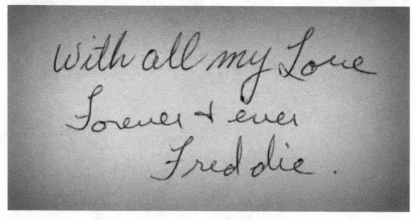

One of Freddie's Letters

About the Author

Leya Delray is a lover of history and literature who has a head full of stories and a closet full of clothing from more eras than she can keep track of.

She lives and breathes whatever time-period she is currently writing or reading about, and has been known to go out in public dressed as anything from a 1940's movie star to a medieval peasant.

She earned a B.A. in English from Thomas Edison State University, and has been writing stories for as long as she can remember. Visit her website at www.leyadelray.com.

9 781732 758711